GOING UNDER

Ray French was born in Newport, South Wales. He has worked with people with disabilities, and as a stagehand, labourer, cartoonist, archivist and in libraries. He now lives in Leeds with his partner and daughter where he teaches creative writing. He is a Royal Literary Fund Fellow and the author of *All This Is Mine*.

RAY FRENCH

Going Under

VINTAGE BOOKS
London

Published by Vintage 2007

2 4 6 8 10 9 7 5 3 1

Copyright © Ray French 2007

Ray French has asserted his right under the Copyright, Designs and
Patents Act 1988 to be identified as the authors of this work

First published in Great Britain in 2007 by
Harvill Secker

Vintage
Random House, 20 Vauxhall Bridge Road,
London SW1V 2SA

www.vintage-books.co.uk

Addresses for companies within The Random House Group Limited
can be found at: www.randomhouse.co.uk/offices.htm

The Random House Group Limited Reg. No. 954009

A CIP catalogue record for this book
is available from the British Library

ISBN 9780099455349

The Random House Group Limited makes every effort to ensure that
the papers used in its books are made from trees that have been
legally sourced from well-managed and credibly certified forests.
Our paper procurement policy can be found at:
www.rbooks.co.uk/environment

Mixed Sources
Product group from well-managed
forests and other controlled sources
www.fsc.org   Cert no. TT-COC-2139
© 1996 Forest Stewardship Council
FSC

Printed in the UK by CPI Bookmarque, Croydon, CR0 4TD

THIS BOOK IS DEDICATED TO PETER BESWICK

'A man who, beyond the age of twenty-six, finds himself on a bus can count himself as a failure'

Margaret Thatcher

1

The moment Aidan walked through the door, he could see he'd put the manager on his guard. He'd only taken a few steps before he left the counter, walked across to where Aidan hesitated, gazing around him nervously at the merchandise.

'Do you need any help at all, sir?'

'I'm looking for a coffin.'

Aidan wished he'd leave him alone; there was nothing worse than someone hassling you when you were trying to buy something. This was difficult enough already without that. He glanced at the name badge on his jacket – Terence Roberts.

Roberts clasped his hands in front of his stomach, softened his voice.

'Who's it for, if you don't mind me asking?'

After thirty-five years as an undertaker, he knew how important this was – the death of a distant relative raised a whole different set of issues for the bereaved to that of a dead spouse, for instance.

Aidan met his eyes.

'It's for me.'

Roberts' shocked expression only lasted a couple of seconds. He composed himself.

'I see.'

Some years ago a man who'd just discovered he had a terminal illness had come and chosen his own coffin and arranged his own funeral, to save his family the distress. It was his way of taking control of what remained of his life, and he had admired him for it. Perhaps Aidan was in a similar position.

Maybe that explained why he was so on edge. He looked like he was in his early fifties at most, seemed to be in good shape, but you never could tell.

'That's The Hartington, a popular model – dark-stained veneer with contrasting cut-away panels, solid gold cremation handles and name plate . . .'

'I'm not really bothered about that – I'm more concerned about what it's like inside.'

'I beg your pardon?'

'I'm going to be stuck in there for a long time. I want to make sure I'll be comfortable.'

Roberts began to wonder how long it would be before his junior partner Clive returned. He'd popped out to buy a couple of Danish pastries to have with their morning coffee, and was taking his time about it.

'How much is it?'

'Five hundred and twenty-five pounds.'

Aidan frowned, pointed to the one next to it.

'How about that one?'

'The Mahogany? That's three hundred and ninety-nine pounds.'

'Can I give that one a go?'

'What do you mean, exactly?'

'Can I get inside, try it out?'

Roberts' gaze hardened.

'I'm sorry, sir, we don't allow that kind of thing.'

Aidan took a step forward, raised his voice.

'Why not? If you were buying a house you wouldn't hand over your money after just looking at it from the outside, would you? You'd want to go and check out what it was like indoors.'

Roberts straightened his back, assumed his most dignified expression.

'And what kind of impression do you think it would create if people walked past and saw you lying down in one of our coffins?'

Aidan considered this. He had to admit, the man had a point. 'OK,' he said, 'how much would it be to hire The Mahogany for a couple of months then?'

Aidan sat in the living room, listening to *Meat is Murder*. It belonged to his daughter Shauna, must have slipped out of her bag when she last visited a few weeks ago. The Smiths were one of the few Eighties bands Aidan rated and he'd been playing it ever since – one track in particular, ten or fifteen times a day. He could do this without any danger of being interrupted now. When Shauna and Dylan had been teenagers, forever running around slamming doors, shouting at each other and hogging the TV and stereo, he'd complained bitterly about never being able to get any peace and quiet. He had more than he knew how to handle now. Once he was made redundant he'd have more.

Here it came, the fourth track, the song that had burnt itself indelibly into his brain, 'What She Said'. It began like a runaway train, careering wildly down the track at a hundred miles an hour. A jagged guitar riff, a red-hot rhythm section pushing it forward relentlessly. You just knew something dangerous and shocking was on its way. When it arrived, it cut him open like a knife. Morrissey at his most haunting, demanding to know why no one had noticed he was dead and decided to bury him. God knew he was ready. After hearing it, Aidan had known exactly what he had to do.

Aidan, Russell, Gwyn and Wilf were sitting in the canteen, eating their lunch. They were watching a man in white overalls re-painting the sign outside the factory entrance.

'How many times is that this month?'

'Five.'

Someone kept altering the sign so that instead of *Sunny Jim Electronics – The Future is So Bright You'll Have to Wear Sunglasses* it read *Slimy Jim Electronics – Take the Subsidies and Run*. The photograph of a beaming Jim Richter, Chairman of Sunny Jim

Electronics, had also been tampered with, several large black holes ruining his perfect set of choppers.

'Maybe they'll hire a security guard to stand under it all night,' said Russell.

Gwyn smiled, he liked that idea. He took a swig from his mug. 'Did you hear the news this morning – Jim Richter, Sunny Jim himself, has been awarded a £750,000 bonus.'

Russell nearly choked on his meatball.

'What for?'

'Successfully managing the global re-structuring programme.'

'Can you translate that?'

'For having the vision to take the radical and courageous decision to shut down their factories here and in Tyneside and the States and to relocate to India, where they can significantly reduce their overheads.'

'That's fucking outrageous.'

'That is business.'

'Bloody hell,' said Russell. 'I've lost my appetite.'

Aidan went pale. '£750,000?'

'Yep.'

'Jesus,' muttered Aidan, pushing a chip around his plate. 'And what will we get? Probably a week's wages for every year we've worked here. Then we'll all be competing for the same jobs in one of the worst unemployment blackspots in the country.' He began ticking them off on his fingers: 'Security guard, stacking shelves in a supermarket, rounding up trolleys in the car park. You seen that bloke in the Tesco's car park at Maes-glas, the one with the little tash?'

'Looks like Blakey from *On the Buses*?'

'That's the one. You should see his face when he sees people just dump their trolley anywhere when they're finished – he looks like he wants to slit their throat. *He's* about our age.' He put down his knife and fork, stared out of the window. 'Rounding up trolleys at Tesco's, that's what we'll all be competing for.'

4

The others didn't say anything for a while. Then Russell started yakking about last night's match.

'That second goal was definitely off-side – and that was the one that killed the game.'

Gwyn and Wilf eagerly joined in the conversation. A few minutes passed before they realised Aidan was just staring into space.

Russell said, 'You all right, mate? What's on your mind?'

Aidan slowly turned to face him, a tortured expression on his face: 'Have you seen the price of coffins these days? It's shocking.'

It was Sunday morning. Aidan had to get out of the house, escape from those four walls. He walked up town, wandered into John Frost Square. Built in the sixties, at the height of Britain's love affair with concrete, it was lined with depressing shops on two sides, a multi-storey car park on another, and the drab Central Library on the fourth. A bitterly cold November wind roared through it, whipping up carrier bags, old newspapers and discarded chip papers, wrapping them round people's legs. Last night someone had smashed the front windows of *Cheap 'N' Cheerful* and *Fags and Mags*, and the ground was carpeted with broken glass.

'Terrible, isn't it? Nothing better to do, have they?' muttered an old lady as she passed Aidan, scowling at the damage and tugging her sickly looking terrier away from the shards.

'No, love, they haven't.'

He wandered around the square aimlessly for a while, then sat down on a bench. The truth was, he didn't know what to do with himself at the weekends anymore. Russell would be on his allotment now. Wilf would be on his way to church – he'd do the weekly shop with Megan afterwards. Gwyn had got over his divorce and was taking night classes, was probably on the Internet at home, he spent hours looking things up. Everyone was busy except him.

5

A £750,000 bonus, he couldn't believe it. How could Richter live with himself? Gwyn had shown him an article about Richter – he had a house in Switzerland, a flat in London, and a ranch in the States. He had his own helicopter and a yacht called the *Iron Lady*. This was the man who had said that demands for a rise would bankrupt the company.

Back in January, when the rumours about the redundancies were building up, Richter had gone on telly. He looked at the camera with studied sincerity and said there was absolutely no truth in this talk of job losses. It was put about by people who wanted to damage Sunny Jim's reputation. Even worse, he felt they were an attack on his personal integrity and nothing meant more to him than that.

Read my lips – there will be no redundancies at Sunny Jim in the foreseeable future. You have my word.

The next day at work, when everyone was saying they wouldn't trust the shifty bugger as far as they could throw him, Aidan had actually defended him.

I just can't believe he'd be so cynical as to say that, then turn around a few months later and give us all the chop.

Don't be soft, mun, he's just buying time.

If that's what he wanted to do he could have just said 'No comment' or 'We can't rule anything out,' couldn't he?

I'm telling you, he's lying through his teeth.

I trust him.

They'd roared with laughter.

But the uncomfortable truth was that Aidan, even without Richter, had begun shutting himself down years ago. It began when Eileen died. That was when he shut down the part of him that believed in the future. When his kids left, he shut down the part of him that took a pride in his home. Doing something just for the sheer hell of it, never mind the risk – shut down. Believing it wasn't too late to meet someone new and start again – shut down. Sticking his neck out for something he believed in – shut down. He'd made so much of himself redundant that he hardly knew what was left of the real Aidan anymore.

Aidan became aware of someone standing next to him. He looked up, saw a smartly dressed man clutching a briefcase and a black book. He smiled at Aidan.

'Good morning, my friend, would you like to hear The Good News?'

Aidan scowled.

'What fucking good news is that then? Have the last ten years been a bad dream? Am I going to wake up now and find out everything is all right after all?'

The man backed away quickly, his smile fading.

A few days later, Pancho was sitting in the corner of the Globe, writing in his notepad, diary and mobile on the table next to him. He wore a Che Guevara T-shirt under his leather jacket, a red bandana around his head. Ponytail, handlebar moustache, three days' growth, gold tooth on the left side. He took a cheroot from his jacket pocket, a match from behind his ear, bent down and in one swift, easy movement struck it first time on the metal heel of his cowboy boot. Aidan smiled. He'd never seen him miss. Pancho was the most colourful thing about the Globe.

The place had hardly changed in the last two decades. A few years ago they'd slapped a couple of coats of sickly yellow gloss over the rank wallpaper, making it easier to keep the walls moderately clean. The grimy windows allowed in little light: the dark brown carpet whose chief purpose was to soak up and hide the countless stains only added to the gloom. There was a permanent cloud of cigarette smoke, a lingering smell of slops and an eye-watering stench from the Gents whenever someone opened the door. Right now there were just a few solitary middle-aged drinkers and a couple of heavily tattooed young bucks playing pool, punctuating every missed shot by a string of foul expletives.

7

'Hi-ya, Pancho.'

He lit his cheroot, looked up.

'*Buenas noches*, Aidan – what can I do for you?'

'I'm after something a little unusual.'

Aidan's budget didn't extend to the kind of prices the under-takers were asking, but he wasn't going to give up now. Pancho took a drag from his cheroot and blew a perfect smoke ring into the air. He fixed Aidan with a wry grin.

'Hey, have I ever let you down before?'

Aidan shook his head.

Pancho nodded, pleased to agree with him. He gestured for Aidan to sit down in the chair opposite.

'Now then, why don't you tell me what you're after?'

Aidan sat, then glanced behind him. Pancho smiled.

'No one's listening – look, don't worry about it, I get all sorts of unusual requests and it's very rare I can't meet them. A couple of months ago I got a big supply of adult-sized nappies and baby clothes for a customer.'

'For dressing up, like?'

'What else?'

Aidan pulled a face. 'Bloody hell.'

Pancho picked up his glass of tequila and slowly took a sip, enjoying Aidan's reaction. Aidan looked around the bar. He turned back to Pancho. 'Who was that for? Are they in here now?'

'There's such a thing as customer confidentiality.'

Aidan held up both hands, palms towards Pancho. 'Of course. I understand.'

'So, this unusual request . . .'

'Was it Brynley Biggerstaff?'

Pancho wagged his index finger at him.

'OK, OK . . .'

'A Design for Life' started playing on the jukebox. Every few minutes, somewhere in Crindau, someone put 'A Design for Life' on a jukebox, it had become a national anthem. It was the

8

unlikeliest of hit singles in these hard-nosed times, a passionate eulogy to the Welfare State by three boys from just up the road in Blackwood. People in Crindau felt an enormous pride in the band's hard-won success.

'I need a coffin.'

Pancho's face fell. 'I'm sorry, I didn't realise you'd had a bereavement.'

Aidan waved his hand dismissively.

'No, it's for me.'

'You?'

Aidan nodded, he was getting used to this now.

'How soon can you get one?'

Pancho's eyes widened. He leaned a little closer, stroking his moustache.

'Have you had some bad news?'

'Yeah, I'm being made redundant.'

'Christ, mun, I know it's a blow, but . . .'

'Don't worry, it's not what you think.'

Pancho shrugged. It wasn't his job to ask questions.

'I'll do my best.'

'How long will it take?'

Pancho glanced down, scribbled something on his notepad.

'I have to admit, Aidan, it is a little on the unusual side. This is going to stretch me a bit.'

'I understand that – but I've got faith in you, Pancho. The thing is, I've had a look in the undertaker's, and the prices are a bit steep. I'm on a tight budget. It's outrageous what they charge for a bit of wood. I'm not fussed about whether it's dark-stained veneer, or finest mahogany, or whether it's got solid gold cremation handles and name plate. I mean, at the end of the day, it's just a bloody box, isn't it?'

Pancho nodded, the customer was always right was his motto. Unless he wanted to return something. Bought as seen was his other motto.

'OK, so nothing fancy, the most important factor being value

9

for money, gotcha. As you know, my prices are always very competitive.'

It was true, he'd bought his video, TV, hi-fi, microwave and fridge from Pancho at a fraction of the price you'd pay in the shops. Aidan held his eyes. 'The sooner the better. I'm in a hurry to get started, understand?'

Pancho didn't, but then he didn't need to, he was just the supplier. His mobile started ringing – 'La Cuceracha'.

'I'll be in touch.'

He reached out, shook Aidan's hand and took the call.

Aidan stood inside the hole, knee-deep now, hands on hips, puffing and blowing like a steam train. The pain in his shoulders and thighs was excruciating. He was desperate to give up, go inside, open a can of beer and collapse on the sofa.

But he wasn't going to.

There were two very good reasons why. He needed to be *doing* something. It was vital not to lose momentum. The longer a plan festered in your mind without you putting it into action, the more unreal it began to seem. Just because he had to wait for Pancho to deliver didn't mean he had to sit around on his backside, doing nothing. He could be getting other things ready. After all, what good was a coffin without a hole to put it in?

Then there was the bedroom curtain twitching next door. Joy was working herself into a frenzy trying to figure out what he was up to. It would be all over the neighbourhood by tomorrow. He wasn't going to give her the opportunity to belittle him.

Hasn't touched the garden for years, an absolute disgrace it is. Then, when he finally decides to get off his backside and do something about the state of it, he gives up after half an hour. Had to go back inside and lie down. Should have seen him, thought I was going to have to call an ambulance.

Eileen had been the one with the green fingers. After she'd died, he could barely bring himself to look at the garden, it reminded him too much of her. Shauna had taken over for a while, she'd picked up the knack from her mother, but when she'd left home, he'd drawn the curtains in the back kitchen, so he couldn't see it anymore, let it go to hell.

There it was again, the bedroom curtain twitching. He'd show her.

He picked up the shovel and went back to work. After a few minutes, Ken came out, whistling very loudly and deliberately. Joy must have sent him down to have a closer look. *Their* garden was immaculate – they stood on guard like sentries when their grandchildren came, in case they spoilt anything. Aidan heard him open his shed, the whistling muffled now as he pottered around in there for a couple of minutes, picking things up and putting them back down again, rattling a few tins. He came out again, shut the door. The whistling stopped.

'Nice evening.'

He was leaning over the garden fence, trying not to stare at the hole, but it was a terrible struggle, Aidan could see.

'It is, aye, very mild for the time of year.'

'You're busy.'

'Just doing a bit of work in the garden.'

Ken waited for more, but Aidan wasn't going to give him any, the nosy bugger. Let Joy come down herself if she wanted to ask him something.

'Well, better get back to work, you know how it is.'

He gave Ken a wink, picked up his shovel and started digging again.

Aidan sat at the kitchen table, a drawing pad open in front of him. He was sketching some of the modifications he'd need to make. He started by drawing a coffin, then adding a square near the top. A window so he could see out, it would be horribly claustrophobic otherwise. A window was a must. But what good was a window without a view? He chewed this over, doodling on the edge of the page. He'd need a shaft from the window to the surface. A patch of blue sky, a soft white cloud drifting past, these were the kind of things that could raise a man's spirits when the going got tough. And people could look down the shaft and see him lying there. It would make a huge difference, being able to look up and see people's faces when he was talking to them. He added these details, leaned back in his chair and reviewed his sketch – yes, it was coming on. He took a swig of lager, wiped his mouth with the back of his hand.

Then he began to have second thoughts. Did he really need a window? Why make extra work for himself? If he just cut a hole in the lid they could lower his food straight down the shaft and he could send the plate back up when he'd finished. *Attaboy, Aidan, now you're getting somewhere.* He picked up his pencil, drew a winch and a couple of stick figures on the surface. It was coming together. Careful planning, close attention to detail, that was the key to success. You couldn't just shut yourself up in a coffin, cross your fingers and hope everything would be all right. He didn't want to discover he'd overlooked some small but vital detail once he was six feet under with the lid screwed on.

He drew a smiley face peering out of the coffin's window. He grinned. He drew a speech bubble coming from one of the stick figures on the surface.

What do you want for your tea?

Then one coming from a smiley face at the coffin's window. *Fish and chips.*

He took another swig of lager, laughed. After the fiasco in the undertaker's the other day, he wondered if he could ever pull it off, but now he could feel his confidence surging back. This was going to work.

Aidan was in the garden, chopping at the knee-high grass, the weeds and the brambles with a pair of shears. A bastard of a job that would probably take him the whole weekend, his hands already cut to ribbons by thorns. Next weekend he'd borrow Russell's lawnmower (a tenner from Pancho) to finish it off, make everything neat and tidy. No point in trying to attract publicity if people had to hack their way through a bloody jungle to get to you.

He'd like to see Russell's face when he'd finished. The last time he'd seen the garden he'd given Aidan a scornful look and shaken his head, then put his hands to his mouth and yelled, 'Sergeant Yashimoto – you can come out now, the war is over. There's a job as a foreman waiting for you in the Honda factory.'

He looked around him now, at the mounds of waste waiting to be bagged up, and felt good about himself, felt a weight lifting from his shoulders. He should have done this years ago. What must he have been thinking of to let it get in such a disgraceful state? How long had he spent sitting on his arse, swigging beer, watching the box, oblivious to the chaos? What kind of awful black hole had he nearly disappeared into? No, stop that. No more looking back, no regrets. From now on he was going to concentrate only on what he *could* change and put the rest out of his mind.

'You're working hard.'

Joy's voice. Aidan tried to straighten up, felt a searing pain shoot from the small of his back up his spine. *Jesus.* He dropped the shears, brought both hands to his back, slowly eased himself upright. Joy was standing by the fence, a concerned look on her face.

'Are you all right?'

As if they were friends, as if she hadn't told anyone who'd listen she'd seen a rat in his garden a few weeks ago. She'd threatened to ring up the council, get Health and Safety to prosecute him.

'Yeah, I'm fine.'

A thin little smile spread across her face as she surveyed his hard work.

'What's brought this on?'

He stared at a point about a foot above her head, like a man gripped by a vision.

'I'm planning some big changes round here.'

'Really?'

She couldn't quite manage to keep a hint of sarcasm out of her voice. He smiled blandly at her, watching her struggle to conceal her impatience. She hadn't come out here to be fobbed off like her husband. She nodded at the hole.

'What's that for?'

'What?'

He was enjoying this now.

'The big hole behind you.'

Aidan wheeled around in surprise.

'Oh, that.'

He hooked his thumbs into his belt loops, looked down fondly at his work.

'It may look like a hole to you, but that's just the beginning. I'm building a wildlife sanctuary.'

'Wildlife,' she repeated.

'Yeah, I get a lot of wildlife in my garden.'

'What sort?'

He winked at her.

'Rats. Big buggers.' He held his hands about a foot apart. 'About that size, some of them – surprised you haven't noticed.'

She shot him a deep-freeze stare, then turned on her heel. Aidan burst out laughing as she slammed the back door behind her.

Strangely enough, though the factory was set to be closed down, the orders showed no sign of drying up and it was another busy morning in the warehouse. It was a harsh, impersonal work-place, the days repetitive and draining. Exactly the kind of environment Aidan had wanted after Eileen's death; somewhere he could spend eight hours a day without any opportunity for dangerous introspection.

Thousands of cardboard boxes of varying shapes and sizes were lined up like faceless recruits on a parade ground. Stapled, tightly sealed in plastic, and labelled, ready for transporting. Yells and shouts, whistles and laughter bounced off the high metal ceiling and walls. The constant hum and whirr of forklift trucks, the smack and thud of heavy loads mingled with the determinedly jaunty sounds of Radio 2 booming out from speakers mounted high on the walls. It was like a greenhouse in the summer, as cold as ice on a winter morning. The harsh strip lighting scalded your eyes if you looked up too quickly; the air was thick with the smell of oil, plastic and stale sweat.

They had been working flat out. After sitting at home, worrying himself sick about the future, Aidan was enjoying the rigorous work-out. He liked to be busy. That way the voices inside your head didn't have time to throw doubts, recriminations and interrogations at you.

What in god's name were you thinking of? That'll never work, give that idea up now, you old fool. What have you done with your life – nothing!

No, if the mind had to work in tandem with the body, it was a much nicer customer. There were all kinds of things lurking in your head that you just didn't want to know about. In another era, he probably would have talked to a priest about them. Nowadays people went on *Trisha* instead and made a spectacle of themselves, spewing their guts in public. But there *was* no easy answer: talking changed nothing. He didn't see what good saying the same things over and over would do, apart from boring your friends to death. Some things were better left unexamined. You needed to keep active to stop them from surfacing.

He liked the banter too, once you got a rhythm going and the job was under control, the jokes would start flying.

'This bloke goes to the doctor, he says, Doctor, every time I have sex with my wife she . . .'

It didn't matter if everyone had heard them before, once someone started telling jokes it was a sign that everything was flowing.

Gwyn came to collect another stack of boxes to load up. He parked his forklift next to Aidan, who was standing with his hands on his hips, taking a breather. Gwyn had noticed a change in Aidan's mood these last few days, he'd been less morose, more like his old self, had even started laughing and taking part again.

Gwyn winked at him, said, 'Still worried about the price of coffins?'

Aidan winked back.

'Nah, not anymore. I've asked Pancho to get me one. He'll save me a fortune.'

Gwyn stared at him blankly for a few seconds, then moved on without a word.

Shauna was browsing in the open-air craft market in Cardiff city centre, looking for a present for Charlie's birthday. She heard someone calling out her name, turned round to find Joy beaming at her.

'How are you, love?'

'I'm fine, Joy. Yourself?'

'Oh, you know me, I never complain.'

Shauna managed to keep a straight face. The spiteful, venomous old bitch.

'So what brings you to Cardiff?'

'Me and Ken are going to see the Band of the Coldstream Guards at St David's Hall. He's in a bookshop at the moment – buying more books about steam trains, I expect.'

Shauna had just spotted a nice watercolour of Cader Idris that Charlie might like, and wanted to check out the price. Joy noticed her distracted air, clamped a concerned expression on her face and got to the point.

'Is your dad OK?'

'Yeah, considering.'

'Considering what?'

Joy's eyes shone with excitement.

'The fact that he's being made redundant.'

'Yes, of course.'

The excitement faded, she knew about *that*. Shauna now realised she'd rushed over to pass on some gossip. She hated giving her the satisfaction of showing she was interested, but couldn't help worrying about Aidan.

'Why do you ask?'

Joy drew closer.

'He's started behaving very strangely.'

She gave Shauna one of her significant looks, then waited.

'How strange?'

'Well, after all these years he's finally decided to do something about the garden. He spent the whole weekend cutting the grass and weeds, I've never seen anything like it. He said he was planning some big changes.'

That *was* strange.

'Isn't that good?'

Joy gave a little angry twitch of her head, 'He was very rude when I asked him about it. He told me he was building a wildlife sanctuary.'

'A *what*?'

Joy looked at her scornfully. 'Well of course he isn't, he was being sarcastic.'

'Oh.'

Shauna was beginning to lose the thread now.

'I mean, naturally I was curious, since he'd dug a great big hole the week before. Ken said that by the time he'd finished, he was up to his neck in it.'

She widened her eyes.

'If I didn't know better, I'd swear it was a grave.'

As Shauna stood in the marketplace, digesting Joy's latest gossip, Aidan was sitting at the dining-room table, an open exercise book in front of him, chewing a biro. The page was covered with crossings-out, exclamation marks, arrows and asterisks, the table scattered with screwed-up pages. There was a knack to this kind of thing, and he didn't seem to have it. It reminded him too much of being back at school, his English teacher asking them to write an essay. *What you did on your holidays this summer, two pages, starting now.* He'd be fine talking about his holidays in the playground before school began – no trouble then – but as soon as he sat down in front of a blank page, he seized up.

He read back what he'd written.

I have taken this desperate step as a last resort. Sunny Jim Electronics have turned down every offer that the government, the Welsh Assembly and the union have made. I think it's about time that employers in this country started treating their workers with more respect and stopped showing them the door when it suits them, without any sense of responsibility for the misery they're causing.

I dread to think what's going to happen to this town if they close down the factory. Every year it gets harder to make ends meet. Every year another town round here goes under. And once they've gone under they never come back. Now it looks like it's going to be us.

It seems no matter how much we bend and twist and stretch we're still not flexible enough for the demands of today's labour market. We have to change, we can't go on as we are, that's all you hear them say now, the politicians. But while they're very fond of telling other people how they need to change, they don't seem very keen to follow their own advice – their pay rises and their bonuses get bigger and bigger.

It had taken him an hour, and he meant every single word, and it was shite. There were so many things he didn't know how to say, that he wasn't even sure you *could* say in a press release.

The phone rang. Aidan walked into the hall, picked it up.

'Hello.'

'Dad?'

'Oh, hi-ya, Shauna, how are you, love?'

'I'm fine, how are you?'

He walked back into the living room, sat back down at the table, staring at the exercise book. He picked up his pen, wrote *His family are behind him every inch of the way*, drew a line underneath.

'Dad?'

'Sorry, Shauna, I'm fine.'

'Really?'

He didn't want her worrying about him; this wasn't her problem.

'Only Joy was telling me about this big hole you've dug in the garden.'

So that was what this was all about.

'Did she now? Nosy cow, I'll bet she's dying to know what I'm doing.'

'Dad – what *are* you doing?'

He'd have to tell her sooner or later, it wasn't fair to keep her in the dark, and he certainly couldn't lie to her. That way he'd be no better than Richter. But something happened halfway through his explanation of his master plan. The more he imagined her anxious face at the other end of the line, the more insane his plan felt. When he'd finished, he said 'So there, now you know – see, there's nothing to be worried about.'

Static and silence greeted his final flourish.

'Shauna? Are you there?'

'Dad, I'm coming to see you. We need to talk.'

The Globe was packed. It was Quiz Night, first prize a £20 Tesco's voucher.

Pancho walked in just as Frank was about to start asking the questions, caught Aidan's eye and beckoned him over.

'Excuse me,' said Aidan, getting up and squeezing past the others, ignoring their startled looks. Pancho stood by the door, looking round him, drumming his fingers against the wall. He had a new T-shirt on tonight, a drawing of a balaclaved Zapatista giving a two-fingered victory salute. Underneath it read *El pueblo unido jamas sera vencido*. Aidan didn't have a clue what it meant, but was pretty sure it wasn't Welsh.

'I've got something to show you.'

Aidan felt a tremor of fear run through him, realising he'd

actually been dreading this moment. Pancho watched him closely.

'You're not going to change your mind after all the trouble I went to getting it?'

'No, course not.'

'Come on then.'

'Now?'

'Yeah – now.'

Aidan looked back at the table in the corner where Russell, Gwyn and Wilf were watching them curiously. If he went now they'd be a man short.

'Can you wait an hour?'

Pancho stiffened. 'I'm going to be tied up for the rest of the week after tonight.' He glanced sideways, apprehensive now, something bothering him. He stepped closer to Aidan, lowered his voice. 'I thought you was in a hurry?'

A couple of blokes standing at the bar had started taking an interest in their conversation, and Aidan could see Pancho didn't like that. He *had* told him he needed it as quickly as possible.

'All right, let's go.'

Pancho's van was parked just outside. As they were putting on their seat belts, Aidan said, 'Where are we going?'

Pancho grinned. 'Tonight I am bestowing a great honour and privilege on you, Aidan. I'm taking you to a secret facility – somewhere no one else has ever seen – not even my senorita, *comprende*?'

Aidan tried to look suitably impressed.

'There's been a lot of speculation about its location, as I'm sure you know. Some people reckon it's in Maindee, others say Gold Tops or Llis-werry, I've even heard it said that it's out in Cat's Ash.' Pancho chuckled at the notion. 'No fear, it's all twitching curtains out there.'

Aidan was wondering how much more of this he'd have to listen to before Pancho got to the point.

'I even heard someone say it didn't exist, was just another part of the Pancho myth.' Dismissive now, trying to make out that what people said about him was water off a duck's back. But Aidan could see he loved it.

'So what is this place everyone's talking about?'

Pancho's leather jacket creaked as he leaned closer. 'Where I store the merchandise.'

He fixed Aidan with a stare.

'We're going to my lock-up.' He paused, as serious and still as someone giving evidence in the Old Bailey. 'There are people who'd sell their grandmother to discover the whereabouts of Pancho's lock-up.'

Aidan was beginning to feel excited now, despite himself. Tried to hide it by smirking and saying, 'Oh aye, do you want to frisk me, make sure I haven't got a hidden camera on me?'

Pancho reached into his pocket, took out a large red handkerchief.

'No, I just want you to wear this.'

'What?'

Pancho was holding it up in front of Aidan, turning it slowly round, so he could see both sides. 'It hasn't been used, straight from the drawer that is.'

'I don't care if you've had it bloody dry-cleaned, I'm not wearing it.'

Pancho lowered the handkerchief. When he spoke again, his tone was hushed, confidential.

'Look, Aidan, don't take it personally, this is all about business confidentiality.'

'What are you saying?'

'Don't get me wrong, I'm not accusing you of anything, I know you're not a grass. But say you had a few drinks one night and, without meaning to, just happened to mention that you'd visited my lock-up.'

Aidan was ready to unclip his seat belt and get out. Pancho leaned even closer.

'You never know who's listening to your conversation in a public place, do you? Did you notice how interested those blokes at the bar were in our conversation?'

Aidan had.

'I came into the Globe one night with a load of Calvin Klein gear — tops and ladies' and gents' underwear at very advantageous prices. Those two blokes were there, wanted a look, then didn't stop bitching — were they genuine? Where did I get them? Even tried to haggle about the price — I couldn't fucking believe it, mun. I had to lay down the law in no uncertain terms, told them to pay up or shut up. They didn't like it, gave me these heavy stares they'd picked up off *The Sopranos*. Did you see how interested they were in what we were saying?' His hand gripped Aidan's leg. 'Just imagine if a couple of blokes like them who'd been listening to you talking about having been to my lock-up followed you home after closing time, pushed you down a dark alley and gave you a good kicking? Wouldn't stop till they got the address of my lock-up out of you?'

He withdrew his hand. He frowned, hating to bring this up.

'I'd feel responsible if you ended up in hospital — and imagine how *you'd* feel if I lost all my stock because you'd given them the address. As if you wouldn't be feeling bad enough already with a broken nose and broken ribs, perhaps a hernia and . . .'

'All right, all right, I get the picture.'

'So, to avoid any security lapses, and any chance of bad blood between us in the future . . .' Pancho held the handkerchief up again. Aidan thought about the hassle of starting the search for a coffin all over again, and at full price too.

'All right, give it here.'

Pancho smiled. 'I'm glad you're being so sensible about this.'

Aidan took it from him, folded it over lengthways a couple of times, then placed it carefully round his head.

'You need a hand tying the knot?'

'No.'

An edge to Aidan's voice this time.

'Fair enough.'

Pancho knew when to stop. He waited till Aidan had finished, then started the van, headed off. He took a right at the end of the street, then straight on for a few minutes, slowed, then circled a big roundabout, joined heavy traffic going west. Aidan guessed they were travelling along Cardiff Road. But shortly afterwards Pancho took a left, another left, then a right, in quick succession, and Aidan began to lose track of where they were. He wondered if Pancho was deliberately taking a complicated route to throw him off the trail. Another left, then they were heading down a road pitted with potholes. Aidan began to bounce around in his seat; not being able to see made it much worse. He gripped the door handle, feeling horribly vulnerable.

'Fucking hell, I feel like Brian Keenan.'

Pancho laughed. 'Don't worry, we'll be there shortly.'

They soon turned right on to a better road, Pancho's mobile rang.

'Hello.'

Aidan heard a lorry thundering past, wondered if they were near the docks.

'I can't do it tomorrow, I'm in Swansea all day. *What?*'

The van swerved sharply to the right. A horn blared, quickly followed by a car roaring past them on their right.

'Christ, Pancho, keep your eyes on the road.'

'You promised me delivery this week, what am I supposed to tell my customers?'

Aidan gripped the edge of his seat and the brakes squealed as they took a corner at fifty.

Ten terrifying minutes later Pancho finally slowed down.

'Here we are.'

Pancho parked the van and Aidan took off his blindfold.

'I'm never getting in this van with you again, you're a bloody madman.'

Pancho grinned. 'I live life in the fast lane, *hombre.*'

23

They stepped out into a narrow road that ran parallel to some railway arches. Pancho walked over to a door, brought out a bunch of keys. Aidan watched him undo three locks, pull open the door, reach inside and turn on a light switch. He waved Aidan inside. The place was crammed to the rafters, boxes piled up almost to the sickly strip lights that hung from the ceiling. Aidan scanned the contents – computers, mobile phones, hi-fis, CD players, video and DVD players, TVs, electric kettles, bread-makers, Walkmans. Plastic bags filled with jeans, jackets, jumpers, tops, coats and skirts and dresses. Aidan gave a low whistle as he wandered past, noting names and labels as he went.

'Not bad, eh?' said Pancho. 'Now you can see why I'm concerned about security.'

'I got to hand it to you, Pancho . . . Who's going to buy that?'

Aidan pointed to a life-size plastic skeleton sitting in an armchair, a Welsh rugby scarf tied round his neck, a pint glass wedged in one hand.

'That's my security guard.'

Further along there were cookers, fridges, a bath, a toilet, a couple of bidets; rolls of carpet and lino, cat baskets, a photocopier, fax machines, karaoke machines, barbecue sets, a wheelchair and a stack of deckchairs.

Pancho touched him lightly on the shoulder as he squeezed past.

'Now then, have I got a bargain for you.'

He bent down to drag a coffin from behind a bright-purple three-piece suite.

'There you go.'

It was much plainer than the ones in the undertaker's. There were no solid gold handles. No handles at all, in fact, just little U-shaped loops of rope where the handles would normally be. He didn't know what kind of wood it was made of, but it looked cheap and nasty. If someone had asked him to describe it, he'd have said the ones he'd seen before looked like they'd come from Harrods and this one looked straight out of the local Co-op.

'Now then, Aidan, what kind of price were the coffins you saw in the undertaker's?'

'The cheapest was £400.'

Pancho beamed. 'Well, I'm going to save you a lot of money.'

'It looks a bit plain. Is it, what do you call it, shop-soiled or something?'

Pancho crossed his arms.

'You are looking at the future. This is a state of the art environmentally-friendly coffin.'

'Is that a fact?'

'Most coffins today are made of veneered chipboard with plastic handles and linings, right? They're a disaster for the environment, they cause air pollution when they're cremated . . .'

'I'm not going to be cremated!'

Pancho looked put out at being interrupted. Aidan knew how much he loved his sales patter; it could go off in any direction, ranging across many different subjects before he got to the matter in hand. Like the time he'd sold him and Wilf video recorders. It was a good price and they would have happily stumped up straight away, but Pancho had talked for a good ten minutes about the benefits of home entertainment, how it kept the family together and saved you money, obscure riffs about why renting a video was better for your health than going to the cinema. Aidan couldn't remember a word of it now, but he'd been completely convinced at the time. He often thought that Pancho enjoyed the sales talk as much as the sale itself.

'And the plastic takes a long time to break down after burial. Now when you think about all the harm done to the countryside in Wales by the coal mines, the iron and steel industries and all the rest, then I think you'll agree it's time we stopped causing any more damage to our fair nation.'

'I didn't know you were so concerned about the environment.'

Pancho nodded. 'Got to think of the future, haven't you? What kind of a world we're going to leave for the kiddies, like.'

'Member of Greenpeace, are you?'

Pancho raised his eyebrows.

'No, but I'm a friend of a Friend of the Earth.'

He talked for another few minutes about the different types of coffin you got these days, how cardboard coffins would disintegrate, allowing the bodies inside to fertilise the soil. Aidan was impressed, he hadn't realised how much things had changed.

'Now, to return to your question, it doesn't look like the coffins you saw in the undertaker's because those are made of wood – a terrible waste of resources; at the rate they're cutting down forests all over the world, there'll be none left soon. Can you imagine a world without trees? Where would the birds nest?'

Pancho patted the coffin and said, 'That's why I'm pleased to say this coffin is made from one hundred per cent recycled cardboard.'

'Fucking cardboard!' Aidan took a step back, looked again. No wonder it looked different. 'Jesus Christ, mun, it'll never hold me, I'll fall right through it.'

Pancho gave him a pitying look.

'This will hold someone who weighs twenty stone, no problem. It's made from extra-tough double thickness corrugated board with an additional internal plastic lining for support along the base.'

'Till it rains, then it'll get wet, go soft and crumble to bloody bits.'

'Don't be stupid.' Pancho leant down, rapped his knuckles hard on the top. 'That's as strong as any wood.'

Aidan looked at him sceptically.

'Cardboard's very strong.' Pancho gestured at the stacks of boxes surrounding them. 'Think of the stuff they put in cardboard boxes these days and ship around the country –

cookers, fridges, all sorts. We're talking about very tough material here, not something made out of cornflakes packets.'

He paused before delivering the *coup de grâce*. 'And it's yours for £40.'

That shut Aidan up.

'£40?'

Pancho nodded. 'That's what I said. I'm telling you, they're all the rage, people are queuing up to be buried in cardboard.'

Aidan banged on the top. It did feel very solid.

'Can I try it out?'

'Be my guest.'

Pancho removed the lid. It wasn't as heavy as wood, but felt very substantial. Aidan imagined some monstrous weight crushing and compacting the cardboard into this dense, tough block. He got inside, lay back, folded his hands across his stomach. It was quite roomy. He slid himself down, so that his feet touched the bottom, then stretched out his hand behind him and calculated that there was about a ten-inch gap between his head and the top. Pancho, the consummate salesman, immediately picked up on his thoughts. 'It's an extra-large model – six foot ten long, twenty-six inches wide, sixteen inches deep. Made by this company that specialises in coffins for the big guys. You'd normally have to pay extra for such a specialist product.'

Aidan closed his eyes. He felt surprisingly calm. There was nothing to be scared of. It was just a box, after all. Perhaps a cardboard coffin was exactly what he needed. If you dispensed with the normal fixtures and fittings, brass handles, metal inscription plate, fancy hinges and all the rest of the undertaker's paraphernalia, it seemed less morbid somehow. Of course Pancho was just a few feet away, and he wasn't actually under the ground yet. Still, he felt OK.

'Stop it.'

'Eh?'

Aidan opened his eyes, saw Pancho standing at the end of the coffin, hands stuffed into his pockets, glaring down at him.

'That's enough, get up now, you're giving me the bloody creeps, mun.'

Aidan grinned, pleased to see Pancho on the back foot for once.

'Like I said, it's not what you think. I'm planning to stick around for a long time yet. Let me tell you what I've got in mind.'

Pancho reached behind him, pulled a deckchair from the pile, unfolded it, sat down at the end of the coffin. He lit up a cheroot. When Aidan had finished speaking, Pancho shook his head, blew another perfect smoke ring. 'You are one crazy *hombre*.' He smiled, slowly nodding his head. 'You know, it might even work.'

'You think so?'

But Pancho was already off, following his own train of thought. He had a faraway look in his eyes. 'The little man against the system, one crazy son of a bitch who just doesn't know when he's beaten.' He tapped some ash thoughtfully onto the floor. 'Yeah, I like it.'

Aidan was delighted. Then a little voice in his head warned him that Pancho probably agreed with whatever a customer said before a purchase. Pancho blew another smoke ring, watched it rising.

'Have you thought of what else you'll need?'

'What else *will* I need?'

'You want the papers and TV to interview you, right?'

'Right.'

'Then you'll need a mobile. How else they going to contact you? And, I hate to say this, but what if *you* need to contact someone in an emergency, how else you going to do it except with a mobile, when you're six feet under?'

'But I've never used one.'

Pancho waved a hand dismissively. 'There's nothing to it, I'll explain how they work. And what are you going to do with yourself when you're just lying there? How are you gonna stop going out of your mind with boredom? Don't tell me you're going to make your own entertainment. Over there . . . somewhere . . .' Pancho craned his neck, pointed to the far corner of the lock-up, 'I got some fantastic digital radios – brilliant sound quality, just the thing for a man in your position.'

'I don't know about that, Pancho, money's a bit tight. I haven't got any to spend on gadgets.'

'You're thinking about this the wrong way, *amigo*. These are not gadgets, these are absolute necessities. I'm sure we can come to some agreement. I've been thinking, you aren't the only one who'll need a mobile, don't tell me Russell, Gwyn and Wilf aren't going to be involved in this scheme of yours.'

'They don't know about it yet.'

'You're going to tell them, surely?'

'Of course.'

'Then they're going to want to help.'

'I hope so, anyway.'

'Well they'll all need a mobile too then, won't they? I mean, just in case you need to reach them in . . .'

'An emergency.'

Pancho treated Aidan to one of those Latin shrugs he did so well – *you said it*.

'So how about this for a deal? If you put those three new customers my way, you can have yours for half price.'

Pancho took another drag from his cheroot, watching Aidan carefully through the smoke. Aidan had to admit it was tempting, and they *would* need a way of keeping in contact.

'Plus, you're going to save a fortune on the coffin.'

His mobile rang again. His face dropped when he answered. Someone started giving him a hard time. Aidan heard a female voice at the other end.

'I know I did, but . . . I know . . . I know . . . I'll be half an hour at most, I . . . listen to me, will you? *Listen to me!*'

He got up and walked away, continued the call further off, out of sight behind a stack of boxes. He came back after a couple of minutes, grinning self-consciously.

'My senorita. I promised her I'd be back by eight. She's not happy, cooked chilli con carne, bought a nice bottle of wine . . .' He shrugged. 'The price of dedication to my customers.' He put the mobile away, dismissed the problem from his mind. 'Now, £40, that's the cash price.'

'I haven't got that much on me.'

'I'll drive you to a cashpoint. Come on, let's get this thing loaded on to the van.'

They carried the coffin outside, Pancho opened the back door of the van. There were half a dozen cookers jammed in the back. Pancho gripped Aidan's shoulder. 'Come on, give me a hand getting these into the lock-up and then we'll put your coffin in and drive to a cashpoint.'

He clocked Aidan's expression.

'Come on, mun, it won't take a couple of fit blokes like us five minutes.'

Aidan crossed his arms. 'Is it just a coincidence that you're bestowing the great honour and privilege of being the first person to visit your lock-up on me on the night when you just happen to have a van-load of cookers to shift?'

But Pancho just laughed, as if Aidan had said something hilarious.

The following night Aidan was having a drink in the Globe with Russell, Gwyn and Wilf. This was it, the acid test. He'd known these guys for years, they'd stuck with him through thick and thin, were more like his brothers. They were cranky, stubborn bastards, but they were the best friends he had and he needed them on his side. His posse, that's what Dylan had called them. The expressions they had these days. His posse.

'What are you grinning at?' asked Gwyn.

'Something my son said.'

'What was that then?'

Russell and Wilf were looking at him too, this was it.

'Oh nothing – listen, I've got an idea about how to stop them closing down the factory.'

Russell paused, the glass halfway to his mouth. He gave Aidan a look he couldn't fathom.

'Do you want to hear it?'

Russell took a swig of his pint and shrugged. Aidan might as well have asked him if he'd wanted to know what he'd had for dinner.

'Aye, why not?'

This didn't bother Aidan though, Russell never got excited about anyone else's ideas. Gwyn looked interested, but wouldn't say anything till Russell had had his say. Wilf looked confused, the course of the conversation changing too quickly for him. It could wear you out, waiting for Wilf to catch up. Aidan rested his arms on the table.

'You see I think we've been going about this the wrong way, sitting around waiting for somebody else to help us. Where's that got us?'

He paused, letting the point sink in.

'Let's face it, the government's not going to do anything, right?'

'Aye,' said Gwyn, 'they've even stopped asking for their money.'

When Sunny Jim Electronics first announced they were closing the factory, several MPs had angrily demanded they pay back the £18 million of government aid they'd received to encourage investment in an area of high unemployment. But that seemed to have slipped off the agenda.

'I wish I could forget about £18 million like that.'

He reminded them how the union had been ignored, how when the Welsh Assembly tried to talk to Sunny Jim about a deal the week before, the meeting lasted barely an hour, Rhodri Morgan coming out grim-faced with nothing to show. He moved quickly on, not wanting to set Russell off on his usual Welsh Assembly rant.

'So who does that leave?'

'We could try sending up the Bat signal,' said Gwyn.

Aidan smiled, you had to allow them their joke. He was pleased with how it was going so far.

'Nothing's going to happen unless we *make* something happen ourselves. And time is running out. People are already forgetting about us. So we need to do something quick.'

They'd briefly made the news and the national newspapers when the redundancies were first announced. But even then, he often wondered if it was mainly because of that stupid slogan.

Sunny Jim Electronics, the company whose slogan was 'We'll give you a free pair of sunglasses when you come to work for us – you'll need them, your prospects will be so dazzling!' today announced it is to close its factories in south Wales and Tyneside with the loss of over 2,000 jobs.

Then, after a couple of days, newer, more entertaining stories came along – someone off *Big Brother* had made a record, David Beckham changed his hairstyle, and they were forgotten.

'We need something that will get us back in the news, put pressure on Sunny Jim and the government to do something.'

'OK,' said Russell, 'so let me see if I've got this right. You, Aidan Walsh, are going to do something that's going to make you a household name and save our jobs.'

He was twisting Aidan's words. He wasn't doing this for personal glory.

Russell put his hands to his mouth, yelled, 'Hey, Frank, how long you had that signed photo of Tom Jones behind the bar?'

Frank looked up from pulling a pint, shrugged. 'About twenty years, probably. Why?'

'Well I reckon you should take it down, he's had his day, mun, he's a dinosaur.'

' "Delilah" was good, mind,' said Wilf.

'It was good thirty years ago.'

'Listen, all I'm saying is . . .'

Russell cut Aidan short again. 'What you need up there behind the bar is a signed photo of a local hero, someone the punters can look up to.'

'Oh aye? Like who?'

He handed the man his pint, took his money. The man turned round and looked at Russell expectantly, catching his tone, waiting to be entertained.

'It just so happens you've got exactly the type of inspirational figure you're looking for in here right now.'

'Yeah? Who's that then?'

Russell pointed to Aidan. 'Him.'

'Him?'

Frank was trying not to laugh.

'Yeah, he's going to put this place on the map.'

Aidan forced a smile, there was no point trying to stop him now, it would only look worse if he got annoyed.

'Can I have your autograph?' asked the man standing at the bar, grinning.

'Piss off.'

There were limits, his friends winding him up was one thing, but he didn't even know the bloke.

'Charming.'

The man grabbed his pint and walked away. Frank went to serve another customer.

'You finished now?' asked Aidan.

'So you're going to succeed where the government and the union and the Taffia's Talking Shop have failed?'

'I know it sounds a bit crazy, but I think it might just work, yeah.'

Russell snorted.

'Yeah – and Wales are going to beat Brazil 6–0 in the next world cup final.'

The others sniggered. Aidan couldn't hide his anger any longer, he'd a right to expect better than this from them. They were his friends and they were all being screwed right along with him. He was the only one who hadn't given up, the one man with a bit of fight left in him, and they were turning on him for it.

'All right,' said Russell, his voice softer when he saw Aidan's expression. 'Come on, tell us about your plan.'

'Forget it.'

'Come on, mun,' said Gwyn. 'He was only pulling your leg.'

'He doesn't know when to stop,' said Aidan.

'All right, all right, I'm sorry I took the piss, I *really* want to hear about your plan,' said Russell, folding his arms too. He sighed theatrically. 'And I promise not to interrupt or crack jokes when you're explaining it, cross my heart.'

Aidan was stony-faced. Russell puckered up his lips and blew him a kiss. 'Go on!'

'Fuck off.'

Now they were all able to laugh, Wilf longest and loudest, delighted and relieved that everything was OK again. Russell stretched out his hand, palm down, and Aidan slapped it hard.

Gwyn said, 'Come on then, we're waiting.'

'OK, it's what you might call an extreme response to an extreme situation. I'm going to bury myself alive in a coffin in my garden, and I'm not coming back up again till Sunny Jim keep the factory open and save our jobs.'

They stared at him for a long time.

'Well,' said Aidan, 'haven't any of you got anything to say?'

Shauna pulled up outside her father's house. She felt a great weariness descending. She'd been dealing with other people's issues all week at work: two clients had broken down in tears, another had spent most of the session talking about suicide. The last thing she wanted to do right now was deal with this. Her family reminded her of those sniffer dogs you saw in films, always tracking down the guy who'd escaped from prison, no matter how ingeniously he'd covered his tracks. Just when you thought you could relax and start your new life, came that awful howling as they picked up on your scent.

She turned off the engine and leaned back in her seat, surveying the state of the place. He needed a new roof. There was a crack running from just under the guttering down to Aidan's bedroom window. Another, like a bolt of lightning, shooting out from the side of the bathroom window. The hedge had long since returned to the wild, blocking the pavement.

He'd let things go. She'd meant to visit more often, keep an eye on things. *So what was stopping her?*

That bloody hedge. Mam was in charge of the garden, Dad took care of the hedge, Shauna was Dad's little helper. That was how it worked. The Sunday mornings she'd been forced to help Aidan, sweeping up the fallen branches, shovelling them into the bin, while he chopped away at it. Aidan stopping every few minutes to chat to people passing.

That your eldest?

Yeah – say hello, Shauna.

She'd rather have been anywhere but out there on show, horribly conscious of her bare arms and legs, her newly prominent bust. Aidan completely oblivious to her awkwardness about her body, grown men running their eyes over every inch of it.

Shauna – don't be rude, say hello!

Darling Dylan, the baby boy, was allowed to stay inside and play while she was dragged out to help.

Shauna knocked on the front door and waited. The curtains were still drawn. She checked her watch, a quarter past eleven. She knocked again, louder, longer. When there was still no answer, she let herself in with her key, stood at the foot of the stairs, calling.

'Dad! Dad?' Still nothing. Strange. She opened the living-room door, feeling uneasy now, and switched on the light.

'Oh my god!'

She gripped the door handle, caught her breath. Aidan was lying in a coffin in his pyjamas, eyes closed. The coffin was on the floor in front of the telly, Aidan still clutching the remote control in one hand.

Sweet Jesus Christ, she should have come sooner! She should never have left him on his own this long.

She walked over to the coffin, her heart hammering. He looked pale and bloodless. Shauna felt a stab of fear, knelt down next to the coffin. She felt for a pulse, found it, breathed a mighty sigh of relief. Then she took in the empty beer cans littering the floor.

He's bloody pissed.

She started shaking him by the shoulder.

'Dad, wake up – it's Shauna.'

His head rolled back and forth.

'Wake up!'

She shook him harder, faster, needing to hear his voice. Aidan began spluttering, 'What?'

'Are you OK?'

He looked up, wincing in the light. 'Where am I? What's happening?'

Shauna sat back on her haunches, glared down at him.

'You're in the living room, lying in a coffin in front of the telly.'

Shauna made bacon, eggs and coffee for Aidan while he had a wash.

After eating he went upstairs and got dressed. She couldn't help tidying up a little and washing some of the dirty plates. But there was nothing she could do about the hideous pale yellow floral wallpaper in the living room, beginning to peel in the top corners, or the worn and sagging furniture. She handed him another mug of coffee when he came back down.

'Thanks, love.'

He knew very well why she was here. To talk him out of it. All the same, just seeing her lifted his spirits. His daughter had grown into a beautiful, confident young woman. He'd worried that losing her mother at such a sensitive age might have scarred her for life. But she was going to be all right. More than all right. She was blossoming.

He sat down in the chair, Shauna settled herself on the sofa opposite. She nodded at the coffin. 'Where did you get it then?'

'Pancho.'

Shauna frowned. 'It's not secondhand, is it?'

'No! It's an eco-coffin.'

'I thought so,' said Shauna.

'You see most coffins are made of . . .'

Shauna was craning her neck to get a better view.

'It looks like one of those cardboard ones.'

'How did you know?'

'Get with it, Dad, green burials have been a big thing for years now.'

Aidan was gutted. He'd been looking forward to seeing the look on her face when he told her.

'One of my clients is obsessed with her own mortality, she's already bought a cardboard coffin and a plot of land in a forest to be buried in. She brought in photos to show me.'

Aidan wished she hadn't told him that. He'd never been able to get his head round the notion that people *paid* Shauna to listen to their problems – just listen, not even prescribe any pills at the end of it. She called it psychoanalysis, but he thought that was just a fancy word for indulging them, when what they really needed was someone to tell them to pull themselves together. He'd tried to move with the times, but every time she let slip what her patients were like he worried about her mixing with such utter bloody lunatics.

Shauna said, 'Well?'

He was looking his age in the harsh morning light, grey stubble, baggy eyes, sickly pallor.

'How long have you been sleeping in a coffin, Dad?'

He swallowed some coffee and slumped back in the chair.

'Last night was the first time.'

'Any particular reason for this change in your sleeping habits?'

He looked at her as if she was thick. 'I'm in training.'

'This isn't making much sense to me, Dad.'

'If you were going to run a marathon, you wouldn't just turn up on the day in your running shoes and shorts, without any preparation, and expect to win, would you? You'd train for it for months by going on a run every day, slowly building up your speed and energy. Well, that's what I'm doing, preparing myself for a marathon. This is going to be a test of endurance, and the first step is getting used to spending time in a coffin.'

'You call getting pissed in front of the telly preparation?'

Shauna saw how much that hurt him and regretted it immediately.

'I needed a bit of Dutch courage, to be honest with you. It felt a bit weird at first.' He shrugged. 'But I soon got used to it. In fact I'm going to spend this afternoon in it, have a break, then settle back down and spend the night in it again.' He looked at her and smiled. 'You know something? I got the idea after listening to one of your CDs.'

'*What?*'

He explained, then wished he hadn't – she looked mortified.

'Dad, why are you doing this? I don't understand.'

'I'm glad you don't.'

'What do you mean?'

'You've got your whole life in front of you, everything is still fresh and exciting to you, I bet you can't wait to get up in the morning.'

'Yeah, I leap out of bed every day singing "The Sound of Music", my life is one long party.'

'All right, all right . . .'

'Dad, I know it must be difficult being made redundant, but there's no need to do something as drastic as this. I can help you.'

'How?'

'If you're worried about money . . .'

'That's your money, love, you've worked damned hard for it.'

Shauna dismissed his objection with an impatient shake of her head. 'I can afford it.'

'No! Anyhow, it's not just about money.'

Shauna clasped her hands between her knees, softened her voice.

'What *is* it about, Dad?'

He didn't know how to tell her. When he woke up in the morning, and watched the minutes tick by till the radio came on, he prayed for the strength to get himself out of bed. To get up and start all over again. To go through the motions, even though he felt like a boxer on the ropes, praying for the referee to step in and stop the bout. Even though there was a gaping hole inside him that he'd never been able to fill since her mother died. The only thing that kept him going was the fact that they were expecting him at work, the one place where his absence might be noticed. Just when he thought he couldn't face doing anything, a voice inside his head would say, 'You can't miss work, what are you going to tell them if you don't turn up?' He'd always hated ringing in sick. *That's* what got him out of bed. Now they were going to chuck him on the scrapheap. He was a fifty-four-year-old unskilled labourer: where was he supposed to go from here? He needed to be able to look at himself in the mirror in the morning and not feel sick at the sight of his own reflection.

He said, 'I might not show it, but I'm worried.'

Shauna winced. The fact that Aidan actually believed he was presenting a carefree face to the world showed a disturbing degree of self-delusion.

'You need to talk to someone,' she said.

It was good to talk, he knew that. He understood it was bad to bottle things up. He also knew that it was bad to drink too much, but he still went to the pub every night. He knew it was a good idea to eat lots of fruit and vegetables, but he lived on chips, pasta and ready-meals. It was one thing knowing what was good for you, and quite another actually doing it.

'I'm talking to you, aren't I?'

'I mean to someone outside the family.'

Aidan flinched. 'You mean a shrink?'

39

'A therapist or a counsellor, yes.'

'I'm not imagining some problem in my head, I really *do* have a problem.'

'All the more reason to get some help.'

He wasn't sure what he heard in her voice then, but his own grew sharper.

'You live in a different world to me, Shauna. I'm just an ordinary working-class bloke, I wouldn't feel comfortable going to one of those people.'

'How do you know till you've tried?'

He looked at her as though she'd suggested he walk through the town centre wearing nothing but a tutu.

'Dad, this idea of yours, it worries me.'

'There's nothing to be worried about.'

'Dad, do you have any idea how stressful it will be to be trapped in a confined space under the ground for any length of time? Stuck down there on your own, all sorts of things could prey on your mind. You say you're worried, well I can't think of any better way to make it worse.'

Russell pulled up outside Aidan's house, left the engine running.

'Thanks, mate. There was no need, honestly.'

Russell put on the handbrake.

'You'd never get a bus at this time and it's a filthy night.'

The rain was hammering on the roof of Russell's Ford Escort. They'd been round Russell's house, watching a match. They'd had a few drinks, a laugh; it had been a good evening. No mention of Aidan's plan, no awkward silences. But behind the banter, Aidan sensed that Russell was brooding. Aidan looked at him now, sunk inside himself, staring morosely at the fat drops wriggling down the windscreen.

'You look done in, mun.'

The words snapped Russell out of his trance. He closed his eyes and massaged them with his fingers. He undid his seat belt, reached inside his jacket, brought out his fags and lighter.

'Want one?'

He didn't; he'd given up years ago. Couldn't decide if Russell had forgotten or was trying to wind him up. What Aidan wanted was to go straight to bed, but he could see that Russell was determined to talk.

Russell sat, sucking the smoke into his lungs. Gone midnight now, the road was deserted. The only noise the sound of a dog barking from somewhere inside the rusting hulk of Jenkins's, the old iron and steel factory that was still waiting to be re-developed. It had probably got in and couldn't find a way out, would be barking all night.

'How long have we known each other now?'

Aidan began to feel anxious.

'It's got to be over twenty years.'

'I reckon it's twenty-four, going on twenty-five.'

Aidan watched the raindrops dance and sparkle under the sickly yellow light of the nearby lamp post.

'Nearly a quarter of a century. It's scary, isn't it?'

'We're getting old, mun.'

'Yeah, we are.' Russell took a long drag, flushing the smoke out through his nostrils.

'Is it OK if I speak my mind?'

'Fuck me, Russell, do you ever *stop* speaking your mind?'

He thought Russell would laugh, felt a right prick when he stared back, deadly serious.

'I reckon I've earned the right.'

There was no need to spell it out. When Eileen died he'd nearly gone under. Russell had dragged him up by the scruff of the neck, forced him back into the land of the living. He made sure Aidan was never left on his own that first year. The kids were always out, playing in the street or park, round at friends' houses, sleeping over, a force field around Aidan warning them to keep their distance. Russell took him to the pub, to football matches, the cinema, racing at Chepstow, on day trips to Cardiff and Bristol. He was absolutely marvellous, you couldn't have asked for a better or truer friend.

After a few weeks, Aidan couldn't stand the bloody sight of him.

When he knocked on the door, he'd duck behind the sofa and hide, thinking *For fuck's sake leave me alone*. Russell would begin to shout, 'Answer the door – I know you're in there', pounding louder and louder. He was a big bastard and after a while Aidan began to worry he'd break down the door if he didn't answer. Eventually he'd pull himself together, open up and make some lame excuse.

I was on the toilet.

I was on the phone.

Russell would smile wearily, not believing it for a minute, then squeeze his shoulder and say, 'Come on, get your coat on.' Aidan wanted to burst into tears then, to lay his head on Russell's shoulder and say, 'Why me? Why the fuck did this happen to me?' But he didn't. He got his coat. He followed Russell out to the car. He strapped himself in. He let himself be taken out for the day. *I reckon I've earned the right.* If it hadn't been for Russell, he'd still be hiding behind the sofa, asking *Why me?*

'Go on.'

'This idea of yours, burying yourself alive – don't do it, for fuck's sake. You'll never be able to stick it. I guarantee you'll be screaming to come back up after a few days. And what will you do then? You know what they're like round here. They love to have a go at anyone who tries something a bit different, especially if it doesn't come off. They'll be queuing up to say "I told you so."'

He paused to take another drag from his cigarette. Aidan was staring straight ahead, expressionless.

'Then you'll have to crawl back to Sunny Jim with your tail between your legs, hope they take pity on you and let you carry on working so you can claim your redundancy in a few months. Have you thought about what that will feel like? Pleading with those bastards, telling them you're sorry you upset them?'

'Yes,' said Aidan, 'I have. I've thought about that and I've decided to go ahead anyway. And I want you to know that if I make a fool of myself, you can be the first one to say "I told you so." How about that? Satisfied?'

A nerve under Russell's eye began to jump. He turned away, rolled down the window, flicked his cigarette out, sparks scattering in the dark.

He turned back to face Aidan, his face tight and strained now.

'I'm trying to help you here.'

Aidan observed him carefully. Maybe he was, but Aidan couldn't help feeling that Russell also wanted to keep him in his place. Russell had always been the one who called the shots, who had the final say on what was and wasn't a good idea. Who cut people down to size when he thought they were getting too big for their boots. Maybe he didn't like Aidan taking the initiative for once. For coming up with an idea when everybody else had accepted defeat.

'Thanks for the advice, mate. Listen, I've got to go, I'm done in.'

He opened the car door. He needed to get away from him now, before he lost his temper. Russell gripped his arm.

'I'll be right behind you if you go ahead with this – you know that, right?'

He looked as though he wanted to punch Aidan.

'Yeah, mate, I know.'

'It's just that . . .'

'I know – it sounds mad. I know it does.'

Aidan stepped into the rain. He'd show him who was mad. He'd show them all.

2

Cardiff made Dylan sick to his guts. Everything so new and flash and brazen compared to Crindau. When he was a kid you knew where you were. Crindau was a dump and, just down the road was Cardiff, an even bigger dump, probably the drabbest, dreariest capital city in Europe. But now teenagers all over the country applying to university were thinking, 'Maybe I'll go to Cardiff, I've heard that's a happening place' – *unbelievable*. Cardiff was like some old lag lying in the gutter who had finally, miraculously, won the lottery, and had immediately tarted herself up with all the worst accessories that new money could buy. Except she'd done it in such a hurry that she'd missed some bits. Around the edges and right in the centre, here and there, were patches of the old Cardiff, drab, dirty and malignant. It seemed the rest of Wales could fall to pieces as long as they had one shiny new place they could put in the shop window where all the bigwigs just happened to have their offices. It stank, mun, stank to high heaven. No amount of new investment could disguise what a festering provincial hole it remained beneath the shiny new trappings. He didn't know how Shauna could bear to live there.

And, on top of that, she was late.

He'd been sitting here waiting for her for over twenty minutes. It was one of those places that Cardiff was full of now, that couldn't make up its mind whether it was a pub or a café. Two women sat at a corner table with bags at their feet, yakking over cappuccinos, while everyone else was stood around the bar knocking back pints of lager, Orbital playing at earsplitting volume.

This wasn't like Shauna. He knocked back his fizzy water and headed for the door. He'd wait outside, give her another five minutes, if she didn't turn up then, that was it. He stood next to the window, peering at the name. *Café de Paris*. He lit up and took a long drag.

'Dylan!'

He looked up to see Shauna, face flushed, running towards him.

'Where you been?'

'I'm sorry. I had a call at the last minute from a client who'd just taken a load of pills – I had to keep her talking while I got a colleague to send for an ambulance. I couldn't leave – why don't you switch on your bloody mobile?'

'It was nicked last week.'

She groaned and shut her eyes tight, sagging. She looked bloody awful.

'Hey . . .' He reached out, touched her arm. She opened her eyes, looked at him. 'God, what a week I've had.' He handed her his fag.

'Thought you'd given up.'

'I have. And now I'm giving up again.'

He checked out a woman squeezing past who looked back, gave him the eye, quite fit too. Shauna was grinning at him.

'Makes a change for *me* to be late, all the same.' She held out her arms. 'Come here, you.'

Dylan smiled and they hugged. Both realised how desperately tightly they were hanging on to each other at the same time. Started giggling.

'So, how you doing, little brother?'

'Pretty good.'

'I need a drink,' said Shauna. 'Come on.'

Dylan suddenly drew back. 'Not in there, five more minutes listening to bloody Orbital and I'll turn into Travis Bickle.'

'OK, where?'

'It's your town – but make it a proper bar, OK?'

A large glass of wine mellowed Shauna. Then, after a bit of Mrs Doyle-type squabbling over who would pay, Dylan let her get the second round too.

'I don't know how you do it,' said Dylan, 'listening to other people's stuff all day. Don't you ever drift off and start thinking about something else while they're gabbing on?'

She shrugged. 'You learn not to. Have you got any fags left?'

'One – wanna share it?'

Shauna nodded. While he was lighting up she said, 'Anyway, I don't know how you could get up on a stage in front of all those people, I couldn't do that.'

'No?' He handed her the cigarette, feeling chuffed now. Shauna wasn't one to lavish praise. Not on him, anyhow. They were getting along much better than they had for ages, it was almost like being out with a mate.

'You feel at home up there, don't you?' She gave him a long, leisurely look, like she was finally seeing who he really was. He moved a little closer so she could see even better. 'I do, I love it. I get nervous beforehand, yeah, but once I'm on . . .' He clicked his fingers. '. . . I'm flying.'

She blew some smoke out of the side of her mouth, tapped the cigarette over the ashtray. 'You've landed on your feet this time – getting your Equity Card just a few months out of drama college, then getting this job so soon after the last one finished. Most actors spend months, *years*, waiting for two jobs in a row.'

He didn't like that, *landed on your feet*, as if he'd been lucky. It wasn't luck, he was good. She handed him back the cig and he took a quick drag before saying, 'Yeah, but I'm telling you this play is *bad*. I don't mean not very good, I mean fucking shocking. It's a piece of tripe.' He suddenly sat up very straight, held his bottle of Budvar like a microphone and did his Hollywood voiceover. 'It's hard-hitting, it's controversial, it's *Wasted* – the latest must-see play by the Streetwise Theatre Company, the most exciting thing to ever hit Llangrotty Village Hall. You'll laugh, you'll cry, you'll kiss six quid goodbye.'

Shauna smiled indulgently. 'OK, OK, it's no masterpiece, but it will help build up your CV.'

Dylan hadn't finished.

'We won't be doing it in theatres either. Too bourgeois, reckons the director. That's not the place to reach *real people*, the gwerin, you know.'

'Ah them, the common people.'

'Right, so I'll be spending the next six months trudging round community centres and schools. *And* we have to stay behind afterwards and have a discussion with the audience about *the issues*.'

'What issues?'

'The issues raised by this scintillating drama about drug addiction and how they relate to, like, the local kids, dig?'

'I'm getting the picture.'

'Shauna, promise not to come and see me in it, or I'll never forgive you, I swear to god.'

'Look, Dylan, you're twenty-six and this is, what, your fourth different career since uni?'

He shrugged. 'Something like that.'

'You walked out of your journalism training after a few months.'

'I wanted to write something *meaningful*, not another 500 words about drunken boneheads kicking lumps out of each other after closing time.'

'So you left to try stand-up.'

'There's only so many times you can stand to hear some drunken Cockney shout, "Get off, you Welsh bastard!"'

'Then there was your band . . .'

He smiled nostalgically. 'Tonypandy Five-0 – could have made it too, if we'd had a good manager instead of that thieving bastard Brynley.'

She let that go. 'Now you're getting regular work, just be happy to consolidate, OK?'

He was drumming his fingers distractedly on the table.

'Please don't do that.'

He placed his hands on his legs, began drumming them instead. 'You're right, I just have to bide my time for a bit. Not

47

another word about the play.' It wasn't worth starting an argument about, they were getting on too well. When you came down to it, Shauna was all right really, once she'd stopped pulling all that big sister crap on him. He could imagine having a good night out with Shauna. He pointed at her half-empty glass. 'Another?'

'OK.'

As he got up he clicked his fingers, pointed at her, grinning. 'I'll get some fags.'

When he came back, Shauna gave him a significant look, said quietly, 'We haven't talked about Dad yet.'

Dylan gazed at his bottle of Budvar and started peeling the corner of the label.

Using her index finger, Shauna delicately traced the beads of moisture on her wine glass.

'I should have gone home more often and talked to him. Found out how he was feeling. The thing is, he's not an easy man to get to talk about himself. It's such hard work – and I've been so busy lately . . .'

'Don't blame yourself, Shauna, I haven't been back for ages either.'

That was true, he hadn't. But then Dylan was the last person you'd rely on to do anything. *That* wasn't much consolation.

'God knows what he was thinking of, it's a crazy idea.'

Dylan raised his eyebrows. 'Yeah, but as crazy ideas go, it's pretty good.'

'What's so good about it?'

Now she was looking at him like he was some kind of criminal.

'Who would have thought Dad could have come up with something as way-out as this? You gotta admit, it's pretty off the wall. I mean, it *could* grab the headlines.'

'No, Dylan, it will *not* be grabbing any headlines, because we can't allow him to go through with it. He'll crack up – just how long do you think he could actually stick it?'

Dylan carried on shredding the Budvar label, avoiding Shauna's eye.

'Are you up to something?'

He looked up. 'What do you mean?'

'I know you. You're always looking for another scheme.'

'*No!* Not guilty.'

'OK, then go and see Dad and try talking some sense to him. I don't want to have to deal with this on my own. I'm *always* the one who sorts things out. I'd like you to take some responsibility as well.'

Man, she was really getting on his nerves now. She always had to have the last word. And that last word always had to be *It'll never work.* Because she always, always, had a downer on anything that involved an element of risk. Surely sometimes you just had to do without the safety net?

'Dylan, did you hear what I said?'

He took a swig from his bottle of beer, staring into the distance. 'Yeah.'

On the bus back to his bedsit in Llantwit Minor, Dylan's heart sank at the thought of tomorrow. A performance in a local school, followed by another riveting post-play discussion. He wasn't sure he could take another five months of this. All that shite about bringing theatre to the people. His dad's protest, now *that* was theatre for the people. The little guy against the system, the ordinary bloke who couldn't take it anymore. Aidan in the lead role and Dylan directing.

No, Dylan, it will not be grabbing any headlines, because we can't allow him to go through with it.

Shauna really pissed him off sometimes. How could she be so certain that it couldn't work? She was angry because nothing she said to Dad was going to make any difference. She didn't like it when people didn't do what she told them.

His Dad needed help. Boy, did he need help.

Dylan had desperately wanted a hip, cool and knowing

father. Someone with a natural, easy authority, who could make his friends laugh and fix anything mechanical, who understood who he was and would help and support him in getting where he wanted to be. What he got was someone he felt sorry for, who didn't have a clue who he was and who bought his depressing and uncoordinated clothes on market stalls. Dylan loved him, but he also felt sorry for the poor bastard. It was a combination that made his toes curl.

Gwyn was helping Aidan to make the modifications to the coffin.

'We're going to need a shaft big enough to send down food and drink, and winch up my, er, waste.'

Gwyn grimaced.

'Well, it's got to go somewhere.'

Gwyn pushed his glasses more firmly on to the bridge of his nose. 'True.'

'And I'd like it big enough so that I can look up and see the sky properly and that whoever is at the top can look down and see my head and shoulders. That will make me feel less cut off.'

'All right,' said Gwyn. 'Let's get started.'

Aidan lay down on the floor and Gwyn measured a rectangle around his head and shoulders.

'OK, if we make that 32 inches across and 22 inches deep . . .' He noted it down on a pad. 'So then we'll have to make a hole in the coffin lid.'

Aidan stood up, brushed himself down. 'I must hoover this place.'

Gwyn said nothing.

'I've been thinking about how high the periscope should come out of the ground. If it's about five feet high, then people will just only need to bend down a bit in order to see me and talk to me.'

'So say the coffin is five, six feet under the ground . . .'

'We'd need to make it eleven feet high.'

Gwyn nodded. 'It's all in the planning. If you've got a good plan, everything else will fall into place.'

Aidan said, 'Let's hope so.'

They went to a timber yard and bought four lengths of MDF. They built the shaft first, then cut the hole in the coffin. They stuck the periscope on top and held it in place. Looked at each other, grinned nervously.

'How are we going to keep it there? Reckon we should nail it down?'

Gwyn looked around him. 'It'd be a bit of a struggle getting it out through the doors and into the garden then. We could take them out separately, then just put the periscope in place and pack earth around it – that should do the trick.'

'Sorted.'

Aidan remembered something. 'We've still got to winch stuff up and down the shaft.'

'We'll just nail a length of wood across the top, get some rope . . .'

'Yeah, and then nail a piece of wood sticking out at the bottom of the periscope to tie the rope around when I winch the basket back up again, to keep it in its place up there. Because there isn't going to be much room in the coffin.'

Gwyn smiled. '*Now* we're getting there.'

'Gwyn.'

'Yeah?'

'Thanks for this – thanks for helping out. I know it sounds a bit extreme, what I'm doing . . .'

Gwyn stuck his pencil behind his ear. 'Times have changed, you've got to come up with something drastic that will grab people by the balls. Greenpeace did it – look at the amount of publicity they got when that guy scaled Big Ben.'

Aidan nodded, that was right, it certainly got everyone talking. He'd thought it was brilliant.

'Listen, in years to come people will look back on this in the same way we look back at the Middle Ages now and can't believe how backward *they* were. They'll be amazed that companies were allowed to act like this. "It was bloody medieval back in the twenty-first century, mun," they'll say. "Fancy having to bury yourself alive, just to get what everybody takes for granted today – that management have to consult with the workforce before they make any big changes." I'm telling you, they'll study you in universities.'

Aidan smiled, he liked that idea.

'We'll see.'

'You never know what's going to catch on, do you? The bloke who came up with the idea of sticking a group of thick, boring people with no opinions about anything that mattered together in a house, then filming them twenty-four hours a day, seven days a week, and putting it on the telly – they probably thought he was completely mad. Look what happened.'

Later on, Aidan was lying down in his coffin, having his tea – oven chips, cod and peas. He was trying hard not to sit up or raise his head, he wouldn't be able to when the lid was on. But it was damned awkward. He was forced to take small bites and chew everything very carefully, otherwise he found it difficult to swallow and got terrible indigestion. The peas rolled off his fork and down his neck and inside his shirt, or bounced away down the coffin.

'Fuck it.'

Someone was at the front door. He got up carefully, put down the plate and went to answer it. Dylan was standing there, a lopsided smile on his face, clutching an overnight bag.

'Hi-ya, Dad.'

'Good to see you, son.'

Dylan grinned, squeezed Aidan's shoulder. 'You too, Dad.'

'Did you get my messages?'

Aidan had left two messages on his mobile, asking him to give him a ring, as he had something important to tell him. He didn't want Dylan to hear about it from Shauna.

'My mobile was nicked – I haven't got round to getting another one yet. Shauna rang the theatre company and got the number of the school we were doing the play in, called me there yesterday. She filled me in about what's been happening.'

Great.

'I was going to ring, then I thought – nah, jump on the train and go!'

'So, you staying for long?'

'No, I'll have to go back tomorrow morning.'

'They're working you hard then?'

'Yeah, five, six performances a week.'

That was good news; Aidan was pleased he was busy. He'd been horrified when Dylan announced he was going to be an actor. According to Shauna 99% of actors were out of work at any one time. This was Dylan's first job since getting his Equity Card in a stage adaptation of *One Moonlit Night*, a very experimental production, which Aidan had travelled up to Mold to see, and found totally bewildering.

'I really want to talk to you, Dad.'

His tone gave it away. Aidan could well imagine what Shauna had said to him. *You try and talk some sense to him, he might listen to you.*

'Well,' said Dylan. 'Aren't you going to ask me in?'

'Oh yeah, of course, come on then.'

He moved aside, and Dylan stepped into the hall. Aidan went into the living room. Dylan followed him, put down his bag. He stuck his hands in the back pockets of his jeans, tried not to look shocked.

'So, this is your coffin.'

Aidan watched him carefully, wondering what line of attack he'd take. Shauna thought Aidan let him get away with murder, being the youngest and a boy. But the two of them had had some terrible rows when he was growing up.

Dylan walked over and looked inside.

'Looks comfy.'

53

'Pancho got me one of those futon mattresses – that's made a world of difference.'

Dylan nodded at the periscope in the corner. 'What's that then?' Aidan explained and Dylan went over and inspected it.

'Hey, sounds like you've worked everything out.'

He nodded at the plate on the floor.

'I've interrupted your tea.'

'It's all right.'

'Go ahead and finish it, I'll put the kettle on.'

'Aye, OK.'

Aidan got back into his coffin, put the plate on his chest, carried on eating. After a couple of minutes, Dylan came back in with two mugs, almost dropped them when he saw Aidan eating his tea in the coffin. Aidan sensed him stiffening.

'Where would you like this?'

'Just put it down on the floor next to me.'

Dylan did, then sat down on the sofa.

'Taken to eating in it now, have you?'

Aidan explained, again, about being in training. Dylan said nothing, just slurped his tea. When Aidan finished eating, he put down his plate and picked up his mug.

'You've got peas in your coffin.'

Aidan looked down, saw there were dozens scattered around him.

'That's probably from when I got up to answer the door. OK, aren't you going to tell me what a waste of time it is then? Isn't that what Shauna asked you to do?'

Dylan grinned, crossed his legs.

'My sister been giving you a hard time?'

'Yeah.'

'Don't take any notice of her, it's a brilliant idea.'

'You think so?'

He wanted to hear Dylan say it again.

'It's a beaut, Dad. The media love something like this, something different, something – hey, I love The Smiths angle.'

'Angle?'

'Yeah, Shauna told me how you got the idea. We can hit the music press with that one. Have you written a press release?'

Aidan shifted uncomfortably. 'I have, actually.'

'Really?'

'Yes. I've never been very confident about writing things down. I know you have to write a press release if you want to get publicity, I'm just not sure if I'm doing the right thing.'

'Let's see it, I'll soon tell you.'

Aidan hesitated, he hadn't shown anyone yet.

'Come on, I'd be delighted to give you my professional opinion.'

Professional opinion. That was a joke. He'd started a journalism course, got a placement on the *Cwmcarn Courier* and quit after six weeks. Said it wasn't what he expected, that there was no chance to do anything creative. All he ever got to write about was thieving and people fighting after the pubs closed. What else did he think went on in Cwmcarn, for Christ's sake?

Dylan got up, leant over the coffin, held out his hand.

Aidan grabbed it, let himself be hauled up. He brushed some peas from the folds in his shirt. Dylan was already walking over to the table, taking a pen from his pocket, clearing some space. Aidan got the exercise book from the drawer, put it on the table in front of Dylan.

'Fancy a beer?'

Dylan grinned. 'Aye, why not? OK, let's see what you've done.'

The first part was pretty grim, too much about the town dying if the factory closed. People didn't want to read depressing stuff like that over their cornflakes. And there were a couple of paragraphs at the end that were real Red Flag stuff.

It's about time ordinary people stood up against these Fat Cats. Have we forgotten our proud history? This is the country of Nye Bevan, the founder of the Welfare State. Volunteers from south Wales flocked to fight for the Republican cause against the fascists in the Spanish Civil

*War, and the Welsh people took Paul Robeson to their hearts when he
came here to film Proud Valley . . .*

'For fuck's sake,' muttered Dylan. 'Thank Christ I got here
when I did.'

Aidan took a couple of lagers from the fridge, came back
humming. Dylan was bent over the page, running his pen
through most of it.

'Is it that bad?'

Dylan shrugged. 'It's . . .'

Aidan's face fell.

'Go on.'

'It's a bit, well, retro.'

'Retro?'

'Very Seventies.'

'What do you know about the Seventies? You weren't born
till they were nearly over.'

Dylan ignored this, he'd seen it on the telly. He clenched his
fist. 'Y'know, power to the people, out brothers out, all that.'

'But I've toned it right down, you should have seen the first
version.'

Dylan nearly wept at the thought. 'And it's too long – you just
have to give these people what they want. Which is as little work
as possible. Keep it short, keep it simple, keep it punchy, make it
easy for them. Give them a nearly finished product they can lift
straight out and slap in the paper with the minimum of effort.'

'You mean do their job for them?'

Dylan nodded, peeled back the tab on his can of lager. 'Exactly.'

Aidan didn't like that. Educated people with decent jobs
shouldn't be that lazy.

'So let's make it easy for them, right?'

'Right.'

Aidan tilted the can back, took a long swallow. He winced as
he watched Dylan cross out some more. 'Do you really need to
do that?' There was a pained expression on Aidan's face.

'Dad, mun, no offence, but you really don't want all that stuff about the ordinary people being betrayed by Fat Cat bosses after all the hard work they've put in.'

'Why not?'

Dylan took a deep breath, spread his hands. 'It's so, *so* . . . Those days are gone, no one talks like that anymore.'

'They do round here.'

Dylan groaned, cradling his head in his hands. 'Trust me on this – if you want to get in the papers, you need to change your approach.'

No one else was offering to help. His son was sticking by him when everyone else was telling him he was crazy. It was a long time since they'd sat down and talked, or done anything together. A long time. And it was a bit long-winded, he'd admit that. Four sides, and he'd probably repeated himself. Dylan had always had a way with words.

'OK, you go ahead and do whatever you think is best.'

Dylan took his head out of his hands, beamed. 'You won't regret it.' He went back to work.

Aidan got up, bent over the page. 'Which bit are you crossing out now?'

Dylan ground his teeth, slapped down his pen, pushed his chair back. 'I can't work like this – you've got to give me some space here!'

'Hey, keep your hair on.'

Dylan reached for his wallet, took out a tenner. Forced himself to smile. 'Tell you what, Dad, why don't you pop out and get some more beers, and I'll finish this while you're gone.'

He rattled it off in half an hour. It was ready by the time Aidan came back.

Six Feet Under

While the rest of you are turning your thoughts to Christmas and what presents to buy your loved ones, spare a thought for Aidan

Walsh. He will be spending the festive season buried alive in a coffin in his back garden. The only Christmas present Aidan wants is a job to return to after the holiday. Aidan will be made redundant by Sunny Jim Electronics when they close down their factory in Crindau, and dreads to think what the future will hold once that happens. Aidan, 54, a widower and father of two, who has worked for Sunny Jim Electronics for the last eight years, said, 'That's where I might as well be when they take my job away – six feet under.'

He will stay underground until Sunny Jim Electronics change their mind and keep the factory open. 'I am not just doing this for myself,' says Aidan, 'but for everyone who works there, for their children, for the community as a whole. I am just an ordinary Joe, with no connection to any political party or union, who is just doing what he thinks is right. Crindau has already suffered so many job losses down the years, and these 1,000 people being shown the door is the final straw. Some people say what I am doing is crazy, others call it the most unequal contest since David took on Goliath, but when you are in my position you don't have much choice. What are my chances of getting another job round here at my age?'

His son, Dylan, one of Wales' most exciting young actors, says, 'My dad brought us up single-handed after our mother died. I never once heard him complain or feel sorry for himself; he just got on with it. If the people of Crindau are looking for a local hero, I can't imagine anyone better suited for the job.'

He added Aidan's home number, then his own mobile and email address. Tomorrow he'd type it up on his laptop, save it on disk, then send out copies to the papers.

But Aidan was getting cold feet over the last few lines.

'You're making me sound like some bloody plaster saint.'

'Human interest, Dad. We're telling a story here, and you're the main character. We're up against a faceless multinational, we gotta make you human.'

'I *am* human, thank you very much.'

'You know what I mean – come on, trust me on this.'

Dylan and Aidan sat up into the early hours, watching *The Big Sleep*, drinking their way through a case of incredibly lousy lager. He should never have let him go to the offy on his own; he always bought the worst thing there. Once they'd got stuck into the drink, Dylan had entertained his dad by doing Bogart impressions.

Hey shweetheart, pass us another drink.

Aidan laughing like a drain. His Peter Lorre went down well too.

Let go, you're hurting my arm.

OK, he wasn't in the film, but he *should* have been, it was exactly the kind of film you'd expect Peter Lorre to be in. Mimicking old film stars, that was what *really* convinced Aidan that Dylan was an actor. He'd always been a good mimic. In school the Geography teacher, Mr Collins, would come in and say, 'OK Walsh – get to the front of the class and do some impressions.' It was Dylan's impersonations of the other teachers he wanted to hear; 'Do Mr Jenkins . . . do Mrs Pugh . . .' Dylan would oblige while Collins sat at the back and bellowed. He'd be a hero for a few minutes, saving them all from another tedious discussion about the difference between temperate and tropical zones, until Collins would suddenly get up and say 'All right. I'm bored now. Open your books.' Performing to avoid the horror of real work, perhaps that was what he'd been doing his whole life, Dylan sometimes thought.

When Dylan woke up the next morning his head was pounding like a Serbian heavy metal band. He'd finished off the lager after his dad had gone to bed, sitting up till nearly three, his mind racing. He heard Aidan getting up, trudging to the bathroom, thumping downstairs. The radio coming on, the bang and clatter and sizzle of breakfast. The door slamming as he left for Sunny Jim. Jesus, how desperate was he to do something like this? Bury himself alive to keep hold of a lousy job in a warehouse? It didn't bear thinking about.

Back when Dylan was still living at home, whenever he had told Aidan about his latest idea, he would always frown and ask the same question.

That's all very well, but will it pay the rent?

God Almighty, if he heard that one more time he would scream. Would it have hurt to say, just once, 'That's a great idea, son, I wish you luck with it'? He remembered the long, empty days when he was growing up. The cloying atmosphere of sadness and loss driving him from the house. Wandering the dirty, grey, dangerous streets of this godforsaken town. No escape from the dreariness and the utter lack of imagination. If you took a bus out of Crindau, the area soon reverted to what it was best at after a half-hearted attempt at countryside – grim estates and ugly factories vomiting noxious fumes.

If you read a book, or watched a film with subtitles you were a poof. If you didn't like Queen or Iron Maiden played at horrendous volume, you were a poof. If you enjoyed going to the theatre . . . Well, you got the picture. During his short career as a stand-up, knocking Crindau was the bedrock of Dylan's act.

Other places get twinned with these beautiful towns in France and Germany. Crindau is twinned with Ostend cemetery.

Shauna, in one of her put-downs disguised as an insight, said she thought the reason he did stand-up was that the audience was replacing his mother's affection. Anything you enjoyed, anything exciting, she liked to rob of its magic. That's what psychoanalysis was, basically, cutting people down to size. The perfect career for a big sister.

Dylan often felt he was nothing but a shadow of some more solid and substantial version of Dylan Walsh. Someone who was living a wonderful life somewhere else. Somewhere cosmopolitan and cutting-edge, someone surrounded by beautiful women and great friends who were passionately interested in the same things he was, the very things that made him an outsider in Crindau. In the mornings he would wake up and, still half asleep, imagine someone walking into his room and saying, 'I'm terribly sorry, Mr Walsh, there's been a dreadful mistake. You don't belong here. You should have been assigned to New York. Get dressed and we'll take you there now.'

He felt the familiar depression beginning to descend as he lay there in his old room. That awful hollowness lying just under the surface of everything. It was his mother who always encouraged him. *Ah Dylan, a stór, you'll be famous one day.*

He remembered sitting next to her in the Atlantic Bar on their holidays in Ireland, the look on people's faces as they came over to her table.

'Are we going to hear you sing tonight?'

'I've just come in for a quiet drink.'

'Ah go on, please . . .'

They treated her like a queen. Basking in all that reflected affection and admiration were his sweetest childhood memories.

'And how's Dylan? Aren't you getting to be the big man? I'd say you're going to be a bit of a performer yourself, Dylan, *a stór.*'

Sometimes he felt absolutely fucking furious with her for dying. For pissing off and leaving them all to it. It didn't make any sense — it wasn't her fault she'd died, it wasn't anybody's fault, it just happened. So why was he so angry?

Enough. *Come on, get up and get out of here!* He got dressed, stuffed his things into his bag, had a coffee, just managed to catch the 8.30 train. As soon as he got back he'd type up the press release and send it out. This was going to be good, he was going to rock Crindau to its foundations.

Aidan was horrified when Wilf burst into tears. They'd known each other over twenty years, but he'd never seen him cry before.

'I don't know how we're going to cope.'

That was how it had started; the two of them sitting in

Aidan's kitchen, Wilf cradling a mug of tea he hadn't touched, Aidan's nearly finished. Then Wilf was off, saying how there'd always been plenty of overtime, and how that had helped him get his debts down to a couple of grand recently. How he and Megan had been planning to go to Australia next year to see their daughter Sharon, take Wilf's mam with them, the holiday of a lifetime. 'Fat chance of that now.' The next moment he was blubbering like a baby.

'There, there,' said Aidan, reaching a hand across the table and rather stiffly placing it on Wilf's shoulder, giving it a squeeze. But Wilf carried on sobbing uncontrollably, and, after a few seconds, Aidan withdrew his hand. He didn't know what to do next. He had now used up all his counselling skills. He'd not had to deal with a grown man crying his eyes out in his kitchen before.

He wished Eileen was there; she'd have been brilliant in this type of situation. He tried to think what she would have done. She'd have got up, gone around to the other side of the table where Wilf was hunched over, sobbing, sat down next to him and put her arm around him. Then she'd have said something soothing in that lovely Irish brogue of hers.

Aidan got up, sat next to Wilf. He steeled himself, stretched out his arm. But then Wilf suddenly sat up straight with a wretched sounding gulp, and smacked into Aidan's wrist. Wilf looked at Aidan in alarm and confusion, wondering for a moment if he'd deliberately hit him. Aidan drew back.

'Sorry, mate, I . . .'

Wilf covered his face with his hands and turned away. Aidan realised that sitting that close was making it worse for Wilf; he needed to give him some space. He stood up again, went to the fridge, pulled out a couple of cans of lager. When he came back, Wilf was wiping his streaming eyes. Aidan opened a can for himself, put the other in front of Wilf.

'There's a lager.'

Wilf was still turned away, desperately trying to get himself back under control. Aidan stretched across the table, pulled back the tab with a hiss.

'There, I've opened it for you. I'm moving it closer to you now. It's just to your right.'

Wilf dragged his hands down his face, blinking.

'Cheers.'

'No problem.'

Wilf found a handkerchief, wiped his eyes, blew his nose.

'Sorry.'

'No, don't be sorry,' said Aidan. 'It's healthy to cry. It's bad for you to bottle everything up. You're more likely to develop a tumour that way.'

Wilf looked startled.

'Is that true?'

'It was on the radio.'

'I never knew that. Christ, a tumour? Are you sure?'

Wilf was looking at him imploringly. Now Aidan wasn't so sure, maybe it was high blood pressure. He wasn't certain.

'How long do you have to bottle things up before you get a tumour?'

Bloody hell, he wished he hadn't bloody mentioned it now. What was he supposed to be, a consultant?

'Oh, ages.'

Wilf still looked petrified.

'The last time I cried was when Sharon left home, seven years ago.'

Aidan didn't know that. He'd been gutted when his kids left home, but he didn't cry. He'd felt like it, but had sat at on the sofa on his own, trying to pretend it was a relief to have the house to himself and got drunk instead. Now he felt he'd short-changed himself. Maybe he should have had a good bawl about it, like Wilf, let it all out, used up a whole box of man-sized tissues. He wondered what else Wilf got up to when he wasn't looking.

'How can bottling things bring on a tumour then?'

For fuck's sake, he was like a dog with a bone.

'They reckon that men find it more difficult than women to, er, express their emotions, and it's a bit like . . . like . . .' He was struggling now, but had to keep going, with Wilf looking at him like an anxious labrador. 'It's very bad for your health to bottle things up – it clogs up your insides a bit like muck building up in pipes and . . .' He took another swig of lager. Jesus, what bollocks. 'And just the same way that a load of gunge can stop water flowing through pipes, so emotions that you haven't, um, flushed out into the open will bung up your system and make you ill.'

'And you'd have to call a plumber?'

'Yeah, that's right, a good cry is a bit like calling out Dyno-Rod, you do it to unblock your insides, keep yourself regular. In fact I might join you, it's been a good while since I cried; why don't I go and peel an onion right now?'

Wilf almost laughed. That was better. But all this talk about growing a tumour was putting the wind up Aidan. He couldn't help running his hand over his stomach. He could swear he felt a lump. Perhaps he should go to the doctor? Wilf was also running his hand down his left-hand side. He caught Aidan watching him, grinned sheepishly. 'They say you should examine yourself regularly when you get to our age, look out for lumps and that. Megan examines her, er, breasts, she says I should examine myself too, especially my, eh, testicles, but I . . .'

'Nor me.'

Wilf stared at Aidan, then looked away. All that crying had made his face puffy and red, old, worn out. A part of Aidan couldn't help feeling flattered, all the same. Wilf would never have sobbed helplessly in front of the others.

Aidan rubbed his hands together, said, 'Anyway, we're not finished yet.'

'Eh?'

'My plan to stop them closing the factory – they'll have to think twice when I bury myself alive.'

Wilf thought about it, said, 'That's right, I mean, they couldn't just leave you down there, could they? They'd have to do something.'

'That's right.' Christ, he hoped not anyway. Aidan banged his fist on the table. 'I'll show them.'

Wilf beamed, raised his can. 'Here's to you.'

'No,' said Aidan, smacking his can into Wilf's, 'here's to you – and to that holiday in Australia next year.'

Wilf's eyes began to water. Jesus, not again. But he got himself under control, gulped down more lager and then banged the table too.

'Australia here we come!'

'That's the spirit. Another?'

'Aye, why not?'

Aidan hoisted another couple of cans from the fridge, brought them back to the table. Wilf opened his, then looked at Aidan sombrely and said, 'You won't tell the others I've cried, will you?'

Pancho was in the Globe, selling mobiles to Aidan, Russell, Gwyn and Wilf. He was having to take them through how to use them step by step, as if he was dealing with kids.

'You have to dial the *whole* number every time, mind, the area code as well.'

'Even if you're just ringing someone in Crindau?'

'Yeah.'

Gwyn looked put out. 'That's not very convenient, is it?' He looked at his new mobile resentfully. 'I thought these were supposed to make life easier for us?'

Jesus, he hoped he didn't end up like that. Nothing that had been invented after the Seventies was ever going to be any good as far as these sad *hombres* were concerned. Pancho shrugged. 'You'll soon get used to it, trust me.'

He explained about pay-as-you-go, top-up cards and messages, but wasn't convinced they'd understood a word of it.

They looked like kids facing a maths test. He tried to perk them up a bit.

'Now, the moment something happens, and you want to pass on the news, no matter where you are, you can just pull out your mobile and tell each other the latest straight away.'

'As long as you remember to dial the area code first,' said Wilf, looking pleased with himself.

Pancho winked at Wilf. '*Si!*'

'This young bloke at work, Dave Edmunds, his wife is always ringing him up,' said Gwyn. '"I'm in the supermarket looking at sausages with a hint of sage, do you fancy some?"'

'Have you seen his wife?' said Russell. 'Tidy she is.'

There was no dissent.

'That's how we found out about losing our jobs,' said Russell. 'Dave Edmunds got a call from his missus. She'd just heard it on the 9 o'clock news on the radio.' He knocked some ash from his fag, nodded at Pancho. 'They told the bloody BBC before they told us.'

Pancho shook his head. 'Shocking.' He looked at their sad, sagging faces and tried to imagine them thirty years ago, full of hope and energy, but dropped it.

'Still,' he said, trying to move it right along, 'mobiles have got lots of other, nicer uses too.' He grinned. 'His missus could have rung him ten minutes before the end of his shift and said, "I'm in the bedroom waiting for you, wearing my little black lacy outfit, get home soon".'

That put a smile back on their faces. Pancho knew how to handle awkward customers. Maybe now he should leave them on a high. He'd been planning to tell them about texting, but he'd probably be there till bloody midnight if he tried that. Then his own mobile rang.

'Yeah?'

His face tightened. 'I'm just finishing here, then I've got one more call, then I'll be back. I . . . half an hour – look . . . Jesus!' He switched it off.

Russell was smirking, 'What did she say – "I'm in the bed-room waiting for you in my little black lacy outfit, get home soon."?'

'Something like that,' said Pancho, not looking at him. He double-checked he had their cash snug in his pocket, knocked back the last of his tequila.

'Now then, gents, lovely doing business with you, but I have to go.'

He got up, slipped on his leather jacket. 'You know what to do if you need to contact me.'

A light came on in Wilf's eyes, 'Ring you on our mobiles.'

'Exactly. *Buenas noches, senores.*' And he was off, striding across the bar towards the door.

'Doesn't half fancy himself,' said Russell, as soon as Pancho had gone.

'He's all right,' said Wilf.

'OK,' said Aidan, tearing four pages from his notebook, and handing them out. 'Write down your name and number, then pass it on to the next person, who'll write down theirs, and so on, till we've all got each others'.' When they'd finished, they sat studying them.

'Here,' said Gwyn, leaning closer to Wilf. 'Is that a 7 or a 1?'

Wilf squinted at it uncertainly. 'Let me check.' He peered at the booklet. 'Actually, it's a 6.'

'Fuck's sake! This is the man you could be relying on in an emergency.'

'Go on,' said Gwyn, nodding at Aidan. 'Ring me up.' Aidan grinned and started punching in the number.

'Don't forget to dial the area code first,' said Wilf.

'Bloody hell,' said Russell, through gritted teeth. 'I can see you're going to say that every time one of us ever gets our mobile out from now on.'

Gwyn's mobile started ringing – 'La Cuceracha'.

'Hello, who is it?'

'It's me, Aidan, er, how's it going?'

'Not too bad like – how about you?'

'OK, OK,' said Russell, cutting in. 'The first thing you gotta do is change that bloody awful tune, because if that keeps going off while I'm standing next to you, there's going to be murder.'

'Here,' said Aidan. 'Why don't I ring you and find out what yours is?'

He did. It was 'La Cuceracha'. A couple more calls established they all had the same ring tone.

'Anyone remember what he said about changing the ring tone?'

'Yeah,' said Aidan, 'I wrote it down here.' He'd brought a little notebook along with him, determined to master this new technology. He read out the instructions.

'Everyone got their menu up? Right.'

They started selecting. They tried out 'the William Tell Overture', 'We are the Champions', 'Staying Alive', 'Mission Impossible' ('That's the one for you, Aidan,' said Russell). They started getting into it, excitedly telling each other when they found a good one – 'Hey, listen, "My Way".' They turned the volume right up, worked their way through the list, laughing. Eventually a lad in his early twenties stuck his head around the corner, wearing a horrified expression. He turned his head back the way he'd come and said, 'It's a crowd of blokes my dad's age playing with ring tones on their mobiles – straight up. Come and have a look.'

Three more lads poked their heads round the corner.

'Bloody hell, what are they like?'

Aidan noticed them staring. 'What's your problem?'

One of them said, 'We're trying . . .'

'Hey listen – "Men of Harlech"!'

Gwyn held his mobile up like a chalice and treated them all to a tinny version of the stirring march.

'Makes you proud, don't it?' said Wilf. 'Knocks spots off the English national anthem.'

'"Land of My Fathers" is our national anthem, you berk.'

The young bloke frowned, put his hands to the sides of his mouth, took a deep breath and yelled, 'CAN YOU KEEP THE NOISE DOWN? WE'RE TRYING TO PLAY CHESS ROUND THE CORNER.'

Russell turned his hard-man stare on them. 'Don't fucking come round here trying to tell us what to do, son,' said Russell. 'This was our local before you were bloody born, so you can piss off.'

They stood their ground for a few seconds, then retreated back round the corner.

'They're great, aren't they?' said Gwyn, inspecting his menu.

'Yeah,' said Russell, 'bloody marvellous. Pity I've already got a stereo at home.'

'I mean, imagine if you were held up, and you knew someone was waiting for you, you could ring them up and let them know you were running late.'

'If they had a mobile too.'

'How many other people do you know who have a mobile?'

'Er, you three.'

'And just think of the downside – now your wife can get hold of you any time she wants, there's no escape.'

'I don't mind that,' said Wilf. 'I love my wife.'

Russell looked disgusted. 'There's no need for that.'

'What?'

'We were having a decent conversation, why did you have to go and introduce a sour note like that?' Russell pulled a face and put on a mincing voice, '*I love my wife.*'

'Can I just say something?'

'No.'

'I'm sitting here now, looking at this mobile,' said Gwyn. 'And do you know what I'm thinking?'

'You've just wasted a tenner.'

'I'm thinking what it represents, like. This little invention could be the thing that saves Aidan's life if he gets in trouble down there. If he's got some kind of a problem and needs to get out quick, then he's going to have to ring one of us, and we're going to have to drop everything and get there double-quick. We'll be like doctors on call.' He looked straight at Aidan. 'And to be honest with you, mate, it's a pretty scary feeling.'

Aidan walked into Personnel, relieved to see only Safina in the office. The young blonde one, Angie, she always made him feel awkward. Safina looked up from the computer. 'Hi-ya, Aidan, how are you? Sit down, love.'

Safina was about his age, but she took good care of herself, always chose colours that suited her, kept her hair immaculate, wore nice perfume. He took a seat. 'Not so bad. Yourself?'

She smiled. 'I'd feel a lot better if I'd just got a £750,000 bonus.'

Aidan grinned. Blondie would never have said that.

Russell reckoned Safina was a typical Asian, didn't mix, but Aidan figured he'd probably once told her some coarse joke, and when she hadn't pretended she found it hilarious, decided she was stuck-up. But that was one of the things Aidan liked about her; she had no front, didn't pretend she was something she wasn't. Aidan thought she was pretty hot too. When she was talking he found it hard not to stare at her mouth, imagining what it would be like to cover it with his.

'What can I do for you, Aidan?'

The look she gave him – feck, had he been staring at her mouth then? He tried to look businesslike as he handed her a slip of paper. 'I want to book some annual leave, it's all written down there.'

She looked at the dates.

'Two weeks.'

'That's right, I want to take everything I've got left, all in one go.'

She studied the dates.

'And you want to take it next week?'

'Will that be a problem?'

She shook her head. 'No, only everyone else is hanging on to their annual leave, hoping to get that bit extra in their redundancy package.'

'Not me.'

He enjoyed the look she gave him, as if she was discovering there was more to him than met the eye. *Yes*, he thought, *there is. About time you noticed.*

'Where are you going?'

'Down under.'

'That's nice.'

'I hope so.'

'Probably the best thing you could do right now is to get away from it all for a bit.'

That, he thought, smiling, is exactly what I'll be doing. He noticed a photo on her desk. He could only see the back of the frame. He wondered who it was. A man?

'Leave this with me, Aidan, I'll take care of it for you.'

'Thanks.'

He hesitated. She smiled at him, her eyes locked on his.

'Is there anything else?' she said.

'What will you do if this place closes?'

'If?'

'Sorry, when.'

'It's hard to plan. You don't want to start applying for jobs in case you get one and then lose out on your redundancy,' she laughed. 'But you know what it's like around here, they're not easy to come by.' She smiled ruefully. 'I'll have more time to spend in my garden.'

'You like gardening?'

He realised this was the first personal thing he'd discovered about her.

'I love it. I forget about everything when I'm working in my garden.'

'Do you talk to the flowers?'

Eileen used to.

She laughed. 'No – I sing to them.'

He'd like to see that, Safina in shimmering sunlight, bending over and singing.

Russell claimed she and her husband had split up years ago. *He was Italian. He wanted bambinos and she couldn't oblige. Married someone else and now he's got five kids.*

Aidan had felt slightly sick, hearing her personal life discussed in the pub like that.

So she didn't always stick to her own.

She doesn't always stick to her own – you just don't know how to talk to her.

Russell had noticed Aidan's expression.

Aye aye, fancy a bit of Asian spice yourself, do you?

He hated it when Russell talked like that.

Years ago, before he shut himself down, he would have taken a chance and asked her out. Why not do it now? What did he have to lose? In a few days' time he'd be sealed inside a coffin, cut off from human contact. A night out with a good-looking woman would lift his spirits. Even if nothing happened, even if they only had a few drinks and got to know each other better, it would be a sweet memory to hang on to when he was underground. There would be something to look forward to when he came up – meeting her again, pushing things along a bit further.

'Safina?'

She sat back in her chair, folded her hands in front of her on the desk.

'Yes, Aidan?'

Her mouth hung open slightly. He imagined taking her face in his hands, running his fingers down her cheeks, kissing her.

Go on, prove you're still alive, go ahead and ask her.

'I was wondering if you'd –'

The door opened and the young blonde one came in. She was laughing in that high-pitched, screechy way. She called out to someone in the corridor. 'Oh yeah? That's what they all say.'

72

The young blokes swarmed around her like flies. She stood with her hand on her hip, about to say something else. He noticed Safina's face stiffen.

'Hello, Angie.'

She looked round, saw Aidan sitting there. 'Oh hi, Safina, hi . . .'

'Aidan.'

She flashed him a toothpaste-ad smile. He got up from the chair, the sharp and familiar pain of regret lodged in his chest like shrapnel.

'Thanks, Safina, nice to talk to you.'

'You too, Aidan, enjoy your holiday.'

He squeezed past Angie, started walking back to the warehouse, clenching his fists.

You're pathetic. You've downsized yourself so much you're barely a man anymore.

3

Aidan brushed the leaves from Eileen's grave and placed a bunch of fresh chrysanthemums in the centre. He stepped back, took a cloth from his pocket and carefully wiped the headstone clean. He unfolded the camping chair that Shauna had got him. *You spend so much time there, you may as well make yourself comfortable.*

He didn't spend as much time as he used to, had wondered if she was making some kind of point. But still, it was thoughtful of her. He hitched up his trousers, sat down.

'Sorry I didn't come last week, I was really busy, getting everything ready. I'm going down on Monday. I'm . . .' He stopped. He bent his head, hunched his shoulders, drew his hands slowly over his face, breathing deeply now.

'I'm scared, Eileen.'

He looked round to check he was on his own.

'Sometimes I think I've come up with an absolutely brilliant idea, other times I'm worried I'm going to make a complete fecking eejit of myself.'

He stared silently at the soil between his feet for a while. Soon he'd be down there. But alive, and fighting for a future.

'I mean what if no one gives a fuck? "You hear Aidan Walsh buried himself alive, says he's not going to come up again till they give him his job back." "Yeah? What a wanker!"'

A woman quickly walked past, very deliberately looking straight ahead.

'I mean why *should* anyone care?'

He inspected his fingernails.

'I used to have a recurring dream when I was a kid. A huge gang of us were playing hide and seek in the woods. When it was my turn, I'd find this fantastic hiding place, inside the trunk of a dead tree. I'd hear the other kids getting nearer. They'd search all around me, even look up amongst the branches, but never think of looking inside the trunk. Heard them getting annoyed. Have to clamp my hand over my mouth to stop myself from bursting out laughing. Then, eventually, I'd hear them saying they were fed up of looking for me now, they were going to let someone else have a go. Another boy ran off and hid, and they all started looking for him. I'm hunched up inside the tree, listening to their excited voices, thinking, "How could they just give up on me like that?" After a while I can't stand it any longer. I come out and run over to where they're playing. I wave, and shout, "Here I am!" But they can't hear or see me. I'd disappeared. Slipped quietly out of the world . . . I started to panic. I was terrified I'd be on my own for the rest of my life, trapped in some kind of limbo, separated from everyone else by a glass wall. Then I'd wake up with a start, my pyjamas soaked in sweat.'

He took his hands from the chair, examined them.

'It would take me hours to get back to sleep. Peter would be dead to the world in the bed on the other side of the room. I'd try and think of some excuse to go into my parents' room and wake them up. Just to check that I could still make people see and hear me, to make sure I hadn't *really* disappeared. Then I got scared that if I did call out to them, they wouldn't hear me, and that would prove . . .' He stared up at the sky again. 'So I'd just lay there, worrying, till it started to get lighter, the birds began singing, and eventually I'd drift off to sleep again.'

He sighed, put his hands between his knees. 'Jesus, the things that go through your head when you're a kid.'

He ran his hands up and down the arm rests, shifting his weight on the seat. It was a fine morning and the sun was high in the sky now, thick shafts of gold splitting the tree trunks. Normally the sight would have cheered him, but not today.

He clicked his tongue, bent over and peeled the price tag from the cellophane wrapped around the flowers, twisted it into a ball, put it in his pocket.

'Shauna's adamant that it's a terrible idea. She just can't get her head around it.'

He took another drag, flicked some ash to the ground, nudged it away with the toe of his shoe.

'Mind you, if I said it was day she'd insist it was night – you can't tell her anything. Remember how she drove us crazy with her questions when she was a kid? *Where does the sun go at night? If god knows everything, yeah, then why did he let all those people get on that plane that crashed?*

'Dylan thinks it's a great idea though – he's written a press release for me, and he's got lots of ideas about how to make it work, apparently. He's always had amazing energy. Remember how he used to be as a boy – always wanting to show you his latest trick. *Watch me do a handstand – look, look! I bet you couldn't do one that good when you were my age.*

He noticed a squirrel running up a tree, and smiled.

'I wish you could see the way they've turned out, you'd be so proud.'

He ran his hand through his hair, gazed into the branches above his head.

'I miss you.'

He wondered when it would stop, this pain. Surely it should have got easier by now? It felt more like a tumour, something eating away at him that needed to be cut out.

He was sure Dylan had got his confidence for performing from Eileen. He remembered the first time they met, at an Irish bar in Cardiff. He wasn't a great one for Irish bars, had been dragged to too many of them when he was a kid on holidays in Ireland. The thick fog of pungent cigarette smoke – Jesus, Sweet Afton, did they still make that? – stinging his eyes, the shocking sight of adults making fools of themselves as the drink took hold, the horrible squawking of auld ones as they launched into mournful ballads with hundreds of verses.

Oh my love is in Ameri-kay.

But he'd passed Mooney's and heard a session going on and had been overwhelmed by the power of that music taking him back to his childhood. He was on the look-out. He'd been with Christine too long, he was itching to get out of that relationship, move on. He got himself a pint, stood at the corner of the bar, soaking up the atmosphere, enjoying stout that had been stored and pulled properly.

He didn't notice Eileen till she started singing 'The Banks of the Bann'. It seemed one of the bravest things he'd ever seen, for someone to just start singing in a room full of noisy, boozy strangers, hoping they wouldn't be ignored, drowned out by laughter and shouts, or slagged off. After a few lines people started shushing – *Hey! Hey! Come on now, give the woman a chance, willya?* He'd heard better singers, better technically, that is, but she had something that couldn't be taught. Her passion and sincerity shone through in every word. There was no distance between her and the song, she was *living* it. You believed that these things had happened to her, that she wasn't singing someone else's words. She was speaking the truth. That was how John Lennon sang 'Gimme Some Truth' and 'In My Life', that was how Ray Davies sang 'Waterloo Sunset' and 'Days'. That was why Aidan adored them.

Aidan felt she was singing just to him. She knew he was out there and had picked him out, he felt sure. Except when he looked around the room he saw that everyone else there felt the same, each and every one of them certain she was singing just to *them*. That was some talent.

When the song was finished Aidan clapped so hard a couple of auld ones gave him disapproving looks. He'd forgotten it wasn't the done thing to make too big a fuss. He was hoping she'd sing another, but a bloke started playing the accordion. He was good too, but Aidan didn't take much notice, just kept glancing over at Eileen. He walked over to where she sat and told her how much he'd enjoyed the song. She smiled politely, told him it was called 'The Banks of the Bann'. But he could see he hadn't got through to her, that she wanted to go back to talking to her two girlfriends. One of them, the blonde one, you just *knew* loads of people had told her she looked like Dusty Springfield. She gave him a withering look. He returned the compliment. He stayed where he was.

'I know the song. I've heard it sung many times. But I liked the way *you* sang it, that's what I'm saying.'

She looked at him differently now, meeting his gaze for longer this time. Her eyes were a deep green. Some would have said her mouth was too large, but Aidan would have called it generous.

'My parents are Irish, I grew up listening to the old songs. But I've never heard it sung quite like that.'

Now he had her attention. Her smile meant something this time. He heard Dusty whispering to the other one, 'Oh god, not another Plastic Paddy.' Snotty bitch, he thought, then quickly buried it. Didn't want Eileen to see how easily he took offence. Didn't want her to think he was one of those blokes who was quickly provoked. She must have heard Dusty say it too, but you'd never know from her expression. She'd always been able to do that – pretend she just hadn't heard things.

'Where are your parents from?'

'County Wexford.'

'I don't know it that well.'

'How about you?'

'I'm from Mayo.'

People from the west of Ireland looked down on the east of Ireland, according to Aidan's father. Reckoned they'd been jumping into bed with too many invaders for too long – Vikings, Normans, the English – weren't really Irish anymore at all.

'Mayo, that's where the fiddle player Michael Coleman's from.' He saw she didn't expect him to know that. 'My dad said he was the best ever.'

'He was so.'

She gave him an amused look, knowing he was trying to impress her but showing him she didn't mind. He didn't tell her what his dad always said about Mayo though.

Sure there's feck all in it but bogs and cow shit.

'Do you sing at all yourself?'

'Christ, no, I'd empty this place in a minute flat.'

'Do you play anything?'

'Only the fool.'

She shrugged carelessly. 'Ah well. There was no escape for us, my parents were very musical, they had us all performing, I had no choice. You'd get sick of it after a while, you know.'

He liked the way she made light of it. He couldn't put his finger on what made her so attractive. She was pretty enough in her own way, but it wasn't that, he'd already noticed one or two prettier girls. She had a warmth about her that drew him in, and a hint of wildness in those green eyes that excited him. *Go on,* she seemed to be saying. *Ask me what you're dying to ask, you never know.* So he did. She let him buy her a drink, then another, then he got her phone number. That's how he was back then. If he wanted something, he went after it. Before he began shutting himself down.

He'd tried telling himself that if Angie hadn't come into the office when she did the other day, he'd have asked Safina out. Who was he kidding? He'd have bottled it. He'd tried going out with other women since Eileen died, but it had been a disaster. Somewhere deep inside he was still bruised and raw, cowering in a corner; he didn't know how to get out of that place.

This protest would be so much easier if Eileen was alive. Feeling that there was somebody behind him every step of the way. But of course if she was still alive he wouldn't be doing it at all.

Dylan was in the school library, waiting for the kids to arrive for the post-play workshop. He was looking at a cardboard display stand for the new children's books. In bright yellow cartoonish letters it read *Let's Rap About It!* Underneath were images of pre-teens – a meticulous selection of different ethnic types, shapes, sizes and styles – talking animatedly to each other, expressions of great joy on their faces. He looked at the titles that made up the display. *Mummy and Daddy Aren't Getting Along*, *I Have Two Dads Now!*, *What's Happening to My Body?*, *Coping With Bullying*.

There hadn't been any books like this when he was in school. *Mummy's Boy! Mummy's Boy! Mummy's Boy!*

Those three bastards in primary school had made his last year there hell. One day his mother had insisted on walking him to school. It was his first day back after being off with flu. He insisted that she leave him at the end of the street; he was far too old to be seen coming to school with his mother. She kissed him and ruffled his hair.

Ah Dylan, a stór, you'll grow up soon enough. It won't kill you to walk down the street with your poor auld mother a few more times.

As he turned away, he saw three boys on the other side of the street, eyeing him with contempt. That was it. They had him.

The torture and humiliation began. Eventually they demanded that everyone else stop speaking to him. If they saw one of his friends talking to him at break time, they'd turn on them. Dylan found it easier to ignore his friends too, to go into a corner and stand on his own, reading. That way he got no one else in trouble. But even that seemed to provoke them. They started surrounding him, digging their fingers into his arms and shoulders, standing on his feet. *Mummy's Boy! Mummy's Boy! Mummy's Boy!* Till one day he couldn't stand it any longer and slipped out of school during the lunch break and went home. For months Eileen had been asking him if anything was wrong and he'd always said no.

No, really. Honest, Mam. Why can't you just believe me?

Now, at last, he decided to tell her. He could talk to his mother about things that he couldn't mention to other people. His Dad would ask once, then look lost when he wouldn't tell him. But Eileen *never* gave up. She always knew when something was wrong. As he got closer to the house, walking across the park, coming in through the back gate, the relief at what he was about to do flooded through him and he ran to push the back door open.

Mam! Mam!

And there she was, lying on the floor. One arm was stretched towards the cooker, as if she was trying to reach the door and open it, the other was trapped under her body. Her legs were splayed, one foot in the cat food. There was a bad smell coming from her. Head thrown back, mouth wide open, eyes staring straight up at the crack in the ceiling. Dylan didn't cry. He didn't move or call for help. He stood in the doorway and stared.

When he went back to school he hated the way everyone knew what had happened. The way the other kids tip-toed around him as if he might shatter if they came too close. Or maybe they were afraid they'd catch something, he wasn't sure which. He didn't care anyway.

One day the three lads who'd been picking on him approached him in the playground. He was standing in the corner reading his favourite book, *The Silver Sword*. They looked cowed and embarrassed. They looked like they'd sooner be somewhere, anywhere else. One of them said, 'We're sorry about your mam.'

The tears stung Dylan's eyes but he wouldn't let them fall. Not now, not in front of them. The other two muttered something inaudible, their heads slightly bowed. Dylan looked past them, saw Miss Austin standing not far away, very deliberately looking in the other direction. Why hadn't she noticed what was going on before?

'Do you want to play something?'

Dylan looked at him, this boy who'd pushed, pulled and provoked him all these months. Who'd shouted, ordered, tugged and threatened. Followed him home, yelling insults and laughing at him. Now he was standing anxiously waiting for Dylan's reply. It was over. All he had to do was say something – and that would be that; he'd have one less thing to worry about.

Yes, that's all. Or even *No, thanks, not now. Maybe another time, thank you*. Something like that would do.

Dylan held his head high and said, 'Get lost.'

Then turned and walked away from them. He didn't look back, didn't look up at Miss Austin either as he walked past her too, just kept on going and walked out of the school gates.

4

Monday morning, 7.20. This was it. Aidan had been up since six, he'd had three or four hours sleep at most. This was what he had been building up to, the day his plan finally went into action. The one thing that might stop Sunny Jim. When he came downstairs and saw the coffin lying there in the living room, the thought of being stuck inside it under the ground turned his insides to liquid.

There's still time to run for it – get a taxi to the station before anyone arrives. You've booked annual leave, go ahead and use it. Go somewhere nice, treat yourself. Come back in a couple of weeks, tanned and relaxed. Brazen it out when they ask where you disappeared to.

Oh, that's right, I was supposed to bury myself alive, wasn't I? Damn, I knew I'd forgotten something. Did you get my postcard?

No, he wasn't going to run away from this one.

He got dressed, washed and shaved. Dylan had come back last night to be there on the day, but there was no sign of life from his room. Aidan made himself a mug of strong tea and a bacon sandwich. Then, a few minutes later, wished he hadn't. His guts, Jesus, they were killing him. An ominous rumbling sent him running back upstairs to the toilet. His breakfast shot straight through him, hitting the sides with a sickening splatter.

He sat there with his head in his hands, his trousers round his ankles.

'Oh fuck.'

His legs were shaking, his forehead streaked with cold sweat.

'Sweet Jesus, please, no . . . not now.'

There was a knock on the door. He groaned, wiped himself, pulled his trousers back up. They were banging now, shouting through the letterbox.

'Wakey wakey!'

Russell, doing his sergeant major act. Just what he needed.

'All right, all right, hold your horses, I'm coming.'

He went downstairs, his stomach lurching, his temples throbbing, and opened the door. Russell, Gwyn and Wilf were standing there, holding shovels. They grinned, but their eyes gave the game away. They said, 'Reporting for duty.' They were as tense as him. Russell said, 'Christ, you look rough.' That annoyed him. What kind of a thing was that to say to someone about to take the biggest risk of their life? He held the door open. Then remembered something.

'Will you give me a hand putting the banner up?'

It was upstairs, in his bedroom. They carried it out to the landing, opened the window and unfolded it. Hammered a nail through the two top corners into either side of the windowsill. This was all done in near silence, Aidan's tension transmitting itself to them all, preventing any smartarse comments.

'OK – let her go.'

They watched it billow out, then settle down.

'Let's go see how it looks.'

They went out the front door, walked across the road and stood looking back at the house. You couldn't miss it: a white sheet hanging from the upstairs window, with letters two foot high reading

SAVE OUR JOB'S

'It looks great, Aidan,' said Wilf.

Dylan appeared on the doorstep, wearing a pair of jeans and a rumpled T-shirt with Father Jack's scowling face plastered across the front, the words 'FECK! ARSE! DRINK! GIRLS!' underneath.

Russell looked him up and down. 'Christ, it's Sleeping Beauty.'

Dylan yawned, scratched the top of his head. 'What's the time?'

Aidan gave him a dirty look. Once, just once, he might have made the effort to get up on time. It brought back all the worst memories of Dylan's teenage years, when Aidan would have to hammer on his bedroom door till it nearly came off its hinges.

For Christ's sake, get up, will you?
What for?
Because I said so!

Dylan caught his look, muttered, 'OK, OK, I'm sorry I spoke.'

He tottered back inside to make himself some coffee. Aidan had hoped someone from the *Argus* would turn up. Dylan said he was absolutely certain they'd send someone to cover it. But he couldn't hang around hoping someone would come, his nerves couldn't take it; he needed to get going.

'Let's do it.'

They carried the coffin out into the garden and put it down next to the hole. No one dared say what they were all thinking. That it was just like a funeral. Russell spat on his hands and picked up his shovel.

'Hello, I'm looking for Aidan Walsh.'

A young bloke looked over the garden wall, behind him an older guy, a fancy camera round his neck. Aidan looked up, said, 'That's me.'

'Hi, Nick Williams. I'm a reporter for the *Argus*. I was hoping to have a quick interview with you before you got started.'

'You've cut it a bit fine,' said Russell. 'Another five minutes and you'd have missed him.'

'I've been ringing the number you gave me but it seems to be switched off.'

'Shit!' Aidan searched through his pockets, brought out his mobile, realised it wasn't turned on. He grinned sheepishly at Nick. 'Sorry about that.'

'No worries. Can we come in?'

'Oh, sure . . .' Aidan rushed over, undid the bolt on the back gate, held it open for them.

Nick held out his hand and Aidan shook it. He was about Dylan's age. When he read the *Argus*, Aidan now realised, he'd assumed the people writing for it were older. What could this kid know about how it felt to lose your job at fifty-four? Aidan noticed a red line on his cheek where he'd cut himself shaving. His jacket was smart enough, but he was wearing a hideous bright-yellow tie with a knot that was far too big, and a gold stud in one ear. For all the world like a boy trying too hard to look like a man. But still, he was here, proof that the media *were* interested in the story. It was a chance.

The photographer was wandering around the garden, squinting, checking angles, lining up imaginary shots. Russell, Gwyn and Wilf went back inside for a brew, leaving them to it.

Nick opened his notebook, said, 'It's a very unusual form of protest.'

'Well, you've got to move with the times, haven't you?'

He looked puzzled. 'Sorry, I don't . . .'

'Downing tools and walking out, wildcat strikes, picket lines, marching behind banners with brass bands – who wants to know about that kind of thing these days? It's so . . . *Seventies*.'

Nick smiled broadly, like he was in on the joke. 'Yeah, like working-class solidarity, it's so *retro*.'

Aidan smiled back. 'But there *are* lots of people who work there who are my kind of age, and they're going to find it very hard to get another job. If they have to choose between me and a bloke in his twenties for the same job, who do you think they're going to give it to? You probably think I'm exaggerating, being a young bloke yourself, but once you're in your fifties . . .'

'My dad's fifty-three, he was made redundant a few years ago when they closed the steelworks at Pen-y-Lan.'

He looked upset about it too. Aidan liked that.

'What's he doing now?'

'He was out of work till a few months ago, then he got a job stacking shelves in a supermarket three nights a week.'

'How's he finding it?'

Nick shrugged. 'It's work, y'know.'

'Right.'

'People used to say if you got a job at Pen-y-Lan it was a job for life – but those days are gone.'

'They are, that's right. Then you have to think of the knock-on effect – there'll be a thousand less people with wages to spend in the shops and supermarkets, pubs and takeaways. It'll be a blow for the whole of Crindau. It's like . . . dropping a big stone into a pond. Long after the splash has gone there'll be ripples spreading out in every direction, eventually reaching every corner of the pond.'

'But Sunny Jim would say they have to adapt to compete in the changing market.'

Aidan grimaced. 'They're nothing but a bunch of blood-sucking parasites. Just look at what they demanded before they opened a factory here – £18 million of government aid, and a no-strike agreement. And if that wasn't enough, they bullied the council into putting up the money for a new road and a new bus route. So everyone who pays council tax has helped bribe Sunny Jim to come here – and they're entitled to ask what they got for their money in the end, apart from lining the pockets of an already extremely rich company. Sunny Jim were happy to take our money then. I don't think it's too much to expect them to feel some responsibility now after all the help they got. We've done everything asked of us over the last few years – we accepted not having a pay rise for the last four years to keep the company competitive. We've agreed to working new rotas and doing nightshifts and overtime to get the orders out on time. You name it, we've done it, no complaints, no arguments, because we were told it was in our long-term interests. We thought it would help make the company more successful and that we'd share in that success – and this is our reward. The final insult was the chairman pocketing a bonus of £750,000 for cutting our jobs. They talk about the global economy and business trends and their duty to their share-holders – but what about their duty to their employees? Well, maybe this will remind them that it's not just the factory they're shutting down, it's people's lives as well.

'Have you ever noticed how it's only people at the bottom who have to face up to the reality of market forces? The people at the top – the managers, managing directors and shareholders –

they never have to tighten *their* belts. When ordinary people object that *their* wages are too high they say, "If you pay peanuts you get monkeys." Well, if they can get Indians to do *our* jobs for half the wages, why stop there? Let's cut costs even more by getting rid of the directors and get some Indians to manage Sunny Jim, as well as work in the factories. That'll save a few million. And while we're at it, let's ask ourselves if we're getting value for money from Tony Blair. We could get an Indian to do his job for half the price as well.'

Nick was struggling to keep a straight face. Aidan was on a roll now.

'He couldn't do much worse than smiley boy, and we could replace Prescott, and all the rest of that shower with Indians too and use the money saved to do something useful, like open some new hospitals, or improve the railways.'

Nick was nodding, scribbling it all down. Aidan remembered what Dylan had said about local journalists. *They're all desperate to move on to a national, and if you're bringing them a story that will help get them noticed, they'll love you for it.* Aidan was determined to give him one.

Inside, Dylan was hunched over the phone.

'Yeah, it must have been that curry I had last night. No, not that place, the one at the end of Vole Street, Goodness Gracious Me!, with the red flames on the window. Yeah, I know . . . I will, yeah. Listen, sorry about this, but I should be OK for tomorrow . . . OK, thanks, see you.'

He put down the phone, noticed Russell, Gwyn and Wilf standing in the doorway, smirking. 'What?'

'A brilliant performance,' said Russell. 'Good to see those years in drama school weren't wasted.'

'I liked the bit about the flames best,' said Gwyn. 'That really brought it alive for me.'

'Yeah, whatever. Oh fuck!' He noticed the bullet points he'd drawn up for Aidan lying on a chair.

'Where's Dad?'

'Outside, talking to a reporter from the *Argus*.'

'*What?* Why didn't you tell me?'

'We didn't want to interrupt your Oscar-winning performance.'

'But he's forgotten his bullet points.'

Dylan rushed over and snatched up the piece of A4. 'He'll be lost without these.'

'It looks like he's doing all right without them to me.'

Yeah, right. Dylan didn't want to diss his dad in front of his mates, but Aidan needed watching all the time. Just look at his press release, for Christ's sake.

He brushed past Russell, Gwyn and Wilf, and rushed outside. There was Aidan, off-message already, talking about exactly the kind of things Dylan had warned him to steer clear of, things that would only make him upset and incoherent, lead him to be portrayed as a loser, rather than a people's champion. He was talking in a quiet, sombre voice, head down, hands thrust into his pockets.

'She died of a brain haemorrhage. None of us had any idea what was coming. There was no warning, she'd always been in such good health, then suddenly one day she was gone. Switched off like a light. I waved goodbye to her in the morning as I went out the door, said, "See you tonight about seven" as usual, then when I got home she was dead.'

Aidan stopped, tweaked the corners of his eyes with his thumb and index finger, took a long deep breath. The hack – solid local boy written all over him – said, 'Are you OK? If you don't want to . . .'

'No, you're all right, it's a fair question. I said I was a widower in the press release, you're only doing your job.'

Dylan stood there, unnoticed, horrified that the very first interview was spinning out of control, unable to think of a way to prevent it happening. Powerless to stop it because he felt his chest tightening, his breath coming short. It had been a long time since he'd heard his dad talk about his mam dying, and he wasn't enjoying it.

'My son, Dylan, came home from school early that day, and found her lying dead on the floor.' Aidan paused. 'That's a horrible thing to happen to a child, isn't it? Poor Dylan. I was devastated, but god knows what it must have been like for the kids to lose their mother at that age.'

Dylan felt as if he was watching an accident unfold in slow motion. His dad was going to get upset, start blubbering, make a complete bollocks of the interview and ruin everything.

'I still talk to her every day.'

No, don't tell him that.

Aidan smiled sadly. 'I probably talk to her more now than when she was alive.'

The hack was nodding. Then he noticed Dylan watching them.

'This is Dylan.'

Nick looked a little concerned.

'Are you OK?'

Dylan was taken aback, then stricken with embarrassment – his eyes were filling with tears, for fuck's sake. He nodded vigorously, held out his hand.

'Nice to meet you, Nick – how's the interview going?'

'Fine.'

Nick looked embarrassed now.

Come on, get a grip, Dylan.

Nick glanced at his notes, then turned back to Aidan.

'What's your greatest fear?'

Aidan looked very thoughtful; Dylan counted as he left three beats before replying, 'Getting diarrhoea.'

Nick burst out laughing. When Dylan recovered from the shock, he laughed too. While no one was looking, he wiped his eyes on the corner of his sleeve. Aidan was smiling now, displaying an easy, confident manner that made you think he was always cracking jokes.

'Can I quote you?' asked Nick, smiling – you could see he and Aidan liked each other.

Dylan had forgotten Aidan could be funny. When he was a kid, Aidan used to make him laugh a lot, would get down on all fours and play on the floor with him for ages, pull faces, pretend to be a horse, do silly voices. He wasn't so good when he got older though.

Do you like Top of the Pops, Dylan?

It sucks.

Is that good?

The thought of him and his dad trying to make conversation when he was a teenager really made him cringe. Looking at him and Nick hitting it off, he felt a pang of jealousy. It was a glimpse of how they could have been if he'd tried a bit harder, been a bit more patient, lowered his defences a little. He'd been so desperate to get away, so utterly single-minded. Pride of place on his bedroom wall had been a poster of Steve McQueen in *The Great Escape*, sitting on his motorbike, eyeing up the barbed-wire fence that encircled the prison camp. Dylan had taken a felt pen and added a thought bubble coming from out of his head.

It's a long-shot, but anything's better than staying in Crindau another year.

Maybe Nick was the kind of son who would have made Aidan happy: sensible, respectful and reliable, happy with his lot. Yeah, he reckoned Nick would be working for the *Argus* for the next thirty years, mortgaged to the hilt, two kids, Nissan Micra parked in the drive, Disneyland sticker in the back window. He decided to leave them to it.

'I'll just go and see if there's any sign of the people from Crindau FM,' he said to no one in particular.

He went and stood outside the house and lit a fag. A car drew up beside him. He looked up, saw Shauna getting out.

'Ah, there he is – one of Wales' most promising young actors.'

Dylan gaped at her.

'Dad showed me a copy of the press release you wrote for him the other day. Thanks for backing me up.'

Dylan shrugged. A gesture he hoped would eloquently convey his position.

You put me in an impossible situation, everything I suggest you always shoot down in flames, leaving me no option but to do it behind your back.

They stood there, gazing scornfully at each other. The photographer appeared behind them.

'Er, are you Aidan's daughter? We'd like you and Dylan to stand next to your dad in the garden for a family portrait.'

Aidan gurned self-consciously, just like he did in all those old holiday snaps. Dylan did his *Spotlight* pose, head cocked to one side, lopsided grin, smouldering eyes. Shauna managed a thin smile, her eyes guarded. When the photos were finished, Shauna reached inside her bag.

'Here,' Shauna said to Aidan. 'I got you this.'

'Another mobile?'

She raised her hand to prevent any objections. 'You *need* two. What are you going to do when the one you're using needs re-charging?' He hadn't thought. 'What if something went wrong and we couldn't get hold of you? I'm not having that, not when you're down there.'

'Thanks, love, this must have cost you, you shouldn't . . .'

'It's a vibrating one.'

'You what?' Aidan wondered whether he was having his leg pulled.

'Like the pagers that doctors use – it rings *and* vibrates, that way, if you want to listen to your Walkman and someone calls you, you won't miss it, because you'll *feel* it.'

Aidan grinned. 'Sounds like the most fun I've had in years.' He winked at Dylan.

'And this,' she continued, handing him a small box, 'is called

Rescue Remedy. You just squeeze three drops on to your tongue if you get anxious.'

'Anxious, me?' Aidan laughed. Too loudly, too long.

'It's very good.'

'Thank you, love, that was very thoughtful.' He kissed her. She hugged him close and whispered, 'I love you.'

Dylan shifted awkwardly, waiting till they'd finished. He shrugged, did his lopsided grin. 'Sorry, Dad, I didn't get you anything.'

Aidan tried not to look disappointed, 'That's all right, son, you've done so much already.'

Russell checked his watch, said, 'Shall we get started? Some of us have to get to work.'

A flicker of alarm travelled across Aidan's face. Everyone was watching him now.

Russell, Gwyn and Wilf carefully placed the coffin in the hole, then took off the lid. Wilf stepped forward.

'Good luck, mate.'

Aidan held out his hand ready for a handshake, but Wilf threw his arms around him and clasped him tight.

'Fuck!'

He nearly knocked Aidan to the ground.

'God bless.'

Aidan steadied himself, tried to speak. The words caught in his throat. Wilf's voice was thick with emotion when he spoke again.

'Megan and me will be praying for you.'

'Thanks, Wilf.'

'I love you like a brother, mun.'

Aidan nodded, his eyes squeezed tightly shut. He patted Wilf's back. These goodbyes were doing his head in.

'Yeah . . . yeah.'

Wilf took took something from his pocket, put it in Aidan's hand.

'What's this?'

'It's a St Christopher medal. It used to belong to my dad. Kept him safe all through the war – he was in the merchant navy, the convoys in the North Sea, you know.'

'Wilf, mun, I can't . . .'

Wilf stepped back. 'Yes you can. You can give it back when you come out, all right?'

Aidan nodded and put it around his neck.

Wilf stepped back, rubbing his finger under his nose.

Russell was lighting another fag. Gwyn put his hands in his pockets, took them out again, folded them across his chest.

Aidan stood by the edge of the hole, gazing down into it. Jesus, it was creepy. How many people stood looking down into their own grave? It reminded him of those poor bastards in Bosnia.

'Are you all right, mate?'

Gwyn was giving him a searching look. He looked anxious himself. They all did.

'This is where we're all going to end up in the end, isn't it? In a hole in the ground.'

He forced himself to laugh.

Dylan looked alarmed.

Aidan looked around him now, at his children and his friends. It *was* like a funeral. As if he was leaving them all for good. He thought of all the things that he'd never said to them. All the opportunities he'd missed to let them know how much they meant to him. There were so many conversations he should have had with Eileen too. *You know your problem, Aidan? You bury things.* All eyes were on him now, but he just couldn't move. Shauna said, 'Dad, you don't have to do this.'

'I'm sorry, love, I've got to. I'll be all right, don't worry.'

'I will though.'

He turned away, thinking this was the beginning of a conversation they should have had years ago.

Russell said, 'What are we waiting for?'

Aidan wasn't sure. Somebody rushing into the garden yelling,

'Stay where you are – they've just announced they've changed their minds – our jobs are safe!' Or maybe a council official bursting in, announcing some new bye-law that prohibited burying yourself in your garden – something to do with health and safety, a new directive from Brussels that had just come into operation this morning. 'Oh well,' he'd say, holding out his arms, as the official uttered dire warnings of prosecution. 'What can you do? Better call the whole thing off then.'

The photographer had lowered his camera, Nick was looking distinctly uncomfortable, stood very stiffly fiddling with the knot in his tie. This was it. Aidan slapped his hands together, cried, 'Let's do it.'

Dylan brightened. 'Remember the photo opportunity we talked about?'

Aidan had forgotten about that. Now he could turn the whole thing into a joke. He took a pair of sunglasses from inside his jacket, put them on. The others watched him, confused. Dylan cleared his throat, stepped forward, looked at Nick and the photographer while he said, 'What are you doing, Dad?'

Aidan, grinning, replied, 'These were a gift from Sunny Jim – you remember their slogan, don't you? "We'll give you a free pair of sunglasses when you come to work with us – you'll need them, your prospects will be so dazzling!" '

That got a laugh, everyone relieved to see the mood lightening. The photographer started taking more shots, asking Aidan to give him the thumbs-up, smile, move his head this way, that.

'How about a few in the coffin?'

It had become a bit of a giggle. Aidan found it easy to clamber in, lie down and clown around, the photographer hanging over him, clicking away. Dylan stood next to Nick, said, 'Great copy, eh?' Wanting to be sure this smalltown boy made the most of this, before he went back to filing stories about rowdy neighbours on council estates and some bus route being cancelled.

Then they handed Aidan his gear – radio, Walkman and cassettes, the bedpan, toilet rolls, pillow.

'I've got all mod cons here. I don't think I'll ever want to come up again at this rate.'

Russell squeezed Aidan's shoulder and said, 'Good luck, mate.' There was the slightest tremor in his voice that only someone who knew him very well would have noticed. But before Aidan could say anything in return, Russell was turning away, picking up the lid and saying in a brusque and businesslike tone, 'OK, here we go. Let's do it.'

Aidan flinched at the sound of them screwing the lid down. It felt like they were boring right into him. He moved his hands down to his sides, stretched out his fingers and touched the sides of the coffin. The top was about just a few inches above his face. He moved his hands up, touched the lid with his fingertips. He had enough room to shift up or down a foot, and maybe six inches either way. A small world. He heard Russell say, 'Lift it up', felt the coffin lurch to one side then the other, instinctively put out his hands to the sides to stop himself from rolling. He heard the lads grunting as they dragged the ropes underneath the coffin, then exhaling as it was lowered gently down again. Russell's face peered down at him.

'You're a heavy bastard.'

'It's all muscle.'

Russell snorted, moved out of sight again. 'Going down.'

Then he was swinging gently in the air. It wasn't a pleasant experience. He looked out of his window to see the sky swaying gently above him. Call him old-fashioned, but Aidan liked the sky to stay still. It was one of those little things he was really quite fussy about. Then, with a slight bump, he was down. The photographer stood at the edge of the hole and aimed his camera at him again, getting one of Aidan looking out of the coffin. He forced a big smile. He heard the first shovel of earth hit the end of the coffin, a dull thump, followed by the whispering sound of earth spreading. Before he could say anything another shovelful landed, splattering him with soil. The fecking idiots. He stuck his head out, yelled, 'Hey, you've forgotten something!'

Russell was already scooping up another shovelful and turned round sharply.

'You just going to chuck the bloody earth on top of me? Someone needs to hold the periscope in place before you start that.'

Russell stared at him blankly for a moment. Then, sensing movement behind him, pushed his arm out in a sudden blocking movement. Wilf gasped as he walked into it, jolting backwards and spilling the soil from the shovel.

Russell pointed to Aidan's startled face rising from the hole in the coffin. 'Use your head, we haven't got his ventilation shaft in place, we'll end up filling the inside of his bloody coffin – and how do you think he's going to breathe, you clown?'

Wilf looked mortified. Gwyn was frozen, a shovelful of soil at knee height. Russell nodded at Dylan. 'Here, make yourself useful and hold it in place.'

Dylan didn't like his tone, and gave him a look designed to let him know it before he carefully positioned the ventilation shaft directly over Aidan's window. It was awkward and heavy, and Dylan struggled to hold it in place.

'So he'll breathe through that?' said Nick.

'Yeah,' replied Dylan, 'and we'll winch his food down to him through it.' Nick nodded, making notes. 'It'll give him a window on the world as well, he can see what the weather's like, who's talking to him. And, of course, it'll allow him to continue to give interviews to people while he's down there.'

Russell, Gwyn and Wilf started heaving earth into the hole again, concentrating on getting a good rhythm going. They wanted to get it over with. If they started thinking about what they were actually doing, burying their mate alive, they'd never manage to do it. But with Nick and the photographer standing just a few yards away watching, they felt they had to put on a good display.

Dylan was stamping down the earth around the periscope with his foot, taking care to keep it in exactly the right position.

After a few minutes Russell felt the pace slackening. He looked at the beads of perspiration beginning to roll down Gwyn's forehead, at Wilf's face reddening.

'Come on, lads, let's keep it going here.'

They put their backs into it, speeded up again.

Soil splattered Dylan's feet. He skipped out of the hole, stood on the edge, leant over to hold the periscope in place. He looked down it, catching his Dad off-guard, his face creased with anxiety, staring straight up, but looking straight through him, lost in some dark place. Dylan felt panic shooting through him, he didn't want to see him like that.

'Hold it steady,' Russell barked at Dylan. Dylan tightened his grip on the periscope as the earth piled up, rising steadily to the top of the hole.

The thud and scattering whisper of the first few minutes was giving way now to the quieter, more sombre sounds of soil falling on soil.

'Well,' said Russell, after another few minutes, 'I think we're done.' He wiped his brow, put down his shovel. He walked over to the periscope, looked down and leered.

'No playing with yourself down there, mind.'

Aidan smiled. This was better, a bit of banter, just like at work. Gwyn pushed his face into the frame.

'What's it feel like?'

'Cosy. Quite warm actually.'

Wilf appeared. 'You look just the same!'

'Really? What the hell did you expect?'

Russell said, 'That's amazing, I'd never have expected him to look just the same as he did fifteen minutes ago.' He tugged his arm. 'Come on, let's go.'

'Cheers, lads – don't forget to keep your mobiles switched on!'

'I'll pop by this evening,' said Russell. He winked. 'Good luck, mate, you'll be all right, don't worry.' He left.

Aidan sighed, closed his eyes, clenched his teeth. He opened them again, then gave a start. 'Jesus! Don't do that.'

Russell was peering down at him, his head blocking out the sky, a quizzical expression on his face.

'You *will* be in tonight, won't you?'

Russell laughed – he always laughed at his own jokes – then he left again. Aidan heard him shouting, 'Come on, get a move on, you two, we'll be late.'

Nick and the photographer left, then Shauna said goodbye.

'I'll come and see you this evening.'

On the way out, she said to Dylan, 'Call me – we need to talk.' She tried to fix him with a meaningful look, but he avoided her eyes.

Dylan stood with his hands on his hips, alone in the garden. How strange it looked now it was empty. Nothing but a fresh mound of earth in the middle with a wooden shaft sticking out of it. It was hard to believe his dad was down there. That this could be the thing that would put Crindau on the map. He plucked a sheet of paper from his pocket, folded it in half, held it above the periscope. 'Here, catch.'

'What's that?'

'Your bullet points.'

He dropped them down the shaft. The paper floated gently into Aidan's hands, his first delivery.

'We've had one hit, now I'll give Crindau FM a ring and tell them the *Argus* has been here. Once the *Argus* covers us, they'll follow, you'll see. This is just the beginning, trust me. People are going to be talking about you from one end of the country to the other. Well, I'd better get going . . .'

'Dylan?'

'Yeah?'

'Thanks.'

Dylan waved a hand dismissively. 'Don't mention it. I enjoy it.'

Aidan smiled. 'Yeah, I know.'

Dylan frowned, he could read his dad like a book, but the thought that Aidan understood what made *him* tick was a new and unsettling notion.

'It's your gig at the end of the day, Dad. If you're not happy with anything I suggest . . .'

Aidan shook his head. 'Not at all, you're doing a great job. You know, I've been thinking.'

Dylan didn't like his tone, as if he really *had* been thinking, and wasn't just going to repeat some old rubbish he'd heard in work or on the radio.

'This could actually bring the family closer together. I've been worrying that what I'm doing is going to put a lot of strain on you all, and it doesn't seem fair, after all it's not *your* jobs that are being taken away.'

'Hey! Don't worry, Dad, mun, I *want* to help you.'

Aidan paused, troubled.

'Well that's great of you to say so, son, but I'm not so sure about Shauna.'

'Naah!' Dylan dismissed the notion with a shrug. 'She'll be all right, she just needs time to get used to the idea.'

'That's what I'm hoping, that the two of you will come to see this as . . . as something *you* can all be a part of too. You've grown up and gone your own separate ways now. It would be nice to see you . . .'

Aidan was struggling a bit now, he'd imagined he'd be getting a bit more help at this point, that Dylan, after listening in respectful silence to his heartfelt words, would by now be joining in enthusiastically, ending his sentences for him, putting into words the thoughts he was finding so difficult to express. Instead he was looking at him like he had started to speak in Albanian.

'I, er, it's been so long since your mam died, and it's been hard for us all and . . .'

Dylan cleared his throat, began nodding rapidly. He didn't want this kind of talk with his dad. 'Yeah, know exactly what you mean, Dad, that's really sound. Look, I gotta go, I want to speak to Crindau FM.'

'Will you have time to come back?'

'I've got to catch the 1.30 train.'

'Oh, OK.'

His dad's face, wracked with worry, looking old and vulnerable, alone down there, made Dylan hesitate. Aidan noticed his unease, slipped into a cheery voice. 'Go on then, you'd better get a move on. Off you go.' Dylan gazed down at him for a long moment, holding his gaze. The look on his face, it reminded Dylan of the time he left home to go to uni. Then he'd walked away quickly, not turning back once, in case he caught Aidan wiping away a tear. He didn't think he could have coped with that.

He said in a quiet voice, 'Good luck, Dad.'

Aidan smiled and, when Dylan had disappeared from view, said, 'I'll fucking need it.'

Now Aidan was finally on his own, screwed down in his cardboard box, six feet of earth on top of him. The day stretched out in front of him like a prison sentence. He was going to have to get used to doing solitary. There would be no more visitors till Frank brought his lunch. He checked his watch; not quite half eight yet, three and a half hours till he saw another human face. It was so quiet. Incredibly quiet, the silence weighing down on him as heavily as the earth on his coffin.

He was alone. He was scared. *Come on, you've only been down here a few minutes, get a grip.*

'Right, Aidan, it's no good just lying here feeling sorry for yourself, let's get organised.'

He didn't want to be scrambling around looking for stuff in this confined space, unable to put his hands on what he wanted. He hummed as he worked. First he got his Walkman and cassettes tidied away within easy reach. He'd made lots of compilations – The Beatles, The Kinks and The Stones, Soul and Tamla Motown, The Animals, The Hollies, Them, Simon and Garfunkel, The Who and Pink Floyd. There was some stuff from the Seventies too, Led Zeppelin, Deep Purple, XTC, The Clash, Joan Armatrading, Joni Mitchell and Cat Stevens. But not much from the Eighties and Nineties, apart from The Pogues, The Smiths and The Stone Roses. He was, as Dylan never tired of telling him, stuck in the past. He didn't care, he liked it there.

He organised his reading material next. He had the *Radio Times*, last night's *Argus*, plus a couple of thrillers he'd got from a charity shop, both Elmore Leonards – he liked him, took one of his on holiday every year, good old Elmore never let you down. Toilet rolls, bedpan, Wet Wipes, a bottle to piss in, batteries, mobiles, torch, bottle opener, Dylan's bullet points. A change of underwear and socks, Rescue Remedy, newspaper, carrier bags. It didn't take long to get everything in order. What next?

Look up above, and contemplate the beauty of the clouds, Grasshopper.

Yeah sure, he'd do that for a few hours and probably write a few poems while he was at it.

Of course – his diary. He was going to keep a diary. He'd bought a lovely notebook in a stationer's up town, a thick blue one with *Notebook* embossed in gold on the cover. Had felt a bit self-conscious when he handed it over to the assistant, he'd never bought anything like that before, half expected her to say, 'We've got some jotters over there marked down to 50p.'

He liked the idea of recording a little bit about what he did and said and thought while he was down there. So he wouldn't forget what it had been like once it was over. After all, nobody had ever done anything like this before, he didn't want to let the experience slip through his fingers. It would give him something to concentrate on, an outlet for his imagination, a task to be completed every day. It could be something that would stop him just lying there and vegetating.

He opened the diary now, propped it up on his chest, smoothed the first page flat with his hand, took the top off his pen and wrote *Monday, Day One* at the top of the page. So, his first entry. He tapped the pen against his teeth, waited for inspiration to strike. *Here I am underground*, he wrote. Then he stopped, began tapping his teeth with the pen again. What could he say? It was so quiet he couldn't think straight. He realised now just how packed with noise his day normally was, how he took it for granted, the way he did light or colours, or there being a floor beneath his feet. He let the notebook fall flat on his chest, lay down his head, held his breath and strained to hear something, anything. He waited patiently. Minutes passed. Sweet FA. Not even a car going past on the road. How he'd love to hear an engine revving, a car door slamming, or school-kids yelling and screeching. A workman drilling a hole in the road, a ringing phone, the rapid bleeping of a lorry reversing, the drone and clatter of a milk van, a dog barking. *Any* sign that life was going on as normal. To convince him he wasn't completely, utterly on his own.

If he was at work, there would be a radio blaring in the background, men grunting and panting as they lifted heavy weights; boxes crashing against each other; forklifts trundling up and down; shouts, jokes and insults flying – the craic that made working in a warehouse bearable, the banter that took your mind off the drudgery. He missed those things now more than he'd have ever thought possible.

He stared up at the lid, less than a foot above his head. All that earth pressing down on it, it must be strong. He rapped his knuckles against it. It felt so solid, you'd never guess it was cardboard. No, he was perfectly safe. He stretched his hand up the periscope, then stretched his fingers to their limit – his hand reached nearly halfway up so he wasn't very far from the surface, not really. If someone standing next to the periscope thrust their arm down, they'd touch his fingers. If he changed his mind all he had to do was ring the lads and they'd be round and dig him out in half an hour. He propped the notebook upright again on his chest, took his pen and wrote, *It's very quiet down here.*

There, that would do for now. He closed the book. Now what was he going to do? He didn't have the faintest idea.

It came from nowhere, sudden and violent. Sheer, unadulterated panic.

What were you thinking of? You'll never stick this. What if I get ill? I could get flu. Appendicitis. A heart attack. Oh Jesus, what if I do get diarrhoea?

What if there's something wrong with this coffin? Maybe Pancho has sold me a dud. What if my mobile breaks? What if my air supply gets blocked?

If any of those things happened, he was fucked. Why had he put himself in such a vulnerable position? He felt the cold sweat trickling down his back.

'No – stop that now!' He musn't just lie there. That was the one thing he had to avoid. His mind would turn and attack him. He needed to keep busy at all times, and if he couldn't be busy, he needed maximum distraction. He switched on the radio – Robbie Williams. Fuck, not *him*. Never mind, it would do. Anything would do. He stuck a Beatles *Greatest Hits* compilation in his Walkman and put it on. Aidan had fantastic faith in the healing power of The Beatles. The uncomplicated joy and energy they transmitted. 'Love Me Do', 'From Me to You', 'She Loves You', 'I Want to Hold Your Hand', 'We Can Work It Out', 'Hello, Goodbye', he had them all. He turned the volume up high. He sang along. He imagined that someone was watching him. Checking to see how he was coping.

OK, I'll put on a show for them.

It took a while, five or six songs, but his mood started to improve. If you made an effort and acted like you were really enjoying yourself, you sometimes found you couldn't actually tell the difference between pretending you were having a good time and actually having one. He often did that in the Globe, when Russell was holding forth about something that he knew fuck all about. Aidan would think *But that's not how it is, not really*. But the feeling that he was the only one there who thought that, that he was out on a limb, filled him with dread. It was as if a jagged tear had opened in his world. He would quickly banish such disturbing thoughts and plunge headlong into a stirring performance of Aidan Walsh enjoying himself. The anxiety didn't disappear, but he'd pressed it right down, till it was only a gnawing pain in the pit of his stomach. A few drinks helped keep it in its place.

Here I am underground, spirits high, singing along to The Beatles.

This was what he'd want people to see if they were watching. He often felt like someone was watching him, trying to catch him out. Aidan didn't need any CCTV cameras trained on him, he monitored himself very effectively.

When one side of the cassette ended, he turned up the radio till the first song on the second side began. *Maximum distraction.* He shouted encouragement to himself.

'Attaboy, Aidan, it'll take more than being shut up in a coffin to break your spirit – you can do it!'

By the time the second side ended, he felt exhausted by the effort of maintaining his spirits. But he felt strong. He felt good about himself. He'd come through his first crisis. He'd lost track of time he was so absorbed in the music. That was a good sign. When you were enjoying yourself, when you were carefree, time flew. He felt confident enough to check his watch now. Fuck no, that couldn't be right, his watch must be crocked.

'I'll give one of the lads a ring, check the time with them.'

He could have switched on the radio again, waited for a time check but what he *really* wanted to do was talk to someone. He took his mobile from his pocket, gave Russell a ring. He was getting the hang of this thing. It took him a while to answer, then, when he did, there were muffled curses and a crashing noise, followed by scrambling sounds.

'Fucking bastard thing – HELLO?'

'Hi-ya, Russ.'

'That you, Aidan?'

'Yeah.'

'What is it?' Russell sounded alarmed. 'Are you all right?'

'Yeah, I am.'

'You sure?'

'No, I'm fine, honest. I've just been lying here, listening to The Beatles, sometimes you forget just how good they were, don't you?'

There was a sharp intake of breath on the other end of the line.

'Did you scratch your arse as well?'

'Eh?'

'Go on, I really want to know.'

Aidan didn't say anything, he was going to get slagged off, that much was clear, but he didn't know why.

'Because that must be the only thing you've left out of your detailed description of your morning so far. Apart from that, I've got the complete picture, thank you very much, Aidan. Now, shall I tell you about *my* morning?'

'Aye, go on,' said Aidan, trying to keep it jokey.

'I got pulled over by the cops. Got a ticket for speeding. Thirty-two miles an hour in a built-up area. Really. So I end up being late for work, and a couple of guys are off sick and there's a big order to load up straight away. So there I am, breaking my back, and you ring me up. I get the shock of my life when the bloody mobile goes off, nearly drop this fucking box on my toes. There I am, searching for the bloody thing, thinking, Jesus, what's happened, something must have gone wrong already. And then, when I answer, you start telling me how wonderful The Beatles are.'

'Sorry to give you a shock, mate.'

Russell muttered something incoherent.

'So why *did* you ring me up?'

'I wanted you to tell me the time.'

'*You rang me to ask what time it was.* Jesus wept. Haven't you got a watch?'

'Ah . . . yeah, but it says 9.34 – that can't be right?'

'No, it's not. It's 9.33 according to mine.'

'Christ, you're kidding.'

'Do I sound like I'm kidding?'

'I could have sworn it was about eleven.'

Aidan couldn't admit that knowing the right time was only half the story, that he wanted to talk to someone. He should have rung someone else.

'So, now you know the right time. Glad to have been of help.'

The line went dead. Aidan felt as if someone had cut off his air supply. The world was carrying on as normal without him. No one needed him. Aidan could feel himself floating away from everyone and everything. *This is what it must be like when you've died. Imagine your spirit coming back to earth after you'd died, and finding that no one talked about you anymore. You find someone new living in your home, your grave covered in weeds or spray-painted obscenities. How would it feel to realise that you'd left no mark on the world? You'd sweated and you'd slaved and you'd dreamed and you'd made plans, all to no avail. Your time was up and you'd wasted it.*

He moved his arm and caught a sharp odour. It was like something you'd smell on a trapped animal. An awful fear. His body felt stretched and pulled, mangled and pounded, every nerve raw and pulsing. He couldn't move more than a few inches in any direction. He was sealed up with his own worst fears. All the things that he couldn't handle, that he'd tried so hard to shut down over the years, were now seizing their chance, and beginning to push their way back to the surface.

He made a pincer of the thumb and forefinger of his right hand and pinched the palm of his left hand till he yelped in pain.

'YOU SOFT BASTARD.'

He had to calm down. If he could just get through this first morning, get used to the situation, he'd be OK. How long to go? He turned to look at his watch again, stopped himself just in time. He put his hand over the face. That way lay madness.

That stuff Shauna had given him, the Rescue Remedy, where was it? He reached down the side of the coffin, found it next to his cassettes. Tore open the box, pulled out the little bottle. *To Comfort & Reassure.* He read the instructions. *Bring spray nozzle up to mouth and apply 2 sprays on the tongue.* Two sprays – that didn't sound much, so he tried six. Not bad, not bad at all. In fact there was something faintly alcoholic about the after-taste. He closed his eyes and started taking deep breaths. Jesus, if he didn't know better he'd say he was getting a bit of a buzz. He unclenched his fists, stretched out his fingers. This Rescue Remedy was kosher. Shauna knew her stuff all right. How often were you supposed to take it? *Take as required.* He gave himself another six sprays. Yes, he felt calmer already, it was definitely working. He took a closer look at the label, checked the ingredients. *Flower extracts.* What kind of bloody stuff had she given him? The extracts had some nice names though – Rock Rose, Clematis, Star of Bethlehem. And Cherry Plum in a grape alcohol solution. The secret ingredient.

'Grape alcohol, yee ha!'

He held it up, shook it. Yes, sirree, he had enough there to keep him going for quite a while. That was better, now he had a little helper to turn to when things got tricky.

'What you having, Aidan, pint of lager? Actually, I think I'll have some grape alcohol. No, really, you should try some.'

He smiled to himself. You couldn't have too much of a good thing.

'Bottoms up.'

Pressed the spray six, seven, eight, times. Closed his eyes again, took some more deep breaths. Then replaced the top, put the bottle back down by his side.

'That's enough for now, you don't want to get a hangover.'

He massaged his temples gently with his fingertips, moaning softly.

'You're warm and comfortable and perfectly safe. If you change your mind all you have to do is give Russell or one of the lads a ring and they'll be here in half an hour to dig you out. You're going to be all right.'

His breathing was deeper, more even now.

'Remember your plan.'

He'd told himself he was going to find definite things to look forward to, events that would punctuate the day and give it some kind of structure – his next cuppa, the news on the hour, someone coming with the paper in the afternoon. That's how people in hospital and prison coped. Look at Nelson Mandela. He spent years in solitary confinement, miles from anywhere, out on an island off the coast of South Africa. He was locked up in the prime of his life – he had a career, a beautiful wife, young kids. Did it break him? Did it hell.

Aidan clenched his fist, raised it as high as he could manage in the coffin.

'Fair play to you, Nelson.'

The human spirit, it was something resilient and beautiful, and it was inside us all – Mandela never forgot that.

'It's even in me. Even a fat old slob like me. It's there all right and if I dig deep enough, I'll find it. Imagine Nelson watching you squirm and blubber after only a couple of hours – for fuck's sake, mun, aren't you ashamed to be carrying on like that?'

Did Nelson have a radio, books and newspapers and cassettes to listen to? Rescue Remedy to get high on? No, he didn't. He had nothing but willpower. Willpower and the absolute conviction that what he was doing was right.

'So, no more feeling sorry for yourself, no more morbid thoughts.'

If Nelson could stick that tiny prison cell, he could stick this. He picked up the *Radio Times*, had a look what was on the radio. He'd plan a schedule. In between the programmes that he really wanted to listen to, he'd write his diary. He licked his finger, turned the page.

'Mmm, Tuesday, Radio 2, now then . . .'

He tap-tapped the page with his pen, wondering what to circle. He started to hum 'Love Me Do'. Then his mobile started ringing. *Christ!* The piercing noise sounded like an alarm going off in that silent cardboard cell. He jerked upwards with the shock, cracked his skull on the lid.

'Fuck!'

His hands shot up towards the searing pain in his head, slamming his knuckles against the lid.

'Shit!'

He fumbled frantically for the mobile. He was too anxious, too clumsy, only succeeded in knocking it further down the coffin. *His first call!* He couldn't miss it. He contorted himself, bending and twisting round till he could just reach the edge of the phone with his fingertips. He pressed down on the end and it flipped into the air. He twisted again, trying to catch it on his leg as it came down. It struck his knee painfully. He shot out a hand. Didn't catch it, just hit the side with his fingers to send it flying right down to the other end of the coffin. It smacked against the bottom with a crack. Oh Christ, he'd broken the fucker. No, it was still ringing. 'La Cuceracha'. He thought he'd changed it to 'Mission Impossible'.

'All right, all right!'

The idiotic tune was driving him mad. There wasn't enough room to turn round and grab it. His head and knuckles were throbbing. He stretched his hands down by his sides, palms against the floor, raised his knees and pushed himself down. Caught the mobile between his feet. Now what? Christ, he couldn't think straight with that bloody awful noise. He slid his feet forward, but couldn't reach it. He let it drop gently from his feet, adjusted his position, started pushing it back up towards him with his heel.

'Yes, come on, nearly there.'

He grabbed it with his fingers. He had it.

'Hello.'

There was a pause.

'Is that Chris?'

'No, it's Aidan, Aidan Walsh.'

'Oh . . . sorry, mate, I've got the wrong number.'

He ended the call, collapsed.

'Fucking hell. Fucking fucking bloody hell!'

The heat. He was starting to sweat like a pig, Jesus, it was stifling down there. He'd never realised it would be so hot underground; it was a waste being fully dressed.

'Right!' It was all coming off. He unbuttoned his shirt, twisted round one way, then the other, to take it off. He slapped his chest. He was still in pretty good nick. Not too bad anyway, for his age.

'Now then.'

He undid his top botton, began unzipping his jeans. Then he caught himself.

Look at you – what are you like? Doing a strip in a coffin?

He started grinning. He began humming 'The Stripper'.

'DA DA DA – DE DA DA DA . . .'

Wiggled his hips, puckered up his lips.

'Mmmmm, you sexy beast.'

He toyed with the zip, down a bit, up a bit, teasing.

You want to see it? Well, do you, baby?

Teasing who? Wham, she popped straight into his head. Her gorgeous brown eyes, her long painted fingernails, the swell of her breasts beneath her blouse. Safina. She was staring right at him, leaning back in her chair, slowly unbuttoning her blouse. Her mouth parted, whispering his name, '*Aidan*', soft as a summer breeze on his burning hot skin. He closed his eyes, arched his back, felt his hard cock pressing against his jeans. It felt good, very very good. She completely unbuttoned her blouse, tugged it out from her skirt, drew it back.

'Come on then.'

Beautiful brown breasts spilling out of a black lacy bra.

'What are you waiting for?'

Jesus Christ almighty, he was stiff as a broom handle.

'You dirty devil.'

He was a sex machine.

Get on up!

He still had it. He wasn't so young anymore, but he knew how to please a woman. In his head at least. But it was harder to keep feeling so sexy when he'd got his jeans down below his hips. Knees up, tug, shift backwards, another tug, shift backwards again.

'Bloody Nora.'

It was getting on his nerves already, the lack of space.

'Fuck.'

He jerked his knees up too hard, banged them on the lid. Rubbing them with his hands, he shifted on to his side, growling like a dog now, and started a jig. Kicking, prising and shoving them off. Gritting his teeth, he painstakingly disentangled them from his feet, then lay back, panting.

'I'm bloody knackered.'

His cock was going soft. His socks.

'Right!'

He rolled on to his side, lifted up a knee, began rolling down the first one. It was tough prising them away from his toes, the buggers clung on desperately. He pulled hard and his knee flew up and struck the lid.

'Bollocks!'

Jesus Christ Almighty, he'd be black and blue by the end of the day. He turned over and went through the same process for the other one.

His toenails could do with cutting. He sniffed his armpit. Not too bad. A lot better than some blokes he could mention. Russell, fuck, he stank like a ferret by the end of the day.

He left his underpants on. Exercise. He'd promised himself he was going to do exercises while he was down there. He turned over and did twenty press ups, slowly, carefully, his head brushing the lid each time.

'Good man. Well done.'

He was going to congratulate himself every time he stuck to his plan. Positive psychology, that was the key to success. He was breathing heavily now, but he didn't want to stop. He'd got a rhythm going. What now? Pelvic thrusts of course.

'Mmmm, you sexy thing!'

He was really getting into it. Started grunting.

'Uuughn!'

His heart was going like the clappers now. He wished he had some music to do it to. People in gyms, they worked out to music now. It was normal. He had his Walkman, but didn't want to put that on in case he missed a call. He'd make his own.

'I believe in miracles . . . MMMMMMMMMMM – you sexy thing!'

A shadow fell over him. He looked up. There was a scream and Aidan jumped, clattering his elbow on the side of the coffin.

'Oh my god!' Joy clutched her face.

'For Christ's sake, you nearly gave me a heart attack.'

She edged closer, eyes wide. '*I* nearly gave *you* a heart attack? What do you think you did to me?'

'You shouldn't have sneaked up on me like that.'

'You . . . you . . .' She shook her head. 'What in god's name are you up to down there?'

'Doing my exercises.'

'Is *that* what you call it?'

She looked as though she'd just swallowed soiled cat litter.

'Why aren't you wearing any clothes?'

'It's very warm in here – it's none of your business anyway.'

'I'm living next door to a naked lunatic.'

'I'm not naked, I've got my underpants on.'

'*What?*'

He flinched, her voice shrill enough now to smash glasses.

'Calm down, for Christ's sake.'

She had a strap around her neck, there was something heavy dangling from it that he couldn't see.

'Calm down, he says. That's a good one. My next door neighbour has buried himself alive – *naked*.'

'I've got me undies on, I'm telling you.'

'He's –' She buried her face in her hands, shook her head. 'God *knows* what he's doing down there, something . . . *disgusting*! And *I'm* the one over-reacting.'

She began screeching with laughter. It sounded like an air-raid siren, frenetic and chilling. He clenched his teeth; felt a throbbing pain in his forehead, as if someone had just rammed a block of ice into it. *Bloody hell, that was some creepy laugh, she could have made a fortune doing the soundtrack for horror films.*

Aidan was holding his hands up now, like a copper dealing with someone about to jump.

'Just take it easy, it's not what you think.'

She held up a camera – that was what was dangling from her neck – and took a photo.

'What are you doing?'

Then another. Aidan covered his face with his hands.

'Collecting evidence – you're a filthy pervert.'

She used up a whole roll of film. Aidan laughed the incident off when she'd finished. Then began to worry about it. What if she called the police and claimed sexual harassment? Arrested, protest over after one day. Oh fuck.

Half an hour later his mobile rang again. He hoped to god it wasn't the vice squad.

'Hi-ya, Aidan Walsh here.'

'Hello, it's Frank.'

At last. For the past hour Aidan had been able to think of only one thing, the obsession that had pushed everything else right back. *Food!*

'Hi-ya, Frank, how's it going?'

'Slow.'

Aidan heard 'A Design for Life' playing on the jukebox, glasses clinking. He could picture exactly how it looked in the Globe, and he longed to be there, a pint in front of him.

'So, what's it like down there?'

'Very quiet and really hot.'

'Hot, is it?'

'Yeah, I've had to strip down to my undies.'

This prompted a low, guttural laugh from Frank.

'You been playing with yourself?'

'Piss off.'

'I would be, there can't be much else to do down there.'

'Well that's where you're wrong, there's plenty to do.'

'Oh aye?'

'Yes, I've been reading; I listened to the radio; made a few phone calls. And I've started a diary.'

'Have you now?'

'And I've been doing my exercises.'

'Exercises eh?'

'That's right,' said Aidan. 'I don't want to turn to flab.'

'Bit late now, innit?'

'You're wasted behind the bar, you could be packing them in at the Pontypandy Palladium.'

'So, are you hungry?'

'I'm bloody starving.'

He'd fixed it that Frank was going to deliver his meals every day. The Globe was only a few minutes' walk away.

'It's all those exercises you're doing down there.'

Aidan heard someone calling to Frank.

'I'll be with you in a minute, I'm taking an order. That's right, I've just started taking orders over the phone – a takeaway service, yeah. It's for a bloke in a coffin if you must know. Right, Aidan, what do you want for your lunch? We got steak pie, chips, peas and gravy, fish and chips, or burger in a bun, chips and peas.'

'Steak pie.'

'You want a dessert?'

'Yeah, I want the works.'

114

'Apple pie and ice cream, jam roly-poly, chocolate fudge cake, or sticky toffee pudding.'

There was a long pause.

'You still there?'

'Yeah. Go on, say them all again.'

'You what?'

'I want to hear about the desserts again.'

'You soft bugger, come on, choose one. I haven't got all day.'

'Sticky toffee pudding.'

'Good choice. Just the thing to fight the flab. What you want to drink with that?'

'One of those J2Os.'

It was tempting to ask for a beer, but he needed to keep focused. It was hot down there, he was gasping and he didn't want to drift off.

'All right, it'll be about twenty minutes. I'll send Donna over with it.'

'Cheers, Frank.' He didn't want the call to end. 'You busy?'

'Not really, just a few old lags, or valued customers as I like to call them to their face.'

'See you later.'

Twenty minutes was nothing. He'd just lived through an eternity, he could easily fill twenty minutes.

When Donna arrived with his lunch she looked down the periscope hesitantly, did a double-take when she saw him.

'Hi-ya, Donna.'

Her hand went to her cheek.

'Oh, this is weird.'

Aidan smiled. 'Yeah, I suppose it is.'

'Er, how am I going to get this down to you?'

'See the winch?'

Donna looked around. 'Oh yeah, and there's a rope and a little basket. Oh that's cute. So I put it in the basket and lower it down to you.'

'That's the way, cheers, Donna.'

'Righty-o. Here you are, your lordship.'

She winched it down to him. The smell of it as it came nearer. Frank had put his lunch in a plastic Tupperware box. His knife and fork and the bottle of J2O next to them. He already had a bottle opener down there in the coffin. That was called planning.

'Enjoy!'

He propped up his pillow, levered himself up a little, so that the top of his head was now wedged against the coffin lid. The Tupperware box containing his lunch was resting on his stomach. Very slowly he began to prise off the lid. The smell of the food in the confined space was overwhelming and he felt himself swooning. His stomach rumbled and moaned, his juices flowed: he squeezed his eyes shut, groaning luxuriously in delight and anticipation. It was a kind of sweet torture. He knew he had to move slowly so as not to spill anything, but his stomach was howling and his hands shook as he removed the lid.

'Hold on, baby, I'm coming, I'm coming . . . Yeah, you look so fine.'

Inch by inch, he peeled back the lid. Then lifted it right off.

'Mmmm, I've waited so long for this. This is going to be *so* good.'

He cut off a piece of the pie, blew on it, lifted it carefully into his mouth. He didn't start chewing it straight away, just held it there, absorbing its warmth and succulent juices. A moment of pure ecstasy, Aidan's whole body absolutely still, head thrown back, eyes shut, a blissful smile on his face. *Man oh man, that is something else.*

Now he started chewing. He cracked, reached into the box and stuffed a handful of chips into his gob. What he would have really liked to do was grab hold of the box and tip the contents straight down his throat, like Desperate Dan. He revelled in the sensation of having his mouth crammed to bursting with food. He opened the J2O, took a slug of that to help wash it down.

He was cutting himself a second piece of pie when his mobile rang again.

'Jesus!'

He jumped with the shock and the Tupperware box lurched sideways, spilling the contents onto his stomach.

'Aaaargh!'

The red hot meat and gravy oozed out of its pastry, scalding him. When he tried to flick the pie off with his hand it burst. Globs of molten meat and gravy flew through the air like buckshot, spattering the sides of the coffin, landing on his arms, face, in his hair.

'Fuck! Fuck! Fuck!'

He shook himself like a dog, and rapped his fingers painfully against the sides. Roaring now, twisting from side to side. He grabbed some Wet Wipes and tried to clean himself. His chest was scalded. The mobile was still ringing. 'Hello.'

There was a pause.

'Is that Chris?'

'NOT YOU AGAIN? No it's not bloody Chris, it's Aidan Walsh. You rang me before and I nearly broke my bloody neck trying to get to the phone and now you've just made me chuck my dinner over myself – for Christ's sake try ringing the right number for once, you bloody imbecile.'

He switched the thing off.

'Fecking eejit.'

He rang Frank, explained what happened. Once Frank had stopped laughing, he said, 'OK, I'll send over another portion.'

'No, better make it the burger and chips, I shouldn't have had gravy.'

'I could have told you that. It's obvious that hot gravy in a coffin isn't a good idea.'

'Why didn't you bloody say that then?'

'Not my business to – the customer's always right, innit?'

Aidan ground his teeth.

'I'll send Donna back.'

'How long will that take?'

'About ten minutes.'

'Frank.'

'Yeah?'

'I'll have the jam roly-poly this time.'

'Right you are.'

'And Frank?'

'Yeah.'

'Have you got any Savlon?'

After finishing his lunch Aidan became very sluggish. His body felt bloated and heavy, the way it did when you were dragging yourself out of the swimming pool. He'd had very little sleep the last couple of nights, had kept going on adrenalin, but the stress of the last few days had finally drained him.

It didn't feel right, falling asleep in the day.

'Come on, Aidan, snap out of it.'

He shook himself, picked up last night's *Argus* and started reading the letters page. Soon his eyes were flickering; his head started to nod. The paper slowly slid from his hands, his eyes shut, and he fell asleep almost immediately.

'IT'S NOT TIME YET!'

Aidan woke with a start, gasping for air. Didn't know where he was. When his hands struck the walls of the coffin a wave of panic and dread filled him. Then he looked up, saw the sky above him and relaxed a little. He wasn't trapped. He was where he was this morning. Nothing had changed. Nothing had happened. He'd just fallen asleep. He checked his watch. It was nearly four; he'd been out for hours.

He felt heavy and drugged. Stiff, cramped and claustrophobic. Desperate for a piss. He moved onto his side, got the bottle in place. Bottle and bedpan, that was how it was going to be from now on. It felt pretty odd, lying there with his todger pointing into a bottle. The sound of his urine streaming into it made him wince. There was no comforting distance between him and his bodily functions down here. When he finished, he put the stopper in the top, lifted it carefully into the basket and winched it up. He was going to have to wait till the lads came before he'd get rid of it. Frank had said he'd take care of that kind of thing, but then he'd gone and sent Donna over, and he couldn't bring himself to ask her.

His neck and shoulders were stiff as a board. He slowly massaged his neck back and forth, then rolled his shoulders. He was dying for a cuppa. It was so hot down there, he'd need to drink gallons of fluid every day. He hadn't thought of that. How many other things had he not thought of?

More importantly, he was dying for a crap. But that he wanted to put off for as long as possible. What if it turned out to be a particularly smelly or messy one? It didn't bear thinking about.

His mobile rang. If it was that bloke wanting Chris again, he'd bloody well scream.

'Hello.'

Someone was laughing on the other end of the line.

'Who's this?'

The laughing carried on. Great, just great. Now he had a bloody maniac ringing him up.

'RIGHT – I DON'T THINK THIS IS VERY FUNNY, WHOEVER YOU ARE. IF YOU DON'T SAY SOMETHING RIGHT NOW I'M GOING TO RING OFF.'

'Can I have your autograph?'

'Gwyn? Is that you?'

'It is. Listen, you're famous, mun.'

'What you talking about?'

'You're all over the front page of the *Argus*.'

Aidan's heart was thumping, it was too good to be true.

'What does it say?'

'There's a photo and everything – *three* photos in fact. One of you standing next to the coffin in sunglasses, another of you with your kids, and one of the banner hanging from the window.'

Aidan let out a roar.

'Bloody brilliant. What's the headline?'

'*This is Where I Might As Well Be If They Take My Job Away — Six Feet Under.* I'm telling you, mun, you're going to be the talk of the town.'

'I want to shag you.' That was Russell, shouting in the background.

Aidan yelled in delight. Then he started laughing till the tears rolled down his cheeks.

'I did it. Jesus Christ in heaven, I fucking did it.'

Wilf was on the line now, his voice thick with emotion.

'Well done, mate! I'm proud of you.'

'We'll be there in half an hour.'

Time was flying by now something good had happened. Just the moment to finally use the bedpan. If he waited much longer they might turn up when he was actually doing it — he didn't know if he could handle that. He lowered his underpants, manoeuvred it into place.

When they arrived Aidan said very sheepishly, 'Er, can you do me a favour?'

He pointed up at the basket containing the bottle and the bedpan.

'If you wouldn't mind tipping it down the bog, like.'

Gwyn nodded in a businesslike way, trying hard not to look disgusted. Russell took a couple of steps back, pulling a face, as Gwyn carefully removed them from the basket and took them inside. Once the awkward stuff was done with, they wanted to know what his day had been like. So he told them about the wrong number and spilling his dinner all over himself when the eejit rang back a second time. It suddenly seemed hilarious, one of the funniest things that had happened to him in years. He told them how he'd given the guy a good bollocking, then ordered another dinner and they laughed till they bent double, wheezing and coughing and spluttering. He was making his day into a story, giving them what they wanted – things they could remember and smile about. No one was interested in someone cracking up on their own under the ground. None of them was interested in him baring his soul. He wouldn't have wanted that either if he was in their position. He was in a story now, and he was loving it.

After they'd gone Aidan spent twenty minutes looking at the front page. He touched the print – *Aidan Walsh*. He grinned.

'I did it. I fucking did it! All I had to do was hold my nerve.'

Tina had been told that she couldn't miss it – number 27, just look for the banner saying *Save Our Job's* hanging from the window. He's in the garden. He's expecting you. But when she came in through the back gate that evening, it felt weird, all she could see was a wooden funnel protruding from the ground.

'Er, hello – is anyone here?'

'Hi-ya,' said a disembodied voice.

'*Jesus!*'

Tina nearly jumped out of her skin.

'Who's that?' said the voice. 'Are you all right?'

Tina stepped back, trying to work out where the voice was coming from.

'I'm Tina Hughes from Crindau FM,' she said.

'Where *are* you?'

'I'm standing just inside the gate.'

'You see the wooden periscope type thing sticking out of the ground?'

'Yeah, I see it.'

'If you look down it you'll see me at the bottom.'

Tina walked slowly across, stood directly over the periscope and peered into it. At the bottom, about eleven feet below, she could see the head and shoulders of a middle-aged man. He waved at her.

'You got here all right then?'

'Yes, thanks.'

It took a few moments to adjust to the situation, but Tina was a professional. Only last week she'd been sent to Abercarn to interview a man who had taught his parrot to speak Klingon. If she could handle that she could handle this. She stuck a microphone down the tunnel and asked him to say a few words so she could check the sound levels. Once the interview had begun, she asked the same kind of questions as the *Argus*, only this time Aidan remembered to consult Dylan's bullet points.

'I pray they don't ignore what I've said. I sincerely hope they'll come and meet me. They know where I am if they want to talk. I'd be very happy to meet someone from Sunny Jim at any time of the night or day. All they have to do is give me a ring, or just walk into my garden.'

'So are you saying that you'd like to see senior management from Sunny Jim come and visit you in your back garden?'

'Definitely. I think that would prove how committed they are to resolving this.'

Dylan had been very keen on that one. *Tell them you want Sunny Jim to come to you, after all you can't go to them. Just think what a fantastic photo opportunity that would be — management coming to talk to a man in a coffin they've just made redundant! That would get on the front page of the nationals.*

'And do you think there's any possibility of that?'

'Why not? I think it would be a great gesture on their part, it would show they're willing to listen and they'd gain a lot of respect here in Crindau for that.'

That was Dylan's tip too — *Appear hopeful that this can be sorted out if you can just get together with management and talk about it like reasonable people.*

Privately, that made Aidan nervous. *Get together with management! Jesus, I wouldn't know what to say to people like them.*

There was excitement in Tina's eyes now, she knew she had the lead story for the news bulletin.

'Would you like to issue an invitation to the management of Sunny Jim Electronics to come here and talk to you, right now, exclusively on Crindau FM?'

He did just that.

It went out on the seven o'clock news, then again on every news bulletin up till midnight. Aidan listened to it every single time. He couldn't get over it – Aidan Walsh, on the hour every hour on Crindau FM. He was pleased with what he'd said too, though he'd never admit that to anyone in case they thought he was getting big-headed.

I could get used to this. Being asked for my opinion, seeing myself in the paper, hearing myself on the radio.

At eight, Frank brought him over a couple of cans of beer, that was another part of the plan.

'There's service for you.'

'Cheers, Frank.'

This was his reward for making it through the first day. He took one of the beers out of the basket and drank it carefully and slowly, savouring each sip, enjoying the way the cold can felt in his hand, watching the beads of moisture clinging to it. When he finished the first, he propped himself up on one elbow and rolled the second can back and forth against his skull. It calmed the thoughts racing in his head. He moaned softly with relief.

By the ten o'clock bulletin he started getting more critical, thinking of the things he wished he'd added. He also began piecing together what they'd cut out, though it wasn't anything important. On the Rob Fleming phone-in programme at ten they asked people to ring and give their opinion about what he'd said. The calls came in thick and fast. All of them were on his side and every last one of them slagged off Sunny Jim. After about half an hour Rob Fleming said, 'In the interests of balance, is there actually anyone out there who disagrees with what Aidan Walsh is doing and thinks Sunny Jim Electronics is behaving reasonably? If there is, then please give me a ring.' But no one did, not a single solitary cranky tosser responded to his plea. Aidan's eyes swam with tears of relief and gratitude. The people of Crindau were right behind him.

He'd spent over fifty years in this world without as much as having a letter printed in the paper, and today, he was on the front page of the *Argus* and Crindau FM were broadcasting him. Who knew where it would end? If he still believed in a god in heaven he'd offer up a prayer of thanks. But he didn't, not since Eileen had died, so he drained the last of his beer instead and toasted the people of Crindau.

He was on such a high it was hours before he went to sleep. He carried on listening to Crindau FM – *All Through the Night With Myfanwy Bassey*, from twelve till two. The buzz from the beer, some more Rescue Remedy and Myfanwy's husky, sexy voice kept him smiling. As he began to get tired he turned the radio down, till it was barely more than a murmur. He often went to sleep like this at home. He liked the voices keeping him company as he drifted off. When Myfanwy's show finished he switched to the World Service. He must have finally nodded off around half-two, satisfied with the results of his first day underground.

5

Aidan woke up the next morning with a fine misty rain falling on his face, his bladder bursting and his heart sinking as it slowly dawned on him exactly where he was. Still sealed in his box.

Still pinning his hopes on this crazy scheme. He felt a tremendous desire to curl up, go back to sleep and forget about everything.

Then he became aware of gurgling water. Aidan looked up at the drops of rain falling dreamily through a sky the colour of putty. Watching them descend put him into a kind of trance. It was a gentle rain, it surely couldn't be the cause of that rushing water? No, it was water surging down the drainpipe next door on the house to his right – Joy or Ken in the bathroom. He heard Ken coughing and spluttering, then Joy must have said something to him, because he shouted, 'What?' He checked his watch, it was 7.15. He heard a car straining to start, a door slamming. Other people, *normal* people, were starting their normal days. He was going to spend his in a coffin. He would lie there all day. He'd piss in a bottle. He'd shit in a bedpan. He'd bring Sunny Jim to their knees.

You must be off your bloody head.

No, stop this, it was vital to start every day in a disciplined manner.

Empty bladder, wash and clean teeth, do exercises.

But the moment he moved a piercing pain shot through his shoulders.

'Fuck.'

He froze. His neck and shoulders felt like they'd been clamped in a vice, his back was aching and his legs stiff and heavy. He moved much more slowly and carefully this time as he reached down for the bottle so he could pee. This, he thought grimly, is what it must be like being old. All the everyday things you used to take for granted now required major, painful and painstaking effort. No wonder some auld ones ended up pissing in their pants, the poor devils. If it required this much effort to reach the loo every time then you'd be bound to have an accident now and then. He got the bottle in place, aimed his stream of piss inside. When he'd finished, he was light-headed with the relief.

He was dying for a coffee. For someone to *bring* him a coffee, so that he could see another human face. He turned on the radio to catch the news at 7.30. An accident on the M4 was the lead item, followed by a report about a brawl outside a club in Pen–y-Lan. A farmer in Tredunnock claimed to have seen a puma attacking his sheep. He came fourth, after the puma, and they played much less of the interview this time. *Down to fourth already, how did that happen?* It didn't matter, he'd be back. He'd started something.

He did his exercises next, stretching and bending his neck and shoulders, his arms and legs, till he gradually felt the stiffness ease. He turned around and tried a few press-ups, his head knocking the lid as he rose slowly on shaky arms. Then he lay on his back again, raised his knees, clasped his hands across his chest and slowly rocked back and forth on his spine. Shauna had taught him that one, she did it in yoga. Next he rotated his neck, breathing slowly and deeply, gently easing out the tension. After a few minutes, he began to feel less irritable and claustrophobic. He washed himself with Wet Wipes, then shaved. It was years since he'd use an electric shaver, but a wet shave wasn't going to be possible down there. He cleaned his teeth with dry toothpaste. There, he was as good as new.

'Good morning, Aidan, fancy some breakfast?'

It was Megan, holding up a flask and looking like an angel sent from heaven.

'Thanks, darling, I'm gasping.'

She lowered the basket and Aidan took out the flask and a bacon butty, still warm.

'Grand.'

'Come on, let's have your doings.'

Aidan carefully manouvered the bottle into the basket and hoisted it up.

'How are you feeling after your first day?'

'Tidy – a bit stiff, that's all.'

Megan smiled and said, 'Me and Wilf listened to the phone-in last night. We were proud of you.'

'Thanks.'

'Do you think they *will* come down here and talk to you?'

'Let's hope so.'

She nodded thoughtfully and took away his piss.

It was good to know that Wilf and Megan had been listening. He wondered how many others had. It was a new, thrilling sensation to think that he had an audience. He switched on the radio, began listening to the *Elijah Stevens Breakfast Show*.

'The Gaeru Road is very slow-moving at the moment, a lorry has shed its load. Roadworks at Llis-werry are causing a tailback and the sheer weight of traffic and those new lights on Cardiff Road at the junction with . . .'

'Christ, it sounds like a nightmare, I'm better off where I am.'

Normally at this time he'd be stood at the bus stop on the side of Cardiff Road. A horrible spot. A thin strip of pavement, barely wide enough for two people to pass, the twenty-foot-high wall of a factory long since closed behind; the traffic just getting up speed there, on the edge of town, roaring past in a choking blue haze.

'Sounds like a terrible morning on the roads, doesn't it?' said Elijah. 'Let's have something relaxing, shall we? Here's "Morning Has Broken" by Cat Stevens.'

That beautiful piano introduction kicked in, a lovely sound, like crystal clear water tumbling down a mountainside. He turned the radio up, just in time to hear Cat's warm, sad voice singing the opening line. Aidan let the music wash over and into him. He thought about the words, about greeting every morning like it was the very first one. Which was exactly what you should do, not let the days slip past one after the other, like numbers spinning on a meter. You could learn a lot from songs.

He looked up through the periscope at his patch of bright blue morning sky. *Blue* sky in November? It must be global warming. He watched the wispy white clouds drift slowly past. When he was a boy, he would lie on his back in Clytha Park on a warm day and spend ages just watching the clouds moving across the sky, everything around him fading into the background. His father used to say a hundred times a day, 'You'll dream your life away, Aidan.' And why was it that adults were never satisfied if kids weren't always *doing* something? Why couldn't they let them be? He was happy to lie there for what seemed like hours, enjoying the warmth of the sun on his face, the feel of the soft, long grass beneath, the unfolding drama of the sky above, till the stench of the nearby chemical factory wafted over on the breeze and made him gag. You were never too far from noxious smells in Crindau.

He wondered if Cat had lain on his back one morning just like this, stared up at the sky and decided to record this song? He liked the idea, decided that he definitely had. He remembered when this came out, he was driving a van for Edwards & Sons, it seemed to be on the radio every morning, lifted his mood every time he heard it. It seemed like every female in Crindau under the age of sixty was in love with Cat Stevens back then. He told Russell how much he liked his music, how he wouldn't mind some of his sex appeal either. Russell looked like he'd swallowed a lump of someone else's phlegm.

'Don't be so fucking soft, mun, he's obviously a homo.'

He began singing along.

'Praise to the new day, praise to the morning . . .'

His hands roamed across an imaginary piano.

'Fair play to you, Cat, that's a great song.' He smiled, then put his hands to the side of his mouth and shouted at the top of his voice, 'I think you're a gorgeous-looking bloke, Cat Stevens!' He burst out laughing, this was great craic. He could say what the bloody hell he wanted down here.

Then the pips for nine o'clock were ringing out and the *Breakfast Show* was over. He didn't know what the next programme was like, he was usually in work by now. 'Morning Has Broken' was replaced by something that sounded like a workman drilling a hole in the road, and a woman moaning like someone with their head over the toilet after downing seventeen Bacardi and Cokes.

'Gooooooooooooood morning, Crindau! This is Funky Phil and Barmy Bethan with two hours of the latest happening sounds, fantastic competitions, the sauciest celebrity news and on the hour traffic reports – we have got *such* a fantastic programme for you –'

'Feck off, you bloody eejit,' cried Aidan and turned off the radio. Jesus, what kind of person would be able to stick that? Whatever happened to conversation – why did young people have to shout all the time? His peace was shattered, he needed to calm right down again. He began taking deep breaths and turned back to look at his precious corner of blue sky. Then started humming 'Morning Has Broken' to try and get that gobshite out of his mind.

A plane glided across the sky without seeming to move. He'd only ever flown twice – to Spain and Portugal. The take-off scared him shitless, but once they'd levelled out he was able, eventually, to relax and enjoy it. How he'd love to be on that plane now, on his way somewhere special, looking down at Crindau spread out below, leaving all his troubles behind, with a decent, secure job to come back to. The pilot telling them they could now unfasten their seat belts, the hostesses rushing to get the drinks served, people flexing their muscles, easing out the tension, looking round expectantly, ready to indulge themselves when the drinks trolley came. Aidan had never got over how exciting it was, having a drink on a plane.

He'd ordered a gin and tonic, because it had always seemed like the film star's drink to him. The kids had grown up and left home and this was the start of a new chapter in his life. He'd never been abroad before, only to Ireland, and always by boat. Russell and Wilf had ordered tins of Carlsberg, and their wives little bottles of sweet white wine. Russell had squinted suspiciously at Aidan's drink when it arrived.

Gin and bloody tonic now, is it? Lager too common for you?

Megan had nodded approvingly. *Why shouldn't he have what he wants? We're on holiday, aren't we?* She winked at him. *You go ahead and treat yourself, darling, you're as good as anyone else on this plane.*

Eileen would have loved going abroad by plane.

Don't start that.

His first gin and tonic, twenty thousand feet up in the sky, served by a tidy air hostess in a shiny blue blazer, a cheesy smile, him thinking, *This is the way to live.*

He had another after his meal, then settled down in his seat and watched the in-flight film, a comedy with Richard Pryor and Gene Wilder. By the time they were approaching Spain, he was as blissed out as a Buddha.

It was soothing, thinking about being up there in that plane. Gradually his breathing deepened, his heartbeat slowed. He clasped his hands behind his head and stared at his square patch of glorious sky, and let his mind wander. And, out of nowhere, he started thinking of the time he and Eileen lay side by side in a field near Spanish Point. It was their first holiday in Ireland together. A long time ago, before they had kids, when everything was fresh and exciting and they couldn't keep their hands off each other. The bikes in a nearby ditch, their clothes strewn across the grass.

'Isn't it grand?'

'It is, aye. Very grand.'

Eileen turned over to face him, gave him a quizzical look. She ran her index finger slowly down his chest.

'You don't know what I mean.'

'Don't I?'

'I'm not talking about what we've just done.'

'No?'

Aidan looked disappointed.

'Oh that was grand too,' she said.

She smiled happily, ran her finger down to his waist, slowly circled his navel.

'I mean being able to lie here without wearing a stitch and soak up the sun. Doesn't it feel just gorgeous on your bare skin?'

She lay back on the grass beside him again, spread her arms and legs and sighed deeply and contentedly. Her left arm fell across Aidan's chest and they lay in silence for a good while. He loved the way they could go for long stretches without saying anything and still feel so close. She beat out a gentle rhythm with her hand on his chest when she spoke again.

'Wouldn't it be great if you didn't have to bother about clothes, and you could just walk around naked all the time?'

'Think of all the nettles and brambles.'

She grimaced, disappointed that he wouldn't play ball, had tried to make a joke out of it. But she didn't let it annoy her, the way she did later on.

'For god's sake, man, don't be so boring, use your imagination. Think how much freer you'd feel, and you'd never have to think about what to wear when you went out, or do any more washing.' She pointed her arms up at the sky, wiggled her fingers like a pianist loosening up before performing, began humming.

'*I* think it would be great, anyhow.'

'Yeah,' he said, smiling at her easy way, the sheer beauty of her. 'It would be.'

'The bleddy priests wouldn't like it of course.'

'They don't like anything.' He shuddered. 'Oh Christ, imagine seeing Father O'Connor without any clothes on.' The parish priest, who'd called round to Eileen's parents house the day before.

'Oh Jayzus.'

Eileen burst out laughing, then reached over, and cupped Aidan's face in her hands.

'The shrivelled up auld gom, he doesn't know what he's missing.'

She rolled on top of him and smiled. He felt himself growing hard underneath her.

'Maybe he's followed us out here to keep an eye on us. I think he suspects you of sinful thoughts. Perhaps he's peeping through the trees right now.'

She laughed and sat up. She clasped her hands behind her head, and arched her back, pushing out her tits.

'Holy Father, are you there? Did you enjoy that?'

Now it was Aidan's turn to laugh.

'You'll be the talk of Ballymichael.'

She smirked and tossed her hair.

'Sure, I already am.'

He ran his hands down her side, then moved them to her waist and shifted her to where he wanted her. His prick was standing tall now, his heart beating faster.

'Let's give the Holy Father another free show.'

And she smiled and leant down to kiss him tenderly.

They'd been so happy then. Just cycling down the rutted, overgrown lanes back to her family's house afterwards, steering the bike with one hand, carrying the unused fishing rod with the other, listening to her hum 'Marie's Wedding', filled his heart to bursting.

The sky looked just the same that day in Spanish Point. He felt glad that he had such a great store of memories to call up and basked in the picture, no pain or loneliness kicking in as it did usually. Suddenly, he didn't know why, he was at peace with himself and his past. After all this time. Who would have thought he'd find peace and contentment in a coffin?

'Fucking pigeons!'

He shot upwards, his hands clutching his face, nutted himself on the lid.

'Bollocks!'

It might be cardboard, but it felt like solid oak, nearly splitting his skull open. Now he had the screaming pain in his head *and* the mess on his face to deal with. A direct hit, right on the bridge of his nose, forcing him to screw his eyes shut before it ran into them. He scrabbled around him blindly with one hand, reaching for the Wet Wipes, then wiping the pigeon shit from his face with the other.

'Filthy fuckers.'

He opened one eye, tugged out a Wet Wipe and started to sort himself out. It took another two before he was satisfied he was clean. Then he stuffed all three into one of the carrier bags and tied the handles into a knot.

Disgusting bloody animals. Now he'd have to wait till Frank came with his lunch before he could get rid of the bag. Jesus, it was a sobering thought that you weren't even safe from fecking pigeons six feet under in a bloody coffin. It certainly made him think twice about staring up his periscope again. The spell was broken now, his daydream about lying in a field near Spanish Point with Eileen drenched in bird shit.

'Thanks a lot, you dirty bastard.'

He picked up his Elmore Leonard novel.

'Good morning, Aidan.'

Aidan looked up, saw the postman grinning at him like an old friend, which was strange. They'd never exchanged more than the briefest of nods before. He waved a couple of letters in the air.

'Here's your mail – no point in putting it through your letterbox when you're down there, eh?'

'Cheers. That's nice of you.'

'No problem. Shall I stick it in this?' He nodded at the wicker basket.

'Yes, please.'

Aidan winched them down.

'Just bills, by the look of them.'

Since when had postmen started getting so chirpy and familiar? Aidan wasn't sure he liked it.

'Wait till I tell the others. I'll bet none of them has ever delivered to a coffin.'

They *were* bills. Aidan looked up to see that the postman was still hovering, looking rather self-conscious.

'Do you think they *will* come down and negotiate with you? *Here*, in your garden?'

So that was it, he'd listened to the phone-in too. Aidan said he was confident that management would.

'No one's job is safe anymore. I worry about what kind of world my kids are going to live in when they grow up.'

'How old are they?'

'My boy's seven, my girl is nine – thanks for asking. This morning, in the sorting office, it suddenly clicked who you are. I told the others, I said, "Hey, guess what? The bloke in the coffin is on my round!"' He shifted awkwardly. 'In fact, that envelope you just opened, would you mind signing it?'

'You're kidding.'

'I'm not. They wouldn't believe me when I told them. This way . . .'

Aidan nodded that he understood, grabbed his pen.

'Could you put "From Aidan the coffin man, to Ivor"?'

'Sure.'

He put the envelope in the basket and winched it up. Ivor read it carefully, then smiled. 'That's lovely. Cheers, Aidan, see you tomorrow.'

'Ta-ra, Ivor.'

Aidan waited till he was sure Ivor had gone, then murmured disbelievingly to himself, 'My first autograph – bloody hell, I'm famous.'

Aidan had devised a programme to stop him getting too stiff. Every half hour he would move a part of his body for five minutes. At 10.30 he moved his left leg up and down. At 11.00, his right. At 11.30, his left arm, and so on. He was moving his right arm up and down at mid-day when he was gutted to discover that he'd been dropped from the news and that Sunny Jim still hadn't responded. He felt a headache coming on, and the excitement of last night beginning to fade. Dylan rang.

'Morning, Dad, have Sunny Jim said anything yet?'

'No. And I've been dropped from the radio news.'

He was disgusted with how fickle the media was – local hero one day, elbowed out by an alleged sighting of a puma the next.

'That's the way it is. You gotta keep feeding them a new angle if you want to stay in the headlines.'

He heard Dylan drumming his fingers against something.

'What we really want is for you to be in the *Argus* again tonight, to keep your profile right up there.'

'How are we going to do that?'

'I'll have a think. By the way, you might be getting a call from *How Green Was My Valley*.'

'What's that?'

'A monthly environmental magazine, they're interested in your recycled coffin.'

'Just the coffin?'

'Like I said, you've got to give them an angle. They've only got a small circulation but if they run something it might get picked up by someone bigger. The journalist is called Fiona, a bit of a hippy but she's all right. Tell her how you're doing your bit to save the planet as well as trying to save your job. She'll love it – a working-class bloke like you from a shithole like Crindau thinking of the environment even when you're faced with redundancy. You'll be their pin-up of the month, mun, proof that the green revolution is about to happen.'

'Crindau isn't a shithole!'

'No, you're right, it's not. Sorry, slip of the tongue. I've got to go.'

Aidan was listening to Radio 2, sucking on a mint, his diary open on his chest, in case inspiration struck. He longed to flex his limbs, to stand up and move around. As well as his half-hourly work-outs, he was remembering to wriggle his toes, bend his legs up, down. Roll his neck from side to side, stretch his arms, his fingers. Got to keep the blood circulating. He was raising his left arm up to his chest, then back down to his leg when his mobile rang.

'Hi, it's Nick from the *Argus*.'

'Hi-ya, Nick.'

'I wanted to ask you about the mood at the factory.'

'What *is* the mood?'

'I've had an anonymous phone call from one of your workmates. Apparently the temperature down there is rising. People are furious that Sunny Jim haven't responded to your invitation to talk. They're saying it proves how arrogant they are. I wondered if you had any comment about that?'

An anonymous call? Aidan's mind was racing, trying to figure out who it might have been.

'Whoever it was said he didn't want to give his name in case there were any reprisals, that he didn't trust Sunny Jim.'

Aidan wondered if it was Russell?

'I think there might be enough here for another story – it would be good to get your response.'

He hesitated, he'd never had to do this before – think of something to say to a journalist right out of the blue. *Come on, quickly now.*

'What was it Churchill said? "To jaw-jaw is better than to war-war." '

'Uhu, yeah . . .'

Keep it moving, that's what Dylan said, try and make things happen every day.

'If they don't respond by tomorrow, it will prove what people have been saying all along is true – they listen to their shareholders and their accountants, but never to their employees.'

'Are you setting them a deadline?'

'Yes, I am. If Sunny Jim don't come and talk to me by the end of the week it will prove to the people of Crindau that they know they haven't got a leg to stand on. What have they got to be afraid of? I won't bite them. If the Protestants and the Catholics can talk to each other in Northern Ireland, if the Israelis and Palestinians can sit around a table together, then surely to god Sunny Jim can bring themselves to talk to one of their own employees?'

'OK, that's terrific.'

Yes, thought Aidan, *it was, wasn't it?* He was discovering he had a talent for this kind of thing.

Frank brought him the *Argus* when it came out that afternoon. He leaned over the top of Aidan's periscope and smiled sardonically.

'Are you never out of the bloody paper?'

He stuck it in the basket and left. Aidan was the lead story on page two.

Jaw-jaw Not war-war!

A photo of Churchill underneath, a huge cigar clamped to his mouth, giving the V for Victory sign. The caption underneath read *Sunny Jim should take a leaf out of Churchill's book, says coffin protestor Aidan.* The article took up half the page.

Today the events surrounding Aidan Walsh's unusual protest against being made redundant by Sunny Jim took another dramatic twist when a worker who refused to be named described the mood inside the factory as 'reaching boiling point'.

The caller was quoted at length, followed by Aidan's reaction. It finished by saying that no one at Sunny Jim was available to comment. 'No comment' – everyone knew that meant *Oh fuck, what are we going to do about this?* It was so brilliant that his workmates were pitching in and backing him up. It made him proud to come from south Wales, where solidarity still meant something. He read it three times, grinning to himself. Then Dylan rang, and Aidan read him the story.

' "No one at Sunny Jim was available to comment" – Ha! I'll bet there wasn't – they'll all be running about like headless chickens, wondering what to say. You've got them on the run, Dad, mun. They can't ignore this.'

'What do you think they'll do?'

'I don't know, but the ball's in their court, that's the important thing, we're piling on the pressure. They know they're in a fight now.'

Aidan liked that, enjoyed imagining *them* feeling under pressure for a change.

'This is great, but something's been bugging me.'

'What?'

'I wish I knew who called the *Argus*.'

'It was me.'

'What?'

'*I* rang them.'

It took a few seconds for this to sink in.

'Then all this stuff about the mood in the factory reaching boiling point – it's a lie.'

'No, it's not. It's bound to be like that, the way Sunny Jim are carrying on.'

'But didn't Nick recognise you?'

'Nah! I pretended I was Russell – '*I'm telling you, people are up in arms about this.*'

It sounded just like him. It was uncanny.

'Jesus, you didn't, did you?'

'*I speak my mind, I do, and if you don't like it, you can bloody well lump it.*'

'Stop that!'

Dylan roared with laughter.

'You can't go around pretending to be someone else, it's not right.'

'Dad, that's exactly what actors do.'

'Not impersonating friends of mine – Christ, Russell will kill you if he finds out.'

'How's he gonna find out?'

'That's not the point. You pretended it was him saying something that he didn't. That's out of order.'

'How do you know he wouldn't say those things?'

'Because he *hasn't*.'

'Not to you maybe. But I'll bet he's said them to Gwyn and Wilf on their lunch break or in the car on the way back from work or in the Globe last night.'

'You don't know that . . .'

'But I do – because I know Russell. And it's exactly what loads of people would say to the press if they weren't so worried about losing their redundancy money. You told me yourself how disgusted everyone was with them.'

'That's different to . . .'

'In fact you told me so many times it felt like the bloody needle was stuck.'

'But . . .'

'And you watch. Now that it's been in the paper, people *will* start saying it in public – someone just needed to start the ball rolling.'

'I still don't like it. It's not right.'

'We've got to keep you in the news and this is the way to do it.'

'But it's lying, Dylan.'

Dylan made an exasperated sound.

'And have they been telling the truth?'

Listen to what I am saying – there will be no redundancies at Sunny Jim in the foreseeable future. You have my word.

'This is not a game of cricket, Dad. These are the people who're taking your job away, why should you be bothered about playing fair and square with them? When have they ever played by the rules? If you're going to make this work, you're going to have to learn to do things you don't like. You're in a tight spot, Dad, and we've got to get you out of there. People have short memories – if you're out of the news for a few days, they'll forget about you.'

That kind of talk made Aidan suspicious, he sensed there was a contempt for ordinary people in Dylan and he didn't know where it had come from – not from him or Eileen, that was for sure.

'You're the little guy on your own, in a hole, in the garden. Sunny Jim is a mega-powerful corporation dedicated to making huge profits. They are *not* caring sharing people, they are not interested in your opinion. They think you're a bloody fool who's going to last a few days down there before you chuck in the towel and go back to work. What they're trying to do is ignore you and hope you go away. And what we're trying to do is show them that they can't.'

What Dylan had done made him distinctly uncomfortable. But he liked the way he was talking now. Fighting talk. Father and son standing together as a team. It hadn't always been that way. When Dylan was a teenager they had terrible rows: about him lying in bed all morning; about missing school; his weird haircuts; staying out all night. One argument ended with Dylan shouting that he wished Aidan had died instead of his mother.

'You little fucking bastard.'

He swung for him. Dylan managed to dodge at the last moment and Aidan only caught the side of his head with his knuckles. But it was still enough to send him flying into the chair behind him. Aidan stormed out of the room. Tears flooded his eyes as he walked up the road. He didn't know where he was going, he just needed to put some distance between himself and his son before he killed him. No, they hadn't always been a team.

'Dad – trust me, I know what I'm doing. Sometimes you just have to stir things up to make something happen. The less time you spend down there the better, right? I'm just moving things along.'

'But it's a lie – they can lie if they want to, that's up to them. But if *we* start lying too, then we'll end up just like them. I want people to know that they can trust me. If people find out that we lied once, then they'll start asking themselves how many other things we lied about.'

He could hear Dylan thinking about this. The silence, heavy with the tension of their many never-resolved arguments, lengthened.

'OK,' said Dylan eventually, 'we play it straight from now on,

I promise, now we've got the ball rolling. Even though we're dealing with a bunch of lying, greedy, heartless scumbags who'd sell their own grandmothers for a quick buck.'

Russell, Gwyn and Wilf called to see him after work. It was embarrassing to see how excited they were, no idea what a con the story was.

Wilf looked down the periscope, smiled and gave him a V for Victory sign.

Gwyn shouted, 'Jaw-jaw not war-war.'

Russell said, 'Yeah, and while you're at it, send up your crap-crap and your piss-piss.'

The next morning a Sunny Jim spokesman made a statement which was played in full on Crindau FM.

'We have no intention of talking to Mr Walsh. The time for talking is over. Sunny Jim Electronics have already held extensive discussions with the government, the Welsh Assembly and our shareholders. We have taken the very difficult decision to close down our operation in Crindau after much careful deliberation, and it is very misleading and unjust of Mr Walsh to suggest that we took no account of the staff. Indeed, the exact nature of the redundancy package on offer is something we are giving very serious consideration to.'

'Yeah,' said Aidan, 'trying to figure out how little you can get away with giving us.'

The reporter said, 'And when will you –'

'If I may just make another point before you cut me off.'

'Hey – it was *you* who butted in,' shouted Aidan.

The reporter gave way, thrown by the spokesman's aggressive tone.

'Go ahead.'

'People have to understand the nature of the global economy. It's a very exciting and demanding market and will, eventually, bring prosperity and opportunities to all. However it will require an initial period of re-adjustment. We in Europe have enjoyed very high standards of living for many years now, but our comfort and wealth is in stark contrast to the living standards of people in the developing world. In many ways our lifestyles have only been achieved through exploiting the natural and human resources of those other parts of the world, while giving nothing back. Companies like Sunny Jim are now in the vanguard of a new trend. Our operations are now migrating to those areas which have previously suffered from underdevelopment. We are committed to adjusting the imbalance, and slowly but surely bringing everyone up to the same level.'

'But –'

'Have you ever been to India?'

'Er, no.'

'Well I have, and the poverty there brought tears to my eyes, I have to tell you.'

'Jesus!' Aidan didn't think he could take much more of this – he bet the last time this guy cried was when he caught his todger in his zip.

'There are so many people there living in the most abject poverty, and the opportunity to work in one of our factories is going to transform their lives – and the lives of their children. Would you really deny these people the chance of a future without hunger and disease?'

Aidan thumped the lid of his coffin. 'Come on, mun, say something, don't let him get away with that – making out he's the new Bob Geldof.' This reporter was shite.

'But would it hurt to actually discuss these matters with Mr Walsh? Don't you think jaw-jaw is better than war-war?'

There was a pregnant pause before the spokesman replied, in an icy tone. 'We do not conduct negotiations through the media. And we do not talk to blackmailers.'

'You're calling Mr Walsh a blackmailer?'

'What other way is there of describing what he's doing? In fact I would question the state of his mental health. You have to ask yourself what kind of person would bury themselves alive to get their own way? It's very morbid. It's reminiscent of those IRA hunger strikers in Northern Ireland who tried to hold the British government to ransom. They said if you don't give us what we want we'll starve ourselves to death and it will be your fault. Mr Walsh is saying if you don't give me what I want I'm staying here in my coffin and on your head be it. It's the mindset of a fanatic. It would be totally irresponsible of Sunny Jim to give in to this kind of tactic.'

'Can you see no way out of this situation?'

'You call it a situation. I call it blackmail. That's all, thank you.'

Aidan rang Dylan.

'They said *that*?'

'Yeah, they compared me to the fucking IRA.'

Dylan gave a low whistle. 'Boy, I didn't think they'd get *that* pissed off.'

That was not the kind of response Aidan was looking for. *Dad – trust me, I know what I'm doing*, that's what he'd said.

'What now?'

There was a lengthy pause.

'Actually,' said Dylan, sounding upbeat again, 'this is probably the best thing that could have happened. Yeah, this is brilliant, now I think of it.'

'It is?'

'Yeah, mun, they haven't even bothered to *try* and sound reasonable, went straight into heartless bastards mode. They're going to lose any sympathy they had by carrying on like this.'

'They don't need people's sympathy, they've got power, that's what counts in the end.'

'That's defeatist talk. Listen, this is about holding your nerve – the fact that they're reacting like this just goes to show how much you've rattled their cage. They're on the run. They can't take the heat, they're getting nasty. They're trying to scare you.'

'They're doing a good job.'

'It's just an opening gambit. They'll start off sounding like they won't budge an inch, but once they see you're not going to crumble, they'll have to shift their position.'

'Call my bluff.'

'Exactly. You've got to ring up the *Argus* and Crindau FM and say you want to respond to Sunny Jim's statement. You can't let it go. You have to come right back with something every time they make an announcement, never let them get a free run. The media like that – it's much better to have a blazing row to report than just one side making a statement, understand? Soon the papers and the radio will start ringing *you* up, asking for a response every time *they* say something, because they'll know you're able to feed them copy at the drop of a hat. Sunny Jim, on the other hand, will be slow and cumbersome, everything that goes out in their name will have to be approved by a committee. You'll run rings around them.'

'OK, I'll ring them.'

'Do it now. What are you going to say?'

'I'm no blackmailer.'

'Yes.'

'And I concentrated on the issues while they went for character assassination.'

'That's right.'

'At no point did I make personal remarks about Sunny Jim management . . .'

'Exactly – so you leave it to the public to decide which approach they prefer. Be sure to say "Do I look like a blackmailer?" That might prompt them to run another photo. OK, sorted, I gotta go, we're doing our play in a school in half an hour, talk to you later.'

Sure enough Frank came with the *Argus* that afternoon.

'You're in it again – I'm sick to death of hearing about you, to be honest.'

He dropped it into the basket.

'Cheers, Frank.'

I'm No Blackmailer – Coffin-man Aidan responds to slur on character.

There was a photo of Aidan flanked by his kids. The first three-quarters of the article was all about Sunny Jim's statement, but the last section covered Aidan's response, so that the reader finished with his words ringing in their ears. Dylan had been right, a quick response was vital. He'd turned the story round to his advantage. There had been no need to panic.

Things were going well, but nevertheless Aidan was exhausted by the end of the day, by the sheer effort of holding it all together. It was a full-time job, keeping up his morale.

He had to keep calm. He had to keep things in perspective. He had to keep on encouraging himself. *Well done, Aidan, that's the spirit. Only another hour to tea time, then you're on the home stretch, attaboy.* He had to remember to do his exercises. Jesus, it made his head swim, trying to remember the schedule he'd drawn up for himself.

It's 3.30 – waggle fingers of left hand for five minutes. Or was it my right hand? Oh this is bloody stupid. No, it's not, don't give up that easily, you must keep your discipline.

He had not to be disgusted by shitting in a bedpan. He had to believe that people would hear about and be interested in what he was doing. He had to believe that Sunny Jim would listen and negotiate. By the end of the day his eyes were drooping. But could he get to sleep? Could he fuck. Once the Globe had closed and the last stragglers had gone home and his neighbours were in bed, Aidan's nerves began to shred. The night wasn't really silent at all. There were unidentifiable sounds, whispers, scrabbling. The swish, swoosh and soft murmur of traffic on wet roads, gurgling pipes, a cat yowling. Ghostly cries nearly lost in the wind. Bumps and thumps and rustlings. Sometimes he heard a faint rattle, like blinds shifting in a breeze. The town never slept. Something was always going on, somewhere. He just didn't know what it was.

Aidan's sense of smell was getting stronger. It was probably because he couldn't move and his vision was so restricted. His nose kept him in touch with the outside world. The pungent smell of confinement was freshly turned topsoil and stale sweat. At other times it was the smell of damp and despair in an empty room. There was a strange odour in the coffin when he couldn't get to sleep at night – like paper slowly scorching. The smell of hope and renewal when Megan brought his breakfast was the sweetest vanilla. It was mad. It didn't make sense. But it was happening.

The slightest noise would make his heart race. It was hard to work out how close they were, *what* they were.

Someone's coming. No, it's just the wind. That was definitely a foot-step. Who's walking around at this time of the night? What are they up to?

If there was someone else there he could have dealt with it. But when you were on your own, trapped in a box, how could you know?

If someone *did* want to get him, he was completely fucked, there was no way out. He was a sitting duck. But that wasn't going to happen, this wasn't America, this town was not crawling with psychos and weirdos. It was inhabited by hard-working, kind and considerate people. He'd listened to the phone-in again tonight, everyone was on his side.

It's just the wind.

That's what he'd tell himself. And the rational part of his brain knew it was true. But his imagination wouldn't listen. It *knew* somebody was out there. Listening, waiting, sneaking up on him, step by stealthy step. *Hello, Aidan, I've been out there all the time. Waiting.* He'd get palpitations. He'd end up soaked in sweat. He'd knock back the Rescue Remedy. Turn the radio up. Then turn it down again, in case he missed any suspicious noises. He'd worry he was turning into a nervous wreck. The voices in his head would start.

Pack it in now, before you go mad. Ring the lads and ask them to come round and dig you out.

There's a lunatic out there, biding his time, taunting you. Enjoying making you squirm.

One evening he had one of the lads turn on all the lights in his house so that the garden was bathed in a glow of light. But it didn't stretch far; it made the night a little less dark was all. The noises still shredded his nerves. Yes, the nights were long.

The next morning ITV Wales rang Aidan up. They asked if he would be prepared to give an interview to Huw Humphreys? *Would he?* Huw, the golden boy of ITV Wales. The perennial runaway winner of *Welsh TV Personality of the Year*. There was no one Aidan would rather be interviewed by. He rang Megan.

'Guess who's coming to interview me – Huw Humphreys!'

'Oh my god!'

'He'll be here in an hour, so could you do me a favour, love, and get my best shirt out of the wardrobe – the light blue one, it's got a tag saying Paul Smith on the bottom.' Shauna had given him it last Christmas, but he'd worn it only once – so many people complimented him and asked if he was on a date he was too self-conscious ever to wear it again. 'I need it for the interview.'

'Oh, good idea, Huw's always beautifully turned out.'

'Exactly, don't want to look a scruff, do I?'

A small crowd of women started to gather on the corner outside Aidan's house. Passers-by stopped to ask what was going on.

'We're waiting to see Huw.'

'Come again?'

'Huw Humphreys, he's on his way here.'

'Never!'

Aidan was a bundle of nerves beforehand, checking his hair and his shirt in the mirror Megan had lent him – he wanted to make a good impression on his first TV appearance.

Huw looked a bit shorter and chubbier in real life, and obviously used a sun lamp, but he was totally charming.

'Hello there, Mr Walsh.'

147

Such a beautiful voice – proper Welsh, so soft and musical, it made the Crindau accent sound like sandpaper on brick.

'Please, call me Aidan.'

'Right you are, Aidan.'

Huw smiled – and Aidan felt a warm glow in his chest.

'Can I call you Huw?'

'Please do.'

Aidan nearly burst out laughing – this was fucking wild, he was on first-name terms with Huw Humphreys. Huw winked at him. 'Nice shirt.'

Aidan realised it was exactly the same as the one Huw was wearing.

'Oh yeah . . . fancy that.'

Huw laughed. 'It's a good job I'm wearing a tie, isn't it, otherwise they wouldn't be able to tell us apart.'

Aidan felt his face burning.

Huw did a lovely interview. The questions were utterly predictable, but the delivery, thought Aidan, was pure class. Just what was it about Huw? The women loved him, and the men wanted to be his mate or have him for their son-in-law. Everyone thought he was an absolute smasher. Though now he'd seen him close up, Aidan thought he could lose a few pounds.

There was only one downer – halfway through the interview, the heavens opened. It started hammering down and Huw was soaked.

'As you can see, the weather's turned.'

It was an absolute bloody monsoon. After a couple of minutes, it turned to hailstones. Aidan felt terrible. The storm was so fierce that hailstones were pinging and rattling down the periscope and peppering his head like gravel. His shirt and the mattress were beginning to get wet. Above him Huw was looking like a drenched rat, his hair plastered to his head, water streaming off his nose, blinking furiously as the icy pellets bounced off him. Clearly, he had not prepared as carefully as he thought. How could he have failed to account for the British weather?

It looked great on TV that night – the cut-aways to Huw listening to Aidan, smiling and nodding at his answers, bestowed an instant credibility on him. Huw signed off the report by saying, 'A remarkable man, I think you'll agree. This is Huw Humphreys, for ITV News, Crindau.' Five minutes with Huw had blown Sunny Jim's attempt to brand him a blackmailer out of the water. Huw wouldn't have any truck with blackmailers, everyone knew that. But when they cut back to the studio after the interview, the presenters at the desk, Steve and Libby, were laughing.

'Huw Humphreys there in Crindau,' Steve paused, turned to Libby and grinned, 'where it's the rainy season.'

Libby laughed as if it was the most hilarious thing she'd heard in years. Eventually she pulled herself together and said with a smirk, 'Don't worry, he had a nice hot bath and a Lemsip afterwards and he'll be back tomorrow.'

Aidan squirmed, the interview had gone brilliantly, but all they were talking about was the bloody weather. Dylan, predictably, was on the phone within minutes.

'Dad, you've got to get a shelter put up, you can't have people who come to interview you in danger of drowning.'

He was right, they should have thought of that. He rang Gwyn.

'We'll go down to Argos tomorrow and buy a gazebo. That should do the trick.'

Gwyn sensed him hesitate.

'Something wrong?'

'I wouldn't be able to look up at the sky then – I always counted on being able to do that. It makes me feel still connected with the outside world – do you understand what I'm saying?'

'Yes, mate, I do.'

He was glad he'd rung Gywn, and not Russell. *Don't be soft, mun.*

'Hang on, I've got an idea. We could get a large square of plastic sheeting – that would keep the rain off, but you'd still be able to see the sky through it. We could put in four poles, about eight foot high. Then we'll get a stepladder and nail the four corners of the plastic sheet to them. That way we'd have an all-weather shelter for TV celebrities and all your other visitors.'

'Gwyn, mun, you're a star.'

'Sorted – we'll do it tomorrow, after work.'

So they put up the shelter, then Russell produced four garden chairs.

'I got these too – they were on Special Offer.'

He arranged them in a row under the plastic roof.

'Now all these media celebrities you're hobnobbing with these days can take a seat while they're waiting to interview you.'

Gwyn stuck a handmade sign to one of the poles.

Aidan is in. Please take a seat.

The days began to fall into a pattern. It was amazing, how you could adapt. How you could work out your daily routines and adjust to the strangest circumstances. It took him so long to get to sleep that he would wake late. To the sounds of water rushing down drainpipes, a whistling kettle, the clank of cutlery against plates, muffled sounds from radio and TV. Then the morning rush would gradually fade and silence would descend. Except it was never quite silence. There would be a car passing, someone walking by on the road outside, a window shutting, the dreamy sound of rain pattering on the plastic roof above. Then his neighbours would start dropping by for a chat. They were great, they'd always bring a flask of tea or coffee, biscuits, a slice of homemade cake, chocolates. He was starting to worry about putting on weight with all these treats and him not doing any exercise, just lying there. But it was hard to resist with so little to do all day. He couldn't bear to say no. He didn't want to offend. He desperately wanted their company.

'Nice talking to you, I'll drop by later, see if you need anything.'

'Cheers.'

He listened to the news on the hour on Crindau FM, but there weren't any more statements from Sunny Jim. What were they playing at? He'd counted on them responding to his reply, which would give him the opportunity to come back at them again. He was ready and waiting. But maybe they'd realised that and had decided the best way to deal with him was to ignore him.

After a few days in the coffin, it began to feel relatively normal. He longed to be able to get out, stretch his limbs, walk around, naturally. But there was a strange kind of comfort in having the world shrink to a few square feet. To having everything within arm's reach, to be able to watch and listen to whatever you wanted. He didn't need to worry about the state of the roof or the cracks in the masonry now that he was living in a cardboard box; no need to trudge around a dreary super-market, with Frank bringing his meals every day. He'd never have thought he could do without the telly, or his pint in The Globe, but it turned out that he could. He was taking a break from the rat race, downsizing, re-evaluating. He'd become a kind of hermit. He liked the idea, remembered Shauna telling him that hermits were held in great esteem in the eighteenth century. How it was fashionable for the rich to hire an ornamental hermit to live on their estate in order to amuse their visitors. *Yes, that's the boating lake and over there, in that clump of trees, is our hermit. Would you care to come and meet him? He's quite harmless.* In fact the tradition was being revived – last year an estate in Staffordshire that advertised for an ornamental hermit received over 200 applications from around the world. Oh yes, people were queuing up to be hermits, desperate to escape the pressures of modern life. Maybe he should grow a beard and cultivate a deep and meaningful stare?

He would wake up and wash himself with Wet Wipes and shave and do his exercises. Megan would bring him his breakfast. He'd listen to Crindau FM, checking to see if he was mentioned. Shauna would ring him on her way to work.

'How are you feeling, Dad?'

'All right, love – I told you not to worry about me.'

During the morning he would get some calls from people wanting to do interviews – newspapers from all over the country now. Dylan was right, the media loved it. Often Dylan would ring with some new idea they'd talk over together. Sometimes Russell, Gwyn or Wilf would ring and tell him some story about what was going on at the factory. People who lived further up the road he'd never said more than 'Good morning' to would call round and offer a few words of encouragement, or ask what Huw Humphreys was really like.

Smashing, a real gent.

After lunch there would be two or three more interviews, the *Argus* would be delivered and he could read about himself in the letters page. Gwyn, Russell and Wilf would visit after work, then Shauna would arrive later on. His days were filled with talk and visitors. In some ways he felt better, more alive, than he had for years. Now he was the centre of attention, his opinion was valued, the public were behind him. The days were good. They were. Sunny Jim hadn't made any more statements and he decided that no news was good news. It proved they had no idea how to respond. No one was on their side. Who was going to root for Goliath?

The days he could get a handle on, but the nights were something else. Just as he'd been learning more about himself down there, so he was learning more about this town, too. It all came out at night.

Once darkness descended, some kind of madness gripped the people of Crindau. A stream of noise filled the air and gushed down his periscope, crashing straight into his head.

Drunks, screaming women, sirens, taxis disgorging drunken revellers, blokes roaring at each other. *Don't say that again, I'm warning you, mind. Fuck off, you twat.*

Someone would open the door of the Globe and let out a thump and clatter of jukebox, yells, groans and laughter, the sour whiff of bitter, a clattering of glasses.

One of his neighbours had a dog that would go berserk every time someone walked past the house. That got much worse at night too. It's high-pitched, self-important yap would set off the owner, telling it off five or six times an hour. The sheer banality of it gave him a twisting pain in his guts and made his head throb. How could anyone stand a dog that stupid? Why couldn't they take it to a dog training class? Or shoot the fucker?

He was forced to listen to it all. He couldn't shut his door, turn on the telly or his music and shut it out. Well yes, he *could* turn on his Walkman, but the truth was he was strangely addicted to every sound now. Life was going on above ground – he needed to know what was happening up there, however irritating or distracting. When he was a teenager he'd read a story in a comic called *Fantastic Tales* about a man born with phenomenal hearing. At first this guy thought it was a tremendous gift and used his power to prevent accidents and crimes that would otherwise have gone undetected. But gradually he began to hear things that he'd rather not. His best friend bitching about him behind his back; his wife telling another man that she loved him. There was no way of preventing all the mean and hateful and sordid things that people said and did from filling his head to bursting every waking minute of the day. He put his hands over his ears and screamed. He begged and pleaded for mercy. But there was no respite, his gift had turned into a curse. Eventually he went insane. Some nights Aidan understood how he felt.

He'd started to get nocturnal visitors too. The lost souls. They flocked to his garden after dark. He would hear the latch opening on the garden gate, its hinges creaking, then the gentle thud and rattle as they closed it behind them.

Here's another one.

He would put down his newspaper or book, or turn off his

radio, and wait, following their footsteps across the garden. Some would cough or say 'Hello', to let him know that they were there. Others would just stick their head over the top of the periscope and peer down at him, a strangely expectant expression on their faces, as if they were gazing at some kind of circus freak. Some were disappointed, he could see that. This wasn't what they expected. He looked just like a normal bloke, lying there in his T-shirt.

Maybe he *was* some kind of act. The last of a dying species – *an employee who thought he had rights*.

He would say, 'Can I help you?' and they would jump. It had never occurred to them that he could actually *speak*.

'I've come to wish you good luck. I think it's brilliant, what you're doing.'

That's how it would usually start.

'I'd love to do something myself but, to be honest, I'm too frightened of losing my redundancy money. Otherwise . . .'

Because they came at night, he couldn't see their faces very well. Maybe that was why they came then. They liked the anonymity. It made it easier for them to talk. He wasn't sure he'd recognise them if he saw them again in the street.

'I admire your guts.'

He told them it was easier for him. That his kids had grown up and moved out, he was on his own, had no one else to worry about.

'It's about time somebody stood up to these multinationals, they think they can do what they want.'

They'd list all the other big employers who'd pulled out of Crindau over the years.

'The steelworks at Pen-y-Lan closing down, that was the last straw. Three thousand jobs gone in one fell swoop. No town could recover from that, not without something to take its place. What did they offer the people who'd been laid off? Free courses in IT and business skills – I ask you.'

Aidan would murmur agreement. He would listen to their

stories about how people who'd been made redundant from Pen y Lan had gone under; some had to move away from Crindau to get work, others couldn't get another job, started drinking, the cracks in their marriage getting wider and deeper till that crumbled too and they were left with nothing.

'This used to be a decent place to live. But now . . .'

Crindau was the arson capital of the UK. The closed-down factories and boarded-up houses were regularly set alight by kids who then attacked the fire brigade when they arrived. When they ran out of buildings to torch, they set cars alight, or, in the summer, woodland. Sometimes those fires got out of control and people were forced to abandon their houses. Younger kids grew up hero-worshipping the arsonists. Then there were the drug addicts who hung around on corners and in underpasses with their eerily blank expressions.

People didn't look out for their neighbours like they used to. Everything was falling apart and no one did a damned thing about it. If Sunny Jim pulled out, what was to stop Crindau ending up like those desperate towns in The Valleys that broke your heart? Those ugly concrete smudges on forlorn hillsides, where the air was thick with the smell of defeat. They didn't know whether to laugh or cry sometimes. Aidan would say, 'I know, it's terrible.' He couldn't think of anything else to say, but that usually seemed to be enough. They didn't expect a solution. Had given up expecting anyone to offer one a long time ago. They'd come because they wanted someone to listen to them. And Aidan fitted the bill. Meeting him made them feel better – he was one of them and he was *doing* something.

'You stick with it, mate, good on you. Everyone I know is behind you.'

It should have depressed him, listening to all these sad stories, but it didn't. To be honest, it made him bloody ecstatic. Night after night he'd lain awake on his own in the house, going over the mistakes he'd made, fretting about the future. He'd look out of the window and see the rest of the houses in total darkness, his the only light still on. I'm the only one torturing myself into the early hours, he'd think. Why can't I relax like everyone else? But now he realised it hadn't been like that. All the time, behind drawn curtains in other houses all over Crindau, there were other people worrying themselves sick about the same things that kept him awake in the long, dark nights.

This town was wracked with anxieties and insecurities. No one here felt safe anymore. No one wanted to think about the future. This had always been a hard-working place, priding itself on community and solidarity, coming down like a ton of bricks on any hint of pretension. There was little sense of Welsh identity or culture – no choirs or chapel-going tradition here, few Welsh speakers. No pride in the past either – anything that took place before the era of heavy industry was pre-history. There was nothing to cling on to if the work ran out. Aidan just happened to be the one who'd finally admitted he was scared shitless by the prospect and had actually done something about it. His cry for help had sent waves of recognition and sympathy through the town. It could have been any one of them down there in that hole.

But when these people left and he was on his own again, his mood would change. He started to feel responsible for them. They actually seemed to believe he knew what he was doing, the poor fools. How could he let them down?

Every night there were more of them, bringing their stories of loneliness and disappointment, their feelings of desperation and loss.

When the gate opened one night, Aidan had a feeling straight away that it was someone in trouble. He had listened to so many people coming into his garden now, he was convinced he could tell something about them just by the way they opened and closed the gate. This was a big man, but he was using his strength sparingly, as if he was nervous about objects snapping off in his hands. Aidan listened to him having to make several attempts to close the gate he was using such little force, and the wind just swung it back open each time. This was a strong man who had been wounded. Aidan turned off the radio. He held his breath. The guy's head and shoulders appeared at the top of his periscope. He shifted his feet uncertainly.

'Hello?'

'Hi-ya.'

'You probably don't recognise me, but I work at Sunny Jim too – on the assembly line. My name's Geoff.'

'Nice to meet you, Geoff.'

'Here –' He put a bottle of whisky in the basket. 'This is for you. It'll keep you warm on these cold nights we're having.'

'Cheers.'

He winched it down and made a big deal out of admiring it – he rarely drank whisky, but this looked like classy stuff. Old Scots malt, in a box with a painting of an island on the front, it must have cost him a fortune. Aidan was touched.

'I saw you being interviewed by Huw Humphreys. That was fantastic, you got the message over very well. The only other time you ever see Crindau on the news, it's about kids starting fires.'

'Thanks.'

'When they're talking about profits and their responsibility to their shareholders they never stop to think that they might be ruining people's lives by putting them out of work . . .'

Suddenly he brought his hands to his face, then bowed his head. A grown man, a complete stranger, breaking down in front of him. Aidan didn't know what you were supposed to do.

'Are you OK?'

He got himself back under control just in time, thank Christ. He let out a deep, long sigh, then uncovered his face.

'Sorry. I don't know what came over me.'

'No, you're all right, mate. It sounds like you've got a lot on your mind.'

He bowed his head again, took another deep breath.

'Yes, I have.'

157

Aidan waited.

'My wife's got cancer.'

Aidan was shocked at how small and pathetic the whimpering noise that escaped from him was. It reminded Aidan of a dog that knew it was about to get beaten again. Geoff's face crumpled, and he didn't try and stop the tears coming this time.

'It's all right,' said Aidan, before realising just how stupid it sounded. How could it possibly be all right if your wife had cancer?

'I'm sorry, mate. I'm so sorry.'

The man dragged his hand across his face, and a long, thick thread of snot clung to his index finger. Aidan instinctively reached for his handkerchief, then realised he had no way of handing it to him. The man tried to flick it off, but it clung tenaciously to his finger till he brushed it onto his sleeve.

'They opened her up last week, she's riddled with it. I . . .'

'It's all right, take your time'.

'She's only thirty-eight, for god's sake. It's not fair. She'll never live to see our kids grow up. The doctors reckon she's got a couple of months at most.'

'You've got kids?'

'Three.'

'How old are they?'

'Garry is two, Helen is five and Cerys is seven. I don't know what to tell them.'

'How about a drink?' Aidan said, desperate to offer him something, since he couldn't think of a reply.

He opened the bottle of whisky. 'Sorry, I haven't got any glasses.'

'You first,' Geoff said.

Aidan took a hefty slug, then put it in the basket so that Geoff could wind it up.

'How did you cope when your wife died?'

Of course, thought Aidan, everyone knows about my life

now. Who the hell was he to give this poor bastard advice? What in god's name could he say apart from get yourself a friend like Russell? Geoff had passed the bottle back down, and Aidan took another swig before answering.

'I think the most important thing is to remember that you can't do it on your own. You need help. And people *will* offer to help, believe me – this is a great town, we help each other out round here.'

Geoff nodded, and took a drink.

'You're right, it *is* a great town.'

He started crying again.

6

Aidan felt pretty rough the next morning. He and Geoff had ended up getting through most of the bottle of whisky. Then, just to help matters, he was woken up by Joy going to the toilet. He heard Ken yelling, 'How long are you going to be?' and then Joy shouting back, 'What kind of question is that? As long as it takes, for god's sake.' It was still dark; there were no other sounds to distract him from the horror unfolding next door. Now he had noticed, he couldn't not listen. He waited, barely drawing breath, for the first plop. Jesus, there it was, a big one, followed by a large splash. He could have sworn he heard a faint sigh escape through the bathroom window. He squirmed, imagining her up there, squatting.

'Come on, come on, get it over with, I can't bear the tension.'

After what seemed like an hour, there was another plop. Was that it? No, another long silence was followed by a sudden burst of frenetic activity as three more turds landed noisily in quick succession in the bowl. The toilet paper was rolled in a very swift and businesslike manner, the metal holder clanking angrily against the wall. Jesus, it was like he had been there with her. Sat cheek by cheek on the seat, pulled the toilet paper and handed it to her. It felt obscene. He was disgusted with himself.

Come on, pull the chain, will you?

A huge surge of relief pulsed through him as the water pulsed and gurgled down the pipes. *Thank god that's over.* He had no desire to be that familiar with Joy's bodily functions, thank you very much. His head was throbbing, he wasn't used to whisky, and the tension of getting involved in Joy's early morning dump hadn't helped. Now that was over maybe he could turn over and sleep it off.

But no. He heard a grunt, followed by a fusillade of ear-splitting farts from the bathroom window next door. Oh Jesus, now it was Ken's turn. Aidan gritted his teeth and waited.

When Megan brought his breakfast she asked how he was.

'I was woken this morning by Joy having a crap – does that answer your question?'

She bit her lip and left.

Half an hour later, when he'd had breakfast and had a little nap, Aidan heard the garden gate open, someone walking towards him humming 'It's Not Unusual'. A badly dressed middle-aged man with bulging eyes looked down the periscope and stared at Aidan. Aidan smiled, said, 'Hi-ya.'

The man kept on staring. Here we go, another one who'd come to see the freak show. Aidan was beginning to get sick of it.

'Can I help you?'

The man grinned mysteriously.

'I heard you on Crindau FM saying how important music was to you – how it helped to keep you going.'

'Yes, that's right.'

'Well then, you'll be *very* interested in my story.' He arched his eyebrows. 'Everything I'm going to tell you really happened.'

'Oh yeah?'

'I'm the real Tom Jones.'

'You what?'

He nodded vigorously, then looked around to make sure he was on his own.

'It happened back in the Sixties when I was touring the States at the height of my fame, playing Las Vegas, all those women throwing their knickers at me – you've heard about that, haven't you?'

'Yeah.'

'It's true.' He nodded, clearly expecting Aidan to ask for further details. When no such request was forthcoming, Aidan could see he was bitterly disappointed. 'The Mafia tried to get me to pay protection money. I told them to piss off, like. That was a big mistake. Here's some advice, mate – never mess with the Mafia.'

Aidan nodded. 'Thanks, I'll remember that.'

'They kidnapped me. Locked me in this room and forced me at gunpoint to sing and do all my moves while this other guy just sat there and watched.' He bent forward, clutching the top of the periscope with his hands, his face now filling it almost completely. A waft of cidery breath made Aidan blink and splutter.

'What they were doing, right, was getting him to study me.'

'Oh aye.'

'Yeah – because I'd told them to piss off, *they stole my identity*.'

'They . . .' Aidan was struggling to follow him now.

'I know, I know, it sounds too fantastic to be true, doesn't it? But hear me out.' He turned his head, checking again that no one was listening. 'They were grooming this other bloke to take my place. They gave him plastic surgery to make him look like me, they taught him to sing like me, move like me – everything. His real name is Brad Plimpton, he's a secondhand car salesman from Minnesota. They couldn't control me, but they could control *him*. It was Brad Plimpton who made 'Delilah', it was

Brad Plimpton who sang at The Royal Variety Command Performance and Caesar's Palace. They gave *me* plastic surgery to look like this.' He pulled at his cheek. 'This is what Brad Plimpton looks like – ugly bastard, ain't he? They swapped our faces! How fiendish is that? How was I ever going to convince anyone I was the real Tom Jones looking like this? Like a fat secondhand car salesman from Minnesota.'

Aidan was praying for someone else to turn up and save him from this. He wondered if he should call one of the lads.

'They kept me locked in a basement in a little town near the Canadian border for twenty years. Eventually I managed to escape. It took me years, but finally I tunnelled out of there with a sharpened dessert spoon. But who's going to believe me now?' He looked pensively at his hands, then held them over the periscope for Aidan to inspect. 'See those hands? Could you really look me in the eye and tell me those aren't Tom Jones' hands?'

'Well I'm no expert . . .'

'They only changed my face, see? If the police took my fingerprints . . .'

'Er, yeah, I suppose so.'

'But the one thing they couldn't take from me was my voice. I've still got it, I've still got that old magic – listen . . .'

He threw his head back and launched into 'Delilah'.

'SHE STOOD THERE LAUGHING.'

Aidan put his hands over his ears. When he'd finished, Aidan said, 'Very good.' But there was more. He sang 'What's New Pussycat?' 'It's Not Unusual'. 'I Who Have Nothing'. When he started on 'The Green Green Grass of Home', Aidan reached for his Walkman and started listening to The Beatles at top volume. Clearly he was not going to get any peace today.

Shauna had a meeting after work, then a diversion on the way out to the M4 added a good twenty minutes to her journey. She arrived at Aidan's tired and hungry, but determined not to let her growing irritation show. She dropped a big bag of satsumas into the basket.

'Here, I got you these, Dad. You've got to take care of yourself while you're down there. You need fresh fruit – all those pub meals you're eating are out of the microwave.'

Aidan started eating one straight away. He told her about the real Tom Jones. She laughed. He enjoyed that, it had been a long time since he'd managed to make her laugh. When she did, she looked just like Eileen. He told her about his other visitors, the interviews he'd given in the last few days. He didn't tell her about the anxiety attacks, the backache, the mysterious sounds in the night that kept him awake.

'It sounds like it's going really well at the moment, Dad.'

She was making all the right noises, but Aidan could see she wasn't as impressed as everyone else.

'But this is your second week already. You haven't got much time left. What if Sunny Jim don't budge by next Monday? What will you do then?'

He gave her a defiant look.

'Have you got an exit strategy?'

'A what?'

'You can't just stay down there forever, can you? It might be good to plan a way of getting out of this situation without looking like you're backing down. Just in case.'

Aidan was offended.

'If I'd started thinking about what might happen if I didn't succeed before I even began then I'd never have done anything. I've been saying to myself for years "Oh that will never work" and "Who are you to think you could do that?" There's no one better at finding excuses *not* to do something – I'm a world-beater at that. Sometimes you just have to *do* something, no matter how crazy it seems, otherwise you'll do nothing at all.'

'Dad, I hate to say this, but if it's a waiting game you're playing, then Sunny Jim are the favourites. All they have to do is sit tight.'

'While everyone turns against them? They're getting a right roasting, they'll have to shift.'

'I wouldn't bank on it.'

'I *can't* give up now – I'd never be able to face people in the street again. God, Shauna, I had no idea there were so many depressed people in Crindau. You wouldn't believe how many people are relying on me to make this work. I'm their only hope. If I give up, they'll have nothing left to believe in.'

Shauna was startled by this outburst; it sounded like he was developing a Messiah complex.

'I'm worried about you, Dad.'

'Don't be, they won't dare sack me – I've been interviewed by Huw Humphreys.'

Shauna rolled her eyes.

'That sounds like something Dylan would say.'

'Yeah? Well at least he believes in me. It's nice to know that at least *one* member of my family is behind me.'

Aidan was left fuming. Here he was, his back against the wall, his last throw of the dice, and all she could do was criticise.

Have you got an exit strategy? For fuck's sake!

She'd got good A-Levels, been to university, had a career, a nice house in Cardiff. She'd moved on up, bettered herself. That was good. It was what you wanted for your kids. But Aidan wondered if it was really possible to move up a class and not look down your nose a bit at what you'd left behind? To think that you knew better. All the time. About everything. He'd noticed the critical looks when she visited his house. Once she brought along an IKEA catalogue, pointed out some furniture, said how nice that kind of thing would look in his living room. It was the kind of stuff she had in *her* living room. He said it was a bit expensive rather than telling the truth, which was that he didn't like it. Then she offered to buy it for him.

'No, love, you're all right.'

'Dad, I'd like to.'

'Please don't.'

Jesus.

She'd invited him round to her house in the Christmas holidays. It was modern, stylish, cool. Stripped floorboards and expensive-looking paintings on the walls, a huge pine dining table, French windows leading to a beautiful garden. Her friends were therapists, artists, musicians, lecturers. He felt awkward and out of place there. One of them said, 'And what do you do, Aidan?' *I'm a pleb.* He longed to be back in the Globe with the lads.

She thought she had all the answers. She'd forgotten that he'd been around a lot longer than her, had seen a lot more of life. She had a theory for everything. He was sure that she had one about what he was doing. But he didn't want to hear it. Maybe she'd realise that she might have to back a long shot herself one day. When she was finally forced to admit that life couldn't be reduced to theories.

Over the next few days the *Guardian*, the *Telegraph*, *The Times* and the *Mirror* all ran short items on Aidan's protest and he did interviews with about two dozen radio stations. But there was a resounding silence from Sunny Jim.

On Thursday, the *NME* ran an article.

Man Buries Himself Alive in Smiths Tribute.

Aidan was angry about that.

'It's not a *tribute*, for Christ's sake. It's a fight for survival.'

By the next day the first Smiths fans were arriving. One of them, a man in his early forties with thinning hair, a poignant-looking quiff and thick black glasses, told Aidan that he lectured in Media Studies.

'I'm presenting a paper at the first ever Smiths Symposium in Manchester next year, on Morrissey and Working-class Aesthetics with special reference to Sixties British cinema.'

'Right.' Aidan had no idea what the hell he was talking about.

'What you're doing here could link into that actually.' He

smiled apologetically as if Aidan was bound to object, though he was too mystified to do so. 'Your protest is a very exciting development. The Smiths are not perceived as being a political band in the same way that The Clash are, for example. Their popular stereotype is one of romantic miserabilism. Yet one of their songs has acted as a call to action against global capitalism.' He paused, and wagged a finger in the air, face tight with concentration. 'Though rather than trying to picket the workplace, or getting involved in a confrontation with the police . . .'

'*So* retro,' said Aidan, shaking his head. The man smiled indulgently.

'Indeed, instead of the macho confrontations that we associate with working-class struggle, you are burying yourself under the ground. In fact your action reminds me of one of the most iconic songs from their first album, *You've Got Everything Now*.'

'Does it?'

And so it went on, for another ten minutes or so, with Aidan required to do little more than nod assent now and then. He seemed a nice enough bloke, this lecturer, just not very good at explaining what he meant. Aidan wondered what possible good this kind of publicity was doing – it was turning into a frigging circus.

Geoff returned the next day, bringing his kids this time, two girls and a boy. He ushered them around the periscope, standing tall behind them, his hands resting gently on their shoulders.

'I want you to meet Aidan. His two kids are grown up now, but their mam died when they were young, didn't she, Aidan?'

He looked at Aidan imploringly. Aidan took the cue.

'Yeah, she did, that's right.'

He really wished he didn't have to do this. His heart went out to the eldest girl, standing there with a mixture of fear and defiance written all over her little face. She would be a mother to the other two, would have to grow up so quickly, her childhood cancelled. The other girl caught in the middle and the youngest, the boy, never getting enough attention ever again – how could a father replace a mother?

'You were all very sad, weren't you?'

'Yes, we were. We were very sad.'

'But you pulled together and helped each other out, didn't you?'

'Yes, we did. When you lose your mother –'

'When she goes up to heaven early,' said Geoff, catching Aidan's eye.

'Yes, because that's what she did. She went up to heaven early, and she's waiting there for me and *our* children, and she's looking down on us and taking care of us from up there.'

Aidan could read the look on the kids' faces – they wanted her down here, not up in heaven looking down on them. What was the good of that?

'You must remember that she'll be able to see what you're doing. So it's very important that you show her how well you can behave.'

Geoff's eyes were filling with tears, but he managed to give Aidan a thumbs-up. Aidan was looking at the eldest girl, whose stare was deeply sceptical, as if she were thinking *Who are you kidding, mister? I'm too old to believe in fairytales*.

Shauna and Dylan met in a coffee bar near the station in Cardiff. Shauna said 'I left three or four messages, why didn't you ring back sooner?'

Dylan blew on his cappuccino.

'I've been *so* busy . . .'

She bit into the Italian biscuit that came with her mocha and waited for him to finish. When he didn't she said, 'Have you seen Dad lately?'

'No, but I've talked to him on the phone a lot. As much as I can manage, anyhow.'

Shauna's expression lightened as a new song came over the speakers.

'Oh, it's Martha Wainwright – I love this.' She looked at Dylan again. 'He's not looking good, I think the stress is getting to him. I don't think he's got any real idea about what he's doing.'

Dylan unwrapped a sugar cube, touched the coffee with one corner, watching it slowly brown, before dropping it in.

'That's why I'm helping him – otherwise he's going to make a complete bollocks of this.'

'And what kind of help would that be?'

Dylan slowly stirred his coffee.

'Help dealing with the media, ideas for pushing the campaign along. This is his big idea; he's going to be devastated if it doesn't work.'

'Is that really helping him?'

'What do you mean?'

'Do you actually think he's got any chance of pulling this off?'

'Yes, I do.'

'I don't agree.'

'Well you're wrong.'

She looked at him sharply. She hadn't expected that. Thought that when it came to their dad, she was the one who took all the decisions, that he would go along with whatever she said. Now she was going to discover that Dylan had some thoughts on the subject too. He took a sip of his cappuccino.

'Dylan, Dad does not need that kind of help.'

'He does if he's going to make it happen.'

Shauna looked at him as though he was a five-year-old excitedly telling her about the money the tooth fairy had left on his pillow.

'How can it possibly work? Do you seriously think a multi-national is going to give in to some bloke burying himself in his garden in Crindau?'

'Just look at the amount of publicity he's got already. I'm telling you, Shauna, I'm really excited by this.'

'That's because you can't stand not to be excited.'

Dylan scrunched up the sugar wrapper, rolled it around his palm.

'How do you know it won't work when you haven't even tried?'

At times like this, Shauna wanted something shocking, hurtful and completely arbitrary to happen to Dylan, just to remind him of his tenuous contact with the real world. She tapped her forehead with her index finger, staring hard now. 'You're not directing Dad in some play in your head, Dylan. This is reality we're talking about here, do you understand the difference?'

'Piss off.'

'It's no good just telling him things he *wants* to hear, building up his hopes.'

Dylan grimaced. 'Here we go, running up against that bloody Welsh disease again. You're doing it, don't you see? Giving up before you've even started, thinking what's the point, it'll never work, they always win in the end. Christ, I *hate* that. Come on, Shauna, being Welsh isn't an excuse for failure anymore.'

Shauna sipped her mocha and smiled sarcastically.

'Oh, you're Welsh now, are you? I seem to remember that you were Irish last year. All the greatest writers were Irish, the best music was Irish, and the craic over there was fantastic. You were going to apply for an Irish passport, because your mother was Irish. That way, you were saying, if you were ever on a plane that was hijacked, they'd be bound to let you go because the Irish were neutral in every war and everyone loved them.'

'Yeah well . . .'

Shauna said, 'Nuala – wasn't that her name?'

'Eh?'

'That didn't last long, did it? I thought you were thinking of moving there?'

Dylan waved his hand dismissively. 'A few weeks was long

enough. Ireland made me sick, everyone you meet is a character, the woman in the corner shop, the bus driver, even the guy in the petrol station – it's like they're all auditioning for a part in a play.'

Shauna adopted her weary, dealing-with-her-kid-brother expression. 'Aha. Too much competition.'

'Ha bloody ha. It's all so *phoney*. It would be like coming to Wales and everyone you meet bursting into song.'

'You thought you'd connect with your roots, but your roots went and let you down.'

There it was again, that patronising tone. This great amusement at everything he said. He decided to ignore it.

'It's sickening the way they fawn and slobber all over every rich Yank who says their great-great-grandfather was from the auld country. But if you tell them your mother was Irish but you were born in Britain you get this weary look. *That* doesn't count, you're a Plastic Paddy. Well, they can piss off.'

'So you're relishing the challenge of being Welsh now, huh?'

He gave her a warning look. He was prepared to accept a certain amount of taunting, but she was trying his patience now. He slurped down a mouthful of cappuccino. It burnt his mouth and it took a huge effort not to gasp and cough it up.

'I wonder what's going on in your head sometimes.'

'Oh come on, this last week has been fantastic – he's caught the public's imagination, everybody's talking about him.'

'Dylan, it's been great, but it's been a *week*. He's used half his annual leave already, and Sunny Jim haven't shown any sign of movement.'

'Just look at how much publicity he's getting.'

'Dylan, *publicity* isn't going to save his job. What rubbish have you been filling Dad's head with? He seems to think that because he's been getting so much coverage in the media, Sunny Jim won't dare to sack him. Come on, you know they're not going to chuck in the towel after a couple of weeks.'

'How do you know? This has never been done before – no

one knows what the rules are. That's what so exciting – anything could happen.'

'You're excited, are you? Well *I'm* worried about what will happen to Dad. Being interviewed by Huw Humphreys isn't going to help him. It's water off a duck's back to them. This is a multinational, Dylan, these are Big Boys, they do what they want. A certain amount of bad publicity is probably built into their calculations, they'll weather the storm, wait for Dad to run out of steam.'

'OK, OK, I hear you. These guys are very powerful. But let's look at it another way – the factory in Crindau is just one part of their huge empire, it's a piddling little thing like, like, one of the Orkney Islands. So if holding on to it becomes a real hassle, then they might decide to give in because it's just not worth the trouble when they've got whole *continents* to think about.'

'Alternatively, if they give in to Dad, it's going to set a precedent. What's to stop someone else from burying themselves alive the next time they want to close down a factory?'

'Yeah, Dad could start a trend, a new way to fight global capitalism. Wild.'

'You idiot.'

'There's nothing wrong with being ambitious.'

'As long as you don't use Dad to try and realise your own ambition.'

'That's a cheap shot, Shauna.'

'Can you actually look me in the eye and tell me you know what you're doing?'

'You think just because you're the eldest you can get away with that kind of horseshit. Well not anymore'

He got up, and started putting on his jacket.

'I'm not your kid brother any longer.'

'Just acting like it.'

'And you can't tell me what to do.'

Shauna watched him storm out, trying to look taller than he was, rolling his shoulders, knocking a chair aside as he passed.

Putting on a show. People turned their heads to stare as he pushed though. She hadn't handled that very well.

On Saturday, with just a couple of days left before he was due back in work, Aidan received a letter from Sunny Jim.

Ivor said, 'It's from them all right – look.' He pointed at the envelope. 'It's got their logo in the corner.'

Aidan's heart leapt. They'd finally cracked.

'This looks like the one you're waiting for, Aidan.'

Ivor showed no intention of leaving. He obviously wanted Aidan to open it while he was there.

'Thanks, Ivor.'

Aidan put it aside, making it clear that he wasn't going to. Ivor looked hurt, but took the hint and said goodbye. As soon as Aidan heard the back gate banging shut, he tore the letter open. He wondered if they would send someone down here to talk to him, or would they offer a meeting in the factory? In that case, he'd have to come up and, if what they were offering wasn't enough, have to bury himself again – Jesus, just think of that! Despite warning himself not to expect too much, his hands trembled as he unfolded the letter.

Dear Mr Walsh,

You are due back in work on Monday. You will be in breach of contract if you do not turn up for your shift.

The Human Resources Manager would like to see you in his office at 9.00 a.m. to discuss your recent public pronouncements about the company.

Aidan felt his stomach lurch violently, as if he was on a boat rocking in a wild sea. He read it again, slowly, searching each word for the possibility of some alternative meaning, some hidden message. But there was no ambiguity; it couldn't be more straightforward.

'That's wonderful, isn't it? They're asking me to come back to work so they can make me redundant.'

He rang Dylan.

'It doesn't sound like they're weakening to me at all.'

'This is like a game of poker,' said Dylan. 'You've got to keep your nerve.'

'You mentioned that already.'

'They'll give in in the end, you'll see. They can't just *leave* you there, you're famous – you've been interviewed by Huw Humphreys! They'll come up with an offer, you mark my words. They're terrified of you.'

'Like a game of poker,' repeated Aidan to himself, after the call ended.

Aidan lay there, the fear slowly growing inside him. Soon he would have used up all his annual leave. *They wouldn't dare do anything – you're famous now.* Oh yes, he'd captured the public's imagination. They stuck their heads down the periscope and gawped. They took photos. They wrote stories about him to amuse people over their cornflakes. *Roll up, roll up, come and see the lunatic who's buried himself alive in his back garden.* But was it doing any good? Had Sunny Jim changed their position in any respect? Had they hell.

There was something else. Strange things were happening to his body these last few days. Frightening things. Things he didn't understand. The sweat rolled off him. He trembled. He shook. He found it hard to breathe. His throat was parched. He couldn't swallow and his eyes burned. His head felt so heavy he was frightened he'd never be able to lift it again. Other times he was convinced he was having a heart attack. With no warning, it would start to beat madly. He could feel it bucking and butting against his chest, desperately trying to force its way out. He imagined it bursting right through him, like the *Alien*. He pressed both hands down hard on his chest to try and keep it inside. He knew it was mad but he did it anyway.

I'll really be fucked if I have a heart attack down here. Even if he rung for help, how long would it take them to come and get him out? *I should ring now, before it gets worse.* For fuck's sake. What would they think if he called and said, 'I think I'm about to have a heart attack, and I'm buried in a coffin in my back garden – can you send an ambulance?' They'd think they were dealing with a lunatic.

He wanted to get out of this coffin before he went completely mental. Or his body went to pieces. Maybe he was worrying about nothing. Maybe everything would be much easier if he just let go and lost it? Give up, lie there drooling, oblivious. Mad might be good. Easier than clinging on to hope. That could drive you crazy. He remembered that badge he'd seen a guy wearing in the Globe a few months ago – *Since I Gave Up Hope I Feel Much Better.* But what else was did he have apart from hope? Fuck, the sweat was rolling off him.

That afternoon Russell, Gwyn and Wilf stopped by. He always knew when it was them coming through the gate, Russell would open it with one swift, familiar lurch and yell, 'Anyone home?'

Aidan told them about the letter.

'Let's see it,' said Russell. Aidan put it in the basket and winched it up. The three of them huddled around and read it. Russell shook his head. 'Nasty.'

'Very condescending,' said Gywn, pushing his glasses back on to the bridge of his nose.

'No one would blame you if you went back to work,' said Wilf. 'You did your best, like.'

'And where will you be if you don't,' said Russell. 'Up shit creek, that's where.'

'Remember what you said? They'll be queuing up to say I told you so if I go back to work with my tail between my legs – no, I'm not doing it.'

'Come on, mun,' said Gwyn. 'You've done what you said you'd do – everybody's heard about us now. The spotlight is right back on Sunny Jim. We've had TV crews and journalists here all week. Now it's time to leave it up to the politicians. Imagine what a scene it'll be when you go back to work on Monday with the media following your every step.'

'Yeah, and where will they be the next day? They'll have packed up and moved on to the next story. The only reason they're here is that I'm stuck down in this box. Once I come back out, I stop being the man who buried himself alive and become that nobody Aidan Walsh again, don't you get it?'

'What would be so bad about that?' asked Russell.

'Because I'd be working in a warehouse, drinking in my local, I'd be no different to thousands, *millions*, of other people. Why would anyone care about me then?'

'You'd be just like us again, is that what you mean?'

There was an edge to Russell's voice. But perhaps he'd hit on an uncomfortable truth. Aidan had left that person behind. That sad bastard who'd been afraid to stick his head above the wall. That fucking loser. He got a pain in his chest just thinking about how he'd been living his life these last few years. Treading lightly, hesitantly, flinching at the slightest noise, expecting another blow to land at any minute. If he went back now he'd look a fool. Besides, what about all those people who'd begged him not to, told him that he was their last chance? And that wasn't all. Getting his face in the paper, being interviewed, he'd loved it. He understood now why people were so desperate to become famous. It was exciting. You mattered. Maybe if he hadn't been stuck in this box with nothing to do all day, he could have kept things in perspective. But visits from friends and talking to the media was all he had to keep him going. They'd become his oxygen.

On Monday Aidan listened to every news bulletin on the hour without fail. There was nothing. He jumped every time the phone rang, but it was never Sunny Jim, it was just friends asking him if they'd rung. *They don't want to lose face, they're stretching it out as long as they can. They'll come up with a last-minute compromise.*

It was a game of poker, he told himself. Though the feeling grew that he'd been dealt a losing hand.

On Tuesday morning when Safina arrived, his heart leapt. Then he realised something was wrong. She looked terrible. She held out a brown envelope.

'Aidan, they sent me down here in a taxi to give you this. I told them I didn't want to do it. I begged them not to make me.' She paused, her voice breaking. She gently shook her head. 'I'm so sorry.'

He asked her to put it in the basket, and manoeuvred it down. He knew, before he opened it; he only needed to take one look at her face. It was a letter of dismissal.

7

Dylan was in the middle of a post-play discussion in the main hall. In a circle of chairs sat the cast, director, a young teacher and the surly members of 10C from St David's High School, Bryn Glâs.

'So,' said Matt the director, 'what do you think are the main issues that this play raises?'

There was a resounding silence, broken only by a girl loudly popping her gum.

'Well, I for one think it was pretty challenging stuff.'

Dylan smelt something foul drifting over from the direction of the young scholars. The teacher pitched in gamely.

'*I* think it was about responsibility.'

Matt nodded enthusiastically. With his tight-fitting black polo neck and little goatee, Dylan thought he looked like someone who'd come to a fancy dress party dressed as a theatre director. He cupped his chin in his hand and, bright-eyed and breathless asked, 'Does anyone else think it was about responsibility?'

The kids stared at the floor, the ceiling, their nails. Matt perched on the edge of his chair, desperately searching their averted faces for signs of life. 'Or does anyone *disagree*?'

Dylan imagined chopping off his goatee with a pair of garden shears and flinging it through the window. Or maybe setting it alight. The teacher, a nervous edge to his voice, said, 'I think the message was that we all have a responsibility for our own lives, and that the . . .'

One of the girls got up and flounced towards the door.

'Sharon, where do you think you're going?'

Sharon turned and stared at the teacher with the kind of intense hatred normally reserved for mass murderers.

'Toilet. Sir.'

'Usually we ask permission if we –'

'It's my period. Do you want blood all over the chair or what?'

The teacher reddened. A gaggle of girls snorted with laughter. Dylan's mobile rang.

'It's Dad – are you busy?'

'No – go ahead.'

Matt flashed him an angry look. Dylan shrugged apologetically and rushed out into the corridor.

'Dad, mun, what's happening?'

'They sacked me.'

Dylan lowered the mobile, threw back his head and screwed up his eyes. He felt a piercing pain in his chest.

'Fuck!'

'Dylan, are you there? Dylan . . .'

'Wilf, wake up.'

Megan was elbowing him in the back.

'What . . . what is it?'

'The phone's ringing.'

Wilf looked at the radio alarm, it said 12.43 a.m. He groaned. 'Let it ring.'

He closed his eyes again. Megan started tugging the duvet off him. He curled up into a ball, shoved his hands between his legs.

'Stop that!'

'It might be important.'

Wilf grunted, pressed his head into the pillow. Megan elbowed him again.

'What if it's one of the kids in some kind of trouble?'

Why did she have to say that?

'Why don't you get it? You're better at talking to them when they're upset than me.'

It was still ringing, actually seemed to be getting louder, though he knew that wasn't possible.

'But Wilf, what if it's a pervert?'

'I thought you said it was one of the kids?'

'I said it *might* be. But it could be one of those perverts. One rang Shirley last week.'

Jesus, there was only going to be one winner there, that woman had a mind like a sewer.

'Just slam the phone down on them.'

'Go on, Wilf, you're the man. It's a man's job to answer the phone when it rings in the middle of the night. If it's one of the kids upset about something, give me a shout and I'll come down and talk to them.'

He swung his legs over the side of the bed, switched on the bedside light, put on his dressing gown and walked downstairs. The phone was in the hall and he picked it up, but didn't say anything. If it was a pervert, he wasn't going to give him any encouragement, he'd let them make the first move. He heard someone breathing heavily at the other end and coiled tight, ready to slam down the receiver at the first lewd suggestion.

'Wilf, is that you?'

'Aidan?'

'Yeah.'

Wilf breathed a sigh of relief.

'Where are you?'

'The Ritz. Where do you fucking think?'

'Christ, Aidan, it's nearly one in the morning. I was in bed, asleep.'

'Sorry, I know it's late.' There was a pause. 'I need someone to talk to.'

'I'm here for you, mate, go ahead.'

'I don't mean on the phone. Can you come over here?'

'Yeah, of course I can. Just give me time to get dressed. I'll see you in about ten minutes.'

'Thanks – and Wilf.'

'Yeah.'

'Can you bring something to drink?'

'Drink?'

'Yeah, some booze.'

Wilf hesitated. 'Uh, I don't know if we've got anything, we . . .'

'You must have *something*. Have a look, for Christ's sake.'

Boy, Aidan sounded in a bad way. When the lads had been round earlier that evening, they had tried to cheer him up. Wilf said, 'They can't just sack you, the rest of us will walk out, in solidarity.'

'No,' said Aidan, 'I don't want that. They'd be delighted, then they'll be able to sack the rest of you and save even more money. No one asked me to do this, it was my own idea.'

'You won't be able to stop them,' said Wilf. 'They'll be too fired up – we stick together round here.'

Russell snorted. 'I wouldn't bank on it.'

'We'll be out that door like that.' He clicked his fingers. 'That'll put the wind up them.'

'People might *say* that, but those days are gone. I wouldn't

179

bank on them doing it when the chips are down. They'd be too scared of losing their redundancy money.'

'Come on, mun, don't be so negative.'

'I'm being, realistic. That's what we need now, cool heads.'

'He's right,' said Aidan. 'People aren't going to walk out now. Don't worry about me, they're just trying to scare me, but it won't work. They'll have to back down in the end.'

As they walked away, Wilf said, 'He's taking it very calmly, isn't he?'

He didn't sound calm anymore.

'What's happening, Wilf?'

He went back upstairs, told Megan. She was sitting up in bed, clutching the duvet around her. He started getting dressed.

'It'll be cold out, wear your warm jumper, the blue one I got you for Christmas. It's in the middle drawer.'

He slipped it on, bent down to tie up his laces. When he stood up straight again, Megan said, 'Your collar's sticking up.'

He grunted and went back downstairs. There were a couple of cans of lager in the fridge. And a motley collection of bottles in the sideboard in the living room: a half bottle of Bells, ginger wine, advocaat, Babycham, sweet sherry and the mysterious, tiny bottle of Croatian liqueur – no one knew where that had come from. He shoved the lot in a carrier bag.

Walking down the road, the bag clanking against his leg, he thought with pleasure, *Aidan rang me, not Russell or Gwyn.*

He opened Aidan's back gate, walked over, called out, 'Aidan, it's me, Wilf.'

'Hello.'

He sounded terrible. Wilf walked over, peered down the periscope. He *looked* terrible. Like a prisoner who's been turned down for parole again.

'Did you bring some booze?'

'Yeah – here.'

Wilf put a can of lager in the basket, winched it down. Aidan opened it and drank about half in one go, his eyes shut.

He looked up at Wilf, said, 'Aren't you going to have one?'

'I don't think I will, if you don't mind.'

'Go on, it's not much fun drinking alone.'

The haunted look in his eyes unnerved Wilf. 'OK.' He opened the other can, took a sip. It only took Aidan a couple of swigs to drain his.

'Can I have another?'

'I've only got two.'

There was panic in Aidan's eyes. Wilf held out his. 'Here, have this one.'

'Have you got anything else?'

'Oh, yeah.' Wilf opened the carrier bag and listed the contents.

Aidan said, 'Let's have the whisky.'

Aidan winched up the basket with the empty can and Wilf winched down the whisky. Aidan started knocking it back straight away.

'Steady on, you'll be smashed out of your head before you know it.'

'Hopefully.'

'Aidan, what's wrong, mun, you said you needed someone to talk to.'

Aidan took another gulp of the whisky, grimaced. He ran his hand over his face, twisting his head from side to side. 'I'm fucked.' When he laughed, it made the hair on the back of Wilf's neck stand up. 'Completely and utterly fucked.'

'You said yourself it was just a matter of holding your nerve, that it wasn't over yet, that there was no way Sunny Jim could get away with sacking you.'

'But they *have* sacked me. I've got no job, I'm skint, and the bastards haven't retreated an inch. I've shot my bolt, Wilf, I haven't got a fucking clue what to do next.'

'I thought you said . . .'

'That I always thought it was a possibility that they'd sack me, that I was prepared for it. I was lying, trying to make out I was ahead of the game. I didn't think they'd have the neck, the bastards. I thought even *they* couldn't be that callous.'

He forced some more whisky down.

'Shauna was right, I should have had an exit strategy.'

'A what?'

'Never mind.' He polished off the whisky, tossed the bottle into the basket, and yanked it up.

'Right.' He took a long, deep breath. 'Let's have the sherry.'

'Aidan, mun, you'll never find the answer at the bottom of a bottle.'

Aidan curled his lip, shot Wilf an angry look. 'Give me a break.'

Wilf looked away as he put the sherry in the basket. He took another sip of lager. Aidan took a slug of sherry. 'Bloody hell, it's disgusting.'

'We keep it for when Megan's mother comes over at Christmas – it makes her fart like a trooper.'

Aidan wiped his lips. 'I'm such a dickhead. Why in god's name did I ever think this would work?'

Wilf didn't know what to say.

'I mean people are always taking the piss out of you for being thick.'

Wilf's face fell.

'But you weren't stupid enough to believe that you could stop Sunny Jim closing down the factory by burying yourself alive, were you? No, that takes a special level of stupidity. That takes . . .' Aidan noticed the look on Wilf's face, 'Christ, I'm sorry mate. No offence, it's just . . . You know the way people talk . . .'

Wilf shook his head, he'd had time to prepare himself now. 'No, no, you're all right, don't worry about it, you're upset. You know me, I never take stuff like that to heart.'

Aidan squirmed in embarrassment and the bottle of sherry fell over.

'Fuck!'

Some had spilt on the mattress. Not much. He looked back, saw Wilf trying to hide how hurt he was. Aidan began to cry.

'Oh Wilf, what have I done?'

'Don't cry, it's not that bad.'

'YES, IT FUCKING IS!'

Wilf couldn't think of a reply to that. Then, Aidan started laughing manically.

'Anyway, it's good for you, crying. Flushing it all out of your system – like Dyno-Rod.'

Wilf laughed too, hugely relieved Aidan could manage to see the funny side of it. Then he started bawling again.

'Aidan?'

He wiped his eyes, forced some more sweet sherry down. He grinned up at Wilf.

'I'm looking forward to that Croatian liqueur.'

Wilf smiled.

'Wilf?'

'What?'

'You won't tell the others I cried, will you?'

When Megan brought Aidan's breakfast at eight, he was fast asleep, his mouth open, snoring. She reeled up the empty bottle of advocaat.

'I never thought that I'd live to see that empty.'

She put the butty and flask in the basket, winched it back down. She'd had a terrible struggle getting Wilf up this morning. He hadn't even undressed, just collapsed into bed, shoes and all.

It was sad seeing Aidan like this. She couldn't see him lasting much longer.

At their tea break that morning Wilf said, 'I've been thinking.'

Russell smirked. 'Here we go.'

Wilf slammed his mug down on the table. 'I know you all think I'm thick, but it wouldn't hurt you to be polite for once, you know.'

183

'All right, keep your hair on.'

Russell glanced at Gwyn. 'Go on, Wilf,' said Gwyn.

Wilf noticed the pool of tea on the table where he'd slammed his mug, took out a paper tissue and mopped it up.

'Well . . . Aidan's not going to be able to survive much longer now they've sacked him. And he's doing this for all of us, after all. So I thought we could get everyone at the factory to chip in to help him keep going.'

'A collection?'

'Or we could call it a levy – just like you pay your union dues regularly, so we could get everyone to pay . . .'

'Their Aidan dues.'

'Yeah,' said Wilf. 'It wouldn't have to be much. Say everyone gave 50p a week – they wouldn't miss that.'

'Hang on,' said Russell. 'There's nearly 1,200 people work for Sunny Jim, if everyone gave 50p, he'd be on bloody £600 a week.'

Gwyn whistled.

'Oh,' said Wilf, struggling now.

'He'd be a Fat Cat,' said Russell, 'living off the sweat of the workers, gorging himself on champagne and caviar down in his coffin, the lazy bastard.'

Gwyn started laughing. Wilf was irritated; they'd no right to take the piss.

'All right, maybe not 50p, er . . .'

'OK, 10p then, go on, how much would that come to?' He winked at Gwyn.

'Look,' said Gwyn, stepping in before it got embarrassing. 'I know what you're saying, Wilf. But it would be a nightmare to organise.'

'And you'd never get everyone to chip in anyway, some of these bastards wouldn't give you the steam off their . . .'

'We could hold a collection outside the factory gates though. You know, get a bucket and hang around after work, I bet we'd do all right.'

Russell took a sip of his tea. 'Yeah, we could do that.' He leant across the table and clapped Wilf on the shoulder. 'Good thinking, Wilf.'

Wilf grinned and slurped his tea, looking away.

Aidan woke up to a raging hangover. Everything hurt. He only had to move his head a centimetre for piercing hot needles to embed themselves in his skull. After about fifteen minutes he managed to move his arms enough to be able to grab his basket. He ignored the cold bacon butty and poured himself some coffee. There were a few letters and a glossy leaflet with a drawing of a butterfly emerging from a chrysalis.

Have You Failed to Achieve Your Goals?

Do you find that nothing you plan works out? Then perhaps you are looking at life in the wrong way. Come and hear Jazz Jackson explain how our consciousness creates our reality. As we begin to look deep within ourselves, we can begin to change the way we think and feel about life. The inner power we experience enables us to have a loving and positive influence on the world around us. When I change, the world changes. You are not a failure, you have just been looking for answers in the wrong place.

You are also invited to stay on and join us for World Meditation Hour 6.30-7.30 p.m. A special time set aside to send good wishes and peaceful thoughts out into the world.

Aidan groaned.

'I am not a failure, I have just been looking for answers in the wrong place.'

He screwed the leaflet up into a ball, tried to close his eyes and go back to sleep, but his mind stirred into life and the voices in his head began again. *Now you'll be the only one without any redundancy money. Why couldn't you have kept your head down like everyone else? Crossed your fingers and hoped something would turn up.*

For god's sake why didn't you have an exit strategy? They'll all be queuing up to say I told you so.

'Shut the fuck up!' yelled Aidan. Or maybe he just imagined he yelled it. He could no longer tell. The difference between inside and outside his head had blurred and broken down.

Loser. Sucker. Clown. He clawed his face with his hands.

'Please stop!'

The taunting was relentless. There was no need to hire an interrogator; he was quite capable of breaking himself. He was forced to lay there and endure jibes and insults, sarcasm and mockery. It didn't stop. It was like having tinnitus. A constant cacophony so loud he couldn't concentrate on anything else. He tried to pull himself together.

'Come on, it's time to do your exercises.'

Exercises – ha! What good are they? They're not going to save you.

He turned over on to his front. He was going to do some press-ups. He tried to lift himself up, his limbs shook like Bambi trying to take his first steps; his heart burned; there was a metal clamp tightening round his skull. He collapsed. His mouth gaped. He began to dribble. Someone was whispering in his ear.

Hello, we are your inner demons, we have come to keep you company.

He was completely fucked.

Respect had reached Abertillery Youth Club, a pre-fab reeking of stale sweat, cheese and onion crisps and cigarette smoke. Dylan was standing like a spare part at the back of the stage while his co-star, Hermione, delivered a long monologue about her descent into addiction. They'd slept together four times now, but once had been enough to convince him it was a mistake. Sheer boredom had driven him to it. Now they had to carry on working together every day. Everyone knew, of course. It was excruciating.

As she paused to wipe away some imaginary tears there was

an enormously loud belch from the audience, provoking the usual hilarity. Jesus, you could set your watch by the belches. What in god's name had the playwright been thinking of, demanding so many pauses in a script expressly designed for performance in youth clubs and community centres? It beggared belief. They were particularly lively in Abertillery tonight – someone had yelled 'Are you gay, mate?' at Dylan five times so far and it was only the first act. The thought of doing this kind of thing in this kind of place ten years from now, in front of fucking gobshites like these *and being grateful for the work* depressed the hell out of Dylan. He missed the buzz of helping with his dad's campaign. Getting the auld fella featured in the papers and on the telly had been great craic. He'd felt like a guerrilla, burrowing under the defences of the establishment, lobbing in grenades.

'Then, the only thing I had left to sell was my body,' wailed Hermione, 'so I sold that.' A ginger neanderthal leered, grabbed his groin and puckered up his lips at her. Ah, the glamour of the stage.

Dylan felt sick about his dad. He'd let him down badly. *Trust me, I know what I'm doing, hang on in there, they won't dare sack you.* There had to be something else they could try. What Aidan needed was a new angle. Something big and bold that would grab people's attention. To see your own father going down the chute like that, it made you sick to your guts.

'Life is so hard on the streets,' sobbed Hermione, 'People have no idea.'

Neither did Hermione, whose parents had sent her to public school in Cheltenham. Theatre was just so *phoney*. None of these wanky plays about 'the kids' were ever any good, because the bloody playwrights and directors thought they were missionaries, bringing the Good News to the savages. Drama as social work, what utter bullshit. These kids may have been pig ignorant yobs, but they all possessed excellent bullshit detectors. Here they were, in *their* youth club, lecturing them about the dangers of drugs, when all they wanted to do was play pool. It didn't matter *what* they said or did, these kids had already made up their minds that they were being talked down to.

And right then, it came to him. Suddenly Dylan realised how his dad could win. Of course, why hadn't he seen it before? It was blindingly obvious. OK, it was a long shot and Jesus Christ, it wouldn't be easy to persuade Aidan to do it. But it was his only hope. And only he, Dylan, could make it happen. There was no one else back in Crindau who had the know-how, the ambition, *the balls*, to make it work. It would mean a huge sacrifice on his part. But now that he'd thought of it, there was no way he couldn't go through with it.

'*So what do you think, Gareth?*'

Hermione was staring at him, saying the line with heavy-handed emphasis, panic in her eyes. Dylan realised he'd missed his cue. The director was in the wings, gesticulating at him. Dylan gazed at the future of Abertillery sprawled, legs akimbo, in the front row. Giggling and smirking, sensing something had gone wrong. What a sheer bloody waste of time theatre was, just another way of convincing yourself you were doing something worthwhile when the real action, the stuff that mattered, was going on elsewhere.

He walked slowly to the front of the stage, stood there with his hands in his pockets and looked into their eyes. He felt astoundingly light, as if he might actually float up to the ceiling if he didn't concentrate very hard on pushing his feet firmly down on to the floor. An exhilarating sense of freedom pulsed through him. Moments like this, when you just *knew* what you had to do next, when all doubt vanished, didn't come very often. And, when they did, you had to savour them.

No one belched, no one yelled 'Are you gay, mate?' The youth of Abertillery knew that this was for real. Dylan took another step forward, and stared into their wary, acne-scarred faces.

'What a pile of absolute crap this play is. I'm sick to death of it, just like you.'

There were a few giggles, a snort of poorly suppressed laughter.

'I'm also sick to death of listening to your foul belching and smelling your disgusting farts. You're a bunch of bloody morons and you deserve to live in a shithole like Abertillery. There are about a hundred thousand things I'd rather be doing with my time than wasting it here with you. Fuck this, I'm off to do something worthwhile.'

He jumped down from the stage and walked straight through the gaping audience, out the door and into the street. There was work to be done. He was going home.

The next day, when their shift finished, Russell, Gwyn and Wilf met outside the factory gates to hold a collection for Aidan. Wilf thought Russell and Gwyn were looking a bit morose.

'Come on, cheer up, it'll be a laugh.'

'What will we find so amusing about it?' asked Gywn. He was hunched up against the cold.

'You only get out of something what you put in. It'll be great craic.'

Russell scowled. 'You're a sad bastard if you think standing around in the cold holding a bucket and begging is good craic.'

'Wait . . .'

Wilf took a red nose from his pocket, put it on.

'TA-DA!'

'What the hell are you doing?'

'If you want to raise money, you've got to create a fun atmosphere.'

Russell stared back at him, stony-faced. Gwyn rolled his eyes.

'You know, like Comic Relief.'

'I fucking hate Comic Relief,' said Russell. 'All those filthy-rich celebrities telling ten-year-olds if they don't hand over their pocket money it will be their fault if children in Africa die. Now take that off.'

'No,' said Wilf, stepping away from Russell, worried he might snatch it off him. 'I won't.'

'Right, that's it, there's no way I'm standing next to you looking like that. I'll see you back in the car.'

He turned and walked away.

'RUSSELL!'

'Leave him,' said Gwyn. 'Come on, let's make a start.'

He chucked some loose change into the bucket, started rattling it around.

'SHOW AIDAN YOUR SUPPORT, COME ON NOW.'

A car drove past, the driver gaping at them with his mouth open.

Russell sat in his car smoking with the window rolled down, his seat pushed back, his feet up on the dashboard. He became aware of someone walking towards him. Looked round, saw Dylan smiling at him.

'Hi, Russell.'

'What are you doing here?'

Dylan leant down, placed both hands on the roof of the car and looked into Russell's eyes.

'I need to talk to you.'

'About what?'

'Let's face it, my dad's campaign is running out of steam, we've got to come up with something new, and quickly.'

Russell gave Dylan a searching look.

'Come on, get in.'

When they drove through the factory gates, Wilf and Gwyn were still shaking the bucket, looking very miserable. Russell slowed down.

'COME ON NOW, DON'T LET HIM STARVE – HE'S DOING THIS FOR ALL OF US – oh, hello.'

'Was it good craic then? No, I thought not. Get in.'

'Hi, guys,' said Dylan cheerily from the back seat.

Gwyn got in the front, Wilf slid in next to Dylan in the back.

'Hi, Wilf, how you doing?'

'Not so bad like, y'know.'

'Why are you wearing a red nose?'

'Because he's a moron,' said Russell, pulling on to the main road.

'How much did we get?' asked Wilf.

'£2.78p,' said Gwyn. 'No, hang on, I put in about 50 or 60p in change to make the bucket rattle, so about £2.30p, I suppose.'

'Brilliant – that'll buy him a saveloy and chips and a cuppa.'

'How long had we been there?'

Russell checked his watch. 'About half an hour.'

'Is that all? Jesus, it felt like hours, I'm freezing.'

They drove on for a while without saying anything. Dylan had thought carefully about how to pitch this to them. They were old and set in their ways, had limited imaginations, and were deeply suspicious of dynamic, intelligent, good-looking young guys like himself. He had to tread softly. He said, 'It's sad about Dai Rogers, isn't it?'

He'd been Crindau West's MP for over twelve years but had died of a heart attack a few months back. There was going to be a by-election in January.

'Aye, a real shame,' said Gwyn. 'He was a good bloke. He was Crindau through and through was Dai, born and bred here, no airs or graces whatsoever.'

'It's thanks to Dai we've still got the Casualty Department here in Crindau. People said he'd never manage to keep it open, but he just wouldn't give up, he was a real battler.'

'He stood up for what he believed in and there aren't many of those left,' said Russell. 'Smart with it.'

'That's right,' said Dylan. 'He was a bright bloke all right, they reckon he could have ended up on the front bench if he'd toed the party line.'

'"That might go down well in Westminster, but it wouldn't wash in Crindau",' said Wilf, quoting the phrase he'd made famous, and the others smiled.

Russell glanced in the mirror, said, 'For Christ's sake take that red nose off, will you?'

Wilf grinned sheepishly and put it back in his pocket. Gwyn turned round to face Dylan. 'If Dai was still around now, you can bet your life he'd be kicking up a right stink about Sunny Jim closing.'

'Yeah, I bet he would.' He glanced out of the window, noticed they were passing Coedkernew Park, where he'd copped his first feel. He was fourteen, thought he'd died and gone to heaven as he unhooked her bra. *Concentrate, Dylan.* 'So what do you think of this new guy they've selected then?'

Gwyn made a face.

'Nigel Watkins – the absolute opposite of Dai, a squeaky-clean New Labour type.'

'A barrister,' added Gwyn with distaste. 'A legal brain, cold and calculating.'

'No personality, a real nodding dog. Yes, Tony, no, Tony, three bags full, Tony. He's even got the same smile.'

'Not as creepy though,' said Wilf. They laughed. Wilf looked startled, he didn't usually get laughs.

'So what's his position on Sunny Jim?' asked Dylan.

'I don't think he even knows where the factory *is* . . .' Gwyn trailed off in disgust.

'No one I know likes him,' said Russell. He made a sour face. 'He'll still get in of course.'

'If they put a red rosette on a donkey in Crindau, they'd vote for it,' Gwyn said.

Dylan smiled, as if he'd never heard that one before. Then Russell put the final nail in the coffin.

'This Watkins bloke, he's from Cardiff.'

'I bet he lives in one of those flats down by the bay. A one-bedroom flat costs a hundred grand down there now.'

'*One bedroom!*'

'As bad as London it is – and you know what? They've all got Internet connections already built in, but no kitchens.'

'No!'

'It's true – I read in the paper, mun. That's what it's like in Cardiff now – you work at home and you go out to eat.'

'That's mad that is.'

'That's Cardiff for you.'

Dylan wouldn't have minded one of those flats himself, it was about the only bit of Cardiff he could imagine himself living in, but they were a bit beyond his means.

Dylan said, 'What you need is a local candidate, someone who understands local people's concerns. Someone you can trust.'

'Yeah? And where are we going to get one of those?'

Russell slowed down for a red light at the Gaeru roundabout. Dylan waited till he stopped the car completely and put the handbrake on. Then he said, 'I know *exactly* the person we need.'

'Oh aye?'

'So do you, actually.'

Russell turned around slowly, rested his arm along the back of his seat. He said, 'OK, what are you up to?'

'Your only hope is if someone stands as an independent. A single-issue candidate. Someone determined to hold Sunny Jim to account, to stop them pulling out and making you all redundant. They'd have a bloody good chance of winning. All we need is the right person, someone who's well known for their opposition to Sunny Jim. And there's only one man who fits that bill as far as I can see.'

Russell said he needed a drink before he could get his head around what Dylan was proposing, and insisted on driving to the Globe. They got a table in the corner, away from the telly, pool table and fruit machines. Dylan hated the Globe; it had an air of desperation about it. He remembered coming here with his dad when he was seventeen. It was supposed to be some kind of bonding session but they'd run out of things to say to each other after a few minutes. There was no football on the telly, so they ended up playing pool to hide the uncomfortable silences. He'd thrashed the living daylights out of Aidan, the one thing he'd enjoyed about the evening.

'OK,' said Russell, putting a pint in front of him and jolting him out of his reverie. 'Let's hear it.'

Gwyn and Wilf had sat down either side of him, Russell directly opposite. Surrounded by jaded bodies and minds. Dylan took a sip from his pint, then laid his palms flat on the table.

'Let's face it, he can't stay down there forever. *We* know that, and *they* know that. At the moment, all they have to do is wait, and weather the storm. If we're realistic about this, we've only got a short amount of time before he *has* to come back up again, haven't we?'

None of them replied, so he ploughed on.

'Now, he can either come up as a loser, having spent all that time underground and lost out on his redundancy money for nothing, or we can give him the chance to come up a winner, and carry on the fight as the MP for Crindau. Which is it to be?'

Russell held up a hand. He was looking at Dylan as if he'd gone and cracked up, just as Dylan had expected.

'He's got no experience of running a campaign, he's never made a speech in his life, he hasn't got a party machine behind him, he's got no budget, no policies . . . He'd lose his deposit and look a right idiot.'

Gwyn nodded and Wilf looked increasingly worried.

'I don't agree,' said Dylan.

'Why not?'

'I'll tell you why – he's got no experience of running a campaign, he's never made a speech in his life, he hasn't got a party machine behind him . . .'

'Eh?'

Russell looked angry but Dylan hunched forward, locked eyes with him. Russell would be the toughest nut to crack; he had to take him on head to head, show the others who was top dog here.

'The things you think are weaknesses are actually his greatest strengths.'

'OK,' said Russell, 'you've been to college while we're just a bunch of plebs, so you're going to have to spell out what the fuck you're talking about.'

'Dylan glanced warily at Wilf and Gwyn, rattled that Russell was playing the class card so soon.

'The fact that he's just an ordinary working bloke without any political experience is *exactly* what we're going to emphasise – what's the point in trying to hide it? Remember that survey a few months back, where it turned out that people trusted politicians less than secondhand car salesmen?'

Gwyn laughed, he'd seen it in the paper and had shown the other two.

'Aidan will be the No Bullshit candidate, the guy who tells it like it is. People will love it, they're crying out for someone like him.'

'The people's choice,' said Wilf.

'Exactly.'

Dylan smiled encouragingly at him. When he was growing up he'd always liked Wilf best. Whenever he came to the house, he'd always slip him a bar of chocolate, find time for a quick kickabout with him in the garden.

'I'm telling you, he's perfect. He'll storm it.'

'You enjoying that?' Russell asked Dylan, nodding at the pint of gassy draught lager Dylan had barely touched. He usually drank bottled lager – Budvar, Beck's, or Cobra, but knew better than to ask for one of those in the Globe.

'Yeah, it's great, cheers.'

'You've hardly touched it – not much of a drinker, are you? I'd say drugs are more your scene.'

Dylan felt his nerve wavering under Russell's granite stare. He didn't smile or reply.

'Because only someone who'd taken too many drugs could come up with an idea as barmy as Aidan standing for MP.'

Gwyn laughed and Russell gave him a high five. The atmosphere improved.

'Yeah all right, very funny.'

Dylan had been shaken up for a minute, god knows what kind of prejudices were festering inside these bitter, twisted old guys. A couple more drinks and they'd be telling him that Jim Davidson was their favourite comic, that the country was being swamped with illegal immigrants, that they should bring back National Service, the birch, hanging. He let them carry on laughing; they had to be given some rope. He drummed his fingers against the table, waiting for them to settle down.

'I'm telling you, the other candidates will be crapping themselves when they find out Aidan is standing.'

They were off again, bellowing. It was almost as bad as being back on stage in Abertillery Youth Club.

'What did I tell you? He's been at the wacky backy.'

Jesus, thought Dylan, the banality of this middle-aged banter. He felt sorry for his dad having to hang out with an ape like Russell. There seemed to be a bit more to Gwyn than met the eye and Wilf was a sweet guy. But Russell, he couldn't see why Aidan put up with him.

'What's so funny about the idea of Aidan standing for election as an independent?'

'He works in a warehouse, he sits right there, exactly where you're sitting, drinking his pint after work, and talking about football. He goes home afterwards and cooks his boil-in-the-bag fish and sits in front of the telly eating it. He's a normal bloke.'

'Not anymore, he isn't.'

'Come again?'

'He stopped being a normal bloke when he started appearing in the papers, and on the TV and radio. Thousands of people know about him now. He's the little guy taking on the Fat Cats. The man who finally decided that enough was enough, that it was time to make a stand. He's become a symbol. Symbols are

very powerful, much more powerful than political manifestos –
no one reads those.'

He paused to let that sink in. *We don't have to play by their rules.*
We can rip it up and start again. Gwyn was nodding, he liked the
idea, had grasped the potential quickly.

'A vote for Aidan will be sending out a message that the
people of Crindau have had enough of being taken for granted,
of turning out like sheep to vote Labour. It will show that they
want to be listened to and treated with respect. I mean, do you
really want to vote for this lawyer from Cardiff?'

'No, but . . .'

'He's my dad, and he's your friend. We've *got* to get him out
of there. If *we* don't help him, who will?'

They weren't laughing now.

'Like I said, I don't think he can last much longer if we don't
come up with something new.'

Wilf cleared his throat, looked around uncertainly, said, 'A few
days ago Aidan rang me up after midnight, very upset, like . . .'

The others stared at him.

'He rang *you*?' said Russell.

Wilf looked uncomfortable, ran his index finger up and down
the table as he spoke.

'Yeah, he wanted me to bring him some booze, so he could
get drunk. Well I only had two cans of lager, and a bottle of
Babycham left over from when Sharon was last home, but then
I found a bottle of sherry in the . . .'

'Do you think we care what's in your drinks cabinet? Get on
with it!'

Wilf told them how distraught Aidan was, how he was sure
he'd made a terrible mistake.

'Shit,' said Russell. 'I didn't know he was *that* bad.'

Neither did Dylan.

'Why didn't you tell us about this?' demanded Russell.

'He asked me not to tell anyone else. He was embarrassed.'

Russell glared at him, then took a long swig from his pint.

'You see,' said Dylan. 'We've got to get him out of there.'

Russell started searching through his pockets for his fags; Gwyn began picking at the edge of a beer mat; Wilf examined his fingernails. There was a long silence.

'So who'd run this campaign for him, since he's stuck in a coffin?' Gwyn asked.

'Me,' said Dylan.

'I thought as much,' said Russell.

'If you don't like it, you run it.'

'No bloody thanks.'

'Any objections to me being in charge? Because now's the time to say so.'

Russell said, 'How are you going to run it while you're off somewhere acting?'

'I quit yesterday. That's how much I believe in this.'

That impressed them.

'I can't do it on my own. This will need to be a team effort. We'll be up against professionals with big budgets and loads of staff. It's not going to be easy, there'll be lots of hard work. *Lots.* Are you willing to help?'

'I am,' said Wilf, god bless him. Dylan flashed him a smile and Wilf beamed back.

'Good on you, Wilf – Gwyn?'

He nodded, a tense, thoughtful expression on his face, then said quietly, 'I'm in.'

'Cheers. Russell?'

He blew smoke through his nostrils and reached for his pint, spinning it out.

'It's a bloody stupid idea. But we've got to try something. Aye, I'll lend a hand.'

'Right, well that concludes the opening session of the Vote for Aidan campaign, unless there's any other business.'

'So how confident is our candidate then?' asked Gwyn.

'I don't know. I wanted to talk it over with you guys before I put it to him.'

'I don't believe I'm hearing this,' said Russell. 'You mean you haven't even told the poor fucking idiot what he's in for?'

'He'll find it harder to say no now he knows *you* all think it's such a good idea.'

'I'll say this for you,' said Russell. 'You've got some fucking neck, son.'

Dylan wanted to tell Russell not to call him son again, but thought better of it. Instead, he gave him a broad wink.

'So when were you planning to tell him?'

'There's no time like the present. I was thinking after we'd finished these drinks.'

Aidan was surprised to see Dylan, Russell, Wilf and Gwyn arriving together and staring down the periscope at him, big smiles on their faces.

'What's going on? How come you're home, Dylan?'

'Oh, I've got a couple of days off.' Dylan didn't want Aidan to get hung up about packing in his job before they'd got on to the main topic.

'I've got an idea,' said Dylan. 'It's a bit crazy, but I think it might just work.'

'Like father like son,' said Gwyn.

'Eh?'

'That's exactly what your dad said to us that night he told us about the coffin.'

Dylan decided to ignore the comparison, he was his own man.

'Have you lot been drinking?'

'Just a quick one,' said Russell.

Russell had insisted on another round before they came to tell Aidan. While he was at the bar he'd asked everyone if they'd vote for Aidan. Before Dylan knew what was happening, there was another pint in front of him from a well-wisher, along with a slap on the back. *I remember you when you were this high – spitting image of your dad when he was young, you are.* Then another and then another, and the quick one turned into a two-hour session, with chants and singing. *Aidan's gonna win, Aidan's gonna win, ee-aye-addio, Aidan's gonna win.*

'The thing is,' said Dylan. 'Now I know how we can beat Sunny Jim.'

That got Aidan's attention. Dylan pitched him the idea, fast and confidently, so he couldn't interrupt. But Aidan appeared to grow more terrified the longer Dylan talked. He looked exhausted and ground down, drained of all belief, thought Dylan. He'd arrived just in time. When he finished, Aidan said, 'You're off your bloody head,' a look of complete alarm on his face.

'No, I'm not – you can beat this other guy. I'd put money on it. In fact I *will* put money on it, once it's official.'

'Piss off. I've got no chance. What the hell do I know about being an MP?'

'What does anyone know? You don't have to have any qualifications, or pass any exams, you just pick it up as you go along. You've got civil servants to show you the ropes. Not having a bloody clue didn't stop the others – Christ, Dad, mun, if John Redwood can get elected, you *must* stand a chance.'

Aidan had to admit this was a powerful argument, one to which he had no ready reply. Sensing a gap in his defences, Gwyn tapped Dylan on the shoulder, said, 'Tell him about being a symbol.'

But despite Dylan's eloquence Aidan still wasn't buying it. 'I'll look a right bloody fool.'

'No, you won't. People round here *hate* politicians, they'll identify with a nobody like you.'

'Thanks a lot.'

'I'd vote for you,' said Wilf. 'Megan will too, you can count on that.'

'Me too,' said Gwyn.

Dylan turned to Russell, who was struggling to light a bent cigarette. He'd sat on his packet in the pub. 'How about you?'

'Aye, definitely, I'm not voting for some bloody lawyer from Cardiff.'

'And I'd vote for you as well,' said Dylan. 'And Shauna.'

'And everyone down at the Globe,' added Gwyn.

'You're the People's Candidate,' said Wilf.

'The pisshead's choice,' muttered Russell, finally giving up and chucking the mangled cigarette on the ground in disgust.

'*And* everyone who works at Sunny Jim will vote for you,' said Dylan. 'There you are, that's over a thousand votes in the bag already, before we've even started. This result will send shockwaves through the country.'

'He's off again,' said Russell. 'More wacky backy talk.'

'I don't know the first thing about politics.'

'But everyone already knows what you stand for – you've only got one policy: keep the factory open. A clear, simple and very popular message that can be summed up in a few words – that's an extremely strong brand image. The other candidates would kill for it.'

'He's a brand now, is he?' said Russell. 'He was the people's choice a minute ago.'

'The people's choice *is* a brand, the best there is. Look at all the publicity you've had already. Imagine how much *more* you'll get if you stand for election – it's a *fantastic* human interest story.'

'You've got to do it,' said Gwyn. 'You're the only one with any chance of pulling this off.'

'Absolutely not.'

'You'll never have another chance in your life to do something like this – to make a difference. Just think how much you'd regret it afterwards if you don't. Imagine having to live with that.' said Dylan.

Dylan saw from Aidan's anguished expression that he was hitting home with this one.

'Do you think that the New Labour candidate, this fancy lawyer from Cardiff, had any doubts about whether he was good enough to stand? You'd make a much better MP than him –

you've lived here all your life. This other bloke, he doesn't give a toss about Crindau, it's just a nice safe seat so he can get on board the gravy train and line his pockets even more.'

'Yeah, the greedy bastard,' shouted Russell. 'Let's show him we don't want his sort in Crindau.'

Aidan went to reply, but couldn't get a word in edgeways.

'Don't let us down now, mate.'

'Yeah, we're counting on you.'

'But I wouldn't have a clue what to do.'

'You just be yourself, leave all the details to your campaign team,' said Dylan.

'And who, exactly, are my campaign team?'

'Us!' cried Wilf, sticking his hand in the air and beaming.

'Oh fuck,' said Aidan.

Afterwards they went into Aidan's house. On the way Russell said, 'Here, make yourself useful and empty this,' and handed him Aidan's bedpan. Dylan shuddered with distaste, took it inside at arm's length, then held his nose and chucked the contents down the toilet. While Wilf was making a pot of tea, Dylan eyed the mess in the living room.

'It's hard to believe that this is going to be the nerve centre of the campaign to elect Crindau's first independent MP.'

He took a quick glance at the mouldy sofa.

'The last time that was in fashion, Harold Wilson was prime minister.'

Russell regarded him scornfully.

'OK, so what do we do now?'

Dylan ran his hands through his hair, looked up at the ceiling and said, 'Christ knows – we've got no experience, no connections, no money. Our candidate won't be able to appear in public because he's stuck in a coffin, and this is one of the safest Labour seats in the country.'

'You just told Aidan he had it all sewn up.'

'I didn't want to worry him.'

'Jesus wept.'

Dylan suddenly felt exhausted. He wanted to crash out. It had been a long day. 'It's not going to be easy, that's all I'm saying.'

'Well thanks for the inspirational words, team leader.'

Wilf brought in the tea and they sat down and poured it, passing around the biscuits. The booze was taking its toll now, and they were all starting to flag.

Gwyn said, 'Aidan didn't look too keen. Perhaps we should ease off, give him a few days to think it over.'

'Christ, no – we've got to keep the pressure on, not give him a chance to back out. Anyway, the deadline for candidates to register is this Friday.'

'Bloody hell, so we've only got three days?'

'Yep.' Dylan dunked a biscuit in his tea, cool as you like. Russell threw him a piercing look.

'So this is something you dreamt up at the last minute. Everyone else has been planning their campaign for months, and we haven't even persuaded our man to stand yet. It's going to be a right shambles.'

'Wrong – because no one was expecting it . . .'

'Least of all Aidan,' Russell pointed out. Dylan ignored this.

'Which means we've got the crucial element of surprise on our side – all the others will have worked out what they're going to say and planned how they're going to respond to the other candidates, but *we* won't have figured in their calculations. Dad is the wild card – they'll be completely thrown when he steps into the ring.'

Wilf narrowed his eyes and wagged his finger at Russell.

'See – the things you think are weaknesses are actually his greatest strengths.'

'*Exactly!*' cried Dylan, winking at Wilf. Russell rolled his eyes and shifted his arse to let a fart escape.

'Three days though . . . That's very tight,' said Gwyn. 'Jesus, was that you?'

Russell grinned malevolently.

'It's enough, you'll never get anywhere if you give my dad too long to think about something. You have to put the heat on. Which is why you need to get all the people in work and from the pub to go see him and tell him how much they want him to stand so they can have someone to vote for.' He brought his fist down on the arm of the chair. 'Let's create a real buzz, so that he just can't dismiss it as a crackpot idea.'

'It *is* a crackpot idea.'

'This is no time for negative thinking. *We've* got to believe he can do it if we're going to persuade other people he can.'

Russell sipped his tea, keeping his eyes on Dylan. 'I hope you know what you're doing, son.' There it was again, *son*.

Gwyn stirred, sat upright and put down his mug.

'Hang on, you said the candidates have to register by Friday.'

'That's right.'

'What's the deposit these days?'

'£500.'

Gwyn winced. 'Where are we going to find that kind of money?'

Dylan cradled his mug in his hands, gazed dreamily at the ceiling. 'I'm working on it.'

The next morning, Megan brought Aidan his tea and bacon butty at eight as usual.

'Here's your breakfast – and good luck in the election.'

Her cheery tone made him cringe. 'I haven't made my mind up about that yet.'

Megan frowned. 'Well you better get a move on – nearly everyone in the road has already said they're going to vote for you. Anyway, better go, ta-ra.'

'Great – thanks a lot, guys.'

The postman came ten minutes later.

'No post today – I just wanted to say I'll be voting for you.'

'I haven't decided whether . . .'

'Wait till I tell the lads in the Sorting Office.'

He winked and clenched his fist as he left.

'Power to the people!'

Frank rang at mid-day.

'Hello, is that the Right Honourable Member for Crindau?'

'Cut that out, for fuck's sake.'

'That's nice language now, isn't it? You're going to have to watch that kind of thing on the campaign trail.'

'Oh piss off, will you.'

He rang off and lay there seething. He held out for nearly half an hour before he picked up his mobile and rang back.

'Frank – what's for lunch today?'

In the evening, a stream of people who worked at the factory came to visit Aidan, urging him to stand.

'I'm telling you, you'd walk it, everyone I know would vote for you.'

'Thanks a lot, mate, I appreciate it.'

It was a set-up, he realised that. Dylan and the others had cajoled them all into persuading him what a great idea it was. None of them would have come otherwise. They must have thought he was born yesterday. All the same, he'd started to feel a little bit better about himself. It might be nothing but a load of old blather, but anything was better than wallowing in the black mood he'd been in these last few days. This lot had been put up to it, but at least they'd made the effort to come after a long day at work. That showed how much they thought of him. Aidan felt the first stirrings of hope, and this scared him. What if he allowed himself to believe that he could actually win, stood in the election and was totally humiliated? He'd be the butt of jokes for years to come. Or the object of pity. *The poor sod, he actually thought people would vote for him; he got the shock of his life, he's never been the same since.* He wouldn't be able to show his face in public.

He needed to talk to someone he could trust. Someone who wouldn't tell him what he wanted to hear, who was strong enough to say what they really thought. Someone who'd be able to stand back and look at things coolly and calmly. He picked up his mobile and punched in the number.

'Shauna – it's Dad. Can you give me a ring when you get this message please, love, I want to ask your advice about something important.'

8

Shauna picked up Aidan's message while she was driving over to meet Dylan. Both of them wanted to see her. Something was going on, that was obvious. At least she could kill two birds with one stone. When she pulled up outside the house, she noticed a couple of blokes pushing open the garden gate, shouting 'ee-aye-addio, Aidan's gonna win' and punching the air with their fists. Crindau was a weird place.

She let herself in to find Dylan in the living room, slouching in a chair, watching *The Simpsons*. He jumped to his feet when he saw her.

'Hi, sis, would you like a drink?'

'Tea would be nice.'

'You got it.'

He was suspiciously perky. She'd barely sat down before he poked his head around the door and said, 'I got some Earl Grey in specially, I know you like that.'

And suspiciously thoughtful. He whistled merrily as he came back in with the tray. He put it down, nodded at the box of wafer thin French biscuits next to the teapot. 'Yes,' said Shauna, wearily, 'they're my favourites. That's very nice of you, Dylan. So – how come this feels like a first date?'

'What do you mean?'

'You're trying so hard to impress me – come on, what are you after?'

'I . . .'

Her look dared him to bullshit her.

'First I get a call from you saying you need to talk to me about something really important to do with Dad, then I get a call from *him* saying he wants to ask my advice about something important.'

'He said that – he wanted to ask your advice?'

'What's the matter, wasn't he supposed to?'

Dylan avoided her eyes, stirred the tea too early, started opening the biscuits.

'Then, when I get here, you start treating me like the Queen of bloody Sheba. Now I don't want to sound bitter and twisted, but I have to say you're not usually this attentive. So – spill the beans, boyo.'

She slid one of the biscuits out of the packet he'd just opened, nibbled a bit off the end and sat back in her chair, watching him intently.

He pitched her the election idea. This was a much different speech to the one he'd given Russell, Gwyn and Wilf. He tried not to get too carried away, and was careful to show he was aware of the mountain they'd have to climb if Aidan was to stand any chance of winning. But he reminded her that no one had given Martin Bell much of a chance when he stood against Neil Hamilton as an independent and of how much publicity and sympathy Aidan had received already. It was, he thought, a terrific performance, combining a grand vision with careful attention to detail and a really quite impressive assessment of the opposition. When he'd finished, Shauna looked out of the window for a long while, lost in thought, slowly rotating the ring on her middle finger with her thumb. Eventually she said, 'And if he doesn't win the election, that's it, he gives up? There's nothing else left to try, he stops the protest?'

'But he *could* win.'

'It's possible, anything's possible . . .'

She didn't sound very hopeful.

'But at least this way, there's a definite timescale, a recognisable process, an achievable objective, instead of . . .' She threw up her hands. '". . . I'm staying down here till you give in." And he might get enough votes to force whoever won to take the issue more seriously. Then he could come up with his dignity intact, having achieved something.'

'He could do more than that, he could win.'

'Yeah, but you also thought Sunny Jim would have caved in by now, so forgive me if I don't share your optimism.'

'You're not going to bring that up every time now, are you?'

'Oh, how unreasonable of me to mention the minor matter of you encouraging Dad in his ridiculous belief that by burying himself alive he could stop Sunny Jim closing down the factory. That was really helpful – he started cracking up when he realised it wasn't going to happen.'

'Don't you think I feel terrible about that? Don't you think part of the reason I'm doing this is to make it up to him, to get things right this time?'

'Don't you think your desperation to make it up to him might be clouding your judgement?'

He was standing now, pointing his finger at her.

'You think you're the only one who can see what's happening, don't you?'

'I often *do* think that, yes. You know why? Because I've got used to being proved right. You can have your artistic tantrums and your wacky get-rich-quick schemes, secure in the knowledge that you can run to me to bail you out when it all goes wrong. How many times have I done that over the years?'

She glared at him. Dylan squirmed. Christ, she expected an answer.

He said, 'Quite a few times. But, Shauna, believe me, I can do this, I can get Dad elected.'

'And how are you going to do that while you're touring?'

'Oh *that*. I quit. Community theatre is a load of shite. This is my chance. You know, I think this is what I've been searching for for years.'

'I can't believe you're telling me this. You only got your Equity Card a few months ago, now you walk out of a tour before it's half over. Your name will be mud. How in hell are you going to get another job in theatre after this?'

'I don't want another job in bloody theatre.'

'Earth calling Dylan, can you hear me? How are you going to eat?'

'My agent has put me up for a couple of adverts, if I get those I'll be laughing with the repeat fees. I'm going to concentrate on film and TV work from now on.'

'So when are you off to Hollywood, little bro?'

He ground his teeth, he hated it when she called him that. Shauna started slowly turning the ring on her finger again.

'I know what's coming next. How much do you want this time?'

He thrust his hands in his pockets, gazed at his feet. 'Shauna . . .'

'You don't want any money?'

'I do. But it's for Dad, not me. There's a £500 deposit to pay before they'll let you stand.'

Shauna became very still.

'£500?'

'Yes.'

'Dylan, that is a *lot* of money.'

'I don't know who else to ask.'

She crossed her arms and closed her eyes for a few seconds.

'I need it by Friday.'

She laughed. 'Jesus, it gets better.'

'It's just a deposit, you'll get it back when he wins.'

She stared down at the floor, chewing her bottom lip.

'This is the only chance Dad has got, Shauna, and I haven't got that kind of money, I'm out of work right now.'

'Whose fault is that? Dylan, it's not the money – well yes, actually it *is* the money too – but what I'm *really* annoyed about is the fact that you put this to Dad first and *then* came and asked me for the money at the last moment. How can I possibly say no?'

'You can if you want, it's totally up to you.'

She laughed scornfully. '*This is the only chance Dad has got, Shauna.* Oh right, no pressure then. I'm bloody sick up to here of sorting out your problems. I've got my own life, I'm not just here to play surrogate mother to you, do you understand?'

'There's no need to get on your high horse.'

'Yes, there is. I cringe when I hear myself talking to you sometimes. I sound like such a nagging bitch. But I don't know how else to get through to you. Unless I shove something right in your face, you'll laugh it off as a joke. It's time you started taking responsibility for things. I'm not your bloody mother, OK? *Our mother is dead.*'

They looked at each other for a long while, but neither of them could think of anything to say after that. Eventually Shauna turned away, opened her bag and got out her cheque-book.

'Who's it payable to?'

He told her. Both of them were speaking very quietly now.

Dylan said, 'Dad will be so grateful when I tell him about this.'

She looked up from writing the cheque, her face tense and drawn.

'I don't want him to know it's from me.'

'Why not?'

'Because then he'll feel he's sponging off his family. Tell him it's an anonymous donation.'

'Hey! That's exactly my approach, we've got to *create* the impression of widespread support first, even if it means being a bit economical with the truth. Get the bandwagon rolling, and then the public will follow.'

'No, Dylan, that's not what I'm thinking.'

'I don't get you.'

'No, you don't, do you? I've got very ambivalent feelings about this whole idea. It could turn out to be a complete disaster. But if Dad *is* going to do it, then I want to him to feel there are people out there behind him, that he's not on his own – that will allow him to give it his best shot.'

Dylan wanted to ask her to explain what the hell the difference was between what he was saying and what she'd said, because it was bloody well beyond *him*. But he decided not to.

'Just remember that it's Dad who has to face the consequences if your brilliant ideas don't work out, OK?'

'Of course.'

She held out the cheque, but didn't release her grip when Dylan tried to take it.

'This is on condition that he promises that if he loses, then he stops and comes up out of that coffin, understood?'

'Understood.'

Dylan gritted his teeth. 'Thanks, sis.'

She let go of the cheque and Dylan walked over and put it under the clock on the mantelpiece. Shauna said, 'I'm going to talk to Dad now.'

'I'll come with you.'

'No, you won't.'

She closed the door firmly behind her on the way out.

'Hi, Dad.'

'Hi-ya, love.'

He sounded exhausted. He looked old and worn out. Haunted by things he'd found out about himself that he wished he hadn't. Yet slowly but surely he became more animated as he talked about the election idea, even though he kept saying what a ridiculous idea it was. She said, 'Maybe it *is* crazy. Do you want to do it?'

'What else is there left for me to try?'

Shauna couldn't decide if it was excitement or desperation in his eyes.

'Nothing.'

That made him smile. 'Don't hold back now, Shauna, you can give it to me straight.' When she smiled back she looked so like her mother that Aidan could hardly breathe.

'My clients often tell me their that their biggest regrets are not about the things they've done, but those things they haven't done.'

Her words opened him up in the same way the song by The Smiths had. Could he live with the regret of not taking this chance? He knew he couldn't. Not now, not after going this far.

'Shauna, I want to do it.'

She gave him a probing look he couldn't figure out. He felt instinctively it was the kind of look she might give a client.

'And here's your exit strategy – you'll come back up once the election is over, no matter what the result.'

'OK, it's a deal.'

They talked for a few minutes more, then Shauna walked back to her car. Dylan was leaning against it, arms folded, tapping his foot rapidly on the pavement.

'How did it go?'

'He'll do it.'

Dylan threw back his head and clenched his fists.

'Yes!' He flashed her a brilliant smile. 'Come on, let's go for a drink.'

She could tell that he wanted to hug her, start telling her again how amazing this was going to be.

'I've got a headache.'

His face fell.

'Excuse me.'

Reluctantly, he stood aside and she got into her car without another word. It took her about half an hour to drive home. She made a sandwich, then lay in the bath with a large glass of wine, the door open, listening to *A Love Supreme* by John Coltrane. She loved Coltrane, the fiercest player since Charlie Parker, yet also capable of producing music of breathtaking beauty. An intense, restless spirit, obsessively searching for the truth, no matter what the cost. There was a church named after him in San Francisco, where he was worshipped as a saint. Shauna didn't consider herself a religious person, but she found it easy to understand why people might want to view Coltrane as a saint. There were times when listening to his music pulled you back from the gathering darkness, gave you the strength to carry on.

She thought about something one of her clients had told her today. 'The Shouting Place' was the name given to a spot on the Golan Heights where the main town used to be. It was destroyed when Israel seized the Heights from Syria. As people fled in panic, and the border was redrawn, whole families were divided. Every weekend groups of locals would gather on opposite slopes of the valley, about 400 yards apart. Some of the people who went there have not been within touching distance of their loved ones since 1967. They stand on opposite sides of the border and yell at each other through megaphones. *How are things with you? Is our mother all right?* It had struck her client, and Shauna, as a parable for family life. The different members separated by an unbridgeable gulf, yet unable to give up trying to communicate, no matter how difficult and artificial the means. Returning to the same spot over and over, trying somehow to convey everything through polite questions and inconsequential talk. It wore you down, feeling like that. Still, she couldn't give up trying. Sometimes she hated it, this desperate need to do the right thing.

On Friday, after registering Aidan as a candidate, Dylan held a press conference on the steps of the town hall. He'd sent out a press release and made a few calls, and there were a gaggle of local reporters, a crew from HTV and a cable channel. He launched immediately into an appeal for donations.

'My father is the people's candidate and he needs the help of the people if he's going to take on the powers that be. We have no money to run a campaign, not a bean. So I'm asking you, the public, to give whatever you can, no matter how small. I know it's coming up to Christmas but there will be one man who'll be spending Christmas on his own in a coffin under the ground at the bottom of his garden. That's the price he's willing to pay for his principles. It's a high price, I think you'll agree.' He paused, emotion flooding his voice, overcome by his own oratory. 'Please don't forget my father this Christmas. Give him the means to have a fighting chance in this election. Give him the chance to leave that coffin a winner. Thank you.'

The handful of passers-by who'd gathered burst into applause. Man, he was good. The director of that godawful play would slash his wrists in envy if he could see him now, inspiring the gwerin with his off-the-cuff eloquence.

A middle-aged woman put down her two bulging carrier bags, opened her purse, stepped forward and stuffed a fiver into Dylan's hand.

'There you are, love.' She clasped her hand over his, her eyes shining. 'You show them. I'll be voting for your dad.' She started wagging her finger at the building behind them. 'It's about time someone stood up for Crindau. I'm sure he'd do a better job than that bloody shower in there.'

The other onlookers and a couple of the hacks laughed. Dylan was absolutely delighted, it would be a great TV moment; he couldn't wait to see it.

That evening he met Russell, Gwyn and Wilf in the Globe. They were just taking their seats when Frank turned up the telly – they were showing his appeal on the town hall steps on *HTV Reports*. When the woman said her piece everyone in the bar laughed and cheered.

'You tell them, love.'

Gwyn put a bottle of Beck's in front of Dylan, a quizzical expression on his face. 'Do you really think people will give money?'

Dylan reminded him about what they'd just seen.

'Yes, it was great. Look, don't get me wrong, but we'll need a lot more than that.'

'I had no problem getting the £500 for the deposit. I just used my contacts. I put the word out that Aidan was going to stand and . . .' he clicked his fingers '. . . someone came up with the money the same day.'

Russell gave him a searching look. 'Who?'

'I'm not at liberty to disclose that.'

'Go on, we're in the bunker here,' said Gwyn.

'I thought we were in the Globe?'

'Metaphorically-speaking – this is the inner sanctum, we're the campaign team – you can tell *us*.'

'The donor wishes to remain anonymous, and I have to respect that.'

Russell started laughing. 'Who do you think you are, son?'

'I'll tell you who I am. I'm the guy who's just raised £500.'

'£505,' said Wilf.

Russell muttered something under his breath.

'£505 – thank you, Wilf. And that's just the beginning. I'm going to run this campaign in a professional manner and get my dad elected. And being professional means that when you guarantee a donor's anonymity, you don't give their identity away the very next day in the pub.'

He turned from Russell's glare, addressed the others.

'Tomorrow I'm going to go down to the bookies and put money on Aidan to win – and I'd advise you to do the same, while the odds are still good.'

'I think *I* might have a little flutter,' said Wilf.

One of the regulars barged his way into the conversation, stuck a tenner in Dylan's face. 'Here you are mate, this is for your campaign fund.'

'£515!' cried Wilf in delight, licking his finger and marking up an imaginary scorecard.

'Cheers,' Dylan pocketed the note, desperately trying to remember the man's name.

'I was going to get a Christmas present for my brother-in-law. But now I'll tell him I gave the money to a good cause this year instead.'

'What a great gesture,' said Wilf. He held up his pint in salute. 'You should be proud of yourself, Tony, that's the true spirit of Christmas.'

'Yeah . . . and anyway I hate the twat.'

They roared. Russell slapped the table in delight. Tony said, 'So are you going to get a battle bus?'

They gawped at him.

'You want one of those – they're fantastic, mun. I watched this thing on the telly about the Lib-Dems' battle bus, in the last election. It had all mod cons – computers, telly, tea and coffee, a bar, the lot. You could have your bloody holidays in it. It'd be a right laugh, wouldn't it? Cruising through the streets of Crindau in a bloody great battle bus, rolling down the windows and shouting "Vote for Aidan!" through a loudhailer.'

'It would,' said Dylan. 'It'd be great. You going to join us?'

'I might,' said Tony. 'I'll just have to check to see if I've got a window in my diary in January.' He winked at Russell and Russell winked back.

Dylan smiled to himself. Once they started thinking it would be a laugh, it would be easy to get them to do all kinds of things. They were big kids at heart, still locked into some kind of retarded playground relationship. This, he realised, was the key to getting the best out of them, to make out it wasn't really work at all, not letting them stop to think about how uneven the contest would be. These guys were novices, he was the only one with any experience of running an election campaign. Admittedly it wasn't about local politics – he'd been elected Social Secretary in Uni, had stormed it, actually. It had been about having a gob on you, promising cheap booze and the best bands. But the principles were the same. Find a strong message that people liked. Make sure you did things with a bit of style, because the *way* you said things was at least as important as *what* you said. Not that he expected these guys to realise that. He needed their help, but there was only going to be one leader.

It was all happening too fast – a few days ago Aidan hadn't a clue what to do next. Now he was standing for Parliament. He was still struggling to take it all in. On Radio Cymru that night, Rob Fleming began the phone-in programme by playing 'Power to the People' by John Lennon.

'Well, we now have a man in a coffin standing for election here in Crindau – whatever next? Ring in with your thoughts on 01 . . .'

Whatever next indeed. It was unreal.

Could he really win? Was it actually possible that someone like him could become an MP? No, what a joke. He was just a new circus act.

Roll up, roll up, see the clown who wants to be king.

But if everyone thought like that and believed they didn't have any right to try and change things, where would we be now? There'd be no holiday or sick pay, no votes for women, no public libraries, no National Health Service. At one time all those things must have seemed too fantastic to be true. Till someone said, 'Why not? Why shouldn't we have it?' They probably called that person crazy too.

Aidan tried to imagine himself sitting in Westminster. Surrounded by pompous, dead-eyed men in grey suits. What would they make of him?

Excuse me, can you bring me a G and T?

Get it yourself – I'm the Member for Crindau West.

He'd hate it there. He'd be like a fish out of water.

No one's asking you to like it – you'd be there to save people's jobs.

It was too late to change his mind now. There were so many people pinning their hopes on him. The die was cast.

★

Over the weekend some of the nationals picked up on the story. It was good timing, a slow news week before Christmas, and they loved the angle – the man who'll be spending Christmas buried in a coffin in his back garden. People wanted heart-warming stories – the little guy standing up to a big corporation, the loyal son running his father's campaign, a family sticking together, the true spirit of Christmas, all that shite.

Aidan was besieged with requests for interviews and was delighted to be kept so busy. But every now and then the absurdity of the situation assailed him once again. He spent all day lying in a coffin. And how did he fill his time? Talking to the media about what it was like to spend all day in a coffin.

The thing was, no matter what kind of paper it was – local, national, tabloid, broadsheet – or a lifestyle magazine or a radio station, they all asked the same questions. *How do you spend your day? Don't you get bored? Isn't it claustrophobic? Do you get lonely?*

And their favourite, he could tell, there was always a smirk in their voice. *How do you go to the toilet?*

Dylan thought it was fantastic. 'I'm going to really work you hard, Dad. I'm talking ten, twenty interviews a day – are you ready for this?'

To Aidan, work meant making something with your hands, or delivering something that other people had made – something concrete. What he was doing now wasn't work.

His kids lived in a different world. His daughter earnt a living by talking to strangers about their problems. His son wasn't actually earning a living at all, but all he *really* seemed to want to do was talk all day too. Aidan wondered what the future would be like, when everyone talked, made speeches or gave presentations, ran PR companies and wrote press releases all day and there was no one left to actually *make* anything. Where would they turn when they needed something? They'd pay people in India peanuts to make it for them. Now Aidan had joined that world. He'd joined it in order to save proper jobs

that entailed physical labour. It was an even more bizarre thing
to do than burying yourself alive in your garden.

The media asked Dylan how they were going to raise the
money.

'One guy is getting people to sponsor him to walk on all-
fours for a week, another's shaving all his hair off, and there's a
bloke who's going to have a totally dry Christmas and give us all
the money he would have spent on alcohol.'

None of it was true – he'd made it up on the spot – but it
made good copy and would get the ball rolling, encourage
people to join in with their own daft stunts. Sure enough, by
Monday Tony had people sponsoring him not to swear at his
brother-in-law over the Christmas holidays. Another of the
regulars, Strange Eddie, was getting people to sponsor him to
kiss Frank on the lips on Christmas Eve.

No bloody fear.

Come on, Frank, don't be a spoilsport – it's for a good cause.

He's a pervert.

*He's not bad looking though. You never know, it could be the start
of a beautiful friendship.*

Fuck off – you're barred.

By Wednesday, Ivor was delivering over a hundred letters a
day to Aidan, most of them with cheques and cash in them.

'Bloody hell, if this keeps up my back will be knackered.'

It seemed nothing short of a miracle to Aidan that he could
attract such support through an act of sheer desperation. He
soon got to know the ones from pensioners by the spidery hand-
writing on the envelope. They made his heart ache.

Dear Mr Walsh,

*I am writing to say how much I admire your stand. It must take
courage to do what you are doing, and I really hope you succeed
and save your job and the jobs of your workmates. It is about time
someone stood up for the normal man or woman in the street, so*

to speak. In my day, you could be pretty confident that once you got a job, it was yours for life. But there doesn't seem to be any stability nowadays. I was in the same job for forty years, driving a train (I could weep when I look at what Thatcher did to the railway system. Now there was a woman who hated public transport). I always turn up the sound when you are on the TV or the radio – your appearance is quite an event in our house. You come across as a very likeable and sincere person, not at all like the usual type of politician, and I say three cheers for you! You have certainly made the high and mighty sit up and take notice!

I am afraid I can't send you much, but I enclose a postal order for £17.50 and I would like to take this opportunity to wish you the best of luck, and to let you know that my wife Doreen and I and all our friends in Morecambe are rooting for you – we only wish we were registered to vote down there in Crindau!

Yours very sincerely,
George Wilson

P.S. My wife and I spent a summer holiday in Wales in 1979, we found the people very friendly and had a very enjoyable two weeks, despite it raining every day!!

Aidan wondered what George and Doreen had had to give up in order to send him the money. He pictured them in their little house, gazing through rainwashed windows at the grey seaside and struggling to understand the way the world was changing. A world of decent, frail, frightened people who nobody visited or found time to speak to. These were the people who gave, the ones with no money. He received hundreds of letters like this. The ones from people who had been bereaved were the hardest.

My heart goes out to you. I lost my husband ten years ago. I still find myself thinking, 'I must tell Ted about that' and then I remember he's not here anymore.

He vowed to write back to all of them. At least two sides

every time. He told Shauna about it when she came to visit that night.

'You've become a symbol.'

'Oh yeah?'

She was making him uneasy. It was hard enough being himself, let alone being a symbol.

'I feel like a fraud, taking these poor sods' money. I worry that they can't afford it, especially the pensioners.'

'You shouldn't feel bad about it, Dad. They *want* to do it, it makes them feel good.'

'You think so?'

'Definitely, they feel they're able to make a difference. Some of them won't have felt like that for years. Didn't you feel good about yourself when you gave to Live Aid and the miners and Children in Need and all the others?'

He did.

'You wouldn't begrudge them that feeling, would you?'

'No, I suppose not . . .'

She was spot on. He *did* feel better about himself after helping someone else. He understood why people devoted themselves to good causes. Sure, they wanted to help people less fortunate than themselves, but it must have given *their* lives meaning too.

Slowly it began to dawn on him that this was giving *his* life a meaning. Please god he could live up to people's expectations.

Dylan put all the cash, cheques and postal orders people had sent into a carrier bag, went into town and opened an account. Within days they had nearly a thousand quid banked, and there were still two and a half weeks to Christmas – they were motoring.

One morning there was a knock on the door and Dylan opened it to find a smartly-dressed elderly man gazing up at the banner hanging from the front of the house. He looked Dylan up and down in a critical manner, as if trying to decide whether to fine him for his unkempt appearance. He narrowed his eyes.

'You're the son, aren't you?'

He had a clipped Home Counties accent.

'Yes.'

'I've just driven down here from Hereford – came off the M4 at the wrong junction, ended up driving through some godawful hole called Brynglas.'

This was considered a desirable area locally.

He checked his watch. 'I'm going to be late for my meeting in Cardiff now.'

Dylan wondered when he'd get to the point, he was expecting a call from Radio Bristol. The man scowled, reached inside his coat and took out a bundle of banknotes. He stuffed them into Dylan's hands.

'Here's a contribution.'

For once Dylan was at a loss for a reply. His mouth hung open, and he stared at the money.

'Now go and give the Socialists a bloody nose.'

The *Socialists*? Dylan wasn't aware of any Socialists standing in the election. It had been many years since he'd met anyone who'd described themselves as a Socialist. In fact he wouldn't have been surprised if Bill Oddie were to introduce a new BBC series called *Socialist Watch*, promising exciting secret footage of this endangered species. Then the penny dropped – he meant New Labour. Dylan made a heroic effort not to burst out laughing. Christ, what a ridiculous old fart.

'The Socialists, yes, a bad lot altogether. We'll do our best. Thank you, sir, I appreciate this.'

The man nodded curtly. Dylan was longing for him to say, 'Jolly good, carry on' – that would have been the icing on the cake. Instead he pointed up at the banner hanging from the front of the house.

'There is no apostrophe in "jobs", young man.'

'You're right, there isn't. My Dad made that banner, he isn't very –'

'If there's one thing I can't stand it's the greengrocer's apostrophe.'

Dylan was gently rubbing the notes back and forth between his fingers, savouring the gorgeous feeling.

'I'll see to it.'

That seemed to satisfy him. He nodded briskly and got back into his Rover and drove off. Dylan watched him go, fervently hoping he would get lost again and be forced to take a detour through the roughest parts of Crindau, where he'd run out of petrol. He shut the door and stood in the hall, counting the money.

'Two hundred quid – most excellent. Thank you, dude.'

He wouldn't tell his dad about this donation, he'd freak at taking money from a Tory. What he didn't know wouldn't hurt him.

By the middle of the week Ivor couldn't cope under the strain and a van was delivering two mailbags a day to Aidan. The letters came from all over the country and beyond. Christmas cards were arriving from Europe, Australia, and North America. Ivor managed to keep hold of a few of the more exotic ones so he could deliver them by hand. He arrived with a huge grin on his face and handed one over that had come from Canada.

'TA-DA! How's that for service?'

To the man who buried himself alive in his garden to save his job
Wales
England
The UK

'Fantastic work, Ivor.'

Aidan gave him the thumbs up.

But, best of all, better than the wellwishers who sent Christmas cards, the people who sent money, were the offers from women. Some of them enclosed photos. Some of those photos left little to the imagination. The one from the woman who lived in Rotherham was his favourite. Her photo snatched the breath from his lungs, lifted his cock to the heavens. She was completely naked, sprawled on a bed, her hands behind her head, staring into the camera, confident as you like. No wonder – she had a fantastic body. On the back she'd written *I'm waiting for you*. The very ordinariness of the surroundings were what made it so exciting. The radio alarm on the bedside table, the tub of lotion next to it, the pillows and sheets that were almost exactly the same as those in Wilf and Megan's bedroom. It was so obviously real, so unlike the soft-focus studio shots of the porn magazines. Rotherham was what, two, three hours away? He imagined going up there, knocking on her door. She'd open it and gasp. He'd go to say something but she'd smile and put her finger on his lips to close them. They wouldn't need words. They'd kiss each other passionately, tearing at each other's clothes. He'd kick the door closed behind him. They'd go straight upstairs. He'd lift her dress up over her head and fling it on to her bed in one swift movement.

I'm waiting for you. The thought of it drove him crazy. It had been years since he'd been with a woman. He spent hours imagining every detail. Eventually he couldn't stand it any longer. He stuffed the photo back into the envelope and chucked it down to the end of the coffin. He had hundreds of letters to write, he was wasting time. It was probably just a tease. He knew the phone number off by heart.

He was too embarrassed to tell the lads. He didn't want them to think he was boasting, so instead he told them about Angelica, the woman from Texas who wanted to marry him. He showed them the two photos of her that she'd sent with the letter. In one, taken in a photographer's studio, she was smiling demurely, one hand on her cheek, dressed in a pink frock. In the other she was in shorts and a T-shirt, hugging Mickey Mouse in Disneyland, a huge smile on her face.

Why was he telling them? Because he could hardly believe it

himself and their reaction would make it seem more real.

'What do you think?'

Russell peered at the one in Disneyland.

'She could do with going on a diet.'

Gwyn said, 'What did she say in the letter?'

Dear Adrian,

That was a great start . . .

What you are doing really moves me inside of my heart. I sure hope you win back your job. A man without a job is like a dog without a bone, my father always used to say!!

I can really relate to you as I too have suffered personal tragedy in my life. My husband walked out on me and I was left to bring up our daughter and son on my own. I have been unlucky in love ever since and sometimes I think I will never find 'Mr Right'!!!! But when I read about you in the newspaper, and saw your photo (has anyone ever told you that you look a lot like Anthony Hopkins?), I just knew that you were a good man.

I'm a very young at heart forty-eight-year-old, who loves to eat out, watch corny movies that make me cry, and stroll hand in hand through the surf on a deserted beach at sunset. I take great comfort in my faith and believe Our Lord Jesus is guiding my every move. I work as a Checkout Captain — my job is to stand near the tills in a superstore and point out which of them has the shortest queue to people wheeling their trolleys up to pay. I wear a giant plastic hand with a long pointing finger which the kids just love. The pay isn't great, but I get a lot of satisfaction from helping people. My son Dean is the assistant manager of a drive-thru McDonald's in Tallahassee, and my daughter Beth is training to be a dental hygienist in Houston. I believe that Our Lord Jesus is watching over you too, Adrian, and that you have nothing to fear. I know that we haven't even met yet, but I really feel that . . .

If he was *really* honest, she scared the bloody shit out of him.

'She said I looked like Anthony Hopkins.'

Russell bellowed. 'Jesus – she needs glasses too. What a catch.'

Gwyn was smiling, a little guiltily; even Wilf was looking amused. They were pissing him off now.

Russell said, 'Christ – Yanks, what are they like?'

Aidan felt cheap and nasty. He hadn't meant to hold her up to ridicule, it was only meant to be a bit of fun. He was ashamed.

'When you write back, don't forget to sign it Anthony Hopkins.'

Aidan knew exactly what was happening here. They were jealous. He wasn't supposed to enjoy being famous. Why not? A couple of weeks ago he was in bits. Now women were throwing themselves at him. Who wouldn't get excited? They wanted him to carry on being good old Aidan. They hadn't grasped it yet – he could never be the same after this.

On Saturday night, a couple of young women staggered over to Aidan's periscope, giggling. He looked up to see two flushed faces gazing down at him. In their early twenties, both pretty tidy.

They waved. Aidan grinned, waved back. Nothing threw him anymore. Why shouldn't drunken young women come to see him at midnight? The election campaign didn't start until after Christmas and, until then, all he had to do was lie there and see what happened next. They laughed. Stopped laughing. Looked at each other, started all over again. The blonde one leant closer.

'How are you doing down there?'

'All right.'

'I bet you get lonely.'

Aidan shrugged. 'Not really. I get a lot of visitors.'

'Do you get visitors like us?' she pouted.

He smiled broadly. 'No.'

They looked at each other, then they were off again, shrieking with laughter once more. Aidan was enjoying this.

Girls like these would never have talked to him when he was above the ground. Even if they were pissed.

Her mate slung her arm round her shoulder, said, 'Fucking hell, Tina, I'm stonking.' That set Tina off again. Aidan, completely sober, felt the charm of the situation beginning to wear off.

'How long you been down there now?' asked Tina, pushing the other one away, who was threatening to topple her over with her dead weight.

'Four weeks.'

'Fucking hell, I bet you're gagging for it.'

Tina's mate snorted and lurched into her again. 'You dirty bitch.'

'Come on now, girls,' said Aidan. 'That's enough, eh?'

'I wouldn't like to go without it for four weeks, I'd be chewing the bloody carpet, mun.'

'You dirty cow.'

'Christ, how many did I have?'

'I'll bet you're horny as hell.'

'I think you should go home and sleep it off.'

'Here, have a look at these.'

Tina opened her coat, threw it down, started undoing the buttons of her blouse. Aidan felt his cock stirring.

'Bloody hell, Tina, what you doing?'

'I'm gonna give the poor bastard an eyeful.'

'You what?'

'To keep up his morale, like. He's been down there for all that time on his lonesome. Look at the state of him. *Four weeks?* I bet the poor bastard hasn't had it for years, have you, love?'

'Hey!'

'I'm gonna put a smile back on his face.' She was still struggling with her second button. 'Bloody things . . .'

Her mate grinned. 'Me too.'

Oh Jesus.

Joy was staring at them out of her bedroom window.

227

'Oh my god. Ken, wake up. Come and look at this.'

Ken shuffled over to the window.

'Good god.'

'We're living next door to a den of vice.'

'Disgraceful. Utterly disgraceful.'

'I mean that is the limit – hiring strippers. What next?'

Ken gasped. 'She's, she's taking off her – OW!'

He banged his forehead on the glass. Joy pushed him away.

'For god's sake!'

Aidan was hating it, loving it.

'Please don't!'

'You're not . . . gay are you?'

'NO!' shouted Aidan automatically.

Tina had wrestled with her second button till she'd pulled it clean off, then set about undoing the next one. Aidan caught a glimpse of her bra. His prick was trying to burst out of his underpants. Her mate was shrugging off her coat now. She had a bright-orange top on underneath, no buttons. She started lifting it up, baring her midriff. There was a pole holding up Aidan's Y-fronts.

'Mmmmm, yeah baby.'

Tina looked up, saw what she was doing, joined in.

'It feels so fine, baby.'

Aidan didn't want to look, he knew they were taking the piss, but his prick didn't. It was trying to leap out of the coffin and introduce itself. Tina pulled her last button clean off, lifted her blouse free from her skirt, undid her cuffs.

'I want you near me, honey.'

Her mate was pulling her top over her head, got it caught in her earrings. Aidan was now goggling at two bras, one white, one black. *Oh Jesus Christ.* Tina was reaching round behind her back, wiggling suggestively, her lips parted. Aidan was trying to keep his face expressionless, give nothing away. Robert Stack in *The Untouchables.* Shifting from cheek to cheek, taking deep breaths, stretching his toes to relieve some of the tension. Jesus, he *was* gagging for it!

'BABY, BABY, BABY, YEAH!'

'Tina! Hang on, I'm stuck!'

But Tina wasn't listening anymore, she was too carried away with her own performance.

'Here they come – TA-RA!'

She chucked away her bra, giving Aidan a perfect view. Jesus, she must be freezing. His prick was going insane. When he moved and it rubbed against his underpants it was all he could do not to moan out load. Tina leant forward, licking her lips, grabbed her tits, squeezed them.

'Mmmmm.'

She smiled, bit her bottom lip. She was taunting him. The bloody cow. Look away. He did. Heard their giggles, looked again, saw the blonde one laughing at him.

'Go on – look!'

He put his hands over his eyes. It wasn't right. He didn't want this. He hadn't asked for it. The bitches.

'Go away. Just – go away!'

Their shrill laughter rang through the night.

The letters kept coming. They were delivered to the house now, and Dylan would open them, put the cash, cheques and postal orders to one side, ready to take to the bank. He took batches of fifty at a time to Aidan, who would ring him when he was ready for some more.

They weren't all supportive. He got a few aggressive ones.

Dear deluded communist scum,

Who do you think you are, demanding a job for life? Get real, the nanny state has gone forever. Why should the rest of us be expected to carry the likes of you? Is it my fault you didn't pay attention at school and get a few more qualifications so that you couldn't find anything better than a job in a warehouse? I

DON'T THINK SO!!! The government has already bribed this company millions of pounds to open a factory in your godforsaken part of the country, i.e. Wales, or Cymru, as you fanatics laughably expect us to call it. This is the only reason you've got a job in the first place — thanks to our taxes being chucked at your employer. Otherwise you would still be languishing on Benefits, sitting at home all day, stuffing your face with beer and crisps, watching your satellite TV and scratching your scrotum. And now you want more special treatment to make these generous employers stay there, when it is clearly good business sense to move their operation elsewhere, where their costs will be lower (could anyone doubt that hard-working, obedient, grateful Indians would be more efficient than a bunch of bow-legged, inbred, foul-breathed, whining Welshmen?). What makes you think you know better than the managers of this company? They are very clever businessmen, and you are nothing but an ignorant pleb stuck in a time warp. Why can't you get it through your thick skull that such important and complicated financial questions are way beyond your limited mental horizons and leave it to the experts? I advise you to give up this ridiculous protest now and go back to what you do best, i.e., copulating with sheep.

Yours truly,
A hard-working taxpayer

P.S. If your ghastly little town really is going to be made economically unviable by these job losses, then may I suggest a sensible solution? Why not flood the place and turn it into a reservoir. Isn't that what they usually do with Welsh towns past their sell-by date?

It was a new and disturbing feeling to discover that complete strangers hated you. Aidan tried to laugh it off. But the doubt persisted. Because maybe, despite all the insults and taunts, the guy actually had a point? If the government were to help them by pouring money into the town, wouldn't it mean that some other desperate place would then lose out? What about the other Sunny Jim factory in Teesside? He wondered what they made of what was going on in Crindau? Actually, he knew, having read an article about them called 'The Forgotten Town' in the paper the other day. One of the workers was quoted as saying, 'We never get a mention in the media. All you ever hear about is that town in Wales where that chancer buried himself alive. We're in the same boat as them, but no one seems to care. We obviously need to come up with some kind of gimmick in order to get the papers to come up here and write about our problems. Maybe one of us should sit up in a tree and refuse to come down till they keep our factory open.'

Aidan was wracked with guilt after reading that. He could understand the guy's attitude. He would have felt the same. But he couldn't fight their battles too. Nor did he like to think about the effect his protest might have in India. *Would you really deny these people the chance of a future without hunger and disease?* But you could drive yourself mad worrying about stuff like that. If he could figure out all the consequences of every one of his actions in advance, life would be so much easier.

He told Dylan about the letter. He shrugged and said, 'The guy's a crank, forget it.'

He told Shauna. She visited every night.

She said, 'Do you know which are the three happiest countries in Europe?'

'What's that got to do with it?'

She raised a cautionary finger.

'Sweden, Holland and Iceland. All countries with strong welfare states. The people in those places feel more secure, well taken care of, valued. Their lives have some kind of dignity and purpose. You can't be happy or confident if you're constantly worrying about the future.'

She was so sharp. He often thought that she should be the one standing in the election, not him.

'A government will actually *save* money in the end by investing in job creation. Unemployment absolutely guarantees you more crime, alcoholism and drug addiction, marriage break-ups, and kids going off the rails. They then have to pump money into the police force, the probation service, and the health service to cope – god, the millions they must spend on anti-depressants alone. So it ends up costing them ten times as much as it would to do something *positive* and keep jobs in the area. Letting a town go down the chute makes no economic sense at all.'

'So I could be saving the government an absolute fortune if I win.'

'You could.'

She smiled; she looked beautiful.

'Shauna.'

'Yes?'

'You should smile more often.'

The smile disappeared.

'I would, if there was more to smile about.'

Dylan pinned some of the other letters and cards expressing support up on the wall. A Christmas card with Aidan's face pasted over Santa's, JOBS written on Santa's sack. A child's drawing of a stick man lying under the ground, *Save Our Town* scrawled across the top in felt pen. There were poems too.

> *Aidan's in a hole, but so are we!*
> *If our jobs go, don't you see?*
> *So lend a hand to get him out*
> *And when he wins we'll jump and shout!*

> *The people's MP, that's what he'll be!*
> *Safeguarding the interests of you and me*
> *Sunny Jim will be forced to listen when*
> *He takes our case to Number Ten!*

'Ah, the land of Bards,' said Dylan, as he pinned that one up. When reporters came, he'd show them the piles of mail and the cards, poems and letters.

'The support is phenomenal. We're getting so much mail now they have to deliver it by van.'

The hacks would look around, impressed, taking notes. Dylan had had some business cards made up and would hand them one as they left. All these contacts he was making would prove useful when the election was over and he was deciding what to do next. He fancied writing a column, or perhaps having his own radio show: then again he might go into public speaking, or run inspirational seminars – 'You too can move mountains – the art of the impossible' by Dylan Walsh. You had to think ahead. He'd chucked in his acting career to help his dad out, was putting in fourteen- or fifteen-hour days. He'd have been crazy not to look out for himself.

For a change, Russell, Gwyn, Wilf and Dylan were in the Globe. It was 8.30, and getting busy. Carrier bags stuffed with Christmas presents were getting trodden on and knocked over, their contents spilling on to the filthy floor. Strange Eddie stood at the bar with a notebook and pen, grinning as people lined up to sponsor him to kiss Frank, who was ignoring him. 'Fairytale of New York' came on the jukebox for the third time in a row and everyone sang along. A lot of them were half cut already and Dylan could see some would be crying before too long. It was an unbelievably depressing pub.

'This is more like it,' said Russell, nodding at the jukebox. 'If I hear that fucking Slade song one more time I'll go stark, staring mad. I'm telling you, if I met that Noddy Holder and I had a gun on me . . .'

'What if you met him *and* Cliff Richard,' said Gwyn, 'and you only had one bullet?'

'I'll tell you what I like most about Christmas,' said Wilf, who hadn't been listening, and was looking glassy-eyed, 'The cranes.'

'*The cranes?*'

'You know, the way they cover them in lights and put banners up saying Happy Christmas written on them. I think it looks lovely.'

'You're right,' said Gwyn. 'That *is* good.'

'Is that your favourite thing about Christmas then?' asked Wilf.

'No, it's *The Snowman*, I never get sick of that.'

Dylan flicked his beer mat high into the air and caught it; then felt ridiculous about how much pleasure it gave him. What a way to be spending your Friday night, drinking with your dad's mates in their crummy local – what was happening to his life?

'Hang on,' said Russell. 'I haven't said what my favourite thing about Christmas is.'

'Go on then.'

Russell gave them a warning look before he spoke: 'The little kiddies doing their Christmas play in school.'

They didn't expect that. Dylan's spirits sagged. Getting sentimental at Christmas was *de rigueur*.

'I was always at work, but one year I was off sick so I dragged myself out of bed and went. Theresa was playing Mary, and Jason was an angel.'

He paused, took a swig from his pint.

'Things are different now. You see fathers taking their kids to school, picking them up from school. But in those days, let's face it, blokes didn't have too much to do with their kids.'

'No time, was there?'

'But it wasn't just that, was it? You didn't want to be seen fussing and worrying over your kiddies, that was what your wife did – you didn't want people laughing at you.'

'I fussed and worried over mine,' said Wilf.

'Yeah, but it's different for you.'

'What do you mean?'

'You're used to people laughing at you.'

Gwyn snorted with laughter.

Wilf tried to rise above it. 'What about you, Dylan?' he asked. 'What's your favourite thing about Christmas?'

'I used to love helping my mother decorate the Christmas tree – she made angels and reindeer and stars and stuff out of papier mâché, then she painted them. It looked terrific.'

'She was very talented your mam,' said Gwyn, gently laying a hand on Dylan's shoulder.

'Yeah, yeah, she was . . .'

He simply had to get out of there, it was doing his head in. He knocked back his drink and pushed his way to the door. The Globe stood on the edge of a patch of wasteground, and Dylan noticed that a car abandoned behind it a couple of weeks ago was on fire. He began walking across the green to his dad's house. It was bitterly cold, the ground underneath rock hard with frost, the biting wind penetrating his coat. The streetlights shed a sickly yellow glow, illuminating the swings, the rusty climbing frame, a drinking fountain that had never worked. The week after his mother died, a couple of boys from down the road called round for him, asked him out to play. He hardly knew them, they had the frozen look of kids sternly told to be on their very best behaviour by their parents, sent round on a mercy mission. They trudged out silently, no one knowing what to say to each other and started playing on the swings. Dylan couldn't bear the unnatural way they were behaving around him, treating him as if he were made of bloody glass or something, terrified of doing or saying the wrong thing. So he swung higher and higher, standing on the seat, jerking furiously on the chains, till the air rushed in his ears like an angry sea. He felt like he was leaving everything that had happened in the last few weeks far below him, as he soared high into the blue. Till he slipped, flew through the air, crashed to the ground and broke his arm. The next thing he remembered was Aidan running out of the house, shouting like a madman. *What have you done to my son? What have you done to my son?*

The agony as he squeezed Dylan so tight he thought he'd pass out with the pain, trapping his broken arm against his chest. Hot tears fell from Aidan's eyes on to his neck as he kept frantically repeating, 'Dylan, Dylan, son, for fuck's sake talk to me, Jesus Christ say something, I'm begging you.'

He hated the green after that and had never played there again.

The music from the Globe emitted a muffled, melancholy sound behind him. Dylan turned and looked back. It looked like an old rustbucket that had slipped its moorings and was drifting away from the shore. The passengers and crew still partying, blissfully unaware of the danger.

'And no lifeboats on board,' he muttered into the wind.

He pushed open the garden gate. A row of bright blue outdoor lights stood like sentries, leading from the gate to his dad's site. A floodlight on the wall of the house. Christmas lights strung around the poles of the shelter. Russell and the lads had done a good job. The effect was quite theatrical and Dylan wished he could capture it on film. He stood under the shelter, lit a fag.

'Who's there?'

'It's me, Dad.'

'Hi-ya – come here so I can see you.'

Dylan peered down the periscope and gave him a wave.

'What's it like in the Globe?'

'Pretty lively. The lads are in good form – Wilf is drunk already.'

Aidan looked anxious. 'Russell's not giving him a hard time, is he?'

Dylan blew some smoke through his nose. 'Not especially.'

They fell silent for a while.

Dylan said, 'Remember how Mam used to spend ages making things for the Christmas tree? She was brilliant at all that. It's a shame we never bothered much after she died.'

He took a drag from his cigarette, then clutched his collar tightly around his neck.

Aidan said, 'You know sometimes I think I'm doing *this* because . . . it's as if I couldn't save your mother, so I'm trying to save something else. Does that make any sense?'

Dylan took a long look at his dad. He wondered if it was like this for all fathers and sons? You longed for your dad to do or say something unpredictable for once. To dare to be different. Then when he finally did, it made you wonder if you had any idea who he actually was. He turned his face away. 'Listen, Dad, Christmas is only ten days away and the money is still pouring in. We need an extra phone line, computers, Internet access, a photocopier, and a fax. We need leaflets and posters . . . But we've got to make every penny count, get the best deal we can.'

Aidan was mortified that Dylan had utterly ignored his attempt to explain how he felt. But he was determined not to show it and adopted a jaunty tone when he replied.

'I know just the man,' said Aidan.

'Yeah?' said Dylan. 'Who's that?'

'Pancho.'

Aidan rang Pancho the next morning.

'Hey amigo – you do me a great honour. It is not every day that the most famous man in Crindau rings me up.'

'Cut that out.'

'So, what can I do for you?'

Aidan recited Dylan's wish list.

'*Si, si,* some of these items I have in stock, but others I will need to outsource. Christmas is a very busy time for me. My goods are flying off the shelves.'

'How soon can you get them?'

'For you, the next MP for Crindau, I will pull out all the stops.' Pancho burst out laughing. 'Hey – power to the people!'

It was late afternoon and the light was fading. Aidan had just finished an interview with the *Observer* magazine which was running a series on people who were spending their Christmas Day in an unusual way.

His mobile rang again.

'Hi-ya.'

'I fucked your wife.'

Aidan felt the words in his stomach. As if something brutal and ugly had been forced down his throat.

'Years ago. It was in the afternoon. You were at work.'

The man had a low, rasping, sandpaper voice. Aidan imagined it scraping his throat raw as he spoke.

'Who is this?'

As soon as he said it he knew it was the wrong response.

'This is Lover Boy – that's what she always called me. She was gagging for it. You ought to have heard her – "Fuck me, fuck me hard!" We did it in your bed. We did it on the stairs. We did it in your kiddies' room, I came on their sheets. She took it up the arse. She sucked my cock. She couldn't get enough of it.'

'Fuck off!' Aidan cut the call. Dropped the mobile, clawed at his face with his hands.

'Bastard!'

His heart hammering, trying to escape from his chest. He felt suddenly sick.

'Fucking cunt!'

He wanted to smash the guy's face in. But he wasn't there, so he punched the coffin instead. Aidan looked at his knuckles. They were scraped and raw: he'd caught the lid at an angle, blood was seeping through the skin already, like ink through blotting paper. He welcomed the pain. It was easier to take than the turmoil raging in his head, the tightening in his gut. He wanted more of it. He clenched his fist and struck the lid again, harder this time.

He screamed out in pain. Flaps of skin hung off his knuckles. The pain filled his mind, obliterating everything else. For a while.

How could anyone bear to say something like that? It wasn't true. That's all he had to remember to make it lose its power. It just wasn't true. *How can you be sure?* Christ no, the voices were back. *Fuck me, fuck me hard!*

It was in his head now though. The disgusting possibility. Something vile and twisted that hadn't been there before. It happened, of course. People had lovers. Sometimes they went to their graves with secrets like that.

No. If he thought like that, the fecker had won. That's what he wanted, to plant a seed of doubt. Torture him. Well it wasn't going to work. He could see through that one right away. His hands were shaking. He picked up the mobile, called the Globe.

'Frank?'

'Yes, your lordship, what can we do for you? Have you had a dump that you need collecting? Or would you like me to recite our extensive menu?'

'I need a drink – a large brandy.'

There was a pause, Frank re-adjusting to the tone of his voice. When he spoke again, he'd dropped the jokey tone.

'Sure thing, mate, I'll bring it over myself.'

'Thanks.'

He ended the call.

Frank brought a hip flask full of brandy. He took a long, careful look at Aidan as he lowered the basket down.

'Something up?'

'No, I'm OK.'

'Suit yourself. I'll add it to your slate.'

Frank left him to it, he wasn't a bloody counsellor. If a bloke didn't want to talk, just drink, that was fine by him.

Aidan opened the flask, took a deep slug. He began spluttering. It took his breath away, made his eyes water.

'Jesus.'

His mobile rang again. He looked down at it, lying next to him, the sickly green screen flashing importantly – *Answer me! Answer me!* What if it was that pervert again? That's what they

239

did, they kept coming back for more. He grabbed it, switched it off. But though he could switch off his mobile, he couldn't switch off his mind.

He needed to tell someone. But who? He couldn't tell Dylan, it would sicken him. First, finding his mother dead on the floor, then hearing vile obscenities about her. No, Dylan had to be protected from this.

He couldn't tell Shauna. A daughter shouldn't have to hear those kinds of things about her mother.

He didn't want to tell the lads either, he knew very well how they'd react. *The filthy bastard – tell him to go fuck himself.* They'd talk tough, they'd act disgusted. But underneath they'd be embarrassed. Deep down, they'd feel sorry for him. He didn't want their pity. He couldn't cope with it.

There was something else too. They'd think that it said something about him. They wouldn't mean to, but they would. He knew because he felt the same. When you got a call like that, you asked yourself *Why me?* You imagined there must be something about you that stood out, drew these people to you; something weak and shameful, dirty and disgusting that other people managed to hide but you couldn't. They knew.

No, he wouldn't tell his friends. He'd tell no one. He'd banish it to the cellar of his mind and throw away the key. He wasn't going to let it bother him. *Say it.* 'It doesn't bother me. It's just some sicko.' There.

Shauna came to visit him later that evening. She took one look down the periscope and said, 'What's happened?'

'Nothing, I'm just a bit tired.'

'Come on, Dad. You're really upset, what is it?'

'Don't go on, love.'

But she did. She wouldn't let it go.

He closed his eyes, folded his arms across his chest.

'I've had one of those obscene phone calls.'

She didn't looked shocked; she didn't look upset or disgusted.

'Dad, I'm afraid this is what happens once you get in the papers. You attract nutters.'

'It was about Mam. He said horrible things, really vile things . . . I don't want to repeat them.'

'I'm sorry, it must have been awful.'

'It was.'

'What will you do when he rings again?'

He looked at her in alarm. His daughter, this beautiful young woman, so familiar with the workings of sick minds.

She said, 'I'll get you a whistle.'

'Eh?'

'Wear it around your neck. When he rings again, give him a blast. That should put him off.'

What a sick bastard, to make a call like that just a few days before Christmas. The last Christmas he and Eileen spent together had been terrible. If only he could have that time again. He'd come home too late, hours after work had finished. The kids were already in bed, and Eileen was sitting in front of the TV, a furious expression on her face.

'Your dinner's in the oven.'

He opened a can of beer and ate on his own in the kitchen. She came in and stood in front of the table.

'Aidan, talk to me.'

He didn't know what to say. It was no good between them anymore and he didn't understand why. He wasn't her husband any longer. He was someone who shared the house with her and the kids, a machine for working. If he didn't work long hours and take the overtime when it was there, then they couldn't survive. There wasn't any choice. You just got on with it. You did the best for your family. And if your family didn't like it they could lump it.

'I know you're tired, god knows I'm tired too. Can you not think of a word to say to me?'

He couldn't. She lost her temper. She said the kind of things to him that only someone who has loved you once can say. He didn't fight back. He did a Muhammad Ali. The rope-a-dope that Ali used against George Foreman in the Rumble in the Jungle. Hunched up in the corner on the ropes, offering no resistance, letting Foreman punch himself out. He took Eileen's blows and waited for her to run out of steam. He wanted her to stop. He wanted another drink. He wanted it to be just like when they first met, before they had the kids, the bloody mortgage, the blazing rows and the nerve-stretching silences. And if it couldn't be like that again, he didn't want to think about it anymore.

She'd stopped shouting. She looked exhausted, ready to burst into tears.

'Aidan?'

'What?'

'Can we talk about this?'

'About what?'

She folded her arms, and her voice was quiet and under control once more when she spoke.

'About how we never talk anymore.'

If he'd known how to talk to her about how he felt he would have done. He believed so anyway. But blokes didn't talk back then. None that he knew. You didn't talk about how you felt. You didn't wear an earring, use conditioner, or drink expensive continental lager from bottles. You didn't wear boxer shorts, dye your hair or have time off work with stress. You got on with it.

She said, 'It's like talking to a brick wall.'

Maybe it was. But everyone else had their wall around them then and he'd have been a damned fool not to have had his wall up too.

'Aidan.'

'Leave it, will you?'

Eventually she did. He was relieved at first. Then the emptiness began to seep into him, like dampness after you've been soaked through and had to walk all the way home in wet clothes. A cloying dampness that never went away again.

'Leave it, will you?' he'd said.

Eventually she did. She was dead three months later.

On Saturday morning Pancho arrived with a full van. While Russell, Gwyn, Wilf and Dylan unloaded it, he sat in the driver's seat smoking a cheroot. A post office van drew up next to his and Pancho watched the driver haul a sack of mail out of the back and dump it on Aidan's front step.

'POST!'

Dylan came out and casually dragged it inside.

Pancho got out, walked over, asked, 'Is all that for Aidan?'

Dylan nodded, looking pleased with himself. 'Some days we get two.'

Pancho gave a low whistle. This was a very interesting development. He went into the garden to have a word with Aidan. A British TV crew was filming a French journalist talking to a kind of periscope thing sticking out of the ground.

'Would you say you represent the voice of the common man that governments and big business would like to ignore?'

This French woman was pretty cute. Milk-white skin, elfin face with jet black hair cut as short as a boy's. She looked as though she'd stepped straight out of a Sixties' film about a cooky sexpot playing off three or four men against each other during a long, hot summer in Paris. Subtitles and a jazz soundtrack, naturally.

There was an Ordinary Joe standing there too, reading the *Mirror*.

'You waiting to see Aidan?'

The guy looked up from the racing page.

'Yeah, we had a collection for him in my local last night, I've come to drop it off.'

Pancho chewed this over, then nodded at the paper. 'Neddy Seagoon – three to one, the 2.30 at Doncaster.' Pancho winked. 'A cert.'

The French woman was now asking Aidan how he went to

the toilet. Pancho asked the guy reading the *Mirror* how long he'd been there.

The guy checked his watch. 'About ten minutes.'

Enough already. Pancho didn't queue to see clients. He pushed open the garden gate and stepped out into the park. Another TV crew wandered around, interviewing passers-by. Neighbours were coming out of their houses and offering them mugs of tea and plates of biscuits. A group of teenagers were draped around the climbing frame, smoking and trying to draw attention to themselves. Other people were pointing out Aidan's house to each other, as if it were some kind of tourist attraction. A guy stood off to one side, taking photos of the whole scene. Wilf rushed out on to the green.

'There you are – we've finished unloading now. Do you want to come and get your money?'

For once, Pancho didn't snap to attention when money was mentioned. There was a glazed look in his eyes.

'*Dios mio* – something big is happening here.'

'It's great, isn't it?' said Wilf.

Pancho narrowed his eyes, tapped Wilf gently on the chest with his index finger.

'No, *amigo*, I feel obliged to contradict you. It's not great, it's terrible, an absolute scandal.'

Wilf looked startled. 'What do you mean?'

'This place is a tip, there are absolutely no facilities for the public. A totally amateur set-up.'

'But they've come to see Aidan.'

'*Si, si* – but what are they supposed to *do* while they wait?'

Wilf looked around for a clue.

Pancho grinned and wagged his finger excitedly at him, as if he had come up with the perfect answer to a thorny problem.

'You go to see a big match, a concert or film, what's the first thing you do?'

Wilf looked at him blankly. Pancho decided to hurry the

process on by answering himself; he wasn't planning to spend the rest of the morning having this conversation.

'You go for a drink, and get something to eat. You want to treat yourself after a hard's day work. You need something for the kiddies too, to keep them quiet.' He hissed through his teeth. 'I feel sorry for these people. They deserve better than this. They're crying out for decent facilities.'

Wilf looked around, bewildered. 'They are?'

Pancho looked pityingly at Wilf. He put an arm on his shoulder and said, '*Muchacho*, they may not be *saying* anything, but inside, believe me, they are crying. I can hear them.' Pancho's eyes were sparkling now. 'They need help. I have arrived just in time.'

At a quarter to one in the morning Aidan's mobile rang. Prime pervert time. His stomach turned over. He answered with one hand, clutched the whistle he wore around his neck in the other.

'Hi-ya.'

'Your wife sucked . . .'

He stuck the whistle in his mouth. He took a deep breath.

'I came . . .'

He filled his lungs. He blew so hard his ears screamed and his forehead felt as if it was cracking open. Aidan spat out the whistle, started bellowing into the phone, 'How do you like that, you fucking bastard?' But the line was already dead.

A couple of days later a red catering van appeared at the edge of the park. On the side in large white letters it said CHE'S CANTINA. At the hatch were two attractive young blonde women in low tops serving burgers, chips, hot dogs, pasties, pies, teas and coffees (50p extra for Winter Warmers, which included a shot of whisky or brandy), chocolate and soft drinks. Business was brisk.

Pancho dropped by after the lunchtime rush for the takings and to check that they were all right for change.

'How's it going, senoritas?'

He counted the notes as he talked. The taller one, Sian, did all the answering.

'Very slow at first, but we had a couple of TV crews and a van full of Japanese tourists at mid-day and things picked up after that.'

'*Si, si*, it's always the way, a crowd attracts a crowd. What's gone best?'

'The burgers and hot dogs.'

He nodded, pocketing the notes, then wrote some figures down on a pad.

'Any people asking awkward questions?'

'No.'

'You know what to do if the cops or someone from the council starts sniffing around, don't you?'

'Act dumb and get out quick.'

'*Bueno*. You'll go far. Catch you later, haven't even had any lunch yet.'

'Hey, why don't you have one of these?' She scooped up a burger on her spatula.

Pancho scowled. 'Christ, no, they look disgusting.'

Aidan hoped he hadn't left it too late. He'd been meaning to do this for so long. Three in the afternoon on Christmas Eve; would there be anyone left at Sunny Jim? When the switchboard operator eventually answered she sounded like she'd had a couple, and was planning to have a few more.

'I'm putting you through now. Merry Christmas, love.'

'Same to you, love.'

He had butterflies in his stomach. His palms were sweating. He felt like a twelve-year-old.

'Good afternoon, Human Resources, Safina Ahmed speaking.'

'Hi-ya, Safina, it's me –'

'Aidan!'

'You remember me.'

She laughed. 'How could I forget? You're in the newspaper and on the radio every day – everybody here is always talking about you.'

He liked the thought that she couldn't escape him.

'I was beginning to think there was no one left, it took ages for the switchboard to answer.'

'There aren't many, no. Angie went to the pub at lunchtime and never came back. I was just finishing up some paperwork . . . well, that Angie should have done, to be honest.'

Aidan wondered whether anyone had even wished her Merry Christmas.

'I wanted to tell you how sorry I am you had to be the one who delivered that letter to me.'

'I'm glad you rang. I felt horrible about that.'

'There's no need – you had no choice. I wanted to ring you earlier, but I bottled it, I guess.'

'Well, you're ringing me now and I really appreciate it.'

The warmth in her voice made Aidan catch his breath. He closed his eyes, it made it easier to imagine her on the other end of the line. Her mouth. Her eyes on his. His mouth on hers. Suddenly he didn't care about all those letters from women offering themselves to him. That wasn't real. *This* was.

'So – you looking forward to Christmas?'

She told him she was. She didn't sound wild about it though. He asked her what she was doing.

'Same as last year, going to stay with my sister in Bristol. I do enjoy it, especially seeing my nieces and nephews, but families can be a bit . . .'

'Too much.'

'Yeah.' There was a smile in her voice. 'I enjoy getting back to my own house. I've become very fond of my independence.'

Not *too* fond, he hoped.

'What about you? Don't you get lonely?'

'No, not at all.'

247

He didn't want her to think he was a wimp, that he couldn't take it.

'I get people ringing me up for interviews and coming to see me all the time – honest, I haven't got a moment to myself.'

He wasn't going to mention how it felt when he was there on his own, late at night.

'Actually, it's quite festive down here – I've got a miniature plastic Christmas tree, and some tinsel – and you wouldn't believe how many Christmas cards I've had.'

'I know, I read about it. Lucky you.'

Even though it was Safina he was talking to, he wanted everyone up there to think it was a breeze, that he could stick it out for months, that Sunny Jim would never break his spirit.

'I'm quite happy to spend my Christmas on my own down here, to be honest. I can remember some terrible Christmas days in the past. Months of build-up, then come the big day all you do is sit around watching awful TV programmes, stuffing your faces and getting on each other's nerves. This year I'll have my Christmas dinner, then I might read a book, or just think. I spend a lot of time thinking about things these days.'

Women liked thoughtful men. And he *was* thinking about things more now.

'No, I won't miss all that commercial crap. Christmas should be a time for reflection, don't you think?'

Maybe that was laying it on a bit too thick? He didn't want to sound like a bloody vicar. Smug men were a turn-off.

'It should be, you're right.'

'We should spare a thought for people on the streets, or in hospital, or spending their Christmas Day in jail just because they oppose the government.'

'That's a nice attitude.'

'Thanks – you know, I enjoy talking to you.'

There was something good happening between them. He could feel it. And for the first time he allowed himself to think that it might actually be possible to achieve the two things he so desperately wanted: keep the factory open and finally feel like a man again.

9

Aidan woke up on Christmas Day to the sound of the 'Hallelujah Chorus' on the radio, lying on his side, nose pressed against the coffin. He desperately needed to pee. He tried to open his eyes, but they'd been sealed shut with superglue. He hated this. Every morning he felt he was hauling a huge weight up the bloody Himalayas when he tried to move. Every sinew, muscle and joint screamed its resistance. Each new day he asked his body ever so politely to please start working, and it said, *Well, if this is how you're going to treat me, I'm going on strike – fuck you.* It took lengthy and painstaking negotiations to persuade it to move a centimetre. Some mornings it resisted him so fiercely he started to worry he might be paralysed. His right arm and right leg were welded to the bottom of the coffin. He tried raising his head. His head didn't co-operate.

Piss off, I'm staying here.

OK, thought Aidan, let's leave the head where it is for now. He re-thought his strategy. Instead he tried slowly stretching his left arm. His arms weren't so unreasonable. His arms he could do business with. There, that wasn't so bad. He pushed it out horizontally, a robot limb, extending, extending, until his fingers struck the far side of the coffin. Pushing as hard as he could against the side, letting his arm take the strain, Aidan slowly rolled over on to his back.

He lay there for a while, breathing heavily, feeling like he'd been hauled out of a crash, dragged to the side of the road and left. When he'd recovered a little, he opened his eyes and looked upwards. He smiled. Flurries of snow were dancing drunkenly in the darkness above.

Aidan adored snow. He could tell, already, that it wouldn't settle. That in another hour or two it would be gone. But he'd have missed it if he wasn't in the coffin.

This Christmas Day was going to be different to all the others. It was going to mean something. He was going to take stock. It would be a time for reflection and contemplation. Not a drop of alcohol was going to pass his lips.

Now he was ready to open negotiations with his legs.

At eight, Wilf and Megan arrived, wearing Santa hats.

'Happy Christmas.'

They lowered him his breakfast – a bacon butty and a mince pie smothered in brandy cream. Aidan nearly choked when he took a sip of coffee.

Wilf winked. 'We put a shot of whisky in it.'

'Bloody hell, Wilf, more like half a bottle.'

'Go on, get it down you.'

Megan began singing, ''Tis the season to be merry, tra la la la la la la la la.'

Oh well, thought Aidan, why not? He slugged back some more. They insisted he open his presents – a box of miniature spirits and *The Little Book of Inspirational Thoughts*.

Love is like a butterfly – hold on to it too tightly and you will crush it. Don't hold it tightly enough and it escapes from your grasp.

By the time Aidan had finished his flask of coffee, he was humming to himself. The Globe opened at ten. Frank brought him a can of beer at ten past.

'No thanks, mate, it's a bit early for me.'

'Don't give me that – get it down you.'

The buzz from the whisky was wearing off and he was feeling a little down. One wouldn't hurt. He still had the whole day to spend in contemplation. But he kept getting interrupted. Not that he was complaining, but people kept coming through the gate and bringing him presents. Then TV crews arrived and began interviewing them.

'Why did you come here today?'

'I didn't want him to feel he'd been forgotten about on Christmas Day. I think what he's doing is bloody marvellous, like.'

'And what did you give him?'

'Aftershave and a box of miniature spirits.'

Cameras were pointed down the periscope, Aidan gave the thumbs-up, put on a party hat from a Christmas cracker, held up his presents and grinned like a lottery winner. Noted commentator Julian Fanshawe arrived. His late-night series on Radio 4, *Musings*, had a small but devoted following. He wanted to interview Aidan for a future edition.

He must have been pushing sixty, tall, thin and ascetic looking, with receding grey hair. Aidan identifed him straight away as an intellectual. He'd often wondered what it would be like to meet one. He pushed the can of beer out of sight and took off his party hat. Aidan found Fanshawe surprisingly easy to talk to. He had a tremendously posh voice, but a gentle, avuncular manner, nodding encouragingly at whatever Aidan said. If only Safina could see him now.

'You know, Julian, it's strange, but ever since I've buried myself down here, I feel much more part of the community than I ever did before. I might as well have been invisible a few weeks ago; no one outside my family and a few friends had heard of me, and now . . .'

'An interesting paradox,' said Julian. He smiled, as if at some private joke. 'It reminds me of Berkeley.'

'Who's he?'

'He was an eighteenth-century Irish philosopher.'

'Oh, him.'

'His most famous dictum was *Esse est percipi*.

Aidan was struggling now. Julian wore a faraway expression, as if he was performing some complicated equation. Aidan understood that intellectuals were different to normal people but, all the same, he was getting a bit frustrated.

'So what does that mean?'

'It's Latin for "To be is to be perceived."'

'So what are you getting at?'

'Well, I suppose you could say, basically, that Berkeley argued that things only existed when someone paid attention to them.'

'I don't understand.'

'Probably the most famous example is the tree falling in the wood – if it happens miles away from anyone, and no one sees or hears it, how can you really prove that it had actually occurred?'

Aidan thought it was the kind of question that only someone with too much time on their hands could come up with.

'A few weeks ago, you were like that tree falling in the wood. When you cried out in despair at your job being taken away, no one heard it. So no one knew or cared about it. Your dilemma simply did not exist for most people. But now you have succeeded in making others aware of you – you have touched many people's lives. And it's their perception of you, in turn, that is making your life more real and meaningful. *Esse est percipi*.'

Aidan grasped that last bit at least. His life did feel more real and meaningful now – he might as well have been sleepwalking before.

Russell, Gwyn and Wilf arrived at mid-day wearing old-fashioned stripey nightshirts over their ordinary clothes and tea towels wrapped round their heads; they carried staffs in one hand and held plastic pint glasses in the other. When they appeared at the top of Aidan's periscope, he grinned and said, 'Hey! It's the three wise men.'

They'd been in the Globe since ten. Their eyes were bleary, their faces dreamy. They winched down their presents – after-shave and a box of miniature spirits from Russell, a book about The Beatles and a couple of compilation tapes from Gwyn.

By lunchtime the queue to see him stretched out of the garden gate and on to the green. Wilf wandered over to one of the camera crews. He wanted to talk to some of these visitors, to welcome them to Crindau. There was a tall, severe-looking guy holding a boom. Wilf said, 'Where are you from, mate?'

'Slovenia.'

He looked Wilf up and down.

'Is this one of your British traditions?'

'I suppose it is, yeah. So what's Slovenia like?'

The man looked at Wilf more carefully now.

'Worse than you think.'

'Right.'

'But this will help.'

'How's that?'

'Showing the people how life in the West is not as good as they think. That things are so bad in UK that a man is forced to bury himself alive in order to try and save job. Will make them realise how lucky they are. Maybe it will persuade some to stay home and help build our own country.'

Wilf smiled and shook his hand vigorously. 'Glad to be of help.'

Meanwhile Shauna and Dylan were in the living room.

'Thanks, Shauna, you saved my life.'

Shauna had just put a parcel on the table. Dylan had forgotten to get Aidan a Christmas present, not an unexpected development. Shauna had come prepared for this eventuality, bringing a couple of ready-wrapped books.

'What are they?'

'Elmore Leonard,' said Shauna. 'Dad likes him. He hasn't read these two.'

Dylan took her word for it. Shauna handed him a label and a pen. 'There you are. Do you need any help in thinking of a message, or can I leave you to do that on your own?'

'Ha bloody ha.'

*

A little girl stared down the periscope at Aidan. Red hair in plaits, huge doll eyes. She stood on one of the plastic garden chairs, her mother behind her, resting her hands on her shoulders.

'Are you dead?'

'No, I just had a bit of a rough night.'

'But you're buried.'

'That's right.'

She turned her head sideways, trying to gain a wider view down the periscope.

'You *are* in a coffin?'

'I am. But it's comfortable, and I *am* coming up again.'

'Like Jesus. He rose from the dead, and made everything all right again.'

'Millie – let me talk to the man for a minute.'

Her mother eased a disappointed Millie off the chair and pressed her own face to the top of the periscope.

'You'll have to excuse her, she's a little confused. When we went to Mass last week the priest compared what you were doing with Jesus' resurrection, you see.'

'You what?'

'Well, in the sense that he was buried and rose from the dead . . . and he said that when you came back up from your coffin maybe *you* could bring new life to the town.' She smiled apologetically. 'She's been begging to come and see you ever since – five-year-olds don't really understand metaphors.'

'I guess not.'

'And she's having a difficult time at school.' She lowered her voice. 'We think she's being bullied, so it's probably to do with that . . .'

'Mam!'

Millie had clambered up and was pushing her way into Aidan's view. Her mother stood back again. Millie peered intently at Aidan's face.

'You look like him.'

'Who?'

'Jesus. Except in my book, he's got a beard and long hair. And he was a lot younger than you. And he wore these long robe things, that looked like a dressing gown.'

'Mmmm.'

There was a fierce expression on Millie's face now.

'When you rise again, you'll be able to get your own back on all the unbelievers, and the baddies, and the bullies. Well, you can forgive *some* of them, but I've got a list of names of people who *don't* deserve to be forgiven. If I tell you who they are, will you smite them?'

'Look, Millie, I'm sorry to disappoint you, but I'm not Jesus. My name is Aidan, and I'm just trying to save people's jobs.'

Millie looked indignant. Her mother winced, then said, 'Millie, why don't you tell him about the cow?'

Millie's face brightened once more. 'We've been collecting money so that the school can buy a cow for a village in Uganda. Then they'll be able to have milk and cheese like us.'

'That's nice. Do you know where Uganda is?'

'Near Aberystwyth. The cow's called Daisy. And you *are* Jesus, I can tell.'

Aidan smiled in what he hoped was a gentle, wise, and all-knowing way.

As they came out into the garden, Shauna said, 'Look at this – we're going to have to queue up to see our own father.'

Dylan, standing next to her, said '*Now* will you believe we can do it?'

The visitors kept coming. A minibus drew up outside Aidan's house, 'The Llandevenny Male Voice Choir' emblazoned on the side. Sixteen men piled out, dressed in bright red blazers, black bow ties, white shirts and black trousers. None of them looked under fifty; most were balding or grey haired; several moved rather stiffly. They looked like the last survivors of some desperate campaign, who had spruced themselves up for a final, poignant reunion. Yet despite the incongruous setting, there was something wonderfully dignified about them. People smiled as they marched smartly into Aidan's garden. The conductor walked to the head of the queue and asked if he could butt in and have a quick word.

'I'll only be a minute, I promise. Lovely, thank you, madam.'

He looked down the periscope at Aidan.

'Merry Christmas, Mr Walsh. My name is Emyr Hughes, leader of the Llandevenny Male Voice Choir. We have to come to salute your magnificent stand and to sing for you on this rather overcast Christmas morning, as an act of support and solidarity.'

Aidan loved listening to him speak. The deep baritone, the impeccable pronunciation of each syllable in his Valleys accent. The pride and sincerity in what he was doing.

'And we'd like to give you this small gift.'

Emyr put a miner's lamp into the basket and lowered it down. Bloody hell, thought Aidan, as he clutched the beautifully-crafted brass relic of a now mythical era in his hands, I don't deserve this.

'Thank you.'

Emyr said, 'We'll get on with it then – we're booked for the Cadogan Hall in Caerphilly at two, but we voted unanimously to come here first.'

They lined up close to the periscope, Emyr herding them into place with military precision.

'Come on now, boys, squeeze up, don't be shy.'

He mouthed something silently to them, face taut with concentration, then made an elegant gesture with his hands and they launched into 'Cwm Rhondda'. Aidan, already fairly sozzled, felt the tears welling up almost immediately. The power of their voices was astonishing. As they soared into the chorus he felt his stomach lurch the way it did when a plane first lifted from the runway. Their singing was beautiful, uplifting, and sad all at once. When he was a teenager he'd thought male voice choirs were totally naff. A load of short-haired blokes in black slacks and smart red blazers from British Home Stores, chests puffed out singing 'Bread of Heaven' on *Songs of Praise* – please. Aidan had preferred The Who, Led Zeppelin, Deep Purple, Jimi Hendrix. But now, standing there above him in his garden on Christmas Day, singing so powerfully, he felt like he'd lost something very precious. He wasn't quite sure what, exactly, but he knew that its loss diminished him. He thought this kind of music would always be there, no matter what. But it was fading away, like the places these men came from. He admired their struggle to keep the tradition going when everything was falling to pieces around them up there in the Valleys. Jesus, he was going to start bawling if he wasn't careful.

They sang 'My Little Welsh Home', 'Land of My Fathers', 'We'll Keep a Welcome', 'Men of Harlech', and 'Ar Hyd Y Nos'.

'Which you might know better as "All Through the Night".'

Which Aidan had always hated, till now. He wiped away the tears running down his cheeks and swore that he would learn Welsh when he got out of the coffin. It was an absolute disgrace to be so ignorant of the language. He would join a choir too and fully embrace his heritage.

The TV crews, meanwhile, were ecstatic, jostling each other for prime position – this was a shoe-in for the main bulletin; Wales in a nutshell.

While this was taking place Julian Fanshawe sat on the edge of the climbing frame out on the green, speaking into a microphone.

'What does it mean to bury yourself? Aidan Walsh has *literally* buried himself, in the hope that by simulating his death he might save his job, and the jobs of others, and, in the long term, the future wellbeing of his community. Is it not reminiscent of *The Golden Bough*, where a human being or animal is sacrificed to the gods in order to guarantee future prosperity? How curious that we have come full cycle and finally returned to the ancient traditions of our ancestors at the end of the industrial age.'

Julian pursed his lips, gazed at the glowering sky.

'But isn't it true that we all bury ourselves regularly in different ways? We let our worries pile on top of us, and say we'd be better off dead. We talk of burying ourselves in our work. When we are fast asleep and cannot be woken, it is said of us that we are "dead to the world", a phrase tinged with envy, as if the sleeper had been transported to some blissful place devoid of all worry and responsibility.'

Julian paused and frowned.

'How extraordinary – I can hear the sound of a male voice choir. If I didn't know better, I'd swear it was coming from Aidan's garden. Funny how the mind can play tricks on you.'

The three wise men were enjoying the choir.

'They're great, aren't they?'

'Yeah, they are, bloody marvellous.'

'It's great being Welsh, isn't it?'

'Yeah, it's lovely.'

Happily soused, they were starting to sway gently.

'It's much better than being English.'

'Oh definitely. The English haven't got anything like this.'

Russell nodded agreement.

'They'd kill for this kind of thing, mun. What have *they* got, the English?'

Gwyn gave the question some serious thought. He tried to adjust his headgear, but sent it sliding off to one side. He decided it could stay there.

' "Swing Low Sweet Chariot",' he said eventually.

'What a dirge,' said Russell. 'That'd soon put the mockers on your party. It's not even an English song – it comes from Jamaica or somewhere. That's typical that is, they're always pinching stuff from other countries and making out it's their own.'

Gwyn said, 'Like us with rugby, you mean?'

'Don't try and be clever – no one likes a smartarse. No, they haven't got anything they can call their own, except that, you know, thing they sing at football matches . . . Engerlaaaand!'

Wilf nudged him. 'Hey, cut that out. People are staring.'

'No, I wouldn't want to be English, being Welsh is at least as good as being Scottish. It's *almost* as good as being Irish.'

'Definitely.'

'That's right, it *means* something.'

'What's that then?' said Wilf.

'Eh?'

'What does it mean?' He was looking at Russell with genuine puzzlement. 'I mean, how would you sum it up, you know? What is it that makes us so different?'

Russell narrowed his eyes at Wilf, then realised he wasn't taking the piss. He thumped his chest. 'You *can't* explain it, mun – you *feel* it in here.'

This seemed a poetic and profound statement to Wilf. He resolved to consider it at length, but the garden gate was jammed open now, and something out on the green caught his attention. 'Here, what's that bloke over there up to? He's sat out there talking to himself.'

'But in a strange way,' said Julian, 'Aidan Walsh has created a very special space where he is neither alive nor dead, but somewhere in between. He is buried under the earth, in a coffin, yet he continues to speak to us. Indeed, people flock to see him, like some latter day Oracle. I have watched them, these believers, on this cold Christmas morning, with almost unbearably intense expressions of longing, line up to speak to this man who is dead yet not dead. This man with one foot in the grave, one in the living world. So what is it that so fascinates them? He holds out the promise of rebirth, of rising again, of starting anew. The second chance that we all long for. Proof that we do not have to accept our fate – even the fate decreed to us by market forces, as powerful now as the gods were to the ancients. That we can, indeed, shape our own destiny. And proof that maybe, after all, only a gossamer thread separates this world from the other. That thread could snap at any moment. Which perhaps helps explain why people are so fascinated by this very unusual protest. This is Julian Fanshawe, in south Wales, on Christmas Day.'

He switched off the microphone as he noticed a man dressed as a pantomime Arab, swaying slightly.

'Are you all right?'

Wilf said, 'You *can't* explain it.' He thumped his chest and nearly fell over. 'You *feel* it in here.'

Then he burst into tears. This really was a most extraordinary place.

Aidan listened to the pips on Crindau FM signalling that it was midnight and, for the first time in many years, didn't breathe a huge sigh of relief that Christmas was over. It had been some day. He was drunk and exhausted, but had enough good memories stored away to keep him going for weeks. The things Julian had said made Aidan feel uncomfortable and out of his depth. But now he was finally alone he felt able to savour them. He'd memorised the Latin phrase that he'd used and quietly recited it to himself: *Esse est percipi*. There was something very comforting about it. Maybe it was the Latin that did it. Aidan remembered how soothing he used to find the priest's recital of Latin phrases, mingled with the sweet smell of incense and the sound of the altar boy ringing the bell. *Esse est percipi*. He repeated it over and over, till he felt his eyelids begin to droop and his head rolled softly to one side.

The next night Aidan was listening to *All Through the Night With Myfanwy Bassey* on Crindau FM. He never missed a show – that woman had the sultriest voice in Crindau. She'd just finished playing 'Midnight at the Oasis' by Maria Muldaur and, boy, thought Aidan, he certainly wouldn't mind tying his camel next to hers.

'That is such a sexy song,' said Myfanwy breathlessly. Aidan pictured her hunched over the microphone, wearing something flimsy and revealing. He wondered where she hung out when she wasn't at work. He imagined her in a smoky jazz club, an enigmatic smile on her face, though he didn't know of any jazz clubs in Crindau. His mobile started ringing. He reached for his torch. Twenty to two. It might be a journalist ringing from abroad, somewhere a few hours behind Britain. Aidan picked up the mobile, answered.

'Hi-ya.'

'I know where you are.'

It was someone he didn't know. Someone he didn't like the sound of.

'Who's this?'

'Number 27 – you can't miss it, it's lit up like a runway at the back, and there's that big sign hanging from the front.'

The guy spoke very slowly and quietly.

'Very thoughtful of you to let everyone know exactly where to find you.'

He paused, and Aidan heard him step into a puddle. He was outside, on the move. Heading this way. Aidan felt a chill run through him.

'I'll probably come in the back way though – you know – over the green, past the Globe, the swings, and the drinking fountain. No chance of being seen if I come from that direction.'

'All right, mate,' said Aidan, trying to steady the tremor in his voice. 'What's this about? Because I'm ready to hang up.'

'We've got a terrible arson problem in Crindau. You must have read about it in the paper.'

He paused, let that hang in the air. Aidan was scared now. He didn't want to say anything in case the guy heard the fear in his voice. He waited. But the guy waited longer.

'What are you getting at?'

'The Crown, that pub on Coomassie Street that burnt down last month – that was me.'

Aidan's mind was accelerating, searching frantically for a way out of this.

'The old warehouse on Newton Lane – that was me too. That was an eyesore. I was doing a public service getting rid of that. Now you, you're always shooting your mouth off. It's really getting on my nerves – I think shutting you up would be another public service.'

Aidan felt his throat constrict. You couldn't imagine this guy ever raising his voice. You'd walk past him in the street without batting an eye. There'd be nothing out of the ordinary about his appearance. He'd be neat and tidy. He'd live on his own. Afterwards, his neighbours would say, 'I hardly ever spoke to him. He kept himself to himself.' No one would be able to understand what had driven him to do it.

'You're a sitting duck, aren't you? All it will take is a small can of petrol – then just a single match chucked into that coffin of yours.'

Aidan's insides turned to hot mush.

'Whumpf! There'll be quite a blaze.'

'DON'T!'

The guy laughed. Aidan had just made his day.

'I'm on my way.'

'WAIT!'

The line went dead.

For a few seconds Aidan was paralysed with fear. Then he began to tremble violently. Where had he rung from? The other end of town? The end of the road? How long had he got? He needed help. Now. The mobile was still in his hand. He rang the phone in the house. Tried to.

'Fuck!'

His fingers wouldn't obey him any more. They stabbed wildly at the infuriatingly small numbers.

'Fuck fuck fuck!'

He squeezed his eyes shut, rammed his head against the coffin. *Come on*. He gulped in air. Filled his lungs to bursting.

Started dialling again, slower this time. Got it right. It began to ring.

'Come on, come on, answer the bloody phone.'

Dylan might still be up. He liked to wind down by drinking in front of the telly. Please god don't let him have it turned up so loud he couldn't hear the phone. It rang and rang. Aidan felt the sweat trickling down his forehead. Running down his back. Breathing was agony. He'd had pleurisy once and that was how it felt. Every breath a razor blade scraping the insides of his lungs.

It was still ringing. Dylan had gone to bed. He was asleep in the chair. He was wearing his Walkman. Aidan began shouting.

'DYLAN! DYLAN! WAKE UP!'

A sob caught in his throat. But no, stop. The shouting was making him panic even more. It was hopeless.

Russell.

He counted ten, fifteen rings. Russell wouldn't let him down. He wasn't going to answer it straight away, not at nearly two in the morning. He had to give him time. Twenty rings, twenty-five.

'ANSWER THE FUCKING PHONE.'

He started slamming his fist against the lid. Beating out a rhythm while he yelled.

'ANSWER IT, ANSWER IT, ANSWER IT, ANSWER IT . . .'

He screwed up his face. He clawed at his hair. He was going to die. A very horrible death. Burnt alive, trapped in a box under the ground, screaming himself hoarse in the dark. How long before someone heard his screams? It would be too late, however long it was.

'Who is it?'

Aidan felt his bones crumble at the sound of Russell's voice. All he could manage in reply was a tortured gasp. Tears and snot oozed into his mouth, scoring a bitter trail down the back of his throat.

'Who the fuck's this?'

Aidan began to whimper.

'All right, that's it, I'm putting the phone down.'

'NO!'

'Aidan?'

'Yes.'

'Do you know what fucking time it is?'

'A bloke's just rung me up – he says he's on his way with a can of petrol – he's going to set fire to me. For fuck's sake, mun, help me.'

'What the fuck . . .'

'Help me.'

'I'm on my way. Call the cops for fuck's sake.'

Aidan's legs were shaking uncontrollably. His breathing shrieked in his ears. He sounded like a big old dog dying at the side of the road. Somehow he managed to make his fingers respond one more time and dialled the police. The operator asked him which service he wanted.

'Someone's trying to kill me.'

He was connected. He begged them to come quickly – the guy was on his way.

'What's your address, sir?'

Aidan reminded them he wasn't in the house, but in a coffin under the ground in his garden.

'I beg your pardon?'

'I'm in a coffin . . .'

'You're that bloke, aren't you?'

'Yes – I'm that bloke. For god's sake, hurry.'

He tried his home number again. He let it ring and ring. He shouted into the darkness.

'DYLAN! DYLAN!'

There was a noise out on the green.

'WHO'S THERE?'

No reply. Where were they now, all those people who came and told him about their problems? Where were they when he needed them?

'WAKE UP! SOMEONE'S TRYING TO KILL ME! HELP ME! HELP!'

If he kept bellowing, somebody would hear him eventually. He pulled off his T-shirt. He poured his bottle of water over it. He held it, soaked now, in his shaking hand. If the guy poured petrol down he'd protect himself with his sopping wet T-shirt. It would soak up the petrol, make it harder to light. He'd use it to catch the match, snuffing it out. No, that would never work. What else was there? Where was Russell? Where were the cops?

I'm on my way. He could be there already, lurking in the shadows, toying with him. Leaving it till the last moment, waiting till he heard the first signs of help coming before he made his move, dropped the match, ran away.

Aidan's throat was raw from shouting. What was wrong with everyone? He was making enough noise to wake the dead. No, his voice wasn't carrying. He was six feet under. People had to stand by the periscope to hear him talk.

A car. *Come on, come on.* Someone driving like a maniac. The engine screaming its resistance. The screeching of tyres, then a loud bang as it struck something – the wall at the front of his house. Aidan put his hands to his mouth and yelled, 'RUSSELL!'

Aidan heard a grunt as he vaulted the garden wall. The heavy thuds as he landed and ran to the periscope. Russell's face appeared, flushed, mad-eyed. Still in his pyjamas. Blue-and-white stripey ones.

'You OK?'

'I'm OK.'

'Thank Christ for that.'

He held up a carving knife.

'Let him come – I'll fucking run the cunt through.'

Aidan couldn't speak anymore. Felt as if he might throw up. He was shaking uncontrollably now, his teeth chattering. He didn't want to cry. Not in front of Russell. Now now, after all these years of managing to hold it back. Didn't want everyone talking about it in The Globe. He started crying.

'It's all right, mate. It's over, you're safe now. No one will touch you – they'll have to get past me first. I'll fucking kill any bastard that tries to hurt you. I'll run them through first and ask questions later, I swear to god.'

Aidan desperately tried to say something, but only a strange gurgling noise came from his mouth. Russell turned away when he saw Aidan gaping frantically like a stranded fish, his eyes swimming with tears. He didn't want to see that. They heard a police siren.

'About bloody time, what's wrong with them?'

Aidan realised that Russell was talking so much to cover his sobs. What if he hadn't answered the phone? What if his car hadn't started? It didn't bear thinking about.

They arrested a man half an hour later. Found petrol, press clippings about arson attacks and a whole scrapbook of cuttings about Aidan in his flat. To be on the safe side, they left a couple of coppers in Aidan's garden overnight.

Dylan was horrified, disbelieving. Shauna took control.

'We're going to hire a security guard.'

There was enough money in the campaign fund for that. She hired a man to guard Aidan from eight at night to eight in the morning. He had been in the army, was enormous and dangerous-looking. You wouldn't want to try and stare him down.

'And they caught the guy,' she reminded Aidan.

But Aidan was badly shaken. If Russell had got there five minutes later, who knows what might have happened?

'Who is this guy? What does he have against me?'

Letters from cranks was one thing, but *this*.

'He's probably psychotic, Dad.'

That didn't help.

'Try not to ask questions like that, Dad. Try and remember that he's just someone with mental health problems. You're safe now. It could have happened anywhere. Everyone is absolutely horrified.'

It was true. The attack provoked massive publicity, and sympathy. There was a policeman outside his gate all day now, and the security guard in the evening. Apart from this maniac, no one wanted to see Crindau's most famous man harmed.

Aidan lay in his coffin, contemplating the horrific events of the previous night. He'd always imagined having time to put things in order before he finally snuffed it. Make his peace with the world. But last night he'd been jolted out of that cosy precon-ception. He could have left this earth very suddenly, without any warning. Without having achieved anything worthwhile or saying goodbye to his loved ones. It had set him thinking. It was time he took a long hard look at himself. Then he saw some-thing in the *News In Brief* section that caught his eye.

Three Simple Words

Psychologists have discovered that simply saying 'I love you' to someone reduces their stress, and yours, by sixty per cent. One of the researchers said 'Poets have known for centuries that nothing makes life worth living more than love. But now it's been scientifically proven.'

He felt the tears welling up. It was that easy. Why wait? Aidan picked up his mobile and rang Shauna. Got her voicemail.

'Shauna, this is Dad. Listen, I just wanted to tell you that I love you.' He paused. It felt so good, he decided to say it again. 'I do, Shauna, I really love you. I'm sorry I haven't told you for such a long time. But I do.'

It worked. He felt fantastic. He rang Dylan next.

'Dylan Walsh, campaign manager, how can I help you?'

'I love you.'

'Eh?'

'I know we're in the middle of the campaign, and you're very busy, but I just wanted you to know how much I care about you.'

'Er, right . . .'

'So . . . I love you. Bye, son.'

He was floating on air. He should have done this years ago.

That evening Russell dropped by. His dearest friend, the man who'd saved his life.

'Hi-ya, anyone in?'

'I love you.'

Russell's face drained of colour.

'*What the fuck?*'

'I'm just telling you how I feel.'

Russell's eyes narrowed.

'Are you all right?'

'Yes, I am. I feel much better for that.'

'I don't.'

'I'm not asking you to say you love *me* or anything like that. I just want you to know that . . .'

'You look weird. You *sound* weird.'

'Why is it weird to tell your friends how you feel?'

Russell stared at him for a while without speaking, then shook his head in disgust and left. It was probably something to do with being cooped up on your own for too long. He'd best warn the others about this unnerving new development.

I love you.

He shuddered at the memory. He needed a pint – quickly.

10

The campaign was under way. Dylan had taped a sign to Aidan's living-room door.

The three-piece suite had been pushed into the hall and stacked up against the wall, a shower of coins, biscuit crumbs, buttons and furry sweets had cascaded out when they put the sofa on its end. Now a dozen volunteers sat at a couple of trestle tables, stuffing leaflets into envelopes. Across the top of the leaflets was the slogan PUT HIM IN TO GET HIM OUT. Underneath a photo of Aidan peering out of his coffin.

Save our jobs. Save our town. Vote for the local candidate.
'A remarkable man, I think you'll agree'
– Huw Humphreys, ITV Wales.

'It's funny, isn't it? Seeing Aidan's photo on all these,' said Wilf.

Russell replied sourly, 'The novelty wore off after the first couple of hundred, to be honest with you.'

Dylan had also taped a sign to the door of Aidan's front room.

DYLAN WALSH, CAMPAIGN MANAGER

That pissed Russell off.

'He's got his own office, while the rest of us are packed in here like bloody sardines.'

Dylan's office had a desk, PC, fax, phone, scanner and photocopier, a coffee machine, radio and TV.

The phone in the hall had been ringing all morning. Gwyn got up to answer it this time.

'I'm sorry, the campaign manager isn't here right now – can I take a message? No, I don't know where he is, I'm afraid. But I'll ask him to ring you back when he gets in.'

Gwyn wrote a few lines down on the pad next to the phone, came back into the living room. 'Another call for Peter

Mandelson?' Gwyn nodded. A few minutes later they heard the front door opening. Dylan bounded in and aimed a video camera at them.

'Here we are at the nerve centre of the campaign,' he said, walking round the trestle tables. 'And this is our election team, the unsung heroes who come in and work for hours stuffing envelopes, taking calls, pounding the streets. I don't know what I'd do without them.' He came to a halt. 'This is Wilf. Say hello, Wilf.'

Wilf smiled shyly.

'Hi-ya.'

'This is Gwyn.'

Gwyn winked, gave a V for Victory sign. 'Where did you get that?'

'The BBC in Cardiff – that's where I've been this morning, pitching them my idea. They loved the concept of a video diary about the campaign – it'll probably go out in the summer. Primetime on BBC1 hopefully.'

He pointed it to Gwyn's right.

'And that's Russell.'

Russell glowered at him and said, 'How about giving us a hand?'

'Ha ha, Russell's a real character, aren't you, Russell?' Dylan moved swiftly on. 'And over here we have Helen – how's it going, Helen?'

Helen, a retired schoolteacher, smiled shyly and muttered something inaudible.

Russell shouted, 'Why don't you make yourself useful and stuff some envelopes?'

Dylan winced; he'd edit that bit out later.

'I've got to go and film a vox-pop in the town centre, I'll be back later.'

'What's a vox-pop?' asked Wilf.

'It's where I ask a random selection of the public what they think of Aidan's campaign, and whether they'll be voting for him.'

'Tell you what,' said Russell. 'I'll do that for you, while you take a turn here, stuffing envelopes.'

'Very funny.'

'No, I mean it.'

'It's not that easy. You have to know how to work this.'

'I bet I could learn in five minutes. I've used a video. Come on, let's have a dekko.'

'It's not that easy getting good interviews, I'm a trained journalist, I've done it before – you haven't.'

Russell gave him a withering stare.

'OK, I'll film you stuffing envelopes then.'

The bloody great ox had ruined the sequence. He'd do it again, when Russell wasn't there.

Gwyn said, 'There are lots of people waiting for you to ring them back, Dylan.'

Just when he was getting into his stride. He noticed everyone staring at him and lowered the video.

'Yeah, I'm glad you reminded me.'

He went and checked the pad.

Lots of the people Dylan had to ring back were individuals offering to help. One, a middle-aged woman, tried to give him a lesson in politics.

'Are you quite ready for this? It's going to be a bumpy ride.'

He didn't like her tone.

'What are you getting at?'

'You've annoyed the party – Crindau West is a very safe seat you know.'

'We're aware of that, thanks.'

'Look, don't be offended, I'd like to help.'

'What kind of help?'

'Advice.'

Dylan was at his desk, his PC in front of him. He noticed he had a new email.

'Right, well thanks all the same, but . . .'

'Believe me, you need it. I've been a Labour Party member for over twenty years, I knew Dai Rogers well, I worked on all his election campaigns. I know how the party machine works. What experience have *you* got?'

Dylan didn't like that. Hadn't he been doing an absolutely terrific job?

'Look, your dad is very popular – people identify with him, everyone round here is wondering if their job is safe, what the future holds. New Labour know they can't attack what he stands for, it's too popular with the voters, so they're going to try and catch him out on his lack of experience, and generate doubt in people's minds. They'll do their best to get him to take part in a debate with the other candidates – you've got to say no. If he goes head to head with Watkins he'll get torn apart.'

'What makes you so sure? I'd say my dad is a media natural.'

'What's his position on Objective One status?'

'What the hell's that?'

'Do you actually *have* any interest in politics?'

He sighed heavily.

'That's pretty basic stuff. If you can't even answer *that* then it sounds like they don't need the Awkward Squad at all.'

'What the hell is the Awkward Squad?'

'They research questions to chuck at people like your dad – that's what they call them in the office.'

'The bastards.' Something occurred to him. 'Does Watkins know the answers to these questions?'

'He will once they tell him – it'll be his homework to learn them. Then, after your father has been caught out, Watkins will reel them off with a big smile on his face and people will think –'

'Dad's a stupid prole and their man is a professional.'

'Exactly.'

'That's pretty low.'

There was an exasperated sound on the other end of the line.

'I've seen you on TV, you're confident and charismatic.

272

That's good, but sometimes too much confidence can be a weakness.'

'What do you mean?'

'Voters can change their minds very quickly, sometimes on a complete whim. One day the candidate wears a shirt just like the one their boss wears. They hate their boss, he makes their life hell, and they start to feel that if *this* bloke wins, it'll be just like having their boss as their MP. So they switch their vote. Or they notice for the first time on the last day of the campaign he has a bald patch and feel the fact that they haven't noticed it before proves he was desperately trying to cover it up – and if he's covering that up, what *else* is he covering up? They switch their vote to the other bloke – and so on. Right now your dad is the little guy with the guts to take on the big hitters, but one day, for some reason, they might suddenly decide that he's too cocky. Or uneducated – you'd be amazed how down working-class voters can be on someone from a similar background to themselves – "He'll show us up, he won't know how to behave in Parliament." And they'll vote for the bloke who's been playing the straight bat. You understand what I'm saying?'

'I see.'

'Don't confuse popularity with voting intentions – there's still a long way to go.'

'Tell me, why are you doing this?'

'Because of Dai. I'll tell you something – usually when you see a public figure up close it's very disillusioning. But not Dai.' She paused, a slight tremor in her voice. 'The more I saw of him, the more I admired him, he was a lovely man. Oh yes, he had a temper and he liked a drink, what people said about him is true – he was no saint. But if you had any problem, no matter how small, no matter how busy he was, Dai would make time to see you. He *hated* letting people down. This lot in charge now, they couldn't stand him. He didn't fit the image. He wasn't smooth enough. They don't like people who can think for themselves.'

Dylan felt sorry for her – she sounded so hurt and bitter. He'd never be stupid enough to put his faith in any party. As far as he was concerned, it showed a terrible lack of imagination.

'You only have to look at the way they rigged the selection process. It happens all the time, anyone with a hint of a personality is frozen out.'

'This Watkins guy, what's he like?'

'He's probably not a *bad* man. But he's happy to toe the line. He'd never give it to you straight like Dai.' She started chuckling. 'This journalist came to the Labour Club once. He said to Dai, "Do you know, this is the first Labour Club I've been to where there isn't a photo of Tony Blair on the wall." So Dai says, "We had to take it down, it was too near the dartboard." The journalist says "Why didn't you just move the photo?" And Dai said, "Wherever we moved the photo, it was too near the dartboard." '

She burst out laughing, and Dylan laughed with her. When she spoke again, she sounded terribly sad and worn down. 'Dai would have liked your dad. He'd have admired his guts. I'd like to think he'd carry on the tradition of being that awkward so and so in Crindau West who never takes no for an answer. Good luck.'

Dylan put down the phone, stared blankly at the computer screen in front of him. The conversation left him feeling uneasy. When it came down to it, what *did* he know about politics? Perhaps he should do some research? He could start by finding out what Objective One status actually was. But his heart sank at the prospect. Attention to detail had never been his strong point. Books about politics were *so dull*. His eyes would glaze over after the first paragraph. Then the phone rang again, and he swiftly pushed this troubling train of thought to the back of his mind and switched back into dynamic campaign manager mode.

'Good morning, Dylan Walsh campaign HQ, how can I help you?'

★

Meanwhile Aidan was also weighing up the opposition. Carefully studying a photo in the *Argus* of Watkins coming out of church with his wife and young son. He looked squeaky-clean, confident, capable. You'd never see his sort in the Globe and Aidan was struggling to grasp exactly what kind of opponent he might be. His bland features revealed nothing, so instead he searched the report for clues. *Mr Watkins said he 'keeps the Bible by his bed', and called on churches 'to play a bigger role in national life'.*

Aidan didn't like the sound of that. He had nothing against people who were religious. But mixing religion and politics made him uneasy. Believing in god, any god, shouldn't give you the right to feel superior to people who didn't. But looking at Watkins' face, that was what he now thought he saw.

He'd often told his friends that he'd stopped believing in god after Eileen died. But that wasn't strictly true; those were words spoken in anger. He'd just needed a break from god. From trying to understand his ways. Aidan had organised a Catholic funeral because that's what Eileen would have wanted, and what her family had expected. But the ceremony sickened him. The priest told him that Eileen dying was all part of god's plan. That we didn't have the right to question these things, that we needed to accept them, no matter how painful. *Don't ask awkward questions.*

When Aidan was twelve, the RE teacher, Mr Flaherty, an anxious and irritable Irishman, had introduced the topic of free will. God loved us so much, Mr Flaherty said, He distinguished us from all His other creatures by giving us the greatest gift of all – free will. Aidan raised his hand.

'If He gave us free will, sir, then aren't we free to not believe in Him?'

Some of the other boys giggled, thinking that Aidan had come up with a brilliant new way of winding up Flaherty. Clearly Flaherty thought so too, for he berated Aidan for his impertinence. But Aidan wanted an answer. He persisted till

Flaherty snapped and sent him to see the headmaster who called him a heathen and caned him. That was the last time he asked any questions in RE.

No matter how hard he tried, Aidan couldn't understand how Eileen having a brain haemorrhage fitted into any grand design or higher purpose. If such a thing made sense to god, then this must be a god so remote from human beings that Aidan wondered if his existence actually made any difference to them? He hadn't lifted a finger during the Holocaust, the famine in Ethiopia, the massacres in Rwanda – what was he doing up there?

You must help god to help you.

How?

You must have faith. If you don't have faith in Him, then His hands are tied. That's what the priest at Eileen's funeral said. He was a kind and decent man, Aidan could see that, but he didn't have any answers.

You needed to believe in *something* in order to keep going. If not justice in the next life, then justice in this. There was some meaning in struggling for a better life for you and your children, your friends and neighbours. There had to be. There was meaning in this painful solitude. The life he'd be going back to, that had value too. People rushing to get to work and drop their kids at school; the crowded streets, the busy shops, the endless chatter of the radio and TV. All the backbreaking, frenetic activity needed just to keep the town running from day to day. It was a miracle of organisation and willpower. *That* meant something. He wasn't clever enough to know *what* it meant exactly, but it felt worthwhile. It wasn't pointless. No, it wasn't only people who kept the Bible by their beds who believed in doing the right thing.

Aidan was beginning to think that when he *did* return to normal life, he would be a changed man. He would question things more, speak his mind and not worry about what people might think. He was growing in confidence, willing to try things he wouldn't have given the time of day to before. He'd begun discovering how powerful his imagination was. He knew he'd put himself in this box of his own free will, but nevertheless for a long time he felt he was being punished unreasonably. His back ached; his neck felt as stiff as an iron bar; his legs throbbed and pulsed, till he was sure he could feel the blood coursing through them; there was a pain in his head when he woke in the morning and late at night; his eyes swam with boredom.

But he was discovering ways to deal with it. He would close his eyes and imagine going on some of his favourite walks. One morning he made his way along the Pembrokeshire Coastal Path. He smiled as he watched white breakers rolling into a bay; swooned as he trekked through headlands carpeted with bluebells, breathing in their strong, heavy scent. He walked past freshly-trimmed verges, drank in the sweet smell of newly-cut grass. Wandered through yellow-flowered gorse, heather and wild flowers, past dancing butterflies with bright orange wings and delicate black spots. He saw a peregrine falcon, twisting and soaring in the clear blue sky; a grey seal sunning itself on a rock; a screaming oystercatcher flying low over the cliffs. His legs grew heavy as he trudged up a sandy track, scattering rabbits; he hummed as he walked down a lane lined with foxgloves, a cool summer breeze caressing his face. By the end of his journey he felt as exhilarated and tired as if he'd actually walked it.

His imagination, like his senses of smell and hearing, was much more powerful now he was lying in the coffin. At first that had scared him. He felt at the mercy of his imagination and had no idea what it would unleash. But, gradually, he was convinced he was learning how to use it. It was stupid not to. That would be like a man who buys an expensive and powerful car, then sits in the driving seat and freezes in fear as he surveyed the bewildering array of knobs, switches and gauges. Clueless how to make it work, hesitant even to touch anything. Sitting in it with the engine turned off, turning the steering wheel from side to side.

They reckon you use only 10 per cent of your brain – god knows what's lurking in the other 90 per cent. Perhaps I'm actually very intelligent and I've just never tapped into the amazing power of my mind. 10 per cent! What an incredible waste. It's like owning a mansion and never going beyond the entrance hall. Yes, the more he thought about it, the more determined he was to discover his true potential down there.

There was a knock on the door. Dylan looked up from the computer.

'Yeah?'

'It's me – Wilf.'

'Come in, Wilf.'

He came in and stood in the middle of the room, looking delighted with himself.

'You know you said you were always happy for contributions, that we were a team?'

'I did.'

'Well, I've been working on a new slogan. You know, something to put on the leaflets and posters.'

'You have?' Dylan said, trying to look pleased. But he really wanted to get back to writing a new press release. *David Against Goliath – The Battle for Crindau West.*

'Yeah, I was up till nearly midnight jotting down ideas.'

'So what did you come up with?'

'OK, here we go.' He cleared his throat and granted himself a dramatic pause. ' "Vote for Aidan – save our jobs." '

Dylan forced a smile and said, 'Yeah, that's good, Wilf. I like it.'

'You do? Me too, I think I've got a knack for this kind of thing.'

Dylan said, 'Sure,' and turned back to the press release.

'OK, here comes the next one.'

Dylan looked up again. He didn't smile this time.

'There are more?'

'Yeah, like I said, I was up till midnight. "Save our jobs – vote for Aidan." What do you think? It's snappier, isn't it?'

Dylan was sitting rigidly in his chair, rolling his biro back and forth rapidly with the palm of his hand.

'I tell you what, why don't you write these all down and show them to me at the end of the day?'

But Wilf wasn't listening. ' "A vote for Aidan . . . *is* a vote for jobs." You know, like, emphasise the "is", so that people . . .'

'Wilf, it's not a good time right now, mate.'

Wilf thought Dylan hadn't got it. So he tried saying it again, hoping it would sink in this time.

' "A vote for jobs *is* . . ." '

Dylan yawned and rubbed his tired eyes. When Wilf didn't take the hint he got up, slipped on his jacket.

'Voting for Aidan is the same as voting for jobs, don't you see?'

Dylan patted him on the shoulder.

'Look, I'm off to meet someone. Just write them all down and leave them on my desk, yeah?'

It was nearly eleven at night when she arrived.

'Hello.'

Aidan saw a heavy-set, middle-aged woman looking down the periscope at him.

'My husband works in Sunny Jim.'

'Does he?'

Unhappiness was seeping through her like damp through a wall. Aidan could tell that she'd stopped worrying what she looked like a good few years back.

'I really hope you'll be able to keep the factory open.'

'I'll do my best.'

It had been a long day. He'd given about thirty interviews, had scores of visitors.

'It'd be very tough without that money coming in. I've only got a part-time job as a dinner lady.'

Jesus, thought Aidan, I bet you put a smile on the kiddies' faces.

'I'll bet that doesn't pay much.'

'No, it doesn't. But that's not what I'm worried about.'

Aidan was thrown.

'It's the thought of him being at home all the time.'

She was blathered, Aidan saw now. She'd been drinking at home, on her own.

'I can't remember the last time we had a conversation. He comes in, I put his dinner on the table, then I go in the other room and watch the telly, while he eats it in silence.'

'I'm sorry to hear that.'

'When he's finished he has a bath, then goes down the pub and stays there till closing time. I always make sure I'm in bed by the time he comes back, and he usually falls asleep the moment his head hits the pillow.'

'Right.'

Aidan couldn't bear much more of this.

'I can't remember the last time he touched me. Or showed any interest in what I said or did.' She paused, staring into space, chewing her lip. 'Do you have any idea how that makes me feel?'

Aidan's throat felt dry and tight. 'I'm sorry to hear that, love.'

'You wouldn't believe it to look at me now, but I used to take a real pride in my appearance.'

She gave him a knowing look.

'I know what you're thinking – "Her?"'

'I wasn't.'

He was.

'I was always having my hair done, buying new outfits. Other women used to come to me for advice about what to choose . . .' She laughed mirthlessly. 'Now they give me a wide berth – who wants to be seen with me?'

'Ah come on now . . .'

She shook her head dismissively. Aidan hated to hear a woman talk like that.

'That man, he's broken me down. I was a pretty confident person, it's taken him years, but . . .' She shook her head, smiling bleakly. '. . . he did it in the end – his life's work.'

Aidan had no idea what to say to her.

'You've got to win. You've got to keep that factory open. Because if you don't, and I have to spend more time with him than I do now, I . . . Jesus Christ, I don't know what I'll do . . .'

'Don't talk like that, love.'

One fat teardrop escaped from her eye. Then she lifted up her face, took a deep breath and somehow managed to stop the rest of them coming.

'It eats away at you, being this unhappy. You look at other couples, start thinking maybe none of them are happy either. Because you just can't imagine people being happy together anymore. If you see a man and a woman kissing in the street, you tell yourself they're fools, that it won't last. In fact you gloat about the shock they've got coming when the excitement fades and it begins to turn sour. Isn't that awful?'

Aidan thought it was. She scared him.

'That's why I admire you so much.'

'Me?'

'Yes – you lost your wife. A wife you really loved. That must have been very difficult.'

If only she knew what those last few months had been like. *Can you not think of a word to say to me?* But as far as the outside world was concerned, it had been the perfect marriage.

Her stare was unsettling.

He would have liked to have been honest with her, to tell her how rocky their marriage had been towards the end. That one of the things he'd found most difficult was not knowing whether things would have got better or not. Telling her would have made *him* feel better, but would it have helped her? For some reason she had decided that his marriage was the one relationship that she could still believe in, that it had been perfect, spoiled only by a tragic, premature death. It obviously helped her in some small way. Did he really want to shatter her illusion? Take away one of the few small shreds of comfort that she still had?

He said 'Yes, it was hard. We were so happy when she was alive.'

She nodded.

'Hard to bring up those kids on your own too. But you've gone on thinking of others instead of wallowing in your own problems. You're putting yourself on the line here for all the people who work at that factory.'

'It's not . . .'

'Usually when people get hurt, they can't see beyond their own problems. But you're not like that. Do you know what keeps me going?'

Aidan shook his head. He found it difficult to believe she *was* still going.

'The thought of you down there, holding out, refusing to give up. I think of you, all on your own, not able to get up and go for a walk, or do all the things that we take for granted, and I think, "If he can carry on, then so can I." '

Aidan was squirming now; he didn't know how to react to this. It was too much.

'People stopped seeing me years ago. I've become invisible. My husband doesn't see me, my kids don't see me, my neighbours don't . . . There have been times when I've wondered if I really exist.' She paused and produced a smile that shocked Aidan, it was so unexpectedly warm and tender and he caught a glimpse of the attractive woman she'd once been.

'But you see me, don't you, love? You see that I'm a still a person.'

Aidan remembered what Julian had told him about that Berkeley bloke – *things only existed when someone paid attention to them.*

'Yes, love, I see you. I see that you're a good person inside.'

Her smile broadened, and Aidan desperately wanted to hug her.

'Here, this is for you.' She put a bottle of Baileys into the basket, lowered it down.

'Have a drink on me, love. I'll be thinking of you. Goodbye.'

'No – don't go. Stay and have a drink with me.'

He couldn't endure the idea of her going back to that empty house on her own. She looked at him suspiciously.

'Please. I'd be glad of your company – it's no fun drinking on your own. I've got a couple of plastic glasses down here.'

She smiled. 'OK then.'

Once she'd had a drink she said, 'Tell me about your wife.'

So he did. He told her about the first time they'd met, how her singing had moved him. About their early dates and how they made each other laugh all the time. They ended up talking till nearly midnight. When she left, Aidan whispered 'No, you're not invisible, love, I see you.'

'Dylan?'

'Yeah?'

He looked up from the computer to see Gwyn standing in front of him, looking rather self-conscious.

'You know you said you were always happy for contributions, that we were a team?'

Unfuckingbelievable, what had he started? This time he didn't manage to sound so enthusiastic. 'You haven't come up with an idea for a slogan, have you?'

Gwyn caught his tone, said hesitantly, 'Actually I have, yes.'

Dylan sneaked a look at his watch, it was 10.55 a.m., a reporter from the *Mirror* was going to ring him back at 11. Please let her keep her word, so he could cut this short.

'You've heard of "Politics is the art of the possible", haven't you?'

'Yeah, of course. I think everyone is pretty sick of hearing that one, to be honest, mate.'

'Well, last night I was looking up political quotations on

Google, and I found a good one from Vaclav Havel, that Czech bloke. I thought we could use it.'

'You've got the Internet at home?'

'Yeah, of course. It's very useful for research.'

'What do you research?'

'I'm doing a night class in twentieth-century history.'

Dylan looked at him more closely. He nodded slowly. 'OK, so what did Havel say?'

' "Politics must also be the art of the impossible." '

Dylan went rigid. He stared at Gwyn with an intensity that unnerved him. Gwyn pushed his glasses further back on his nose, wondering if he'd offended him in some way.

'Are you OK?'

Dylan gritted his teeth and thumped the desk with his fist. He jumped to his feet so rapidly his chair crashed to the floor.

'Gwyn – fuck me, that is brilliant. YOU ARE THE MAN.'

He reached across the desk, holding his hand palm out, smiling. He and Gwyn did a high five. Then he burst out laughing.

'Politics must also be the art of the impossible – *ALL RIGHT!*

Aidan was determined not to let his mind turn to flab; he had to keep sharp if he had any chance of winning his battle. For the first time he was able to read the newspapers from cover to cover and he promised himself he would keep up with all the latest stories. He wanted to feel fully involved in the world above him. So if someone asked him his opinion about something in the news, he'd astonish them with the depth and scale of his knowledge. Gwyn had said he should try the *Independent* and the *Guardian*, that they were the best. So he asked Frank to bring him them both. Frank had a face on him when he chucked them into his basket.

'I hope you aren't getting ideas above your station down there.'

Aidan gave up on the *Guardian* after the first day. It was too bloody big; it was a nightmare trying to turn the pages and fold them over in his coffin. He got into a foul mood and started cursing as the pages got hopelessly creased and mixed up.

'Fecking bastard thing!'

He chucked it down the end of the coffin. Then, afterwards, when he'd calmed down, he had to perform a series of painful contortions using his feet in order to get it back up again so that he could stuff it into his basket. He stuck to the *Independent* after that, which was about the same size as the *Mirror*. It was an eye-opener. He read about problems in countries he wouldn't have been able to find on a map before, and that he developed a tremendous sympathy for.

'Jesus, they've got it rough in Uzbekistan – what in god's name are our government doing supporting those bastards?'

He became a fan of Robert Fisk, a man who wore his heart on his sleeve and whose furious reports reminded him of John Pilger in the *Daily Mirror* back in the Sixties. Aidan studied Fisk's photograph. He looked like a right bad-tempered old fecker. A man desperate to give a bloody good kicking to whoever was responsible for the awful mess the world was in. Aidan wouldn't like to get on the wrong side of him. But Christ, the man could write. Yes, he liked old Fisk. There should be more like him.

He read everything. Once he'd finished all the serious articles, letters, editorial and cartoon strips he'd turn to the *News in Brief* stories. Some of them were priceless: *Researchers found 476 items of manufactured rubbish per hour on an uninhabited Pitcairn Island beach 5000 kilometres from anywhere in the Pacific.*

That sounded like an interesting job. How would that look on your CV? *June 2000–June 2001 – counting items of rubbish washed up on uninhabited island, Pacific Ocean.*

He couldn't wait to tell the lads about some of them: *The number of calories used in the 'average sex act' is 200 when accompanied, 60 unaccompanied.*

That got a laugh. He knew it would.

He tried listening to new radio stations too – there was some interesting stuff on Radio 2 and Radio 4. When he was still awake in the early hours he'd listen to the World Service. They had some brilliant programmes. He listened to one called 'The Biggest Desert in Europe', about Iceland. Apparently it was so similar to the moon that the Apollo astronauts went there for training. It used to be covered with trees and grass, but the Vikings burnt the lot, and the fierce winds whipped away the thin layer of soil that was left, turning it into the bleak place it was today. Aidan was staggered to learn how one act of vandalism had shaped a thousand years of history. Why hadn't he known about that before? There were so many things he didn't know. Maybe the same applied to individuals too – the one rash decision, one moment of unthinking anger that could have disastrous lifelong consequences. He'd spent years shifting heavy boxes, festering in ignorance. He had a lot of catching up to do. He didn't want to be shown up if he became an MP. The people of Crindau didn't want some ignoramus representing them. A few weeks ago he thought they'd been out of their minds when they suggested he stand for Parliament but now he had a clear lead with polling day just a couple of weeks away. He needed to be prepared.

He even tried Radio 3 once, but they were playing something that sounded like an animal in terrible pain, accompanied by crashing cymbals. Jesus, he might want to expand his mind, but he had his limits.

'Yes!' Dylan punched the air in delight. He wouldn't have believed things could possibly get any better, but they just had. He sprang out of his seat and danced around his desk, doing his best James Brown moves.

'All right – get down!'

Then he stopped and read the front page of the *Argus* again, slowly this time, savouring every word. He burst out laughing.

'Gotcha!'

He couldn't wait to tell his dad. No, the video diary first. He rushed upstairs, switched it on, sat down, a huge smile on his face.

'Here's the front page of today's *Argus*.'

He held it up in all its glory.

Labour Candidate's Anti-Crindau Jibes

'Isn't that a sight for sore eyes?' He grinned and began reading out the story.

' "Today Nigel Watkins, the Labour party candidate for Crindau West, sought to limit the damage caused by his off-the-record remarks made late last night at a hotel in Cardiff." That's journalese for shouting his mouth off while pissed as a fart. "Mr Watkins was heard to make disparaging comments about the Independent candidate, Mr Walsh. 'Everyone tells me the local candidate is the favourite – well he would be, wouldn't he? The voters probably feel intimidated by anyone from outside Crindau, especially somebody halfway intelligent. After all, it's the kind of place where you are regarded as an intellectual if you can read the *Sun* from cover to cover in less than a day.' " He went on to describe Crindau as "A bloody awful hole." '

Dylan looked up from the paper and eyeballed the video, grinning.

'Oh boy, is he screwed. *"This morning Mr Watkins insisted he had been quoted out of context and that he had been under tremendous strain at the time. He apologised for any offence caused by this unfortunate misunderstanding. He claimed that he had actually said that some people regarded Crindau as a bloody awful hole, but that he thought it was a fine town."* '

Dylan snorted with derision. 'Oh boy, is that lame. Too bloody late – you're history, pal.' He laughed again. 'Oh man, this is sweet.' He checked the paper. 'Story by Nick Williams – good work, Nick. The solid local boy came good.'

He carefully folded up the newspaper and dropped it on the floor. He clenched his fist.

'They'll never recover from this.'

He got down on his knees, clasped his hands as if in prayer, then raised his eyes to the ceiling.

'Thank you, god. Thank you so, *so* much.'

'How *dare* he.'

Dylan was taken aback by how furious his dad was. In his excitement he'd forgotten that Watkins had insulted him.

'This is a great town – he's insulted me and everyone in it. Who does he think he is?'

'Sickening, isn't it?' said Dylan. 'I was *so* pissed off when I read it.'

This genuine anger, it was priceless. It would push his dad to new heights. Dylan imagined the headlines – *Now it's personal.* They were flying.

In the Globe they'd ripped a photo of Watkins out of the paper and pinned it to the centre of the dartboard. Russell stood at the bar, pint in hand, holding forth.

'The arrogant bastard. Well if Crindau is a bloody hole, why does he want to be our MP then?'

Wilf said, 'We've got some very clever people living here. A few years back a team from Crindau won *Blockbusters* four days in a row.'

'There you are,' said Tony, opening his bag of pork scratchings. 'I bet they've never had a team that good in Cardiff.'

The next morning Dylan stood listening to Aidan give an interview to the *Argus*.

'I think this proves that beneath the cool, professional manner there's a real contempt for ordinary people. As far as Mr Watkins is concerned, winning this election would be no more than the first step to a successful parliamentary career. The place itself means nothing to him. He would be just as happy standing for a safe seat in Rotherham, or Dundee, or Ipswich. But this is my home, and I care very much about what happens to this town.'

Nick was furiously scribbling it all down in his pad, secure in the knowledge he had today's front page story. Dylan was delighted; he thought Aidan was hitting just the right tone. He also had a startling revelation while he was listening.

My father is actually a really decent, honest guy.

Dylan was proud of him. He liked himself for feeling proud too. But he also felt uneasy. He seemed to be both standing there in the garden, listening to Aidan speak and, at the same time, was years ahead in the future, looking back, and mourning the loss of this moment. Why couldn't he just *be*? Why in god's name could he never relax, even when things were going so well? He loathed these moments of doubt and dislocation, did what he always did when they occurred. Poured all his energy into doing something concrete, redoubling his efforts to bend the world to the shape he desired.

Watkins was on the defensive, and that's where they needed to keep him. Dylan sent the volunteers out tramping the streets, shaking hands, handing out leaflets and posters and talking to the voters. *You can trust Aidan, he's Crindau born and bred, he won't look down his nose at you like Watkins.*

That night Dylan recorded his video diary to the sound of a group of Aidan's supporters singing 'Power To The People' outside in the garden. It was nearly midnight. They were pissed out of their heads, had been at it for over an hour and were showing no signs of winding down. Dylan had allowed himself to be sucked into the celebratory mood, was clutching a nearly empty bottle of wine as he addressed the video.

'Do you hear that? This place is being rocked to its foundations. I feel like this is something I've been building towards all my life. I've finally discovered what I was meant to do. You start thinking you can change things, that you can do anything.'

He paused, trying to collect his thoughts, his head swimming.

'The other candidates may have party machines and big budgets, they may have loads of experience and sophisticated manifestos – but they'll never have my imagination. They'll *never* be able to think outside the box. Stuff just comes to me – it's like Mozart waking up with whole symphonies in his head, no idea how they got there.'

He ran his hand through his hair, staring into the distance.

'There have been times in the past when I've just wanted my brain to fuck off and leave me alone. It was torture, having so many ideas. Far more than I could cope with. Something would flash into my mind and I'd think, "That's brilliant!" But, before I had a chance to run with it, I'd have a new idea – and then another, and then another. I just couldn't keep up with myself.'

Power to the people!

Dylan inclined his head towards the window, smiled. 'Hear that? They're still at it.' He began raising the bottle to his lips, thought better of it.

'But now, at last, I'm focused. I've got one clear goal and I'm going to see it through to the end.' His face lightened again and he broke into a lazy grin. 'Man, we have got them on the run. Something beautiful is finally happening in this dirty, downtrodden old town.'

Aidan lay in his coffin, thinking about his friends. He bet they'd be surprised, shocked even, to know the kind of things he worried about late at night. So it followed, didn't it, that there were probably all sorts of things preying on their minds that *he* didn't know about. Behind the banter and the jokes, the leg pulling and the laughter, lay dread and fatigue. They were like actors who knew their lines and had perfect timing, but would always struggle with their character's motivation. Aidan watched them in action, fascinated and, sometimes, horrified. He thought, *I was just like them until recently*. But not any longer. He remembered something that Shauna had told him. Until the middle of the nineteenth century the word 'worry' was used to describe what hunting dogs did to their prey. But a hundred years later the word had acquired a quite different meaning: we were hunting ourselves.

Aidan felt he had discovered something crucial down there in his coffin, though he couldn't say exactly what it was. He only knew that he would no longer be the same person when he came back up again, and it concerned him. He'd never been in this place before, and he didn't know what the rules were.

Maybe one of his friends was lying awake now, fretting about him. He hoped not. He hoped they were all sleeping soundly. He hoped their friendship would survive this.

He had these sad thoughts often now, late at night, when there were no more visitors and he struggled to get to sleep. He wished he had someone to talk to about these things. Someone like Julian. He'd listen carefully, smiling, as if at some private joke, then compare what Aidan was thinking to some sixteenth-century Dutch philosopher, or a line of Chinese poetry, and Aidan would no longer feel so lost, so alone. He'd never be able to tell someone like Russell.

Have you ever felt that you were invisible?

What the fuck?

No, he'd keep them to himself, the things that were going on in his head, he didn't feel safe sharing them. The previous night he had had a startlingly vivid vision of himself as a small boy sticking his newspaper cuttings about Spurs into his Woolworths scrapbook. He'd been so gloriously, uncomplicatedly happy back then, as he cut out a photo of his hero Jimmy Greaves dribbling round the United keeper Alex Stepney at White Hart Lane. He had seen this younger version of himself so clearly he felt he could have reached out and touched the young Aidan. But he couldn't, of course. It was probably just his mind playing tricks on him, something that was bound to happen when you were in his position, on your own under the ground. But, all the same, trick or no, the wave of grief as the image faded was real enough. As if he was remembering a dead son. He wished he could go back in time and help him. Did these kind of things happen to anyone else in Crindau?

11

Frank came to collect his bedpan after his evening meal. He raised it up, and asked, 'Is it true about them starting a tab on me at the bar?'

Frank carefully took it out of the basket, placed it on the ground. Then he put Aidan's dessert in and sent that down to him.

'Aye, you're two to one on to stop them closing the factory.'

Aidan smiled. Frank should have gone on the stage. He would show no sign he'd heard your question, then, just as you were about to give up he'd answer without even looking at you.

'That's great.'

Frank sighed, bent down to pick up the bedpan.

'It's funny the things you end up doing for your regulars, ain't it?'

'You're a star.'

'You're in the window of the betting shop too.'

'Yeah?'

'Uhu, you're odds on favourite to win the 3.15 at Chepstow. Enjoy your Spotted Dick.'

Wilf was shattered. It was nearly ten and he'd spent four hours tramping around Crindau, pushing election leaflets through doors, asking people if they'd be voting for Aidan. What was good though was the number of posters supporting Aidan he'd seen stuck up in windows. *Put Him In To Get Him Out* and *Politics must Also be the Art of the Impossible.*

He didn't mind that Dylan had decided to use Gwyn's slogan and not his. Not really. God, he was tired though. It was no joke, trudging the streets after a full day's work.

Dylan had made campaigning sound great fun. But it wasn't, not really. A lot of it was boring. Opening letters, folding up leaflets, stuffing envelopes, flyposting, photocopying. He didn't begrudge it, in fact he felt guilty admitting that he wasn't enjoying it that much. After all, if getting someone elected was a barrel of laughs, everyone would be doing it. *Fancy coming for a drink? There's karaoke on tonight. Nah, I'm bored with karaoke, I'm off out canvassing, I'm standing for Parliament.*

They were doing something momentous here, something that could benefit everyone in Crindau. He had no right to expect he'd *enjoy* it. All the same, it was hard to keep going sometimes. He'd fallen asleep in his lunch hour today, nodded off in his afternoon tea break; Megan had to shout and shake him awake in the morning. But it would be worth it in the end. It was vital to remember what it was all about, exactly why they were doing this. Which was why he hadn't gone to the Globe with Russell, Gwyn and the others for a couple of pints. What he *really* wanted to do, before he went home and collapsed into bed, was go and have a chat to Aidan. He hadn't been able to get near him lately, what with the media swarming around him all the time. It wasn't the same without him. Russell was starting to get on his nerves with his sniping. Wilf knew he didn't really mean the things he said. But it hurt all the same. Aidan had always been the one who'd stood up for him when Russell went on too long. 'Come on, mun, give it a break – leave him alone, will you?'

He thought that was one of the reasons he'd make such a good MP – he stood up for others. Aidan was a special kind of person – Wilf knew he didn't go to church any longer, but that didn't mean he wasn't a believer at heart, he'd just lost contact with that part of himself. Wilf was sure god was guiding him to victory. He wanted to tell Aidan how many people had smiled when he'd handed them a leaflet on their doorstep tonight. 'Ah – the bloke in the coffin. You bet I'll vote for him.' Make him realise just what he'd given this town – hope. It was moments like that, seeing a stranger's face light up with joy, that made it all worthwhile. After years of people saying, 'It doesn't matter who you vote for – they're all as bad as each other', the people of Crindau had someone they could believe in.

But his heart sank when he walked into Aidan's garden. There were three other people queuing to see him, even at this time of night. Wilf sat down in one of the chairs under the plastic sheeting and waited. And waited. He'd been up since six, and soon he began to droop. He woke with a start to find himself sitting on his own, beginning to slump off the chair. He checked his watch. It was just gone 10.30, he'd only nodded off for a few minutes, but he felt like he'd snapped out of a long, deep sleep. He massaged his face and eyes then swayed as a wave of dizziness gripped him. He waited for it to pass, then got up and went slowly over to the periscope. He looked down it and saw Aidan rubbing tired eyes with the fingers of one hand, clasping his mobile with the other.

'Yeah, that's right, I'm ahead in the polls with a week to go, it's looking good, but we're not counting our chickens yet. You know what they say, a week is a long time in politics. Eh? Yes, I will be wanting immediate talks with Sunny Jim management if I'm elected, absolutely!'

This is what it would be like when Aidan was an MP. It wouldn't matter how long you'd known him, how good a friend you were, you'd just have to wait your turn. Aidan would probably spend the week in London, returning to Crindau at weekends. Then he'd be tied up for hours in surgeries and meetings and god knows what. He'd probably stop going to the Globe too, because he'd never get a moment's peace there either.

Wilf wondered when he'd actually get to see him. He feared he'd become a stranger, someone whose life you followed in the papers and on the TV. Then he felt guilty. *Come on, mun, don't be so selfish. He's doing this for all of us.*

He waited for another five minutes, but the call showed no sign of stopping, and Aidan didn't look up and see him. Wilf decided to go home. Tomorrow would be another long day.

'And out of all those songs, which *one* would you choose as your absolute favourite? The one you just couldn't imagine living without.'

Aidan was on Crindau FM's *Lazy Sunday Afternoon* show, picking his favourite records and talking about them. He was on Crindau FM most days now, had come to enjoy it.

'There *is* one song I love more than any other. It's "Days" by The Kinks.'

'Really? And why's that?'

Aidan hesitated. He knew exactly why, but he'd never spoken about it before. This was his chance to be the new Aidan, who would talk about the things that mattered to him. Maybe it would help other people, to hear how it had helped him.

'I played "Days" over and over after my wife died. As soon as it finished, I'd pick up the stylus and start it again, and again, and let the tears roll down my face.' He paused, shocked by his ever-growing ability to talk about himself on the radio, sensing the DJ's anxiety too, on what was meant to be a pleasant Sunday afternoon show. 'I knew, after listening to that song, that Ray Davies had lost someone very precious too. I wasn't surprised when I read later he'd written it after splitting up with his wife. God, that sounds depressing, doesn't it?'

'Well, it's sad, perhaps, rather than depressing.'

'Yes, I think that's a better way of putting it. But you know, as I've played it over the years, it's changed its meaning for me. Now I see another side to it too – as a kind of celebration of someone who's gone. Remembering all the good things about them, as well as the pain of losing them. And I think that it's crucial not to forget, isn't it? I actually think that everything that's happened to you, good or bad, whether you've brought it on yourself or whether it's been forced on you by circumstances, or someone else, is, in the end, yours. And, that you'll never be able to really find peace until you accept ownership of all the good *and* the bad things in your life.'

'And you found all that in a three-minute pop song?'

'Well, I think all that *is* there in that song. It has to be one of the most beautiful ever written.'

'Thank you very much for a fascinating half-hour, Aidan Walsh.'

'You're welcome, I enjoyed it.'

He did too. In fact, he felt much more at home talking on the radio than he did standing for MP. He'd always preferred radio to TV, the feeling it conveyed that the person on it was talking directly to *you*. It was somehow much more intimate than TV. That's how Aidan handled it; he pictured one individual, someone very like Gwyn, somebody quiet and thoughtful, and imagined that he was speaking straight to them. It worked every time.

But there was one thing on the radio that really bugged him. Watkins. It was getting to Aidan. Every day his opponent was on Crindau FM saying the same thing.

'Why won't Mr Walsh appear on a phone-in like the rest of the candidates? What, exactly, is he afraid of?'

That wheedling tone, the insinuation that he wasn't up to it. Whenever he mentioned it to Dylan, he got the same response.

'Forget it, Dad, he's winding you up.'

But Aidan *wanted* to do it. He listened to the phone-in programme nearly every night. He was devoted to Crindau FM. It had helped keep him sane down there. It felt like an old friend. The people who rang in, they were just like him. They were the same people who had lined up to give him Christmas presents, who came here to promise him their votes. He'd *enjoy* talking to them.

He was very grateful to Dylan for all his help. When he was overbearing at times, when he got on Aidan's nerves with his motormouth act, he tried to remember he was still young and desperate to make his mark on the world. He was investing as much of himself in this as Aidan. Which was a concern in itself. But Dylan would just have to learn that Aidan had his own mind. Accepting the invitation to appear on the phone-in felt the right thing to do. He felt bad turning them down all the time, especially when they'd been so helpful, and he'd been on so many of their other programmes. He was going to accept this time. What *was* there to be afraid of?

But Dylan nearly had a coronary when he told him.

'Christ, no!'

Dylan noticed a journalist waiting to interview Aidan staring at him. He lowered his voice, leant down closer to the periscope.

'I thought we'd agreed you would steer clear of phone-ins?'

Aidan told him how sick he was of Watkins asking what he was afraid of. Dylan rolled his eyes.

'Why should you care what *he* thinks? You're twelve points ahead of him in the polls.'

'It's a matter of principle.'

Dylan clutched his head in his hands; this was a *bad* sign, now he'd started talking about bloody principles. He wrinkled his nose as a powerful smell of burgers and fried onions drifted over from Che's Cantina.

'I have worked *so* hard to get you that twelve-point lead.'

Aidan felt the bile rising in his throat.

'*You* got me the lead?

Yes, thought Dylan, it *was* me. All this is down to me, but you seem to have forgotten that. Where would you be now without me telling you exactly what to do and say? Leading you by the bloody hand.

Aidan felt it was time he took the plunge and moved things on a little with Safina.

'Maybe I could take you out somewhere and buy you a glass of wine when all this is over.'

'Oh yeah? Where would you take me?'

She said it easily, without a moment's hesitation.

'What kind of places do you like?'

'Maybe you could figure that out.'

That made him smile. She was teasing him, a good sign.

'Let me see . . . Someplace quiet, without any loud music, so we could have a proper conversation. Not in the town centre, somewhere a little off the beaten track, away from the crowds.'

'That's a good start. Go on.'

As if they were playing a game; except it was and it wasn't.

'There's a nice place in St Brides called the Argel, do you know it?'

'No, I've never heard of it.'

'Not many people have. It's at the end of a really narrow road right next to the Severn. It's still got a coal fire in the lounge, a coal scuttle next to it, all these horse brasses hanging over it. They have those old-fashioned table lamps on all the tables. There's no jukebox, the couple who run it play their own records. They have a record deck behind the bar and a stack of albums next to it. They put on whatever they fancy but they play it very low, so it's just in the background.'

'What kind of music do they play?'

'Not the usual kind you get in pubs. Not really the kind of stuff I'd listen to at home either, to be honest, but I enjoy it when I'm there. For example, sometimes they play classical music – nothing heavy, like, but stuff you could hum along to. I couldn't tell you what it was called, apart from "The Blue Danube"; even I know that one. Other times they play jazz – ragtime piano and Louis Armstrong, Acker Bilk and Dave Brubeck – his big hit, what was it called?'

'"Take Five"?'

'That's the one. If it comes on the radio it sounds dead corny, but whenever I hear it there, I love it. Like I said, not usually the kind of thing I go for, but do you know what I really like about it?'

'What's that?'

'It's so obviously stuff that they really love, that they've been listening to for years, and that they'd be playing anyway, even if no one else was there. Sometimes I've looked around and seen one of them humming or nodding their head when they're serving and they're always really pleased if you ever ask them what it is that's playing. That makes it kind of special, like you're visiting someone's house, you know what I mean?'

'I do. It's hard to find a place with character these days.'

'That's spot on, every bar you walk into now, you feel you've been there before. But not the Argel – "quaint", my son calls it. They have some tables outside too, so in the summer you can sit at the water's edge and watch the lights flickering in the darkness on the other side of the Severn.'

'It sounds lovely.'

'It is. The only thing is, it's a bit of a pain to get there, there's only one bus an hour and they don't run very late.'

'I've got a car.'

'Hey, you're sorted.'

'Sounds like it.'

Aidan smiled to himself. It had been so easy. He should have done it years ago.

Russell stepped into the garden for a fag. It was nearly ten, he'd spent the last two and a half hours blowing up balloons emblazoned with *Vote for Aidan*. He was tired; he was bored; he was thoroughly pissed off. He looked around – for once there was no one waiting to see Aidan. Just the security guard, standing by the open gate, having a smoke himself. Russell sauntered over to the periscope, peered down.

'Hello, anyone home?'

Aidan smiled. 'How you doing, mate?'

Russell sighed, massaging his brow. 'I'm knackered, to be honest.'

'Listen, I really appreciate all this, I . . .'

Russell cut him off irritably. 'Don't go on.'

'No, really, mate, I . . .'

'Forget it, you'd do the same for me.'

Aidan frowned and shook his head. 'No, I wouldn't.'

Russell was so tired it took him a second to cop on. Then he laughed and Aidan winked at him. A gust of wind ruffled the plastic sheeting above their heads. Raindrops began tapping on it.

'So – you been practising your victory speech?'

Aidan's mobile rang. It was as if an electric current had surged through him. He held up his hand to Russell, an apologetic smile on his face.

'Sorry, mate, I'd better get this.'

Russell said nothing. He took a drag from his cigarette, watching carefully as Aidan answered, and began exchanging pleasantries with someone called Ed. Then he put his hand over the mobile, turned back to Russell and said, 'It's the *New York Times*!'

'Is it, now?'

Aidan looked uncomfortable. 'They want to interview me – we're talking about a half-page profile.'

Russell said, 'They can't vote in the Crindau by-election over there, can they?'

'Eh?'

'You could tell them you were busy, ask them to ring back in twenty minutes.'

Aidan laughed, as if he'd said something funny.

'Yeah right – it's the *New York Times*, Russell.'

Russell didn't reply. He didn't say anything either when Aidan removed his hand and started a conversation. But as he turned away, and flicked his glowing cigarette into the night, he said, 'Well, fuck you, Aidan.'

Russell went back inside. Gwyn and Wilf were the only ones left in the living room, still unpacking boxes of leaflets and sorting them into neat piles on the tables. Wilf was yawning. Gwyn sighed heavily, gazing into space.

'I feel like bloody Cinderella.'

Russell said, 'When did the others leave?'

'Just now.'

'Where's Dylan?'

'Upstairs, recording his video diary.'

Russell scowled. 'Doing something practical, as usual.'

'Oh bloody hell.'

'What is it?' asked Wilf.

Gwyn held up one of the leaflets, pointed to the heading.

'I've just noticed. Do you see what it says – "A special massage from Aidan Walsh." He picked some more up from the box, moaned and threw them back, then scanned the piles already stacked on the tables. 'Would you believe it – they're all like this. What a bloody farce, mun.'

'Come on, it's knocking-off time, let's go and have a drink.'

'What about all these?' said Wilf, nodding at the piles of leaflets.

'They can wait. Let Dylan sort it out.'

They caught his tone, glanced at each other, then went and got their coats.

Russell got a round in and they found a table in a quiet corner. They watched an old guy wearing a *Put Him In To Get Him Out* badge pour some of his pint into an empty ashtray, then put it down on the floor for his Jack Russell.

'What's up?' said Gwyn. Russell told them about Aidan cutting him dead when the *New York Times* rang.

'I'm telling you, he's getting too big for his boots.'

'What you have to remember,' said Gwyn, twirling a beer mat slowly between his fingers, 'is the reason Aidan's doing this.'

'That's right,' said Wilf. 'He's trying to save our jobs.'

'That might have been the reason at the beginning,' said Russell, 'but not any longer. He lost sight of that a long time ago. What he's doing now is securing his own future.'

Gwyn looked at him sharply. 'What are you getting at?'

'Do either of you know how much an MP earns?'

They didn't.

'Well, I do – I looked it up.' He paused, took a swig from his pint. He licked his lips. 'Fifty-two grand a year.'

He watched them take that in.

'Not bad, eh? He'll be all right, no matter what happens to the factory.'

They stared at him, trying hard not to look shocked.

'He couldn't have done it without us, working our bollocks off for nothing. Let's hope he remembers that.'

'Come on, mun,' said Gwyn. 'You're making out he's some sort of cynical conman. You know Aidan's not like that. We've known him for years, it's not in his nature.'

'I never thought it was in his nature to cut an old mate dead when some journalist rang him up, but that's what he did to me tonight. You ought to have seen him when his mobile rang – everything else went out of the window. He's loving every minute of this. Do you really think he's going to be the same old Aidan at the end of this?'

Neither of them answered, so he asked again.

'Well – do you?'

'Welcome to tonight's phone-in. My name's Rob Fleming and we've got a very special guest tonight – Aidan Walsh, the man who's buried himself alive in his garden and is hoping to force Sunny Jim to reverse their decision to close their factory in Crindau. Aidan will be here for the next hour to answer your questions, so please do ring in. According to the latest polls, he is in the lead by *twelve* points, which is an astonishing achievement for an independent candidate with no previous political experience, in one of the safest Labour seats in the country. But then your campaign slogan is "Politics must also be the art of the impossible".'

'That's right, Rob. And I'm looking forward to this.'

'So am I, *and* so are the people of Crindau, I can tell you, because the switchboards are jammed. So without further ado I'd like to introduce the first caller – Stephen Prothero from Somerton.'

'Hello, there. I'd like to ask Aidan this – you've been in that coffin ages now. What's the first thing you're going to do when you get out?'

Aidan laughed.

'Walk straight over to my local and have a nice cold pint.'

'Aye, nice one, mate – and I'll be there to buy it for you.'

'Cheers, Stephen.'

Aidan was elated, this was going to be a breeze.

'And next we have Alan Williams from Maes-glas.'

'Good evening, Rob, love the programme.'

'Thanks, Alan. And what is your question for Mr Walsh?'

'I'd like to ask Mr Walsh what is his position on sustainability?'

There was a long pause. Eventually Rob said, 'Did you *hear* that question, Mr Walsh.'

'Yeah, I heard it, thanks.'

More silence followed. Every second felt like a month of unendurable torture.

'Ah . . . and would you like to answer it?'

There was another lengthy pause.

'Sustainability, well now, it depends really.'

'On what?' said the caller.

'Which particular aspect of sustainability did you have in mind?'

'I was thinking about the whole concept actually. After all, it's very pertinent to the situation here in Crindau, wouldn't you agree?'

'Some people would probably say that, yes.'

'So – what's your position?'

'Well . . .'

'You *do* know what I'm talking about, don't you?'

'Yeah, of course I do. It's hard to say, really, because it's such a very big area, sustainability, isn't it? An enormously complicated subject. And so it's not easy to just, you know . . .'

Rob Fleming cut in again.

'Just to make things clearer for our listeners, you're actually referring to a clause in the Wales Act of 1998, aren't you, Mr Williams?'

'That's right. You seem to have a greater knowledge of recent legislation than the candidate. It is the first *ever* bill in Britain giving a legal and a statutory obligation to any part of the country to develop a sustainable economy. I find it astonishing that the candidate doesn't have a clue what I'm talking about.'

'I didn't say any such thing.'

'You didn't have to.'

Back in the house, Dylan was lying in the foetal position on the floor.

'Oh fuck. Oh fucking fuck.'

He unfurled himself, slowly clambered to his feet, he couldn't stay still any longer.

'It is a hugely important question for the region. With or without the Sunny Jim factory, it is one that will have to be addressed by whoever wins this election, and it's very clear that Mr Walsh is not capable of addressing it.'

'I am!'

Dylan paced up and down, snatching drags from a cigarette. This caller knew his stuff.

'For Christ's sake, Dad! Get off the ropes.'

Why was he just lying there and taking it? If you couldn't answer the question, you attacked the questioner's motives. Surely to god he knew that much?

Aidan failed to answer the next five questions and was

obviously floundering so badly that Rob Fleming had to step in.

'OK, we don't do this very often on the phone-in pro-gramme, but I'm going to play some music now. Here's "Electioneering" by Radiohead.'

Dylan slumped on to the sofa, rolled a bottle of cold beer slowly back and forth across his forehead. They said a week was a long time in politics, but right now an hour was beginning to feel like a life sentence.

Dylan could hardly bring himself to talk to his dad, he was so furious with him. He went to see him once the phone-in was over, and the Crindau FM crew had packed up and left. Aidan was still trying to work out what had hit him.

'Where did all these bloody know-it-alls come from? Watkins didn't get difficult questions like that when he was on there.'

'You were set up.'

Aidan gaped.

'It must have been the Awkward Squad – remember I told you about them?'

'But that's disgraceful – we have to let the press know about this.'

'We can't prove anything. We could even make things worse by making allegations – people will say we're desperate.'

'We *are* desperate.'

'Yes, we are. But we can't let on. What we need now is a period of stability, no more nasty surprises, and hope and pray that it will blow over.'

'That's easy for you to say, I was the one who was shown up.'

'And whose fault is that?'

Aidan looked ready to erupt.

'OK, OK, what's done is done. But *don't* try any other initiatives without talking it over with me first.'

When Dylan left, Aidan lay in his coffin, his head splitting. He'd shot his bolt. He was finished. Washed up and humiliated. His son had spun him a fairy tale and he'd taken it as gospel. Now it was time to get real. He crashed down hard on the ridiculous notion that he might still win. For believing for one second that a no-hope outsider could sweep to a famous victory on a wave of righteous anger. A pathetically soft-centred, comforting notion. *Don't be a fucking idiot. Life's not like that.*

He was disgusted with himself. As a punishment, he made a fist and struck the lid of the coffin with all his might, crying out in pain as he opened up the scabs on his knuckles that had only recently healed. *Did that hurt? You fucking idiot, it serves you right. I'm thick, let's face it. You're a stupid pleb, Aidan Walsh.*

He grimaced as he made a fist again and prepared to punish himself some more.

The next day everyone in the Globe was talking about it.

'It was like blood sport,' said Tony. 'Those callers tore him to pieces.'

'Well, he's not exactly Einstein, is he?'

Tony took a sip from his pint, came back for more. 'Remember that last pub quiz? He thought the capital of Mexico was Los Angeles.'

'Come on, he'd had a few,' said Gywn.

Tony laughed derisively. 'So had I, but I still knew it wasn't Los Angeles.' He leaned back in his chair, yelled, 'Frank – are you sure these pork scratchings aren't past their sell-by date?'

Frank looked up from his paper. 'No way – they're the finest money can buy, I get them from a little place in Paris.'

Tony shouted back, 'There's no need for that, I only asked.'

'What *is* the capital of Mexico?' asked Wilf.

'Mexico City.'

'See – no wonder he got it wrong, it's a trick question.'

'Everything's a trick question to you.'

'Hang on,' said Gwyn. 'Let's keep this in perspective. That's hardly likely to come up in *Question Time*, is it?' "Can the Right Honourable Member for Crindau tell me what the capital of Mexico is?" I mean, if that's how you're going to judge whether someone's fit to be an MP, then . . .'

A couple of them chuckled. Tony didn't. He said, 'I'm telling you, every time he opens his mouth in public we'll be holding our breath, hoping he doesn't say something bloody daft. Because it won't just be him they'll snigger at, it will reflect on us all; the whole town will become a laughing stock.'

'The Labour bloke, Watkins, did you hear him on the phone-in the week before? He was very professional, cool as a cucumber.'

'A barrister he is. That could be handy – say if you were in dispute with the council or a landlord . . . He'd be able to tell you where you stood right away. Aidan wouldn't have a bloody clue.'

'But remember what he said about Crindau. He called it a bloody awful hole.'

'Maybe he *was* misquoted – you know what journalists are like.'

'It's not easier being a barrister, mind, they have to study for years. You need fantastic attention to detail – every little thing, no matter how insignificant, can be crucial in a court of law, see, so you have to have a razor-sharp brain.'

'Like Rumpole of the Bailey.'

'*He* wouldn't let himself be shown up like that.'

'Or Perry Mason.'

'Who would you rather see representing us? A professional with a trained mind, or an uneducated pleb whose only claim to fame is that he buried himself alive in his back garden?'

'Come on,' said Gwyn. 'Aidan isn't an uneducated pleb.'

No one would catch his eye. Tony checked his watch, looked around, a puzzled expression on his face.

'So where's Russell tonight?'

Wilf left work early the next day and came to see Aidan. He was concerned about him. When he looked down the periscope, Aidan was very gently examining the knuckles of one hand – Jesus, it looked as if he'd been in a fight.

'Hi-ya, mate.'

Aidan jumped, as if he'd been caught doing something shameful. His damaged knuckles disappeared from view. Then he started interrogating Wilf.

'What are they all saying about me then?'

Wilf's expression was disconcertingly similar to Father Dougal's.

'What do you mean?'

Aidan clenched his teeth – *Jesus.*

'About how I did on the phone-in last night – what the hell do you think?'

'I haven't heard anyone mention it, to tell the truth.'

'Fuck's sake, Wilf, can't you do any better than that?'

Wilf reddened. 'I haven't!'

Aidan looked at him scornfully.

'You'd be hopeless on that panel game.'

'Which panel game?'

Aidan couldn't remember what it was called. It used to be on years ago.

'The one where you have to guess which person is lying.'

'I don't know that one.'

'WHAT DOES IT MATTER WHICH ONE? Bloody hell, why do I always have to spell everything out for you?'

'Sorry, Aidan.'

'It doesn't matter anyway, I can imagine for myself what they're saying.'

Wilf didn't know how to reply.

'I'll bet they're loving it.'

'Ah now . . .'

'There's nothing they like better than slagging off someone they know. Get the knives out to break up the boredom.'

His mobile was ringing. He answered it.

'Here we go.' He sighed. 'Aidan Walsh . . .'

Wilf watched his face grow taut.

'No comment.'

He clicked the mobile off.

'Bastard. See what I mean?'

Wilf didn't, but he didn't want to upset Aidan again, so he kept his mouth shut.

'That's about the fiftieth call today. They're trying to make out I'm some kind of moron. Well, I'm not!'

There were fewer volunteers the next day and they kept their heads down when Dylan walked through the room. He shut the door of his office behind him, took the phone off the hook, read the papers. Watkins had played a cool, knowing hand, honing in on weaknesses no one had stopped to consider before.

'A vote for Mr Walsh will be a vote wasted. That much was clear after last night's abysmal performance on the radio. You have to have your wits about you in Parliament. Sending Mr Walsh there may have seemed a great idea before. After all, who wouldn't enjoy sticking two fingers up at the powers that be? The little man against the system, David against Goliath. We all love an underdog. But what about the long haul? If he won, he would be representing you for four or five years. What has he got to offer you, beyond saying no to closing the factory? Let's just say it does close — now I know you don't want to think about that, and, believe me, behind the scenes the Party is doing everything possible to persuade the owners to reconsider, away from the glare of publicity. But let's just say it does — what other policies does he have? Let's face it, the media love a clown, it's so much more fun, so much easier, to report his knockabout comments rather than tackling the in-depth issues. But if you want someone who can get things done, who's going to be an effective, disciplined and hard-working representative, then I would suggest you think again. Four years is a long time for the same joke to still seem funny. The people of Crindau deserve a different sort of candidate.'

Dylan collapsed on top of the paper, moaning quietly. He felt the walls closing in on him. He had to get out, go for a walk, clear his head. He didn't want to talk to any journalists; he didn't want to deal with volunteers; he *certainly* didn't want to talk to his dad right now. He picked up his jacket, threw back the last of his coffee, ploughed through the house and garden, and out the gate.

This used to be a scrubby little park with a couple of swings and a slide, but now look at it. TV vans, reporters, stalls. That had been on Dylan's list of things to do, to go and see Pancho about this little operation he was running on *their* patch. Now he noticed that next to Che's Cantina was another stall selling election souvenirs. It had been there for over a week, and Dylan hadn't minded too much, it all added to the happening atmosphere. But this morning it was annoying him. He decided to take a closer look. Spread out across a table were baseball caps with *Put Him In To Get Him Out* emblazoned on them.

Fucking hell, the bastard was ripping him off. He picked one up and examined it.

'They're £4.99, love, do you want to try one on?' said the woman behind the counter.

'No,' said Dylan, 'I bloody don't.' He pointed angrily at the front. 'Who gave you permission to use these words?'

The woman took a step back, her face closed down.

'And what the fuck's *this*?'

Next to the baseball caps were model coffins, no bigger than a matchbox, with the top cut away to reveal a crudely painted model of a man lying inside. He appeared to be smiling. Or possibly screaming. It was so badly painted it was almost impossible to tell. *Save Our Job's* was painted in white on the coffin lid. Dylan picked one up and thrust it at the woman.

'How long have you been selling these?'

She shook her head robotically. 'No comment.'

'Where's Pancho?'

She nodded at the corner of the field, 'Over there.'

Dylan headed for the van, clutching the miniature coffin in

his hand. Pancho was sitting inside, taking a call on his mobile. Dylan opened the door on the passenger side, chucked the coffin into Pancho's lap. Pancho casually looked down at it, then across at Dylan. He didn't look pleased at having his call interrupted. 'We need to talk,' said Dylan.

He stared at Dylan and Dylan stared back, intimidated, resentful, angry. Pancho held his gaze for long enough to let him know that he wasn't bothered, then calmly said to the person on the other end, 'I have to go, I'll call you back later.'

Dylan climbed in and sat in the passenger seat next to him.

'I turned a blind eye to the burger stall –'

'I didn't realise you owned this park.'

Dylan faltered, but only for a second.

'But *this* is way out of order.'

Pancho picked up the coffin lying in his lap, looked at it fondly.

'Very popular with the Japanese tourists, my girls tell me.'

'Oh do they? And what about the baseball caps with *my* slogan splashed all across them? Are they popular too? You've been ripping me off. You've been ripping my dad off. It's got to stop.'

Pancho put his mobile back into his jacket pocket with slow, deliberate movements, keeping Dylan waiting.

'I have to tell you, *amigo*, after your father's performance last night on the radio, the bottom has fallen out of the market for souvenirs. I am going to be left with a large amount of unsold stock on my hands. I'll be very lucky to break even.'

'Oh *please*, spare me. That's not the point and you know it. You have been ripping us off.'

Pancho took out a cheroot, lit it. He took a puff, then held it up in front of his eyes, slowly twirling it round in his fingers.

'And what about you, *amigo*?'

Dylan didn't expect that.

'What do you mean?'

'You need to take a good look at your own self before you go accusing other people of exploiting your father.'

Dylan straightened up, gave Pancho his most macho stare. 'Is that so?'

Pancho held his eyes. 'I see you are making a film about yourself.'

'A video diary – about the campaign.'

Pancho smiled. 'Starring you, with script and direction also by you, *si*?'

'Listen . . .'

'And I've found some of your business cards on the ground. You walk around as if you own the place. You think you're a big star now. People who've lived here all their lives, they feel offended, to tell you the truth. They are asking me, "Who is this *hombre* going around saying the people of Crindau think this, and the people of Crindau won't put up with that? I've never seen him before."'

'I grew up here.'

'But you left pretty quick, no? I'm a part of this community, you're not. You left here years ago to become a ballet dancer.'

'An actor.'

'Whatever. You've forgotten how things work here. You don't just swan in from your travels when you feel like it and rewrite the rules. You think you can come along and tell me what to do, just like that?'

'Piss off.'

Pancho stiffened and, when he spoke again, it was very quietly and slowly. 'I'll ignore that, since your father is a friend of mine.' He set the miniature coffin carefully on the dashboard.

'We've got the lowest wages in the country here in Wales, but the prices are the same as anywhere else, right? So some bloke in London, he wants a designer top that costs a hundred quid, he doesn't think twice, he goes out and buys it. But the powers that be, they think a bloke here, who earns barely half his wage, should pay the same. Where's the fairness in that? He can't afford to do it, can he? And why shouldn't that bloke be able to afford decent gear? Who's got the right to say he doesn't deserve it just as much?'

'Is this relevant?'

'And these big companies that make this stuff, how much do you think *they* pay for the gear? They got these poor devils in India and the Philippines, working fifteen, sixteen hours a day for fifty pence a week making their stuff, so they can keep the costs down. So when you go into a shop and pay the full whack, you're just propping up a rotten system. The people round here, not only do they hate injustice and exploitation, they like stylish goods, and I am able to provide those for them. Now these souvenirs, they are a very small part of my operation. But they are my way of putting something back into the community.'

Dylan burst out laughing – 'Oh yeah, how's that?'

'I'm spreading the word. I want your father to win as much as anyone. In fact I went down the bookies the day after he announced he was standing, and put two hundred quid on him to win.'

Dylan folded his arms and fixed him with a meaningful stare.

'I want you to pay a percentage to the campaign.'

'You are beginning to annoy me, *amigo*.'

'And you're annoying me. Let me ask you something – have you got a licence to trade?'

Pancho sat bolt upright, pointed a finger at Dylan.

'Get out of my van.'

'Look, I'm not going to –'

'GET OUT!'

Dylan got out.

Aidan had asked Gwyn.

'Where's Russell?'

He'd asked Wilf.

'Where's Russell?'

They'd both looked shifty, said they didn't know. So he asked Dylan. He looked down the periscope at his dad's pale,

313

worried face, and decided to give it to him straight; it wasn't fair not to.

'He got the hump and left. I'm not sure why.'

Aidan knew why. It had been preying on his mind. He hadn't seen him since that time he interrupted their conversation to take the call from the *New York Times*.

Dylan said, 'Listen, Dad, he was a negative influence. I hate to say this, but the campaign is probably better off without him. To be honest I think he was just jealous. He's used to being the top dog, he didn't like seeing you in the papers.'

Aidan suspected he was enjoying it right now though.

'Look, I know he's not perfect, but he's been a good friend to me. Stuck with me through thick and thin down the years.'

Dylan remembered him coming round to the house, behaving like a bully. Aidan taking it.

Aidan noticed Dylan's sceptical expression.

'As you get older, you learn to give and take, because you're never going to get exactly what you want from your friends and your loved ones. That's something you'll learn.'

He could see that Dylan didn't think he'd ever have to learn anything from him. Sometimes that boy was too cocky for his own good. Aidan wanted to ring Russell. But he knew it would be no use. Knew him too well. He'd leave it, wait till all this was over. He didn't want to be below him when they next talked, with Russell staring down at him through a periscope.

That evening Watkins appeared on the TV news, announcing that Sunny Jim had agreed to a period of consultation with the government.

'I think this is a very significant development. It just goes to show how seriously the government is taking this matter. This party and this prime minister are absolutely committed to protecting people's jobs whenever possible. The people of Crindau can rest assured that New Labour have their best interests at heart.'

Dylan flung a cushion on to the floor. 'Oh *please* – pass the sick bag.'

The reporter asked, 'Did you, as the prospective MP for Crindau West, ask the prime minister to intervene?'

'Well, let's just say that he's been kept very well informed about what's happening here in Crindau.'

The look of smug triumph on his face had Dylan on his feet and yelling, 'You slimy fucker!'

The message couldn't be clearer – I have connections; if you vote for me I'll get things done. Dylan began stabbing his finger at the TV.

'Who are you kidding? It's nothing but a bloody PR exercise.'

He turned off the TV in disgust. *A period of consultation.* The voters would never fall for that. Surely?

In the Globe, Tony put down his pint, wiped his mouth and said, 'You've got to hand it to Watkins, he's making things happen.'

The others round the table nodded. Wilf did too, then caught Gwyn's sombre expression and regretted it. Gwyn pushed his glasses back on to the bridge of his nose.

'You really think so?'

Tony rocked back in his chair, a disgusted expression on his face.

'At least he's getting them to come to the table – Aidan never managed that, did he? They won't give him the time of day.'

'That's right.'

Gwyn looked rattled, but leant forward, swallowed hard and began speaking again.

'Look, all I'm saying is –'

Tony cut him off immediately. 'Oh give it a rest, mun, no one wants to listen to your nitpicking.'

The others started jeering Gwyn, and he dropped it.

★

Dylan came downstairs in a foul mood the next day. It was 7.30, he'd slept badly, his mind pulsing with negative energy. How was he going to repair the damage his dad had done? What was he going to do about Pancho? There were so many other problems, was it really worth taking him on? But how could he back down now without Pancho thinking he'd scared him off? He couldn't have that. He picked up the pile of newspapers lying in the hall. Only a few days ago he couldn't wait to find out what they were saying about the campaign, but now he chucked them on to the living-room table without looking at them.

He made himself a pot of coffee. He spread some jam on his toast, then brought his plate and mug through to the living room, sat down and glanced at the front page of the new determinedly downmarket Welsh daily, the *Dragon's Tongue*.

Coffin Protestor's Dope-smoking Lesbian Daughter

'Jesus fuck!'
The slice of toast dropped to the table. Dylan grabbed the paper with both hands.

Shauna Walsh, daughter of clueless underground protestor Aidan Walsh, who is running as an Independent in the Crindau West by-election, has a criminal record for possession of cannabis, it emerged today.

The story dated back ten years, to when Shauna was at university. There was an old photo of her in a *Meat is Murder* T-shirt, wearing shades, looking like the archetypal drug-smoking student. Dylan was gripping the paper so tightly it began to tear. He let go, gulped down some coffee. This was a catastrophe, an absolute catastrophe.

Shauna Walsh, 30, has a live-in lezzie lover, 'Charlie' Robson, who plays saxophone in controversial all-female band Offa's

Dykes. Their CD includes tracks such as 'The Ladies of Llangollen' (the notorious lesbians who settled in the town of that name in the nineteenth century), 'Shirley Bassey Wouldn't Like It' and 'I Lost My Cherry in Caerphilly.'

There was a more recent photo of Shauna next to one of Charlie – *the sultry sax-playing girlfriend.* But the killer line was at the bottom. *If Mr Walsh has failed to come clean about his own daughter's criminal record and unconventional lifestyle, then voters are entitled to ask why they should trust him about anything else?* At the end of the story it said, *See Editorial, page 18.*

Dylan turned to it. The headline was *No Respect.*

The name Offa's Dykes is one that seems calculated to cause maximum offence. It's making a mockery out of our heritage. King Offa built his notorious dyke to keep the Welsh out of England. Any Welshman found on the English side of the dyke was deemed to be plotting insurrection against the English and had his right hand cut off, so that he would not be able to use his sword. It had nothing to do with sex at all! To use the name in this fashion is disgraceful. It is an insult to the Welsh people. It is something that the electorate of Crindau West should bear in mind when casting their votes this Friday.

For fuck's sake, that was rich. This was the paper that always called Plaid Cymru 'the language fascists' and only last week had run an article claiming the Eisteddfod was a 'monstrous waste of money'. Where had this newfound deep respect for Welsh heritage come from?

'OK, OK!' said Dylan, tossing the *Dragon's Tongue* to one side. 'Let's not panic. This is a time for cool heads. How are we going to limit the damage?'

He took a long, deep breath and tried to focus. He gazed out of the window and was silent for several minutes. Then he growled and slammed his fists down hard on the table. Fuck, he had no idea.

Aidan's mobile rang just as he was about to bite into his breakfast butty.

'Good morning. Les Richards from the *Dragon's Tongue* here. What's your policy on drugs?'

'Come again?'

'Dad!'

Aidan looked up to see Dylan making a desperate cutting motion with his hand, mouthing, 'No comment.' He held Aidan's questioning stare, then repeated the gesture and shook his head rapidly.

'Hello? Are you there, Mr Walsh?'

Aidan, still looking at Dylan, taking in the panic in his eyes, said, 'No comment.'

'Have you seen the *Dragon's Tongue* this morning?'

Dylan helpfully held up the front page of that very organ.

'Oh fuck.'

He switched off the phone.

It was terrible. They were using his daughter to get at him. Why? Last week they were describing him as the people's candidate.

Dylan said, 'It's a tabloid rag, Dad. That's why.'

Dylan knew she used to like the odd joint – so what. But he'd never known she had a conviction. And how the hell had they found out about her being gay? God, what a nightmare. He should have vetted her carefully before the campaign began for any skeletons in the closet.

'Did you know she was taking drugs, Dylan?'

'Dad, going to university and not smoking the odd joint would be like going into a pub every night for three years and never drinking anything but mineral water. It's no big deal.'

'She could have said no.'

Dylan took a deep breath. He knew that getting sarcastic wasn't a good idea, but oh man, it was difficult not to sometimes.

'Dad, it's harmless. Didn't you see that programme on TV about those old people in Wales who smoke it because it helps with their rheumatism?'

He had. What an eye-opener. Pensioners in sensible cardies smoking a big spliff with their cuppa. *Lovely it is, just the job.* Fair play to them though, if nothing else had worked. It was improving their lives. Still. That was different. That was *medicinal*.

'Look,' said Dylan, 'I'll get her to put out a statement – "I experimented with soft drugs for a brief time when I was a student, but it was just a phase, blah, blah, blah . . . The name Offa's Dykes is not intended to cause offence, blah blah blah . . ."'

But something was bothering Aidan.

'Have *you* smoked drugs?'

'Yeah, course I have. But I'm like you, Dad, mun, I prefer a drink.'

Aidan decided not to ask any more questions. There were things he was happy not knowing. He'd had enough revelations for one day.

The press soon started arriving in his garden and poking their snouts down the periscope, asking the same gloating, sneering questions. When Aidan said 'no comment', they kept on plugging away; when he shook his head and said he wasn't giving any interviews at the moment, they'd point a camera at him and take a photo of him scowling, or shielding his face with his hands. He had no choice but to lie there and take it. It sickened him, the way the media had turned against him. He'd given hundreds of interviews and not once had they been nasty or unpleasant. But now they scented blood, and had turned.

'What do you think of your daughter's lifestyle?'

'No comment.'

'Are you a fan of Offa's Dykes? Do you think their name is in good taste?'

'No comment.'

'What is your policy on cannabis?'

'No comment.'

'We've seen a lot of your son Dylan during this campaign, but this is the first time we've heard about your daughter. Have you been deliberately keeping her out of the limelight because you knew she was a liability?'

Aidan snapped.

'How dare you — I'm very proud of my daughter. How she lives her life is her own business. Now fuck off out of my garden.'

After they'd gone, he realised he'd given them just what they wanted, another juicy headline. *Foul-mouthed Candidate's Outburst!* Still, he liked himself for losing his temper. For standing up for Shauna and being a good father. Protecting her. Even though this was ruining his campaign.

He tried ringing Shauna again. Every time he'd tried before her number had been engaged. This time, he finally got through.

'It's Dad. Shauna, have you seen the paper?'

'Yes, I have.'

Her voice was strained and tired. She sounded miserable, on the cusp of anger.

'Are you OK?'

'How could I be, after having my face splashed all over the front page of that rag?'

Which made him feel like an idiot. That had been a dumb thing to say.

'You've got to get your side of the story out.'

'I'll talk it over with Charlie tonight and we'll decide what to do together. I'm not going to rush into anything.'

'No, Shauna, listen to me, you've got to do it immediately.'

Now there was an edge to her voice. 'What's the rush?'

Aidan answered too quickly. 'They're going to the polls tonight.'

As soon as he said it he knew it was a mistake. There was a silence, and he held his breath.

'So that's what's really bothering you?'

Aidan had fallen in her estimation. He could actually feel himself falling. He feared he would break open when he finally landed. There was such hurt and disappointment in her voice. He knew the anger would follow. And he didn't blame her.

'Well, I'm sorry if this affects your standing in the polls, Dad, but I have to tell you that it's having quite a negative effect on me too.'

'Shauna, love, listen to me please, you don't understand.'

'No, Dad, I understand perfectly. I'm the one who sorts things out, I'm the one you and Dylan can always rely on when you need help. And now, when *I* finally need some support from my family, all you can do is accuse me of ruining your chances of victory. Well, thank you very much.'

'Shauna.'

'Good luck in the election, Dad. I've got to go now.'

'Shauna –'

She'd cut the call. He pressed redial. She didn't answer.

'Well done, Aidan.'

What he hated most was the way they tried to make him ashamed of his own daughter. *Was* he ashamed? He told himself he didn't care what Shauna did as long as she was happy, but did he mean it? If he wasn't ashamed of what she was, how come he hadn't told his friends? He imagined Gwyn and Wilf reading about it. Russell too. They'd want to know why he hadn't told them. What could he say?

You never told us she was a lesbian.

Well, you never asked.

That rag was right. They'd wonder what else he hadn't told them about. The public, the voters, they'd all think the same. *If he can't come clean about his family, then how we can we trust him with our vote?*

He hadn't known what to do for the best. Shauna had told *him* about it, not his friends. It wasn't any of their business. It was a private matter. There'd been no one to talk to about it. If he'd known someone else with a son or daughter who was gay, it might have been different. *Yeah, Shauna says that too. It's hard, isn't it? You don't want to say the wrong thing, so you say nothing. I don't mind as long as she's happy, I just worry sometimes that she has to deal with prejudiced people.*

But he'd said nothing. When his friends asked about her, he always said the same thing. *How's Shauna getting on? Oh, great.*

In fact, he couldn't remember the last time he'd sat down with Shauna and asked her about herself – asked properly, in a way that made it clear he really wanted to know, even if it would make for uncomfortable listening. His kids had their own lives now and he didn't want to interfere. That's what he told himself. But maybe he was scared to hear about how hard life was for them.

It had been a long time since they'd talked to him about any of their problems. The realisation suddenly made him feel very sad, and lonely as hell.

He was a lousy father. He hadn't given Shauna the kind of understanding she needed. His heart began drumming as he thought about it. If she or Dylan were suffering, if they were unhappy or confused, then it was because he'd failed them. All the bad things that had happened to him since Eileen died he deserved. He'd done so much harm to the people he loved. Let them all down. Collapsed under the pressure. He was a useless fucking bastard.

And he had the gall to ask people to vote for him. What a joke.

Then Safina rang him.

'I've just seen the paper, Aidan. How awful. That poor girl, how must she feel, having her personal life raked over like that?'

Aidan ground his teeth, scraped his calloused knuckles along the coffin lid.

'And I've just made it worse.'

He told her about their row.

'I've really screwed up now.'

'No,' said Safina, 'you haven't – don't you dare talk like that. You don't know how lucky you are, Aidan Walsh.'

'Come again?'

'Lucky – yes, *lucky*.'

She sounded furious.

'How I wish I had a daughter to fall out with. Or a son. But I couldn't have children.' Her voice, hoarse with emotion, froze the breath in Aidan's lungs.

'Safina, I'm sorry . . .'

He was shocked now. Didn't know how to react to her bringing up something so personal, right out of the blue like that.

'I don't want your sympathy. *That's* not why I'm telling you.'

He'd never heard her so angry. He wondered if he'd offended her without realising. It felt like they'd fast-forwarded through the early stages of a relationship – the flirting, first dates, romantic weekends and staring into each other's eyes – and gone straight to the bitter recriminations and boiling resentments.

'And don't think I'm going to offer *you* sympathy either. It's your daughter who needs help and understanding most right now. So stop feeling sorry for yourself and *do* something about it, alright?'

Aidan was beginning to squirm. How many more women were going to lose their temper with him today? At this rate he wouldn't be surprised if Megan turned up later and tipped the contents of his bedpan down the periscope.

'Well . . .'

'Well what?'

'How important is your daughter?'

'There's nothing more important to me. But I don't know if *she* realises that.'

'Well now's the time to let her know. You feel bad now, you're regretting what you did. But you'll never forgive yourself if you just lie there and wallow in misery and let Shauna think you don't care about her.'

Aidan stared up at the grey sky above, the plastic sheet rippling gently in the wind.

'But she won't answer her phone, what can I do?'

'You'll think of something if it's that important to you.'

She was right. It was time for him to stand up and be counted. He had to do the right thing, no matter how much it might cost him.

The phone in Dylan's office didn't stop ringing all morning. He tried stalling, kept saying that he'd be releasing a statement shortly, had no comment to make until then. Only he hadn't written one yet. How could he, when Shauna wasn't returning his calls? How did she expect him to help her when she just ignored him? It didn't matter what he did, she'd always treat him like her kid brother. The mess she was in now, and the damage it had done to the campaign, he could still sort it out, he knew he could; if she'd just give him the chance.

The phone rang again. He snatched it up, then put it straight back down. Took it off, laid it on the desk. He couldn't think straight with that constant clamour. He checked his watch — nearly half-eleven. If she didn't ring back soon, he was going to have to write something without speaking to her, and if she didn't like it, tough. They were running out of time and he couldn't stand this anymore.

When she hadn't rung back by mid-day, Dylan decided to call Nick at the *Argus*. He would be the most sympathetic journalist and damage limitation was the name of the game. Dylan would say that Shauna regretted her youthful dalliance with soft drugs, and was totally opposed to legalising cannabis; she was in a stable, long-term, deeply loving relationship; she had a deep knowledge and love for Welsh culture and was very sorry for any offence caused by the name Offa's Dykes, and so on.

Nick answered.

'Hello.'

'Hi Nick, it's Dylan. I've got that statement in response to today's story in the *Dragon's Tongue*.'

'Right – listen, can it wait?'

'Well not really, no.'

'I'm in the garden right now, interviewing your dad, getting *his* reaction.'

Dylan flew outside, saw Nick standing next to the periscope, scribbling shorthand. He ran over, stood just behind him like an anxious minder, trying to catch up with what was being said. Standing on tip-toe, he could look over Nick's shoulder and just see his dad's face at the bottom of the shaft. He didn't see Dylan though, or at least he didn't seem to. His first words were not encouraging.

'Nick, I'm going to be absolutely honest with you. Make sure you get all this down.'

This made Dylan weak with nerves – absolute honesty was a new and frightening concept in political interviews. What the hell was Aidan playing at?

'I can't put my hand on my heart and say I would be a better MP than Nigel Watkins. I hope I would. And I certainly believe that I have more commitment to this town than he does. But no, I'm not going to promise people that I would do a better job than him. I'm sick to death of listening to politicians promising the earth. And what happens when they get into power? They never give a straight answer to a straight question. I won't pretend I have the solution to every problem, and I'm not going to make any promises I can't keep, because I wouldn't be able to live with myself afterwards if I did that. I respect the voters too much. All I can say is that if you vote for me, I will do the very best I can for you. Maybe Watkins is smarter than me, but there's one thing I can say with absolute certainty, he doesn't love this town like I do, he doesn't care about its people like me. It will be a long and hard struggle to keep the factory open and I don't honestly know if it's possible. But I *can* promise you that no one will try harder than me to do it. I don't know if that promise is enough to make you vote for me, but it's all I can offer you.'

Nick was nodding as he wrote all this down; behind him, Dylan hung his head. He couldn't believe what he was hearing. What in god's name was Aidan thinking of?

'But if you disapprove of my daughter's lifestyle, then I don't want your vote. She's a fine young woman, and I love her very much.'

He stopped for a moment to get his voice back under control. Dylan had his head in his hands now.

'I can think of no one in this world who means more to me, and if the price of getting elected is to see her suffer at the hands of that disgusting rag, then it's too big a price to pay.'

Dylan had to turn away and mouth a silent scream. They were ruined. It was all over. After all his work.

There was a long pause. Nick looked up from his notebook. He said in a very quiet voice, 'Is that it?'

'Yeah, Nick, I think that's it.'

Now all Aidan could do was wait. He would keep his promise to Shauna. He was coming up out of the coffin, no matter what the result. He rang Gwyn and Wilf, asked them to come around after work and dig him out. He asked Dylan to help. Dylan seemed to be in shock, but mumbled his agreement, then disappeared.

12

Later that afternoon Gwyn, Wilf and Dylan dug Aidan out. They unscrewed the lid, grabbed his hands and hauled him up. When he took his first steps his legs were as weak and wobbly as a newborn kitten, the light blinding him, the space around him making him feel dizzy and disorientated. He was freezing so Gwyn wrapped a coat around him. Aidan looked agog at the garden. Hard to believe that it was his – it was too big, too unfamiliar. He leaned on Wilf as they walked back into the house.

'Sorry, I must stink to high heaven.'

'No, you're all right, mun.'

When he stepped inside his unease grew. He saw objects – a kettle, cooker, table, curtains, and knew, in an abstract way, what they were, had some dim memory of their name and function lurking at the back of his mind. But their sheer otherness threatened to overwhelm him. Gwyn gripped his shoulder tightly.

'Are you OK?'

'Everything feels strange.'

'Bound to, mun, after all this time. Come on, let's get you sat down.'

Aidan admired the chaos: the trestle tables with hundreds of leaflets still scattered across them; dirty mugs and plates; posters; letters and drawings pinned to the wall. It looked as if everyone had been evacuated because of some terrible crisis.

Aidan felt dazzled by all this space. There was nothing to stop him from getting up and walking wherever he wanted. But he stayed in the chair, not yet ready to explore any of the other rooms yet. That felt far too daunting. It would take him months just to get used to this one again.

'How does it feel to be back in your house after all this time?' Gwyn asked

Aidan looked at him, so large, so solid, after being nothing but a head and shoulders at the top of his periscope for weeks.

'Scary, to be honest with you, mate. It's like I've been to outer space and back and now I've got to get used to life on earth all over again.'

Gwyn stared at him. 'It'll take time. There's no rush. You haven't got to do anything.'

'Yes, I have,' replied Aidan, a sliver of fear running through him. 'I have to be at the town hall for the result tonight.'

'Yeah, there is that.'

'Yeah,' said Aidan, 'that.'

There was an uncomfortable silence. 'Where's Dylan?' Aidan said.

Wilf pulled back the curtain, looked through the window.

'He's out in the garden, making a call.'

Aidan gripped the arms of the chair. 'He's taking it badly. He put so much into this.' He looked at Gwyn and Wilf. 'You all did. I'm sorry I let you down.'

Wilf said, 'You could still win, couldn't he, Gwyn?'

They both looked at Gwyn.

'That's true. I'll go and put the kettle on.'

As they were drinking their tea Shauna arrived. When he saw her standing in the doorway, Aidan felt his chest constricting. Gwyn and Wilf sank further back in the sofa, wishing they could escape to another room, but not knowing how to leave this one without drawing attention to themselves. Shauna took a step forward.

'Thank you, Dad.'

Tears pricked his eyes. She dropped her bag, came over, crouched down and hugged him tightly.

'That must have been a really hard thing to do.'

'No, not nearly as hard as losing you.'

She pressed her face to his.

'You'll never do that.'

Then for the first time Aidan was crying in front of his friends.

Shauna found Dylan upstairs in his old bedroom. He was sitting in front of the video camera, staring blankly into the lens.

'Dylan?'

He turned slowly round. His face was drained and pale.

'Don't you think you should come downstairs and spend some time with Dad? I think he'd like that right now.'

He looked as though he was straining to hear something that Shauna couldn't, laughter possibly, or music from somewhere far away. 'In a minute, I . . .'

'What's on your mind, spit it out.'

He gazed at her for a long time, then said, 'Why didn't you return my calls?'

'I didn't have time.'

Her expression warned him not to push it. But he did.

'I could have helped.'

'Dylan, I wasn't looking for the kind of help you would have offered.'

'Thanks a lot. You don't even know what I was going to –'

'What I needed was support – would you have offered me that?'

His mouth gaped open.

'I didn't want any ingenious ideas about how to turn round the story in the paper, or a carefully worded apology for breaking a tacky tabloid's moral code. What I wanted was someone to understand what I might have been feeling like. That was what I wanted, more than anything. Could you have given me that, Dylan?'

He stared back at her, horrified; she was nearly in tears.

'No, I thought not.'

She turned away from him, left the room.

Aidan had a long, hot bath. He put in some drops of lavender that Shauna had brought and lay back and closed his eyes. After about twenty minutes his stiff and battered body gradually relaxed and he began to feel some of the pent-up tension slowly subsiding. He flexed his fingers, gingerly moved his legs from side to side, delighting in the gentle ripples he created. Ran his big toe over the tap, savouring the contrast between the cold metal and the soothing warmth that enveloped the rest of his body. After weeks of having to use Wet Wipes to keep clean this was pure, unadulterated luxury. He could have happily stayed there all night and was actually beginning to nod off when Shauna gently knocked on the door and told him they needed to leave soon. He towelled himself dry, then went upstairs and got dressed. He chose the shirt he'd worn in the Huw Humphreys interview, a pair of black trousers and a navy blue jacket. He didn't own a tie and wasn't going to start wearing one now. When he went back downstairs he rang Safina.

'Hi-ya.'

'Hello, I hear you're back in the land of the living.'

'Yeah, but I'm not sure it feels any better. I'm dreading getting up on that stage.'

'You should be proud.'

'I've made an arse of myself.'

'No, you've been very brave. It was wonderful to hear someone speak the truth in public for a change.'

'I couldn't have done it without you. The things you said . . .'

Dylan opened the door, saw Aidan's expression, quietly closed it again. But the spell had been broken and now Aidan didn't know how to talk about what had passed between them on the phone. Instead he said, 'I might get a roasting tonight, and you know what the media are like, the way they can ruin your private life. So I don't think we should meet until the heat dies down.'

'I understand. Maybe we *both* need a bit of time.'

Aidan wondered what that meant? Had she said too much, did she regret it? Would they both now be too embarrassed to face each other?

'I'll give you a ring soon.'

He put down the phone and sat on the step for a long while. Maybe the real reason he hadn't arranged a time to meet her was because he wasn't sure if it would work out, and he just couldn't face being hurt again. He was nervous. He was scared. He was afraid of being found wanting. Wouldn't it just be easier to quietly settle into his disappointment, with a minimum of fuss, just as he usually did?

When they arrived at the town hall they were immediately crushed by a pack of journalists and photographers. Aidan was sandwiched between Gwyn and Wilf, clinging on to Shauna's arm. Faced with an audience, Dylan sprang into life again, burrowing through the pack like a dervish, a blur of limbs. *No comment. Excuse me. No comment.*

They walked down a long corridor lined with overbearing oil paintings of former mayors and council leaders. Inside the hall there were TV crews from France, Italy, Spain, Poland, India, Australia and beyond. The voices echoed off the walls and ceiling, reverberated painfully in Aidan's head. It was utterly overpowering after being boxed up for so long. The crowd pressing in on him, the bright lights, the noise, the size and scale of the place, its municipal pride and self-importance rammed down his throat. He wanted to be back under the ground again, with nothing but a periscope connecting him to the booming, buzzing, dangerous world above.

Shauna said, 'Are you OK?'

He steadied himself against her.

'I need to sit down.'

She guided him to a chair, hunkered down next to him and held his hand. Aidan felt people staring at him. There were a couple of blokes in cheap suits standing nearby, quite obviously sozzled, swigging booze from plastic glasses. They began talking about Shauna at the top of their voices, as if she were deaf. *Is that his daughter? Well I'll say this for her, she's got guts all right, turning up here.* He went to say something but she tightened her grip, whispered, 'Leave it, Dad, it's not worth it.' Her tone saddened him, as if she was used to being pointed out as different. Once again he wondered how much he really knew about his children's lives.

Dylan was scurrying around the room, barging in on conversations, asking how Watkins had done. Aidan knew it was his way of coping, but he just wished that for once Dylan would calm down and come and sit with him and Shauna. He tried to blot out the thought that immediately flew into his head: *he'd sit down if Eileen was here*. Every time he got annoyed with Dylan, each time he pushed too hard, Aidan would remember how close he'd been to his mother and how, no matter how he tried, he could never replace her.

Someone handed him a cup of tea and he settled down to wait.

When the time came for the result to be announced, Aidan felt dizzy. His throat was dry and his palms were clammy. He stood in a line with the other contenders, the only one not wearing a rosette; the only man without a tie, flanked by Shauna and Dylan. It felt weird, to be standing in a line like that at his age, heart racing, anxiously waiting for his name to be called. Reminded him of the times he was forced to wait outside the headmaster's room with the other miscreants back in school. Just as in those days there was no doubt that he would be caned, so too now he knew the outcome already, could tell from the glances people were giving him, the look of huge relief on Watkins' face. The joy of doing the right thing by Shauna had now disappeared. Aidan felt utterly drained and horribly depressed. He stood there, stony faced, and listened to the announcement.

Nigel Anthony Watkins, 22,837; Aidan John Patrick Walsh, 21,077

When the applause and cheers had died down, Watkins stepped forward to make his victory speech. He began by thanking the mayor and all the officials for their splendid efforts and Aidan made a mental note to do the same. The least he could do now was to bow out with dignity and decorum.

Watkins continued, 'This has been a hard-fought and close-run contest. Indeed, just a few days ago I was being written off as an also-ran. But I've always been someone who's relished a fight, no matter how great the odds stacked up against me, and I never had any intention of giving up.'

Aidan felt the bile rising in his throat. He was disgusted to hear this wealthy lawyer, backed by the might of a party machine, portray himself as a plucky underdog.

'And I promise the people of Crindau that I shall be just as tenacious when representing them in Parliament.' He paused, and right on cue a gaggle of party hacks cheered and yelled as if he'd just scored the winning goal in the world cup final. 'In the end, this was a victory for realism and common sense. It proved that the people of Crindau were able to make a sober and intelligent assessment of what is the best way forward for this town.'

No, they didn't, thought Aidan, they switched their vote at the last minute because I was ambushed on the radio by your dirty tricks squad and the papers dug up some dirt about my daughter.

'There is a tendency to romanticise the past, to think that everything was better in the old days. But the world is changing rapidly and we cannot rely on the old certainties anymore. At one time south Wales was famous the world over for its industrial might, but those days can never return. We must learn to adapt. As Tony Blair has said, there is increasingly little difference these days between the manufacturing and the service industries.'

Aidan stared at his shoelaces, wondering what the fuck that was supposed to mean. Still, the overall message was clear, don't hold out too much hope for the factory remaining open. Watkins continued in this vein for several minutes, till even his most loyal supporters began to glaze over. Aidan's attention began to wander too, though every now and then he picked out certain phrases of Watkins' that he'd become very familiar with over the last few weeks: *Centrally driven approach . . . incentives promoting user choice . . . inbuilt flexibility and capacity to push forward . . . contestability of service.*

'Shauna', he whispered, leaning closer, 'this is all way above my head. I haven't a bloody clue what he's on about.'

'It's utter bullshit', she whispered back.

That made Aidan smile. And relieved too. He elbowed her playfully. She lowered her head, whispering again. 'Or the language of management consultancy, to put it more politely. That's what politicians talk in now.'

'Why?'

'So people won't understand what they really mean.'

'What *does* he mean?'

'That he'll privatise anything that moves.'

Aidan looked at her gravely. That was the moment when he realised that he'd been fooling himself all along, that he'd never had a snowball in hell's chance of winning. Even if he hadn't made a fool of himself on the phone-in, or they hadn't run that story about Shauna, there'd have been something else that would have tripped him up. He just wasn't cut out for this. To be a successful politician these days you had to be able to stamp down on expectations, butcher idealism and call the dismantling of the welfare state 'radical'. And do all this as if you were addressing an office meeting about the need to cut down on unnecessary photocopying, rather than talking about our children's futures. It wasn't for him. He was ready to go back to being invisible. But first he must face the public for one last time – the applause for Watkins was dying down and it was Aidan's turn to speak.

He stepped into the lights. A wave of beery breath wafted up from the crowd, a baby cried from the back of the hall, there was a brief and furious outbreak of coughing. Then an expectant hush descended – how was the disgraced loser going to handle this? He began with a series of thanks, just as Watkins had done. He looked into the crowd and noticed Geoff, the man whose wife was dying of cancer, standing about twenty feet away. He looked utterly distraught. Aidan flinched under his mournful stare. His eldest, Cerys, was sitting on top of his broad shoulders, gazing up at a red balloon nestling against the ceiling. He had let them down, left them with no defence against the remorseless

334

need to adapt endlessly to the new reality. He grabbed the microphone with one hand and clung on to it tightly.

'I don't think I romanticise the past, and I don't believe that everything was better in the old days. But I was born and bred in this town and I'm not ashamed to say that I want the very best for everyone who lives here. If you want to call that unrealistic, if you think that shows an inability to adapt, then so be it. But I'm proud to have that dream, no matter how unfashionable.'

There was a huge cheer and wild, prolonged applause. Gywn cried out, 'You tell them, Aidan!'

Aidan could feel a lump forming in his throat, the tears threatening. He took a deep breath and continued.

'I believe that politics should be all about expressing your deepest dreams and hopes and about promoting belief in your fellow man. It should aim high, it should dare to be unrealistic and it should use the kind of language that everyone can under-stand, because it affects everyone.' He paused and glanced sideways at Shauna, who nodded at him encouragingly.

'I wonder if any youngsters will be inspired to go out and get involved in politics after listening to the kind of leaders we have today? I doubt it, to be honest. I remember watching a speech by Martin Luther King on the telly when I was a teenager. It was mesmerising. I was sitting on the edge of my seat, hanging on his every word. When he'd finished I felt the world was a better place because we had people like him in it. Can you imagine Martin Luther King saying "I have a dream . . . that one day we will achieve inbuilt flexibility and the capacity to push forward"? Or "I have a dream . . . that one day we will achieve incentives promoting user choice"?' There were a few giggles.

'Well, can you?'

'No!' cried Gwyn.

Aidan nodded at him. 'Do you know what "incentives promoting user choice" means?' Gwyn shook his head. 'No, neither do I, and I'm not ashamed to say it. In fact I feel a whole lot better for *not* knowing what it means. So if anyone out there does know, then please keep it to yourself.'

That got a laugh and a smattering of applause.

'Politicians wring their hands and wonder why fewer and fewer people vote. But we all know why, don't we? Because it's so hard to choose between the parties now, it hardly seems worth making the effort. It's like that old joke – no matter who you vote for, the government always gets in.'

The clutch of Watkins supporters at the front were growing uneasy now, but Aidan ignored them and focused on the people farther back.

'Do you know what I'm hoping? That there's someone out there watching or listening tonight who will be inspired to stand themselves in the future, after seeing how close I came to winning. That someone else will learn from my mistakes, and go on to win next time. Because it *can* be done. All it takes is one person who won't take no for an answer. One awkward so and so who doesn't believe that the people at the top know best. I really do think that a time will come soon when the people of this town will rise up and demand a greater say in how their lives are run.'

He paused to get the growing tremor in his voice back under control.

'It was Vaclav Havel who said "Politics is also the art of the impossible". Lots of people said I had no chance of saving our jobs, lots of people said a man like me had no chance of being elected an MP. Well, the people of Crindau very nearly made the impossible happen. I would sincerely like to thank everyone who voted for me. I'm sorry if you feel I let you down by not getting in – I did the best I could.'

He stepped away from the microphone and embraced Shauna. As the applause died down he said, 'Let's go home, love.'

Aidan spent the next couple of days getting used to being in his house again. Rising from his chair and walking from his living room into his kitchen felt like a major expedition, making tea and toast a daunting new task. *Jesus!* Nearly jumped out of his skin when the toast popped up with a loud clatter and bang.

He walked into the garden and felt the fresh, cold air on his skin. If he'd known how, he'd have written a poem about that moment, it moved him so much. He was out. He was free. The hole had been filled in, Gwyn and Wilf had taken the coffin away and the earth had been stamped down. The park outside was empty once again – no doubt Pancho had already moved on to some new money-making scheme. Each time he raised his head and looked up at the sky he felt less dizzy. Things were slowly returning to normal. He was gaining perspective. Soon he would feel he belonged in this world again. In a day or two he would go out for a walk. Shauna had got food in for him so he didn't have to go up town yet, and have people looking and pointing and smirking. But he knew he'd have to do it sooner or later. He had to sign on too, and think about looking for another job. He wasn't looking forward to that. *Reason you left your last employment? To bury myself alive in a coffin.*

Looking for a new job would be fun too. Who would take him on now?

And he needed to decide whether he was going to ring Safina. Not yet though. First he had to talk to Dylan.

'Son – I want to thank you for everything you put in. No one did more than you.'

Dylan looked up from the music magazine he was reading, slumped there on the sofa, where he spent most of the day, sullen and withdrawn, hardly saying a word. He moved his head very slightly, and Aidan decided it was a nod.

'You know you can stay here as long as you want.'

The truth was, he was making Aidan feel uncomfortable. He'd never said anything, but knew that Dylan blamed him and Shauna for losing the election. Hanging around the house with that long face on him felt like a terrible, constant rebuke. It wasn't good for either of them to be cooped up together like

337

this. Dylan needed to snap out of it, and Aidan needed to rebuild his life, and he couldn't do that with Dylan hovering.

'It upsets me, seeing you like this, son.'

'Like what?'

Acting just like you did when you were a teenager.

'Just sitting around all day, doing nothing.'

He licked his finger, idly turned the page of his magazine.

'Something will turn up soon.'

Dylan felt sure of that. It was only a matter of time: he'd made loads of contacts, handed out hundreds of business cards. Everyone had seen what he was capable of. In a day or two he would start ringing round, set up some meetings. He didn't want to do it yet, in case they thought he was desperate.

When the phone rang the next day Dylan got there first.

'Hello, this is Bryn Thomas, manager of Crindau FM.'

This was it. The first call.

'This is Dylan Walsh.'

What would they offer him? His own show? It would mean staying here in Crindau for a while, but it would be a start.

'So – how can I help you?'

'Is your father there?'

'Pardon me?'

He'd heard, but it hadn't made sense.

'I'd like to speak to your father, if I may.'

'Right . . .'

Dylan went and got his dad, then stood in the living room, lit a fag and paced anxiously up and down. When Aidan came back a few minutes later he had a startled expression on his face.

'Well?' said Dylan.

Aidan said, 'You'll never guess what he just said . . .'

Dylan was getting annoyed.

'Go on.'

Aidan shook his head.

'I still can't believe it.'

'*What?*'

Aidan sat down.

'They asked if I'd like my own programme.'

'*You!*'

Aidan laughed. 'I know, incredible, isn't it? Twice a week, from eight till ten. They want to call it *The World According to Aidan.*'

'The *what?*'

'I said so what kind of programme would that be then? He goes, "That's something for you to work out with your producer. We were thinking of having you reacting to whatever's in the news – just be yourself – playing some of your favourite records and doing some interviews. And talking about your time in the coffin, of course." Can you believe that?'

Dylan couldn't. He felt something vital slipping out of him. For a moment he thought he was going to be sick.

'You know, I could use this programme to keep up the pressure on Sunny Jim. A lot of people seem to think that things are looking up now that they've agreed to talk to the government, but I don't trust them – nor New Labour.' He narrowed his eyes, clenched his fist. 'I'm going to stay on their case.'

His expression softened again and he shook his head in bewilderment.

'I can't get over it.'

Aidan was staring at Dylan, as if he might explain why this enormous piece of luck had fallen into his lap. But he couldn't. He said weakly, 'Congratulations Dad. It sounds brilliant.'

The following evening, Dylan stood in Shauna's consulting room. He'd never been there before. It wasn't what he expected. He'd imagined it would be cold and clinical. But the walls were light blue, there were fresh flowers in an elegant vase on the small table next to Shauna's armchair, a beautiful Persian carpet on the floor. The couch was pretty cool too, covered with a gorgeous Indian throw of bright colours, with plump,

339

inviting cushions piled high in one corner. Dylan could see himself screwing on it. The room was arranged so that whoever lay on it faced a framed Paul Klee poster on the wall opposite. The one with a fisherman standing up in a boat holding a spear, a big fish lurking under the water.

Shauna closed the door behind her and said, 'Why don't you sit down?'

There wasn't another chair, just the couch. Dylan wondered if she was playing some kind of practical joke, but didn't want to remain standing awkwardly in the middle of the room clutching his bag, so he put it down and perched himself on the very edge of the couch. Then had to get up again almost immediately as Shauna came and thrust a thick brown envelope stuffed with cash into his hands.

'Thanks.'

She sat in the armchair opposite. He avoided her eyes as he stuffed the envelope into an inside pocket in his jacket. On the wall opposite he noticed a small framed photo of George Eliot, with a quotation by her that read *It is never too late to become the person you could have been.*

'Where are you going this time?'

'Ireland – remember Nuala?'

'Last year's red-hot love.'

'Yeah, her – well, she has this younger sister who . . .'

'. . . you slept with behind Nuala's back.'

Dylan snapped, 'It was *her* who was chasing *me.*'

Shauna nodded in an offhanded way. Then, Christ, this *really* pissed him off, stole a glance at her desk diary, open on the table next to her.

'So you're going back to Ireland to start something with her.'

'Yeah, she's a musician, and they're setting up these, like, happenings, in village halls and small venues, and at festivals in the summer – a kind of mix of music and storytelling and drama. They all live in this converted bus and . . .'

'Sounds a bit hippyish for you.'

Dylan spread his arms. 'Well, I fancy a change. And I thought it would make a good video diary – perhaps a comedy. I still love that video diary concept, I just need to find the right subject.'

Shauna clasped her hands in her lap. Dylan noticed a box of tissues on the occasional table next to the couch, presumably for clients who spilled their guts then started to bawl.

'Is that something you want to do? Do you think you'll actually *enjoy* it?'

'You gotta keep moving.'

He flashed her his best ironic smile, but Shauna didn't smile back.

She said, 'Can I say something?'

Dylan stiffened; here we go. He thought he kept his voice cheery when he replied, 'Feel free.'

'I know you think you're preserving your precious freedom by never sticking to one thing, but in fact you're so frightened of *real* change –' She placed a hand on her heart. '– any change *inside*, where it really matters – that you're just as tied down as someone with four kids and a mortgage. You're *stuck*, Dylan.'

'Oh come on, stop giving me a hard time for once.'

Shauna straightened up, a steely look in her eyes. 'I can't help it, that's my role in this family – I'm the angry mother. I've been the angry mother since I was fourteen, when our *real* mother died. You've been the little boy lost ever since. Don't you think it's time to grow up?'

'Oh fuck this!'

He jumped up, grabbed his bag. Shauna stood up too.

'I'm sick and tired of the way we are, Dylan. What I'd really like is to have a proper, adult relationship with you.'

'*Bullshit* – you just want everything your own way.'

He took a step forward but she blocked his way and gripped the hand that held the bag.

'There's so much more to you than you want to admit. I just don't buy this motormouth geezer act you put on. You're much more interesting than that.'

341

He moved to her right, and she moved with him.

'The question is, can you handle being more complicated than you'd like?'

He stared at her, saying nothing. Dying to swear at her again, or push past. Instead he sighed and closed his eyes. When he spoke again his voice was barely a whisper, and he was gazing into the middle distance.

'Look, sis, I gotta go.' He leaned forward and kissed her cheek. 'I'll give you a ring.'

He stepped past her and opened the door. When he turned to close it behind him, she was stood with her arms folded tightly across her chest, her eyes brimming with tears. The resemblance to his mother, it took his breath away.

It was raining hard outside and bitterly cold. He walked the streets in a daze for twenty, thirty minutes, not even bothering to zip up his jacket. The rain began to soak into his clothes, his bag was cutting into his hand. He faced a long, miserable journey on his own. He stopped in front of a bar. Why not have one for the road? Was he capable of having just the one? He decided he was.

Aidan was in a cab, on his way to the Argel. It was a filthy night, the fierce wind driving sheets of rain that sprayed the windows like pebbles. The windscreen wipers thrashing, headlights on full beam as they twisted and turned along the narrow country road. For the last couple of hours Aidan felt as if a ball of lead were lodged in the pit of his stomach. He'd been telling himself that tonight was the beginning of his new life, the fresh start he'd promised himself when he was trapped in his coffin. But now that he was actually on his way to meet Safina, he was fast losing his nerve. What if he'd read it all wrong, and she had only felt sorry for him and just wanted to be friends? He'd lean forward to kiss her and she'd pull away, a disgusted expression on her face. *What in god's name are you doing?* Jesus, imagine that.

He wasn't so sure he wanted to put himself though this

342

anymore. Right now the thought of sitting in his armchair in the living room, a can in his hand, watching something on the box, warm and snug in his own house, felt a very attractive option. If he turned around now, he could still have that. But if he met her and blew it, his house wouldn't feel cosy and familiar anymore when he returned later. It would feel like a sad bachelor's house. A place haunted by an absence. Stinking of failure.

'Terrible weather, isn't it?' said the cab driver, interrupting his thoughts. *That's it, start a conversation with the cab driver, take your mind off it.*

'So, you do this run often?'

But before the driver could reply Aidan's mobile started ringing. He fumbled frantically to retrieve it from his inside pocket. He knew it would be Safina. Something was up; she was pulling out at the last minute.

'It's Russell.'

Aidan was completely thrown.

'I'm down at the Globe with Gwyn and Wilf – you want to join us?'

The relief at hearing his voice made Aidan lightheaded.

'It's great to hear from you, mate. I've been thinking about you a lot. I was going to ring you, but –'

'Don't go on, for fuck's sake. You coming or not?'

Aidan burst out laughing.

'What's so funny?'

But Aidan didn't know how to tell him. How to say that it was *him*, Russell, that was funny. The hard man. The know it all, seen it all, done it all, taunting, goading bastard who delighted in cutting everyone down to size. But the first man you'd want by your side when the chips were down and everyone else was making themselves scarce.

'Sorry, mate, I can't make it tonight.'

The silence on the other end of the line was charged and dangerous.

'I'm in a cab on my way to meet someone else.'

'Oh yeah.'

'Not a journalist or anything like that. I'm . . .' He wasn't quite ready to tell him about Safina yet. 'Just someone else.'

He heard Wilf in the background asking, 'What's he saying?' Russell clicking his tongue at him. The clack of balls on the pool table, 'A Design for Life' on the jukebox. For a moment he longed to be there with them, everything back to how it used to be.

'How about tomorrow night?' said Aidan.

There was a pause, then Russell said, 'Nah, I'm busy.'

Aidan smiled at that. Well, naturally. If Aidan wasn't free every night, then Russell certainly wasn't going to be.

'What about Friday?'

'Yeah,' said Russell.' Friday might be OK.'

'Great – the Globe at eight?'

'See you there.'

He was put out, Aidan could tell. Would probably be late, to teach him a lesson. But he'd come, and they'd talk, and they'd be as honest with each other as they could manage.

When the cab stopped outside the Argel and Aidan asked the driver how much it was, he turned around and smiled broadly at him. He was a similar age to Aidan, thick-set, grey, lined face, crooked nose.

'You're him, aren't you?'

'I beg your pardon?'

'The bloke who buried himself alive.'

He was absolutely beaming now, like he'd won a prize. Aidan smiled back, said, 'Yeah, that's me. So how much do I owe you?'

'You know what?' said the cabbie, ignoring Aidan's question, resting his arm across the back of his seat and making himself more comfortable. 'I was really hoping you'd win.'

'Thanks. So . . .'

'I mean, so you got caught out on that phone-in.' He pressed his thumb and forefinger to the bridge of his nose, laughed, a wheezy, thirty-a-day cackle, his shoulders shaking. 'Boy oh boy, you were really taken to the cleaner's, weren't you?'

Aidan shifted uneasily on the back seat.

'Yeah, all right . . .'

'And your daughter sounds a bit . . . But who cares about that? I mean, what *really* matters is whether you believe someone is sincere, know what I mean?'

Aidan said nothing.

'And I tell you what – for a while there, Crindau was a really exciting place to live. Suddenly everyone wanted to talk, and every night it was the same question – "What do you think about this bloke in the coffin then?" People thought things were finally going to change.'

He shook his head mournfully.

'I'm telling you, you see the worst side of people when you're a cab driver – it wears you down. People shouting and swearing and threatening you, running off without paying, trying to shag each other on the back seat, throwing up. You wouldn't believe what I have to put up with.'

He shrugged.

'But for a few weeks, people started behaving decently. It was all "How are you, mate?" and "Have you had a good day?" and my tips went through the roof. Every one was on a high. There was something in the air. No, mun, it was good, *really* good.'

He paused, smiling to himself at the memory.

'Did you vote for me then?'

The driver gave Aidan a scornful look. 'I never vote, me – complete waste of time.'

Aidan took a fiver from his wallet, held it out. 'Here.'

The driver dismissed it. 'No way, this is on me.'

'No, please – take it.'

The cabbie turned swiftly round, took the handbrake off, made as if to start driving away.

'Here,' said Aidan, trying again. 'Keep the change.'

The cabbie reached behind, opened Aidan's door with a swift downward push of his hand.

'Go on, get out of here.'

Aidan stepped out into the driving rain. As the cabbie was pulling away, he rolled down his window, stuck his head out. He clenched his fist and cried, 'POWER TO THE PEOPLE!' and burst out laughing.

Aidan went into the Argel and ordered a pint. He felt people glancing his way but no one said anything, or met his eyes when he turned around. He took his drink and sat near the door, so Safina could see him easily when she came. He was early and soon began to feel awkward sitting there on his own, imagining that people were talking about him.

He noticed a man nod in his direction to his mates. A couple at a nearby table took turns to check him out, and started whispering to each other. Then Safina came through the door, elegant in a black coat and gloves. She scanned the room anxiously, searching for him. He stood up and waved.

'Safina – over here.'

Too loud, too urgent, startling her. She walked over to the table, looking flustered.

'It took me ages to find it. I had to ask directions in the end.'

'Sorry about that.'

He pulled out a chair for her. Used too much strength, almost slammed it right into her. Christ, his heart was going like a jackhammer. She looked pretty tense herself. Perhaps she was thinking this was a mistake? Maybe it was.

She did look gorgeous though. He could sense heads turning all over the pub. She sensed it too, seeming painfully self-conscious as she took off her coat and gloves without looking at him. He stood to one side like a spare part, unable to sit back down again in case he appeared rude. Christ, he didn't have a bloody clue how to behave with a woman anymore. He was going to make a complete arse of himself. Cold sweat trickled down his neck. She began draping her coat over the back of her chair.

'Here,' said Aidan, holding out his hand. 'Let me hang it up for you. There's a coat stand over there.'

'No, it's fine here.'

'No, it won't take a minute.'

She sat down, shaking her head. 'It's fine, really.'

She ignored him, started searching for something in her bag. He was annoying her. He sat down again. He didn't think it would be like this. They'd got on so well on the phone. But then again, perhaps they'd said too much, too early and now, facing each other across a table, it felt very different. As if all the talking they'd done before was just a dream. A game. Like teenagers messing about in a chat room.

She found what she was looking for; some lip balm. Dipped her little finger into the tub, spread some on her lips. Aidan took a nervous swig from his pint and managed to spill some down his chin. Used his hand to wipe it off quickly, before she noticed. When she'd finished with the lip balm he said, 'Can I get you a drink?'

'Yes, please, a glass of red wine.'

Her tone was polite, formal; as if she was meeting him for the first time. But then this *was* the first time they'd met outside work. It was uncharted territory for both of them. She was keeping her distance. Hedging her bets. Leaving enough room to withdraw at the end of the night.

Aidan went back to the bar, ordered her drink. As he was pocketing the change, the barman placed a record on the deck. The first track started playing just as he reached their table. The opening chords of 'Days' stopped him dead in his tracks. He looked back at the barman who stared straight at Aidan, smiling warmly. Aidan realised he'd put it on specially for him. He felt himself blushing and turned quickly away. He put the glass down in front of Safina.

'There you are.'

'Thanks.'

She took a sip, then looked at him properly for the first time and smiled.

'I love this song, don't you?'

Acknowledgements

Thanks to the Arts Council Of England, whose Time To Write grant helped me complete this novel.

My sincere thanks to the following people:

Clare Alexander and Sally Riley at Gillon Aitken. Sophie Hannah Jones, James Nash and Tom Palmer in Leeds. Stuart Williams at Harvill Secker. And, once again, Joanna and Anna.